The Rainbow Promise

LORY LILIAN

Meryton Press

Oysterville, WA

Also by Lory Lilian

RAINY DAYS

REMEMBRANCE OF THE PAST

HIS UNCLE'S FAVORITE

THE PERFECT MATCH

SKETCHING MR. DARCY

This book is a sequel to *Rainy Days*—a popular *Pride and Prejudice* variation. It can also be read as an individual book, but it has references to characters and events in *Rainy Days*. This book contains scenes for mature audiences.

This book conforms throughout to UK English spelling.

THE RAINBOW PROMISE

ISBN: 978-1-68131-009-1

Graphic design by Ellen Pickels
Cover roses: Shutterstock and Depositphotos.com

Dedicated to

Loyal readers who turned *Rainy Days* into a
best-selling book and asked for a sequel

Glynis Whitelegg and Michelle Baines for their
constant encouragement and support

Margaret Fransen and Ellen Pickels for their
support and assistance in publishing this book

Chapter 1

Happiness. That was the foremost word that occupied Elizabeth's mind—a full, complete, overwhelming, heart-melting happiness that kept her awake in the middle of the night and made her soul fly around the beautifully furnished room.

My apartment. She was now Mrs. Elizabeth Darcy, the most fortunate woman in the world, married to the man who taught her the meaning of love, passion, and felicity.

The man was sleeping soundly, his arms circled around her. She was tired too, but her body still shivered in the delight of their lovemaking while her soul burst with joy. She was too happy to feel her tiredness and too tired to sleep.

Their shared passion kept them awake for most of the night. It was almost dawn, but her eyes refused to close as her mind, body, and heart wondered at the reality of everything she had discovered and felt since she had fallen in love with him.

She could hardly believe that only three months had passed since that cold, rainy day they spent in a small cottage—three months that changed her life as she never could have imagined.

Our love. It was more than she imagined, more than she ever dreamt. And this was only the first day—the first night—of their marriage. They had a lifetime to love each other. And yes, they would be—no doubt—the happiest couple in the world; she was certain they already were.

Elizabeth touched his cheeks and whispered "my husband," staring at him a few moments. Then she slowly left the silky sheets of the bed, and immediately her bare feet felt icy. She smiled as she tiptoed toward the window. It was snowing steadily, and the wind shook the windows.

She returned to the bed and sat on its edge. Her eyes caressed his face, and her fingers gently brushed a lock of hair from his forehead. He looked younger while he slept profoundly. As her tender gaze rested on his lips, her skin burned then shivered as she remembered their soft, warm, maddening touch.

He was her husband—Mr. Fitzwilliam Darcy of Pemberley, the man whom she once believed to be aloof, haughty, insensitive to the feelings of others, selfish, and unfair. Called her barely tolerable and refused to dance with her—she laughed in recollection.

The man who proved her first impression of him to be completely wrong had filled her soul with joy and bliss. She always hoped and prayed to marry a man she could love and respect—and be happy with—but only now did she realise how little understanding she had of "felicity in marriage" until that night.

Despite the steadily burning fire, her feet felt frozen. She tried to slowly glide under the sheets without disturbing him, but she failed.

"Elizabeth? What is wrong, my love? Are you unwell?"

Her eyes and lips smiled at her husband. "Do I look unwell, sir?"

Darcy kissed her eyelashes, and his arms closed around her, remembering they had had the same conversation a few hours earlier. "No, you do not. But why do you not sleep?"

Her feet—as well as her entire body—suddenly warmed in his embrace. "I am too happy."

His gaze deepened into her eyes—moist with tears of joy—and his lips rested on her temples then brushed over her bright smile.

"I cannot tell you how much I love you, my beautiful Elizabeth. And how happy I am."

"You need not tell me, my dearest. You have showed me enough."

"And it is only the first day and the first night of our marriage. I have a lifetime to show you my love, Mrs. Darcy," he answered, and she marvelled again that he could actually read her thoughts.

The wind shook the windows again, and its sound made Elizabeth shiver. She cuddled to her husband's chest, feeling warm and safe, briefly wondering whether it was equally cold at Longbourn and what her family was doing. She also wondered whether their relatives had arrived safely, with her aunt taking care of four children and Georgiana not fully recovered from her injury.

"I shall send an express to Bingley tomorrow. Perhaps you would like to write to Jane," Darcy said while he briefly kissed her hair.

"Yes—I will do so first thing in the morning." She smiled to herself; once again, they had thought of the same thing.

"And, although we decided to neither attend nor accept any visit, we could briefly call on your aunt and mine—just to be certain everyone is safe. Very briefly…"

"I would like that very much. You always know what I want…always…"

"It is my pleasure to at least try to guess your desires, Mrs. Darcy."

She sighed, and her fingers entwined with his while his arms tightened around her. She slowly allowed sleep to envelop her, being more certain than ever that her husband was truly a mind reader. *Her* "mind reader"—as he had said a few days before.

ELIZABETH WOKE UP UNDER A SWEET, SILKY CARESS, AND SHE OPENED HER eyes, gasping in disbelief. Her husband was gently touching her face with a stunning red rose, no doubt part of the beautiful bouquet waiting on her cabinet.

She remembered the first time he sent her roses: it was the second day of their engagement, just as this was the second day of their marriage.

"Thank you," she said, tears dancing in her eyes. "This is such a wonderful surprise!"

He embraced her tightly and placed a tender kiss on her temple.

"You are welcome, my love."

"But when did you have time to purchase it? Have you been awake for so long? Is it so late?"

"It is almost noon; I am glad you rested longer. I woke early because—as you said last night—I was too happy to sleep."

Elizabeth's head leant on his shoulder while Darcy continued, caressing her hair. "I sent short notes to our relatives to announce our calls. As for the flowers—I confess I ordered them before we departed for Longbourn, and they were delivered as scheduled. I do not deserve much credit."

Elizabeth smiled and caressed his face. "Of course, you do." She closed her arms around his neck, and he kissed her. In his embrace, the sheet fell from around her, exposing her silky skin to passionate caresses.

"I will go to the library until you get dressed, or you will be unable to leave the room today," he managed to whisper, struggling to withdraw from her.

Elizabeth chuckled while he carefully put the sheets around her and hastily pressed his lips to her bare shoulder then spoke warmly against her ear. "I eagerly expect to return home and to remain alone for at least a week."

"As do I." She covered herself tighter as her husband left and Molly entered.

THE DARCYS CHOSE TO HAVE A LATE BREAKFAST DOWNSTAIRS AS PROPRIETY required. The servants' obvious efforts to please the mistress were rewarded by Elizabeth's warm smile. She was not a stranger to them as they were not strangers to her—and yet, her position as Mrs. Darcy and the presence of the master added more solemnity to the staff's behaviour.

The master's anger following Lady Catherine's impromptu visit and her fight with Elizabeth was something that none of the servants was likely to easily forget, and their decision never to repeat the error was as strong as ever. Fortunately, the master and the mistress appeared to be content—and so was their staff.

Elizabeth's smile never ceased, and the expression of utter delight on her face brightened the entire room. Mrs. Hamilton, the housekeeper, admitted to herself that she had never seen the master looking more pleased—nor more handsome—in the fifteen years she had known him.

After breakfast, they retired to the library to write the necessary letters.

While Elizabeth was diligent, paying attention to the paper in front of her, she barely contained her laughter as she felt Darcy's stare burning her face. She finally raised her eyes to him.

"Sir, have you already finished?"

"Not at all. I barely started."

"Then may I ask why you look at me so intently? Is there something wrong? Do you disapprove of anything in me?" she teased him.

"Madam, you cannot possibly still presume that I disapprove of anything about you. In fact, you should know by now that I look at you because I heartily approve of everything."

She laughed, and he abandoned his chair, moving to her, then sat and pulled her into his arms. Her hands found their way around his neck while his stare lowered to her lips.

"Do you remember when I told you that, once we are married, I would not have to be worried about your lips being swollen from my kisses?"

"Of course, I remember." She blushed while his hands tenderly stroked her back.

"Well, sadly, I still have to worry about that since we will visit our relatives soon," he said, hastily kissed her, and then resumed his proper seat.

Elizabeth's amused gaze followed him. A moment later she stepped toward him and daringly sat on his lap, their faces only inches apart.

"Luckily, I can blame the cold wind for any inconvenience regarding my lips," she whispered against his ear then gently placed countless small kisses on his face, the line of his jaw, then closer to his mouth, which hungrily captured hers.

Never did a letter require such a long time to be written and sent, nor did Darcy loathe more the prospect of a visit to his relatives. He wished nothing but to be alone with her and desired nothing but to love her again and again. He knew he had to show more patience at the beginning of their married life, as he was well aware of the discomfort Elizabeth had felt the previous night. But he was also well aware of the pleasure she learnt and of her own passion and willingness to share their love—and that made his restraint more difficult. Yes—the best solution was a visit to their relatives through wintry weather. This way the day would pass sooner and the evening would come and…they could be together alone again without his being too demanding and too impatient.

Therefore, in the early afternoon as soon as the letters to Hertfordshire were finished, Mr. and Mrs. Darcy went to pay their first visits as a married couple.

Wrapped in heavy clothes, Elizabeth took her husband's arm; her shoes slipped while the wind stung her cheeks. She smiled and breathed the fresh air as Darcy hurried to help her inside the carriage.

He joined her, closed the small door, and put his arms around his wife. Her hands searched for his, and their gloved fingers entwined while the horses stepped hesitantly along the snowy street. Glancing outside, Elizabeth smiled at her husband, her eyes sparkling with joy.

"William, I was thinking…can we go to Pemberley for a few weeks? I am sure Georgiana will not be upset to stay with Lady Ellen a little longer. With the Season starting and Jane's wedding, I do not see how we can leave for Derbyshire until the summer."

His surprise was obvious. "My love, I would like nothing more than to show you our home. But it is not wise to travel so long for such a short time. The journey to Pemberley takes almost three days even in the best of weather. Now it gets dark very early; the roads are in very poor shape. We could be trapped in the middle of nowhere any time by snow and a blizzard."

Her eyes shadowed, and she lowered her gaze outside.

"You are right, of course. It would be very unwise."

He brought her gloved hand to his lips. "I hope you know my only concern is your well-being. It is my pleasure to comply with your every desire, but more important is your safety. But this does not mean that I am not touched by your request, my dearest," he concluded, turning her face so he could claim a kiss.

Trying to fight her disappointment, Elizabeth could not resist her husband's passionate attentions for too long. Fortunately for the propriety of their appearance, the sweet interlude was soon interrupted as the carriage stopped in front of the Matlock townhouse.

They were received with warmth by both Lord and Lady Matlock, and Georgiana's joy was openly displayed as she embraced her brother and sister.

The colonel kissed Elizabeth's hand then teased Darcy about paying calls on the second day of his marriage—a joke that drew embarrassed glances from Elizabeth and Georgiana and a sharp, wordless scolding from Lady Matlock.

"I am glad that you decided to visit us. The weather is quite bad, but I imagine neither of you is bothered by that. I was expecting Thomas and his wife, but he postponed the call until a more suitable day. I easily recognise to whom these words belong." Lady Matlock concealed her displeasure behind the cup of tea while smiling elegantly to her guests. Georgiana exchanged an amused glance with Elizabeth.

"You know, Beatrice resembles Caroline Bingley very closely," the colonel said with a laugh. "Both are handsome and annoying. The difference is Beatrice has a title. Oh yes, and both chased Darcy at some point."

Elizabeth almost choked on the hot tea while Lady Matlock put aside her cup to avoid dropping it. The earl frowned, and Darcy cast a most disapproving look at his cousin.

"Robert, so many years of education and such a long time in the army, yet you still do not know what can be said and when," Lady Matlock said coldly.

The colonel's amusement increased. "Mother, I apologise if I upset you. But we are among close family, and I am sure Mrs. Darcy can appreciate a good joke—especially when it is true."

"Cousin, I always wondered at your ability of always making fun of the very few women who had 'chased' me, but never of the many others whom you keep chasing," Darcy intervened.

The colonel laughed again. "Point taken, Darcy. But it is amusing, precisely because you loathed the chase while I truly enjoy it. And you must admit that I am right about Beatrice and Caroline. They are very much alike."

"One can hardly reject such an obvious truth," Darcy admitted, meeting his wife's mocking gaze. She seemed to have something to add to the conversation although she chose to remain silent.

"I know men speak much nonsense when they are by themselves, but I was hoping to avoid it while in our company," Lady Matlock interfered once again. "I am exceedingly pleased that I have Georgiana with me to carry on a sensible and elegant conversation."

She turned to her niece then again to Elizabeth. "I hope to have Georgiana staying with me a few more weeks. She already agreed—I hope you will not mind. Besides, I believe it would be best for you to spend a little time alone."

Elizabeth exchanged a glance with her husband and blushed.

"Aunt, I approve of everything that Georgiana decides," Darcy answered, swallowing some more brandy.

"Of course you do—especially when it suits you." The colonel laughed again, and it was Darcy's turn to choke on his drink.

Elizabeth desperately attempted to change the delicate subject at which everybody—except Darcy and her—seemed to be amused.

"I was just talking to William about this...about Georgiana staying with your ladyship. I tried to persuade him to go to Pemberley for a few weeks. I long to see it. I am sure it is wonderful in winter. Unfortunately, I received a decided refusal." She smiled.

"Going to Pemberley now?" Georgiana asked. "But Elizabeth, the road is difficult, the weather is bad, and it turns dark very early. It can be dangerous. Can you not wait a little longer? Forgive me for interfering. I would be worried about you."

"Do not trouble yourself; it was clearly an unreasonable idea. Since you are staying with Lady Ellen, I thought it a good time for us to travel. I am not scared of bad weather or roads. But I admit you are both right." She glanced at her husband then at Lady Matlock, whose expression was stern.

"Elizabeth, I am completely against such an idea too. You will have a lifetime to stay at Pemberley—no reason to put yourself in danger. Besides, with the Season opening, we still need to order more gowns. There will be many occasions for you to attend. I already informed the modiste. Mrs. Gardiner will come for tea tomorrow with Becky and Margaret. I am sure she will agree with me. She is a lady with remarkably good taste and wisdom, and I truly enjoy her company. Would you join us?"

"I thank you for your kindness to my Aunt and cousins…and for the invitation. Your ladyship is correct; I need to order more gowns. But I am not yet certain of our plans." Elizabeth blushed, glancing at Darcy once more. She could not declare that they did not intend to leave the house for the next few days.

"We will briefly call on the Gardiners today too. Tomorrow we intend to stay at home," Darcy answered. "But we will take very seriously your advice regarding the Season, the modiste, and all."

"Good. Elizabeth will be my guest at Almack's balls as soon as they start. I am confident that she will be accepted as a permanent participant in no time," Lady Matlock continued.

"I, too, am confident since the patronesses are your friends, Lady Ellen." The colonel laughed once more.

Lady Matlock frowned at her son. "This is not a subject for mockery, Robert! Mrs. Darcy deserves all the appreciation due to her position."

"Forgive me, Mother, for mocking your excellent strategy, but I have never been too fond of Almack's balls and all those stiff rules around them. And neither has Darcy."

"That is because you are both stubborn and always wish to have your way. You are a colonel, and yet you often lack discipline. Darcy is a man of rules and self-control, but somehow he mostly uses the rules for his convenience."

"Well, Mother, let us be grateful that you will no longer have to worry about Darcy since he will have Elizabeth to bear him for the rest of his life. As for me, any sort of worrying will be pointless; therefore, you must avoid troubling yourself entirely. I am a hopeless case."

"I am glad you find a reason for amusement in anything, Son. Amiability should be limited at times," Lady Matlock concluded, and her son, even more amused, bowed humbly and kissed his mother's hand in a gesture of love and respect—and begged her forgiveness for his teasing.

Lady Matlock rolled her eyes, declaring herself defeated. There was little to be done with her younger son at the age of thirty.

The conversation flew for another half hour, mostly around the modiste, dresses, and balls, and the gentlemen wisely retreated to enjoy a drink in the library.

Chapter 2

After a warm farewell, the Darcys headed toward Cheapside. It was around three o'clock, the snow and the wind grew stronger, and the streets were almost empty.

The carriage was freezing inside, so Darcy carefully arranged the curtains then warmed his wife in a tender embrace while his lips claimed hers.

"I missed kissing you," he whispered. "I missed kissing you, and I missed loving you. I am so sorry we promised to call on the Gardiners too. I want nothing more than to lock myself away with you in our chamber."

"Oh, I…" She decided to cease speaking and abandoned herself to his kiss. She briefly wondered whether the curtains allowed them to be seen; then she put away any concern, trusting that her husband knew how to protect their privacy. As if guessing her thoughts, he pulled a few inches away, gently arranged her bonnet, and then stroked her lips with his thumb.

"I cannot afford to ruin your appearance before visiting your relatives. I fear Becky would notice any detail, and I still do not know how to handle most of her remarks," Darcy said as Elizabeth laughed.

"Well, you have no reason to worry. She has already proved how 'very good at compliments' she is—especially towards you. And she confessed she has found you 'pretty' since the first day she met you."

"Indeed. That was one of the most important days of my life. I walked with you, arm in arm, and I invited you to visit Georgiana…and I was overwhelmed by the storm of compliments from Becky."

She laughed again; then her eyes moistened while she leant and placed soft kisses on his face. "Becky is so right—dimples are good," she said, caressing his cheeks, his forehead, the strong line of his jaw…

He turned his head so that their mouths met, then his hand slid inside her coat, around her waist, climbed slowly, and stopped upon her heart.

"I am starving for you. I am sorry if I frighten you and if I am not as patient as a man should be with his new wife, but this is true. I can think of nothing else but being alone with you—and loving you."

"I would not want you to be different in any way, my husband. Not more patient, not less starved…"

"You are a dangerous woman, my dear wife. You find great pleasure in torturing me…"

Their teasing was completed with daring caresses and touches, their words broken by kisses.

"You already knew that when you proposed to me, sir, so you cannot put the entire blame on me."

"I never blame you, madam," he concluded, then hastily separated from her as the carriage stopped at their destination.

With the snow falling and the wind blowing, Elizabeth's imperfect appearance was no surprise to their hosts, more so since the children surrounded her, claiming her attention.

Becky kissed Elizabeth's cheeks then turned her interest toward Darcy, who raised her in his arms and followed the others into the drawing room.

Refreshments were ordered, and their conversation began with the weather and the journey from Longbourn to London while Becky hurried to tell them how she played with her brothers in the snow and they pushed her down. The boys protested and asserted their innocence.

Darcy bore the din bravely, grateful for the glass of wine Mr. Gardiner offered him, but he refused an invitation to the library.

"We cannot stay long. It was a pleasure to see you all, and I hope to have dinner together soon."

"Lady Matlock said you will have tea with her tomorrow," Elizabeth added.

"Yes, her Ladyship is exceedingly kind and generous. She insisted I bring the girls too. I hope *someone* will not be too tiresome and will behave properly." Mrs. Gardiner glanced at her youngest daughter, who returned an apparently puzzled look.

"I am sure Becky will be as sweet as she always is." Elizabeth kissed her youngest cousin. "You will tell me how the visit was when we next meet. And please be careful how you play in the snow, my dear."

"But, Lizzy, are you leaving? Do you not stay to sleep with me tonight?"

"I cannot sleep with you, dearest. I must go home."

"Home? To Longbourn?"

"No, here in London."

"But you always stay with us when you are in London!"

"Becky, Elizabeth is now married. We already talked about this. She must stay with Mr. Darcy."

"But this is easy: Mr. Darcy can stay here too!"

"That would not be possible. They must return to their own home."

Becky looked at her former favourite with disappointment and disapproval.

"I did not know you planned to take Lizzy from me. I liked you better when you were not married."

"Becky!" cried Mrs. Gardiner, pale with embarrassment. "We shall end the discussion this moment!"

Darcy nodded discreetly to Mrs. Gardiner and turned to the girl. "Becky, I am sorry you are upset, but I promise you will have many opportunities to see Elizabeth from now on. And although she will not remain to sleep at your house, we will arrange an apartment for you and your sister and brothers in case you might come to visit for a few days. That is—if your parents will allow it."

"Really? In that beautiful house? Do you have dolls? If not, I can bring some in case I come and visit," Becky said, quickly changing her point of interest. "I hope you will keep your promise," she concluded, and Mrs. Gardiner scolded her again.

"Do you not trust me? I always keep my promises. Elizabeth may testify to this," Darcy said, smiling.

The girl was silent a moment. "I trust you."

"More so, your father agreed that you all will spend the summer at Pemberley with Elizabeth and Georgiana and me. You will learn to ride, you can fish, play in the garden—everything you enjoy."

All four Gardiner children hurried around him, asking for more details.

Becky suddenly had a second thought. "Well, Lizzy does not like to ride, so I shall stay with her."

"I trust that both you and Elizabeth will learn to ride properly at Pemberley.

I will teach you, and I am sure you will like it," Darcy answered.

Becky glanced at Elizabeth, who nodded in approval.

"Very well. But you have to remember that I am a small child and you must take care of me. You may have to carry me in your arms quite often as I cannot walk for too long," Becky concluded in earnest to her parents' shock and embarrassment and Darcy's complete amusement.

"It is quite strange, young lady, how it is possible that the more you are offered, the more you demand. You are quite ungrateful," Mrs. Gardiner said sharply, throwing Becky a meaningful gaze.

The girl turned to Darcy and whispered in his ear. "When she calls me 'young lady,' it is not good, you know. She is upset with me."

"Yes, I would imagine so," he whispered back. "You should not upset your mother."

"I know, but I am stubborn and disobedient—Mrs. Burton said so," the girl of four and a half years wisely explained, and Darcy could not restrain his loud laughter, soon joined by Elizabeth and Mr. Gardiner. The lady of the house, though, was still watching her young daughter severely.

For half an hour, Darcy did little else but to answer the children's enthusiastic questions about Pemberley. Elizabeth watched him, enchanted, her heart melting at his warm kindness and the patience he generously showed to her relatives.

Finally, the visit came to an end, and the children reluctantly separated from their guests. While her aunt and uncle thanked them for the call, Elizabeth felt ashamed to admit even to herself that she was eager to leave. The mere thought of soon being alone with her husband caused her to shiver more than the cold wind. She held his arm, and he tenderly covered her hand with his; she could feel his warmth even through the thick fabric of their gloves.

Again, the carriage started slowly, the horses barely progressing through the fresh snow.

Darcy embraced his wife, and Elizabeth touched his face with her gloved fingers.

"You have been wonderfully patient with my cousins. You are the kindest and most amiable man ever."

"Not at all—I am only doing it to impress you, my love." He smiled.

"You cannot accept a compliment graciously, Mr. Darcy. Why would you want to impress me?"

"Well, since I was so hasty in showing you all my flaws from the beginning of our acquaintance and I offended you from the first evening we met, it is my goal to do anything to improve your opinion of me. As I told you a few months ago, I hope in fifteen years I will succeed in changing the first poor impression I made."

"Please rest assured, sir, that my impression of you could not be better. However, I am delighted by your effort to impress me. Please continue to do so."

"That is precisely my intention, madam, as soon as we get home," he answered, stealing a kiss.

Elizabeth laughed and blushed. She was still unaccustomed to this surprising side of the aloof Mr. Darcy: his teasing, his flirting, his improper small gestures and words, his passion that seemed difficult to control. And she could not help wondering—and worrying—about what would have happened had they not met that rainy day in the cottage. Was it possible that their love—their happiness—was entirely due to a mere coincidence? Would she ever have gotten to know his real disposition if not for that chance encounter? Would he have been willing to show his true character to her—to admit his feelings for her and follow his heart, despite the differences between their families? Or would such a deep love have remained forever undiscovered?

"What is it, my dear? Why are you suddenly so serious?"

"Oh, it is nothing, really…just some silly thoughts. I am so happy to be your wife."

"If happiness makes you solemn, I am afraid I will rarely be able to guess your feelings."

"I doubt that, my darling husband. You have proved to me that you can read my mind." Elizabeth smiled then leant her head on his shoulder. It was already dark, and she counted the minutes until they would be in the comfort of their home.

Through the small window, she spotted a beautiful image: large snowflakes fell quickly, gently blown by the wind, so dense that it seemed like a thick, white curtain.

When the carriage entered the main street, Darcy unexpectedly ordered the footman to stop.

"Would you like to walk from here, my love?"

"Yes, very much! I was just about to suggest it. Please do not deny that you can read my mind, Mr. Darcy."

She held his arm tightly, and he put his hand on hers while taking short steps. The snow was fresh and soft, dancing on their shoes and clothes. From time to time, Elizabeth lifted her face, and snowflakes caressed her cheeks and her closed eyelashes and rested in the dark locks escaping from her bonnet.

Darcy admired her playfulness, completely bewitched by her joy, which only brightened her beauty. Just as they reached the main gate of their house, he leant and tasted her lips, washing away a few drops of melted snow. Fortunately, nobody observed Mr. Darcy's shocking behaviour.

Attentive to each other and their own steps, neither noticed a carriage stop in front of them until its owner called to them.

"Darcy! Miss Bennet!"

They turned in surprise, and Darcy frowned.

"Lord Felton!"

"Good evening—what a lovely surprise. Miss Bennet, are you well, I hope? You look wonderful."

"Thank you, sir. Your lordship is kind. I am quite well." She felt distressed as she noticed Darcy's growing displeasure.

"I am being completely honest! Darcy, I thought you had left London since I have not seen you at any gatherings lately."

"I hope you were not affected by my absence. I can scarcely remember more than three events we attended together in the last ten years," Darcy replied coldly. "And even more, we never shared the same interests."

"True. I know you are not fond of balls and parties although there were times you were a regular presence at the opera and theatre."

Elizabeth sensed the tension in Darcy's arm.

"Felton, I have no time for your foolishness, and I must restrain myself from saying what I would like to at this moment. By the way, as I am sure you know but rudely chose to ignore, there is no 'Miss Bennet' any longer but Mrs. Darcy. I expect you to address my wife properly from now on."

"Oh, yes, of course, silly me—it must have slipped my mind. I remember reading something in the newspaper a few days ago. Congratulations—it was not my intention to offend anyone."

"Very well then—we must leave. Good evening."

Lord Felton bowed to Elizabeth with perfect politeness then turned to Darcy. "I hope to see you often in the future. As well as the Hothfields. Good evening."

"Felton!" Darcy called in a low, sharp voice, but the man entered his carriage and departed in haste.

Darcy's frown and his reaction were impossible to miss. Elizabeth took tighter hold of his arm.

"William, please—do not allow him to torment you! You know very well that he would do anything to start a quarrel with you. Do you remember when you told me about the duel with Lord Hothfield? And you admitted that Lady Ellen demanded that both you and the colonel avoid a scandal with him."

Darcy breathed deeply several times to regain his composure then smiled.

"You are right of course. Forgive me for losing my patience, my dear. What a cur! He made those shameless references to the theatre and to the Hothfields. He is a slick bastard! I am sorry for the trouble he caused. I do not want our walk to end like this."

Elizabeth answered with a large smile. "My love, I noticed that he tried to suggest a connection between you and Mary Ann Alton, the present Lady Hothfield. Please do not worry about me. I was silly enough to allow myself to be affected by Wickham's mischievous words a few weeks ago, and I even quarrelled with you about it. If I ever fell into the same trap again, I would be a completely ridiculous fool, unworthy of your love. Let us hope this is not the case."

Darcy gazed at her with heartfelt admiration, closing his arms around her in the middle of the street.

"Your beauty matches your wisdom perfectly, Mrs. Darcy, and I could not be more grateful for it. Please allow me to show you into our home. Our walk has ended, but our evening has just begun."

THEY WERE WELCOMED BY THE STAFF, AND MRS. HAMILTON INFORMED them dinner would be ready whenever they wished. However, they hurried to their apartments, their faces red and their clothes wet.

Immediately, Miles helped Darcy remove his coat while Molly offered her services to Elizabeth, whose clothes and shoes—thinner than Darcy's—left her chilled.

The two servants closed the doors between their apartments, and Elizabeth only had time to glimpse Darcy's intense gaze and his hidden smile.

"Ma'am, I took the liberty of preparing hot water for your bath. The tub is placed in the adjoined room. I hope you approve."

"Thank you, Molly, it is a perfect arrangement. I really need a hot bath. Mr. Darcy and I walked only a few minutes, but it is quite cold outside."

"Yes, ma'am," the maid said, glancing at the wet gown. "When should dinner be ready?"

"I am not certain…please have Miles ask Mr. Darcy. We had many refreshments during our visits, and I am not hungry."

"Very well…"

Elizabeth wrapped herself in a thick robe while the servants brought the hot water.

She wondered what her husband was doing and was tempted to enter his room, but there were several servants about, and she felt uncomfortable walking around so improperly attired. Was he taking a bath too?

They were finally home, and they soon would be alone. He had told her all day how much he missed her and how much he wanted to love her. Her skin shivered in anticipation of what would follow. Yes, now she truly knew what to expect, and her eagerness matched his.

He said he knew that she was in some discomfort and that he must be more patient during the first days of their marriage. But from the previous night, she remembered nothing unpleasant, only the delight, the passion, the tenderness, the overwhelming joy of being united with him, and the happiness—full, deep, and complete.

"It is ready, Mrs. Darcy."

The maid's voice startled her as though Molly had guessed her thoughts. Of course not—only her husband could. She smiled to herself as she entered the tub and allowed herself to be spoiled by the warmth.

Elizabeth closed her eyes and leant her head back. The small room—with only a table and a couple of chairs—was lit by several candles. There was no fireplace, and it was rather cold, but the hot water made a perfect and most enjoyable combination.

At Longbourn, she rarely had the chance to take a long bath in the tub. With six ladies in the house and only a few servants, it would be impossible to indulge in such delightful activity.

Now she could do whatever she wanted, and all she wanted was to be in the company of her husband as soon as possible. No other delight was as sweet as his presence.

She called for Molly, and no answer came for a few minutes. She thought the maid did not hear, but the door finally opened.

She paled then blushed when she met her husband's gaze and watched him stepping closer to her.

He was only wearing trousers and a shirt, open at his neck. His eyes darkened while his lips twisted in a smile; his gaze never left hers. She crossed her arms to cover her chest, and he knelt by her tub then gently removed a lock of hair from her brow.

"Did I alarm you?"

She smiled, but her voice was trembling slightly. "No…a little…I expected Molly."

"I dismissed Molly and Miles for tonight. Dinner is already arranged in my room. Are you hungry?" His thumb brushed over her lips.

"No…are you?" she struggled to reply.

"Yes, very hungry…but not for food…" he whispered close to her ear, and she shivered then turned her head to meet his eyes. Her lips were hastily captured by his.

His hand slid into the hot water and met her hands, still crossed, then stroked them gently. After a brief hesitation, she uncrossed them, and his tender fingers found their way to her soft breasts, claiming their beauty.

Both moaned at the same time, their lips still engaged.

As he knelt by her tub, his left arm encircled her shoulders while his right hand abandoned the sweet capture and travelled lower along her belly, her hips, and then glided along her thighs and slowly between them. Her body shivered even before she felt the caress inside her, and her mouth fought for air. His lips allowed her to breathe and moan in delight while spreading soft kisses along her throat and shoulder. Then he suddenly trapped her mouth again, just as the maddening pleasure from his strokes made her entire body tremble.

His kisses returned to her face, allowing her to resume breathing. His hand still rested on the warm softness and started caressing her legs.

"Oh, William…" she whispered, allowing her eyes to tell him what she wished.

"Come, my love," he said, gently pulling her out and wrapping her in two large towels.

She briefly thought she should be ashamed to be fully exposed in the full light of so many candles, yet her mind was as weak as were her knees, which refused to support her. But she did not need to either think or walk as his arms carried her into the bedchamber and placed her on the bed.

This room was much darker than the other one although brighter than the previous night. Two candles at each side of the bed and two others, together with the firelight, allowed clear sight of their bodies.

He leant over her, supporting himself on his elbows, then smiled as he caressed her face.

"I am a selfish man, my love. I knew you were ashamed of my presence in the bathroom, and yet I did not stop...and I feel you are still uncomfortable with having more light in the room, but I cannot help begging you to allow it. I want to see your beautiful face while we enjoy pleasure together...to admire every spot of your body that I already touched and caressed and kissed. I want to love you with my eyes and with every part of my heart and of my body...but I shall blow out the candles if you want..."

She smiled, tearful from his confession of love, her body still trembling and yearning for more.

"You are a dangerous man, sir. You pretend you allow me to choose, yet you know very well I can refuse you nothing."

She pulled his head closer to her and whispered, her lips touching his ear. "I was ashamed of your seeing me in the bathroom, and I am ashamed of your seeing me in the light; I am ashamed to think of what happened between us last night and of what I felt and what I have discovered. And there is nothing that I want more than to feel it again. My heart and my body are craving to feel your love again, all the time...and what my mind thinks matters little."

A passionate kiss silenced her and slowly, his lips, his tongue, and his whispers started building the fire inside her again. Then her mouth was suddenly abandoned as his lips lowered to her chin then to her throat and her shoulders. He rose to his knees, looking at her with an adoring gaze that burned her. She forced a smile, her breathing heavier.

He gently started to dry her skin with the towels, inch by inch, then he lowered himself on top of her again, kissing, tasting, savouring every newly revealed spot. His kisses were first sweet, patient, and tantalising, making Elizabeth shiver at each touch. Soon his fingers explored the beauty of her breasts, dancing around them, then his thirsty lips joined, and his tenderness burst in released passion. His patience seemed to evade him as his caresses, kisses, and strokes became more and more eager, conquering her body. He removed the towel from around her hips and legs then took off his clothes. His dark gaze made her skin tremble; her face and her torso arched toward him, and he captured her mouth in a deep kiss as his desire found its way inside her.

Elizabeth released a small cry and tensed, so he stopped. She could feel his strength pulsing inside her, and she attempted to breathe as he whispered in her ear.

"Are you well, my love?"

"Yes…yes…"

He trapped her lips again, and his deep kiss matched the rhythm of his thrusts inside her. The whirls of sensations, stronger than ever before, made her head spin while her heart beat wildly in anticipation of the pleasure she knew would come, and it shattered her fiercely.

Elizabeth felt suddenly cold and realised he was no longer covering her. She struggled to open her eyes and saw him sitting on his knees. When their eyes met, he smiled, and his thumbs brushed her red lips for a moment; then he gently stroked her legs and pulled them apart. Her breathing stopped, and she stared at him, wondering what he would do next. He slowly lifted her legs around his waist and leant a little, so he could enter her again. She gasped, feeling him stronger and deeper than before, slowly taking possession of her being. He kept smiling while his thrusts renewed, longer, slower, more powerful. Her body arched toward him while his hands caressed her shoulders, her arms, her face, then brushed over her breasts, and his palms captured both while his thrust increased. Another cry escaped Elizabeth, and she tried to control it, biting her lips, but his fingers parted them gently.

"Do not hold anything back, my beautiful wife. I want to see you, to listen to you, to feel you taking your pleasure while I show you how much I love you…"

He bent only a moment to steal a kiss, then he resumed his position while his palms returned to their sweet possession and his thrusts grew harder and faster.

She called his name and attempted to move to him—with him—then stretched her arms to touch him and he finally leant over her, overwhelming her with his weight and his passion, throwing her into another storm of feelings until they reached their fulfilment and exhaustion together.

Some time passed in complete silence, and their bodies were still united, their arms still tightly embraced.

"Elizabeth, I never imagined love could be like this. I do not know how to explain…if only I could find the proper words to tell you how full I am of you, my beloved wife. You are in my mind, in my body, in my heart, and I am frightened to even think that I could have lost you before even getting to know you. What would my life have been without you?"

"I do not think there are many words left nor needed between us, my beloved husband. I can easily understand your fears as they are mine too. I often think of that. But this is good, you know? If we share the fears, they will be split in half."

He withdrew from her a few inches so he could meet her eyes.

"You are very wise, my love, but I cannot split the responsibility in half with you, as my share of blame is much, much larger. I was so determined to fight against my own heart—against my love for you—that I likely would have succeeded. If not for that day in the cottage, I would have left Hertfordshire and probably never seen you again."

"Perhaps…or perhaps not…who knows? Maybe we could have met…in Kent when I would visit Charlotte and you, Lady Catherine…or maybe in London when I stayed with my uncle and aunt…or maybe we would have happened upon each other in Derbyshire if I had ever gone there…"

A large smile lit his expression. "True…the more I think of it, the more I realise that we would have found a way to each other. I would have found a way to bring you into my arms—right where you belong."

"I am sure you would have, my dearest Mr. Darcy," Elizabeth answered, her lips, her eyes, and her heart smiling at him.

Yes, it was happiness. A full, complete, overwhelming, heart-melting happiness.

Chapter 3

On the third day of their marriage, the Darcys woke around noon and were still reluctant to leave their apartment. Eventually, Elizabeth insisted they should have breakfast downstairs.

"I think the servants should see us—if only for a little while." She laughed and blushed at the implications of her words. "I do not even dare imagine what they must think has happened to us."

"I am sure they imagine something very close to the truth: we are a couple who married for love and wished to protect their privacy in the first days of their marriage," Darcy said before kissing her hand. "And no, the servants need not see us. There is nothing we should do out of concern for anyone else. But I agree with you about breakfast. Besides, I am quite hungry!"

"Yes, so am I."

He gently kissed her cheek, glancing at the trays of food that remained untouched from the previous night. "This time, I am hungry for food..."

"Yes, so am I," she answered daringly despite her still-crimson cheeks.

The delicious breakfast was much enjoyed and praised to the satisfaction of Mrs. Hamilton. The master and mistress were informed about the courses selected for dinner, and they both approved them although they barely paid attention to the subject.

Afterward, the couple retired to the library. Darcy declared he wished to look through some papers and invited Elizabeth to choose a book and keep him company.

"Is there something urgent you need to attend? I imagined you had been neglecting your business lately with all the problems caused by my family."

"No, I only need to review some papers sent by my solicitors."

She glanced over his shoulder. "May I help you in any way? Can you tell me more about it?"

He was surprised by her request then pulled up a chair for her.

"I am afraid this is quite boring for a lady, but I would be happy to explain it to you. Here is where we register everything related to our income and expenses. For each tenant, we have separate records. For instance, these calculations are for Mr. Benton and his family…"

Two hours passed as Darcy shared all sorts of details related to his estates, things Elizabeth had never heard before from her father—whose interest and diligence in the management of Longbourn were significantly lower. She was equally curious and content to hear everything her husband had to say, and with each word, she found more reasons to admire him.

Finally, Darcy started writing a letter to the Pemberley steward while Elizabeth walked around in search of something to read.

"I was astounded by this library the first time I saw it. I felt too overwhelmed to select one book."

A mischievous smile spread on his face. "I vividly remember the first time you saw it. And the second time."

She blushed then shivered. Yes, she also remembered every moment of that time.

"The day after Lydia's elopement is fresh in my mind. My heart still aches from that pain…the pain that I might have lost you forever."

"I could not imagine you would think that," Darcy answered, taking her in his arms. "I thought my feelings for you were already clear at that point—as well as my intentions."

"They were…but I did not dare hope you would overcome the horror of becoming so closely related to Wickham…that you would still make me an offer despite my sister's elopement…"

"It seems, my love, that my feelings and my intentions were *not* clear to you at that point. If they were, you would not have doubted them."

"Perhaps my mind did not dare believe what my heart already felt—and hoped for," she said, returning to him. He gently pulled her onto his lap and closed his arms around her.

"Enough of sad memories, my beloved. This is such a wonderful day—the perfect day for me. The peace, the silence—and you by my side." As he spoke, his lips moved closer and touched her earlobe. She shivered, and her fingers slid through his hair.

"I perfectly understand your meaning. I imagine how pleasant it is for you to be away from the din at Longbourn."

"More so, from the din at Netherfield. Although it might have been less noisy than Longbourn, it was certainly more irritating. I hope Bingley will settle new rules for his sisters once he is married. But I wonder what was in his mind to schedule the wedding in three months' time. Three months?"

"He and Jane are more patient—and surely more proper—than we were. Three months is a reasonable engagement time. Besides, there will be some lovely weeks for them to know each other better, to become accustomed to being together. I am sure Jane would enjoy being courted by such an amiable and handsome gentleman." Elizabeth laughed while Darcy lifted his eyebrow in challenge.

"There is no better time for a man to court the woman he loves than after they are married. For instance, if we were only engaged, I could not do this," he said, claiming a kiss. "I hope you do not regret that I insisted on having such a short engagement," he whispered, brushing his fingers along her throat then touching the roundness above her dress.

"I do not regret anything you insisted on doing…" She slowly leant back, waiting—hoping—to feel his lips on her skin.

He tantalised her with gentle caresses, pleased to hear her soft moans, until he forced himself to stop, his hand lingering on her half-bare shoulder.

"We should go upstairs," he said hoarsely. "Unless you wish to finish selecting a book…"

"Yes…no. We should go upstairs…"

"Or I could just lock the door so that nobody disturbs us…"

Elizabeth looked at him in disbelief—uncertain whether he was speaking in jest—her breathing heavy, her lips red and moist. He pushed the dress down from her shoulder and tasted the soft skin then gently bit it; his strong palm cupped her face, holding her head to bear his gaze.

"So what would you prefer, Mrs. Darcy?"

"Upstairs…" she said, her mind trying to imagine how it would be if she chose otherwise.

He kissed her hand and attempted to rise when a vigorous knock on the door startled them.

Elizabeth turned pale, struggling to stand and arrange her appearance, her heart beating rapidly. What if they had continued their...activities... and a servant had discovered them!

Troubled, she glanced at her husband who seemed rather amused, no doubt by the same thought.

As if to prove her wrong, the knock repeated, but the door remained closed. Only when Darcy called the person inside did Miles enter hesitantly and hand his master a letter.

"It is from Hertfordshire, sir. Otherwise, I would not have disturbed you with it."

"Thank you."

Elizabeth barely dared to lift her eyes to the valet, but his expression was as calm as ever. His only concern seemed to be to serve his master and gain his approval. Undoubtedly, no member of the staff would ever dare enter a room where Darcy was without permission. There was no danger from that point of view, but the thought of locking the library door—as Darcy had suggested—turned Elizabeth's cheeks red with shame and left her wondering.

"Let us see what it says... Here—this is a note for you from Jane. Very considerate of her—Bingley's letters are rarely readable."

Elizabeth laughed and sat on the settee, pulling the candle closer. She barely had time to look at the first lines when Darcy interrupted with enthusiasm.

"So—Bingley finally came to his senses. It seems the wedding will take place in six weeks after all."

"Yes, Jane wrote me the same. I am very happy for them," Elizabeth said, but her husband pulled the paper from her hand quite unceremoniously and sat beside her.

"Since there is nothing urgent, we can speak of this later."

Elizabeth laughed within his kiss, and her hands encircled his waist.

"We should read to the end, though," she whispered, but her suggestion met with little attention.

Darcy blew out the candle near her, and the room was suddenly half-dark. They were both sitting, and he gently pushed her back then lowered to meet her eyes—and her lips. Small kisses covered her face, tantalised the corner of her mouth, then the tip of her ear, her jaw, her chin, and then returned to her lips.

"You must believe I am a savage, but I can think of little else than kissing you…touching you…tasting you…loving you. I know a gentleman should possess better control, but I have lost it…completely."

"You are not a savage…" she murmured. "And you know that I think of little else but you too. A lady should also possess more control."

Darcy smiled at her willingness to share the blame with him and ended the debate with another passionate kiss.

"You are right. Let us finish reading our letters, and then perhaps we can take a stroll near the house before dinner."

"That is an excellent idea," Elizabeth said, but—to her mortification—she found herself disappointed at not following his first plan.

She scolded herself for such wantonness while trying to concentrate on the letter—filled with more feelings and confessions of happiness than with information.

"If the weather turns better, Jane said she will come to Town for a week. She wishes to order wedding clothes. Perhaps I could schedule a visit to the modiste after she arrives…"

"My beloved wife—I trust you will find the best way of solving this problem. I am sure Lady Ellen will be happy to assist. As for me—I am ready to provide any support you might need, but I do not require further details."

Elizabeth laughed. "You sound like Papa when he speaks of lace, and you are only half his age."

"I am uncertain whether I should take that as a compliment or a censure. However, I doubt any man—whatever his age—has much interest in modistes or lace. We prefer to admire the final result of these efforts."

She continued to laugh, enjoying her husband's teasing and his small kisses tantalising the back of her hand. She vividly recollected the first time he kissed her hand—in the Netherfield library—and that evening in his house when she first felt his lips on her wrist. She shivered just remembering her feelings then and the growth of those feelings, emotions, and sensations during the last weeks.

"But our conversation has made me realise that there are two things I need to purchase without delay."

"What could they be? I cannot imagine anything missing in this house."

"One would be a small piano for your apartment. I would like to admire your playing later at night."

"I would love that very much. And the second?"

Although the room was almost dark and there was no one around, Darcy leant to whisper in her ear.

"A large bathtub."

She was genuinely puzzled and withdrew a few inches, staring at him. "But there are two—one in each of our apartments."

"Precisely. I think a larger one—fit for two people—would be more appropriate. One for here and one for Pemberley."

Her eyes opened widely and her cheeks coloured while amusement spread over his face.

Elizabeth thought of something to reply, but she felt uncertain at how to debate the subject. She tried to put a trace of mockery in her voice as she responded.

"You must know best what purchases are needed in either of our houses, Mr. Darcy. I trust your judgement."

"I thank you, Mrs. Darcy. Your trust pleases me exceedingly."

THE DAY, SPENT IN SWEET TEASING AND STOLEN IMPROPRIETIES, WAS SLOWLY coming to an end.

It was late in the afternoon, and it was getting dark when the couple left the house for a short walk.

It was no longer snowing, but the weather had turned colder. The sky was serene, lit by the stars. As they walked, the snow crunched under their shoes.

Elizabeth walked carefully to avoid slipping. She was holding Darcy's arm tightly, and from time to time, she intentionally stepped through a pile of fresh snow. Before long, her shoes and lower gown were frozen. Her cheeks turned red as she glanced at her husband frequently.

"There is something else that I must purchase for you," he suddenly said.

She turned her wondering gaze toward him, her cheeks even more coloured as she remembered their previous conversation. Immediately, her mind was filled with the image of them both, warming together in a large bathtub…

"What is it?"

"A pair of thick, winter boots. And perhaps some trousers to wear under your dress from November to March whenever you walk outside."

He was so serious that she burst out in laughter.

"You are very thoughtful, sir."

He put his hands over hers to warm them, his broad smile matching hers.

"Are you cold? Shall we return?"

"Let us stay only a little longer, please."

"Very well—we will do as you like."

They took the direction of Hyde Park, with the intention of not going far.

The streets were mostly empty; some fast walkers passed through the park toward their own homes. The prospect of walking in such freezing weather appealed to very few people.

As they spoke quietly, Elizabeth's attention was drawn to a small bench where an unknown person sat hunched over, apparently trying to fight the cold.

She directed Darcy's attention to the person, and they approached the bench together. Darcy gently pushed Elizabeth behind him—in an attempt to protect her—then slowly touched the person.

"Hello there. Are you well? May we help you in some way?"

There was a slight movement; then, from behind a thick shawl, the small face of a young woman appeared.

"Are you hurt?" Darcy insisted, and he received a gesture of denial.

"What are you doing here?" Elizabeth spoke with a soft voice, trying to encourage the strange woman. "It is dangerous to stay outside in this weather. Where do you live?"

"Nowhere," was the weak response. "I mean..."

"Are you waiting for something here? For someone?"

"No..."

Darcy and Elizabeth looked at each other in puzzlement; then he gently took the girl's arm.

"You cannot stay here in the cold. You will come with us, have some hot tea, and warm yourself."

An astonished gaze expressed the girl's disbelief.

"Come with you? But why?"

"Why? Because you will freeze to death here," Darcy answered decidedly, almost forcing the girl to rise. She seemed unsteady on her feet and fearful to move, but Elizabeth took her other arm.

"Come—do not be afraid. We are Mr. and Mrs. Darcy. Our house is just around the corner. You will be properly attended. Do not be afraid."

As they walked together, the cold was so sharp that Elizabeth could barely feel her feet and cheeks. With horror, she wondered how long the girl had been sitting there and what might have happened to her had they not found her. She already could barely move; if not for their support, she would have indeed fallen after the first step.

Eventually, they entered the house, and the footmen stared at them in shock.

"Fetch Mrs. Hamilton! And Miles!"

Only a minute later, both appeared, and the housekeeper gasped in surprise. Darcy allowed no time for questions.

"We just found this girl on a park bench. She seems frozen, and she might be hurt. Please take proper care of her and let us know how she is. We will be ready for dinner in an hour."

"Yes—of course. Right away, sir."

Miles supported the girl to walk downstairs while a maid took her small luggage. The girl still did not speak; she seemed lost and frightened.

"Mrs. Hamilton, let us know if we need to fetch a doctor," Elizabeth added.

"Of course, ma'am."

Elizabeth and Darcy returned to their rooms, hand in hand. Elizabeth was preoccupied with the strange girl; Darcy was even more affected by his wife's distress.

"What could be the meaning of this? Poor girl—did you see her face? I think she is no older than Lydia or Georgiana."

"Yes…it was fortunate that you spotted her."

"She was lucky, indeed. If we had not gone for a walk…I cannot imagine finding her there in the morning, frozen to death."

"Do not worry; she will be safe now. We will help her any way we can if she needs assistance."

Darcy stole a kiss then caressed her hair. "Come, we should change our clothes too."

He continued to place small kisses along her face—then stopped as he noticed that she was preoccupied. No doubt, the incident affected her deeply, so he cupped her face with his warm palms and made her look at him.

"What is on your mind, my beloved wife?"

"Forgive me…I was just thinking…had you not involved yourself in forcing Wickham to marry Lydia, he might have abandoned her somewhere. She could have been in the same situation…"

"Please, stop! First—I do not think even Wickham would have done something so horrible. Second—even if Lydia were in such a dangerous situation, she would never stay outside to freeze. She is a decided young woman who knows to fight for her well-being if needed. And she has a loving family who would have sheltered her, despite her errors."

She forced a smile. "True...but your help was no less valuable, nevertheless. Now let us change for dinner. Forgive me for being in such a poor mood."

His lips rested on her neck and tasted it tenderly.

"I do not want to impose on you just now, but once you are certain the girl is fine, and we have had a quiet dinner, I intend to change your mood, Mrs. Darcy."

Her smile widened, and she put her arms around his neck.

"For this, you will not have to work very hard, Mr. Darcy. I have longed to be alone with you."

They called for Molly and Miles and retired to their rooms. As they were quickly ready, Elizabeth found herself having some time on her hands before dinner. She hesitated a few moments, listened at the door, heard Darcy talking to Miles, and left the room in some haste.

From the time spent in the house—even before their engagement—she knew the surroundings well. She went toward the kitchen and asked about Mrs. Hamilton and the girl.

"They are in the third room down the hall, Mrs. Darcy. Shall I fetch them?"

"No—no, I will go there. Thank you."

As she approached, she heard Mrs. Hamilton, another maid, and a small, lost voice.

"You must not be afraid. You are fortunate: you happen to be in the house of the most generous mistress ever. Mrs. Darcy is the most kind and considerate young lady," the maid said.

"And so is the master," Mrs. Hamilton quickly added, and Elizabeth smiled to herself.

"I...I do not want to intrude...I will leave right away. Thank you for your care..."

"But where will you go? Do you have family in London?"

"I have an aunt...she works at a small inn...but she is not in Town now. She will help me go back to my family. They live near Oxford...in a small village..."

"But you cannot leave now in the middle of the night. The mistress will not allow it. You may leave tomorrow if you want."

"But I cannot give you so much trouble. I thank you, but—"

"Nonsense—I am going to talk to Mr. and Mrs. Darcy now," Mrs. Hamilton concluded, and Elizabeth stepped forward, knocking on the open door. Immediately, everyone rose to their feet. Elizabeth smiled kindly and asked them to sit. The maid brought a chair for Elizabeth then apologised and left.

Elizabeth looked at the woman; she was young and handsome. Her cheeks, recovered after the cold, were red and complemented her dark eyes. She mostly looked at the floor and barely held Elizabeth's gaze.

"I thank you for your kindness, Mrs. Darcy. I beg you to forgive me for all the trouble. I told Mrs. Hamilton…I will leave at once…"

"Do not worry…there is no trouble. What is your name?"

"Maud…Maud Lovell, ma'am…"

"And how old are you?"

"I am eighteen."

"Maud, will you tell me what you were doing in the park? I just want to know how we can help you."

"I thank you, ma'am…I am sorry…"

"Do you know someone in Town? Can we offer you a carriage to go somewhere? Or to send for someone?"

"I have an aunt…I went to talk to her, but she is not in Town. She will return in two days and…"

Elizabeth could see that the girl was too distressed to carry on a reasonable conversation, so she smiled and ceased her inquiry.

"Maud, this is what we will do: you will stay here for the next two days until your aunt returns. You will eat something then rest, and we will talk more tomorrow. I can see you are in a difficult situation, and you are distressed by it. I shall not insist further now. As long as you are honest with us, we will give you all the help you need. Good night."

"I…thank you, Mrs. Darcy…I will not…I thank you…" The young woman was tearful, and Elizabeth gently touched her arm.

"Mrs. Hamilton will take care of everything. Good night."

She left with the housekeeper following her. Upstairs in the main hall, Elizabeth asked with no little concern, "Mrs. Hamilton, what is your opinion? Did you manage to learn any more details?"

"She did not speak much. She is very troubled—and chilled—but mostly very troubled. She has an aunt who works at a small inn—a questionable one, I would say. The woman was out of town, sent by the inn's owner. For some reason, Maud did not remain there to wait; she preferred to stay in the park—in this weather!"

"Well, I can suspect why a young girl would rather depart from the inn's owner," Elizabeth said bitterly.

"Indeed, ma'am, she is very pretty. And her speech is articulate. I suspect she worked as a maid in a good household, but for some reason, she was dismissed with severity. She said she was given no payment at all. Strange…I will try to learn more tomorrow…"

"Mrs. Hamilton, I value your experience and your wisdom. Do you think she might be a danger to others in the house? Was I wrong to host her? I would not want to cause any distress to our staff."

"No, ma'am—not at all. I think it was a gesture of mercy and kindness. Although I cannot imagine how many other ladies would have done it."

Elizabeth ignored the praise. "Very well. Let her rest now. Please have dinner served. Mr. Darcy and I will be there at once."

She hurried to Darcy, her heart still unsettled. She knew she made the best decision for the lost girl, but not knowing the whole truth was troubling to her.

Elizabeth met her husband in the main hall where he had wandered in search of her. He kissed her hand then placed it on his arm while they moved to the dining room.

As soon as the first course was served, Elizabeth shared with Darcy the brief encounter.

"Mrs. Hamilton believes Maud was a maid. She must have done something wrong to be thrown out of the house in such weather and without any wages. I hope she did not do anything horrible. She is so pretty and looks so well behaved. I wonder why someone would expose her to the risk of death."

Darcy said nothing—only responded with a smile to reassure and calm his wife.

While Elizabeth continued her speculations, Darcy took her hand gently.

"My darling, let us eat now. There is no need for more distress. I suggest talking to her tomorrow. I hope she will tell us what happened. If I am content with her honesty, I will let it be your choice to either help her find her aunt or offer her a job in our house. I think we can afford another maid."

Elizabeth's eyes brightened. "Thank you, my love. Your generous kindness never ceases to amaze me."

"I only try to do what is right—and what gives you pleasure." He smiled then turned serious again. "I am happy and proud to comply with your wishes, first because I love you so much but also because your requests are continuing proofs of your character. You never ask for anything to spoil yourself. You have complete liberty to order gowns, to make changes in the house, and to use your pin money as you wish—about which, by the way, you did not even ask. And yet, you prefer to help a strange young woman or go to Pemberley—but that I already refused."

"You are too kind to me and too severe on yourself. What could I possibly want when you give me everything? And why would I try to spoil myself when no other woman is so spoilt by her husband?"

"It is rather pleasant to be so praised, so I shall not interrupt you." He attempted a joke, and she laughed.

"Well, sir, I was under the impression that you were already accustomed to praise. Even I had the chance to hear certain ladies praise your exceptional qualities," she answered, raising her eyebrow.

"I warn you, madam, that I intend to complain to Mrs. Bennet about any more teasing on that subject."

"You are free to do so, sir, as I cannot promise to cease teasing you. I look forward to seeing how Miss Bingley behaves in your presence now that she knows she has no chance of winning you for herself."

"I beg to differ: there was nothing to win as there was no competition." He took her hand and placed a soft kiss on her palm. "You won my heart from the second time I saw you. And that is only because, the first time, I did not look at you with enough attention."

Their hands remained entwined for a few minutes, and his fingers gently caressed hers, sending chills along her arm.

"I love the feeling of my hand in yours," she whispered, their eyes locked.

He kissed her palm again. "I think we should go upstairs. I shall ask for some sweets and drinks to be sent to my apartment."

"Yes, we should. Although, I do not believe much more food will be needed."

THE REST OF THE EVENING WAS SPENT IN TENDER LOVEMAKING AND SWEET teasing.

Sometime after midnight, they both felt hungry, proving to Elizabeth once again that Darcy was wise and cautious in asking the rest of the dinner to be brought to his suite. The room was cold, despite the roaring fire, so they dressed and wrapped themselves in thick night robes. Darcy brought a tray of food to the bed and offered it to his wife.

They started eating, but their gazes proved they were more preoccupied with each other than with the meal.

Darcy could hardly keep his eyes away from her beautiful face glowing with happiness, framed by long, dark locks flowing over her shoulders. His intense look soon made her blush, and her eyes laughed at him.

"You are staring again, sir."

"I know; I am sorry." Neither his mischievous glance nor the little smile twisting his lips confirmed his words.

"May I ask why?"

"Because you are so beautiful, and I still cannot believe you are my wife."

"Oh…" The pleasure of his confession made her heart race.

They continued eating, and it was Elizabeth's turn to watch her husband with growing insistence.

"And may I ask why you are staring at me, Mrs. Darcy? And I beg—do not say that I am pretty."

The word used with so much determination by Becky turned Elizabeth's smile into laughter.

"And yet—you are, Mr. Darcy. But that is not the reason. I was thinking of the first night we ate together on the bed…after Lady Catherine's visit…"

His face shadowed, and he leant to gently caress her hair.

"I thought of that night too. If not for the horrible distress you had to suffer from my aunt—and from my selfish pride—I would say that night was one of the most beautiful of my life."

"Yes, mine too…"

There were a few moments of complete silence—sweet, tender memories contending with the recollection of that terrible afternoon.

"I would not have imagined your being so scary," Elizabeth attempted to joke. "The staff was completely frightened."

"I have a bad temper—very much like my aunt and uncle. Even Lady Ellen said so. Robert declared it was a wonder that you still wanted to marry me."

Elizabeth touched his face with immense tenderness.

"I love everything about you, including your bad temper. And you are, without a doubt, the best man I have ever known. And the most perfect husband."

"I only hope to be the husband you deserve, my beloved."

"You already are. Not to mention that you are very pretty and have dimples. 'Dimples is good, you know,'" Elizabeth teased him with Becky's words, but her laughter was suddenly crushed within a passionate kiss and the tray of delicious food found a most undeserved place on the floor.

Chapter 4

Elizabeth woke the next morning spooned in her husband's arms. She smiled to herself and sighed then put her hands over his. She felt rested and wanted to rise from the bed, but she could not abandon his closeness.

She slowly turned to face him. Their bodies still wore the warmth of the previous night's lovemaking, and she shivered as her breasts brushed against his chest. Her left hand glided around his waist. Through his deep sleep, he released a moan then turned on his back. Elizabeth's smile widened while she watched him with great interest. His breathing was steady, and his expression showed peace and contentment.

He looked even more handsome in his sleep. Elizabeth withdrew a few more inches so she could have a better view of the man she loved. Her fingers travelled—without really touching—along his face, his neck, his shoulders, then stopped upon his heart and her lips joined them, resting warmly on his skin.

Darcy felt a chill shattering his body, and his sleep vanished when Elizabeth's hair touched him. A moment later, her soft fingers burned him and he captured her hand—making her let out a soft cry of surprise. He brought her hand to his lips as she laughed with delight.

"Forgive me for awakening you, my love."

His arms trapped her.

"I am glad you did, my dearest. For so long I have dreamt that your beautiful face would be the first thing I would see in the morning and the last at night…and several times between…" He covered her cheeks with small kisses.

She chuckled, delighted by the sweet indulgence.

"It must be almost noon—I cannot remember when I last slept so much," he continued, and she laughed.

"I would rather say you slept *late* but not much."

"True. Last time I remember it was almost dawn. Did you sleep well?"

"Very well. Not much but very well…" She cuddled against his chest, and he kissed her hair.

"I love your teasing, Mrs. Darcy."

"Then you may depend upon my teasing you as often as I can, Mr. Darcy."

THE DARCYS APPEARED FOR BREAKFAST AT NOON

At Elizabeth's request, Mrs. Hamilton informed them that the young woman found in the park was feeling unwell. She had been feverish the entire night, and it appeared she had caught a very bad cold.

"Send for Dr. Harris," Darcy said. "See if there is something to be done for her."

"Very well, sir." The housekeeper was about to leave then turned to her master. "Sir, I was just thinking: in the ten years I have run this household, no one on the staff has been severely ill. Except Spencer, but he was already sixty when I came to the house."

"True. This proves your excellent management, Mrs. Hamilton." Darcy smiled with a glance at Elizabeth, but the housekeeper continued in all seriousness.

"No indeed, sir—it proves that, in this house, the staff is treated with care and fairness. Thank you, sir."

"Mrs. Hamilton, just see what can be done in the present situation and let us know."

When they were alone, Elizabeth smiled at her husband.

"You receive thanks and gratitude very poorly, Mr. Darcy. Your kindness and generosity are indeed praiseworthy—only I failed to notice it at first."

He returned the smile and took her hand. "Let us not speak of this any longer. Since we brought the woman into our home, it is our duty to offer her proper care. It is the only honourable thing to do. Now, can we have some music? I would love to hear you play."

"I admire you as much as I love you, William. I am sure the girl will owe her life to you, even if you do not want to admit it. And yes, I would happily play for you."

An hour later, the doctor's report was as good as could be expected. Two days and a night spent in the icy weather did not happen without consequences, but the physician was confident that it was no more than a cold, which would pass with tea, good food, and some rest in a warm chamber—requirements that were quickly provided.

Elizabeth felt strangely affected by the young woman, and she had to fight with herself to be reasonable about the entire situation. She realised that Maud would have found better care nowhere else.

With a heavy heart, she tried to be as good company as possible for her husband. However, a sudden headache lowered her spirits even more, but she sought to hide it behind a polite smile.

She played for Darcy, they read together, and then, in the afternoon, he took care of some letters from his solicitor while she wrote a note for the modiste to establish an appointment in a few days.

Darcy repeatedly inquired whether she was well as she looked pale and tired, but she assured him everything was fine. However, it was not as her back started to ache too, and her stomach felt sick. Later on, he proposed a short stroll before dinner, which Elizabeth gladly accepted. The fresh air lifted her spirits, and while the headache did not dissipate, she still enjoyed walking by her husband's side.

When they returned home, Elizabeth fetched Molly to help her dress for dinner. She felt tired and wondered how it was possible as it was still early and she had not done anything that would explain her state.

She lay down for a few moments, and when she rose to dress, she heard the maid release a small cry.

"Mrs. Darcy, are you hurt?"

Elizabeth was puzzled and followed the maid's gaze; then both came to the same understanding, seeing the red spot on the sheets.

"Oh, forgive me, ma'am. Let me help you change," Molly said, and Elizabeth barely succeeded in concealing her distress.

The door between the apartments opened without warning, and Darcy appeared, obviously concerned, and then became surprised and worried as he noticed the same red spot. He attempted to speak, but Elizabeth shouted at him:

"Please leave us!"

He left in haste and closed the door as she pulled the robe around her.

Silly, silly me! She had not thought of her courses at all although she should have known it would happen. What was she thinking? What a shame! And the expression on his face—no doubt he was appalled. What was she to do? How does a woman handle this with her husband? If she had remembered to ask Mrs. Gardiner, her aunt surely would have known how to advise her. *Silly, silly me.*

The door from their rooms opened halfway, and Darcy spoke from the opening. "Elizabeth, are you well? Should I fetch Doctor Harris?"

"Oh no—no, not at all. I am very well…I only need some time…I am well. But I will not have dinner tonight…I am sorry."

"I see…as you wish. I will be here in case you need me."

"Thank you," she whispered, and he retired while her cheeks burned from embarrassment.

It was around eight o'clock in the evening, and Elizabeth rested on the bed, covered in blankets, just as she used to do at Longbourn. Except that at Longbourn it was her mother and her sisters, who all knew about her "several days discomfort," and she did not need to worry about what to do or say.

Now, she kept glancing toward the closed door. She dismissed Molly and refused to eat or drink anything except a cup of tea. She only needed to rest and calm down.

The knock on the door startled her although she was expecting it. She shyly invited Darcy to enter, and he stepped in. She forced a smile then averted her eyes.

"Are you well?

"Yes. Please forgive my improper reaction earlier. I was just…I did not want you to…"

"Please do not apologise. May I enter?"

"Yes, of course."

He stepped closer and waited a short distance from the bed. She held his gaze a moment then averted her eyes again. Such heavy tension between them she did not remember experiencing since before their meeting at the cottage.

"I did not want to disturb you. I just wanted to know if you need anything. "

"No, thank you…I just need to rest."

He watched her, obviously wondering how to proceed further, then decided to leave. Elizabeth looked at him in silence; a sudden lump in her throat prevented any words she might have wanted to say. It was the first night they did not share, but it was only natural this way. And yet, the silence of her elegant room seemed hard to bear, and she wished and hoped to see him return. Then she furiously scolded herself for such silly, improper thoughts.

The door opened once more.

"Elizabeth, I…forgive me, may I stay with you?" Without waiting for the answer, Darcy took a seat on the bed. "I am sorry if I embarrassed you. Should I leave? Would you rather be alone?"

"No…your presence is always dear to me. But I am afraid I will not be a joyful companion."

"My love, I do not seek your company only for joy. I simply want to be with you if you will have me."

"I would like that very much," she said with a tearful smile. "Forgive me—this is rather silly. I mean, it is nothing of consequence. I am not ill or anything, and I do not want to worry you. I shall be fine in a couple of days. It is just that…it is very embarrassing. I have never before spoken to a man about it."

"Nor have I ever spoken with a lady…I mean…I do know what you mean, but…I was worried…"

He kissed her hand then caressed her hair. "I noticed you were unwell the entire day. And then I saw the blood, and I was frightened. I imagined it was my fault somehow…that I have not been patient enough or—"

"Oh, this is silly." She laughed to hide her emotions, stroking his face. "We are both silly, truly. I admit it was the most embarrassing situation, and I was not prepared to handle it properly. But we shall not bother to speak of it anymore. I shall stay in bed for a day or two and that will be all."

"May I sleep with you? I mean—near you?" She was at a loss of what to reply, attempting to guess his meaning. He leant and kissed her forehead.

"It would be nice just to sleep with you in my arms as we did before we were married. But if you are uncomfortable, I will return to my room."

"I would love that very much…to sleep in your arms. I could not be more uncomfortable in your absence than I am in your presence. Of that, you must have no doubt."

It took another couple of hours until they finally fell asleep. At Darcy's insistence, Elizabeth ate a little then had some more tea. Afterward, she lay with her eyes closed to subdue her headache, and he read to her.

Eventually, the candles were extinguished, and Elizabeth rested with her head on her husband's chest while he gently stroked her back, her arms, and her hair until all her discomfort was gone. She was almost asleep when she heard him laughing and gazed at him through the darkness of the chamber.

"Forgive me for disturbing you, my love. I was just thinking of how silly we both were about this entire situation. Although, I doubt this will be the most embarrassing moment we have to face in our marriage. I am quite confident that there will be many others even worse than this."

Her eyebrow rose in mocking reproach. "I am glad you are amused, sir."

He quickly stole a kiss. "I confess I am now that I have no reason for concern. But I am mostly pleased that we overcame an incident that was equally stressful and unusual for us. I hope this will happen with any unpleasantness in our life together. I will certainly do whatever I can for this to happen."

"And I can easily promise my share of commitment to it, my dearest husband."

The night passed easily and restfully for Elizabeth as her husband's closeness dispelled any previous discomfort. She slept more and deeper than in all the other nights since she married, and she only rang for Molly around ten o'clock.

Darcy found even less sleep than before as he was careful not to disturb his wife, and he found her presence in his arms rather disturbing to his rest—as happened so many times before they were married.

Therefore, he woke up around eight, drank a large cup of coffee while reading the past week's magazines, then moved to his office to look through his business papers. He knew he needed to keep his mind occupied for a few more days.

THE NEXT THREE DAYS PASSED UNEVENTFULLY. THE YOUNG WOMAN FOUND in the park was slowly improving, and she was able to leave her bed and perform small tasks.

Elizabeth stayed in her room, and Darcy kept her company at breakfast and dinner. She sent another long letter to Jane and one to her father then exchanged a few notes with Georgiana. She also wrote a few words to her aunt Gardiner but kept the description of the "awkward intimate situation" to a moment when they would be able to speak—and amuse themselves—face to face.

The embarrassment completely disappeared between Darcy and her. And, as she was feeling better, she also grew daring with her teasing and admitted—first to herself and then to him—that she missed their passionate interludes.

The third night, as they prepared to sleep and he was again reading to her, Elizabeth tentatively stirred him by touching his face with her lips and his arms with warm fingers—and his restraint soon abandoned him. Passion turned the chaste embrace into caresses and touches and kisses, which became a maddening torture since they could not bring it to the desired ending, and it needed all Darcy's strength to put an end to it.

Elizabeth knew she should be ashamed of her wantonness, but she was not; quite the contrary, she enjoyed realising that she had the same power over her husband as he had over her, and if his caresses and kisses always made her dizzy, it was no different for him.

The following morning, Elizabeth awoke late and found herself alone. The fire was burning steadily, and fresh water for tea was placed on her table. She smiled and rose from the bed with a feeling of easiness. She was rested and well humoured, and she realised her difficult days had passed.

In haste, she called for Molly, washed, and dressed as quickly as she could. She wished to have breakfast with her husband downstairs, but she was told that he was out on business but would return soon.

Elizabeth was disappointed and curious about his early business, but all she could do was to wait.

She used the time to inquire after Maud. Mrs. Hamilton informed her that the girl was much better and proved to be truly skilful at sewing and stitching and was diligent in her duties—news Elizabeth received with much contentment.

She returned to her apartment and started to read then moved to the window. Her heart raced, and a smile lit her face when she observed their carriage and then her husband entering the main gate.

Elizabeth lost all patience and almost ran downstairs. Darcy's expression brightened when he saw her, and he did not hesitate to embrace her tenderly in the main hall and claim a kiss.

"Are you well?" he whispered, and she nodded in agreement.

"I am glad. Come—I have a surprise for you," he said, taking her hand and heading toward the library. He closed the door and invited her to sit. His excitement was contagious, and she kept smiling, wondering what to expect.

"My love, do you remember when I brought you to the library to give you the ruby jewels?"

"Of course, I do. It was only a month ago. How could I forget? I also remember the way you kissed me then," she said teasingly.

His lips only touched hers briefly then he pulled a small velvet box from his pocket.

"This is the first set made especially for you. Not from the family, but my gift for you."

Elizabeth struggled with her emotions as she tried to overcome her surprise. She opened the box and discovered a stunning topaz cross pendant with matching earrings.

"It has your initials engraved on the back—both the cross and the earrings."

She gasped and stared at it while Darcy pulled out the cross and placed it on her neck. The pendant was made from small teardrop-shaped pieces, combined to form a stylish cross that caressed and lit her skin.

"This is so beautiful," she whispered.

Elizabeth moved to the small wall mirror and admired her gift. He put his arms around her, his lips lingering on her shoulder. While she wondered about the reason for such an exquisite gift, she finally realised and turned into his embrace.

"It is our one-week anniversary!"

"Yes, it is. I am glad you like it."

"I most certainly adore it, my love. But I would have loved anything that comes from you—and your mere presence more than anything."

Darcy caressed her face tenderly then captured her mouth in a long-desired kiss that took her breath away.

Some moments later, Elizabeth suddenly broke the kiss. He watched her, puzzled, as she seemed intent on leaving. However, she only moved to the door and locked it then returned to him, a smile twisting the corners of her lips. Daringly, she took his hand and made him sit in his large armchair at the massive wooden desk, pulled the curtains closed, then sat on his lap.

"This is where we stopped a few days ago…when we went upstairs," she said breathlessly while his hands eagerly stroked her roundness.

She did not really know what was going to happen, but she trusted he would guide her—and he did. It was their first "anniversary," they had yearned for each other for many days, and there was not an instant longer to be wasted nor a second thought to ruin her pleasure.

He hastily took off his waistcoat, then pulled her gown up and made her sit astride him. She gasped as the newly discovered position raised different feelings inside her. Only now did she realise how much she had missed his kisses, his caresses, his passion, and the sensation of his being inside her.

Darcy's desire grew stronger as he witnessed her increased trust, daring, and confidence. The notion that she had agreed and even instigated this most delightful intimacy in the library—a place with so much significance for them—aroused his passion more than ever.

He lowered the dress from her shoulders, exposing her skin to his eyes and touches. The pendant still shone on her throat, and he placed a kiss upon it.

Elizabeth's emotions became overwhelming, and her mind could hardly understand what was happening. She only noticed that he removed his clothes and hers. His whispers burned her ear, then a sweet bite on her earlobe made her spine shiver, and she released a small cry as she felt him enter her—gentle, but stronger, deeper, warmer and more gratifying than before.

"Should I stop?" he whispered, and she forced herself to say no although her lips were not free to speak.

There was a small distance between their shared armchair and the desk, and he gently pushed her back. While the cold wood chilled her back, his hands burned her skin with long strokes then cupped her breasts with tender possessiveness. His thumbs tantalised her nipples, which hardened under his touch, and her body arched toward him.

He slowly pulled her up again and her breasts brushed against his torso while their hands encircled each other. Their moves became faster and deeper, and her moans betrayed her growing pleasure, which only fed his own. He suddenly stood with her in his arms, their bodies still joined and her legs around his waist, and moved across the room until she found herself placed on a small table near the couch. She struggled to regain her breathing, and he stopped, watching her carefully for a sign of discomfort, which was not present.

He started kissing her again, stroking and tasting each bare spot of skin, and her own desire quickly defeated the last traces of reservation.

A barely audible knock on the door startled them both, and Elizabeth attempted to escape from his embrace, but his arms closed tighter around her.

"Shhh…do not move," he whispered in her ear, his fingers stroking her hair.

"What is it, Miles?" he asked severely.

"Sir, I apologise for disturbing you. Colonel Fitzwilliam is here to see you."

Elizabeth looked positively frightened, and he could barely contain his laughter while he caressed her shoulders and bit her earlobe.

"Please invite him into the drawing room. I have something to finish and will join him shortly."

"Very well, sir."

Miles's steps could be heard retreating, and Elizabeth was about to say something, but her lips were immediately trapped in another deep kiss while his palms held her thighs and moved slowly together with her.

"William, we cannot…the colonel is waiting," she whispered in a weak attempt to escape his embrace.

"My love, not a full regiment of colonels would be enough to make me stop now," he said. "Unless you insist upon it," he continued, his movements stronger against her, his kisses matching the rhythm of his thrusts inside her.

She moaned, and her legs pressed tighter around his waist.

"I shall never be able to face the colonel again…but I beg you…do not stop…"

It took a few more minutes until their bodies finally came to satisfaction together while their moans were crushed within their joined lips. Their passion, unleashed after several days of restraint, warred with embarrassment for the impropriety of their situation, and their mutual happiness fought against shame and remorse. However, the delight, the contentment, and the silent promise for more soon defeated any other feelings, and they ended the interlude with a last, passionate kiss.

In some haste, Darcy arranged his clothes, then brushed his hair, and went to greet his cousin.

Elizabeth headed upstairs, her gown somehow arranged but far from presentable for guests. On the way to her room, she bit her lips to stop her smile. How did she dare do such a thing? Yet she did it and could not be happier about it. And it was just noon—their "anniversary" only half over.

Chapter 5

For the first time in his eight and twenty years, Darcy met his cousin Robert Fitzwilliam with uneasiness and held his gaze for no longer than a moment. He was afraid that his expression would betray the reason for his delay. Colonel Fitzwilliam knew him well enough to notice any particular disposition—and yes, Darcy was indeed in a delicious mood. The colonel was also very perceptive; he had quickly observed the small gesture of Darcy's touching Elizabeth's shoe under the table at the first dinner they had together. The same evening Mr. Bennet arrived with the shocking revelation of Lydia's elopement. The same evening his plan to propose to Elizabeth was ruined by Wickham.

Happily, all was past now, and Darcy attempted to hide his thoughts behind a glass of brandy after he filled Robert's half-empty one.

"Forgive me for barging in uninvited. I hope I did not disturb you."

"You need no invitation to visit us, Cousin. I am always pleased with your company—and so is Elizabeth."

"I am relieved to hear that."

Darcy felt the colonel's intense gaze; he did not say that the impromptu call did not disturb them. Without a doubt, the colonel caught his meaning.

"Elizabeth will come to greet you shortly. She was not ready to receive guests."

"I understand. I do not want to bother either of you. I just want to ask whether you are open to going to the theatre tomorrow. Mama is very eager to see the new performance of *Hamlet* with some new actor in the leading role; apparently, he is the latest 'most admired man on stage.'" The colonel's voice expressed complete boredom, and his plea to Darcy was full of hope.

Darcy laughed. "So why are you so displeased?"

"Well, there will be my parents, plus Lord and Lady Pemberton with their daughter Marianne, the Countess of Wellford with her second husband and her stepdaughter Sophia, and of course, Thomas and Beatrice."

"Only friends and family." Darcy laughed again. "So you came to beg me to keep you company and save you from Lady Marianne."

The colonel rolled his eyes. "You are very amusing and full of humour now that you are married. I remind you that you have promised my mother to attend this spectacle since December."

"I did no such a thing."

"Of course, you did—when Georgiana started feeling better. But that was before Miss Bennet came to Town and before you decided to wed in a few weeks. I can see why you forgot."

"Do not be jealous, Cousin. A determined man does not delay things unnecessarily. Since I was convinced I must marry Elizabeth, there was no reason to wait longer. But yes, now I remember my promise. I cannot disappoint Lady Ellen. I shall speak to Elizabeth, and if she has nothing against it, we shall come."

"Against what?" Elizabeth smiled from the doorway.

Her appearance was beyond reproach; only her cheeks were still crimson. The cross pendant and the earrings glowed on her skin as she graciously greeted the visitor.

The colonel bowed to her then kissed her hand with warm politeness.

"Mrs. Darcy, please allow me to tell you that you look more beautiful every time I meet you."

"You are very kind, Colonel. It is always a pleasure to see you. And I hope you will address me by my given name from now on. We are family."

"Of course, Elizabeth—I would be honoured. And I must say those jewels are exceedingly flattering to your figure."

Elizabeth's cheeks and neck coloured even more, and the colonel thought it was a lovely sign of her modesty. Darcy took her hand and helped her to the settee as she replied to their guest.

"I thank you. I just received them earlier from William. It has been a week since our wedding."

"I see…" The colonel seemed suddenly uneasy, and he looked from one to the other, realising that he indeed had intruded.

Darcy indicated he should sit and filled his glass once again.

"My dear, Robert reminded me that I promised to attend a play tomorrow night. It is a performance of *Hamlet* with a new actor. Would you like to go? My aunt and uncle will be there with several other guests and also my cousin Thomas and his wife, Beatrice."

"But please do not let that discourage you," the colonel intervened, and Elizabeth laughed aloud while Darcy threw him a reproachful glance.

"Mrs. Darcy…Elizabeth, please forgive my improper mockery. The truth is I am very fond of my brother; he is an excellent man. But I am not equally happy with his choice of a wife. My sister-in-law and I are not the best of friends."

"I am sorry to hear that, Colonel. I met your brother, Lord Buxton, and Lady Beatrice at Lady Ellen's ball. From what I heard, Lady Beatrice is the daughter of a marquess and one of the most admired young heiresses in Town with a considerable fortune and excellent connections. Perhaps she just needs more time to adapt to your family. I am confident that things will turn out well in the end."

The colonel did not miss the subtle reference to Lady Beatrice's situation in life, and he could not deny that both his parents had approved of her enthusiastically at the beginning and highly supported Thomas's intention to marry her. Unfortunately, Lady Ellen proved wrong in her estimation that time.

"Well, they have been married for quite some time now, and things have not improved in the slightest," he said, taking another gulp of brandy.

"If your brother is happy with his choice, that is what matters most, is it not?" Elizabeth added.

"Indeed…if only he were happy."

Elizabeth continued with a slightly sharp, teasing voice. "I imagine you were not very happy with Mr. Darcy's choice of a wife, either, but I dare say things improved in time between us."

"I cannot deny that. But I will tell you what I told my mother even before she met you: my opinion about you changed the moment I saw how happy Darcy was in your presence. I would be very content if my sister-in-law would look at my brother the way you look at my cousin."

Elizabeth's smile paled with emotion, and she found nothing more to say. Darcy took her hand to his lips.

"It will be a pleasure to spend a lovely time with all of you at the theatre," Elizabeth concluded politely, and she quickly turned the conversation to Georgiana, whom she had not seen in a few days and truly missed.

They were interrupted by the sudden entrance of Dr. Harris. At seeing the colonel, the doctor apologised even before he had time to greet them and attempted to leave the room.

Darcy invited him to join them, and the doctor hesitantly accepted.

"Forgive my intrusion, Mr. Darcy. I came to check on my patient, and I wished to take this opportunity to give my regards to you and Mrs. Darcy. I shall not bother you any longer."

"Sir, please stay only a moment and have a drink with us," Darcy replied.

"And how is the girl?" Elizabeth inquired.

"She is improving. Her state is still not entirely satisfactory, but Mrs. Hamilton reported to me that she refuses to keep to her bed. Fortunately, she is warm and benefits from proper food and care, so I trust she will be her usual self in a few days."

"Did Mrs. Hamilton offer you the remuneration for your services?"

"Yes, ma'am, of this I never worry in regard to Mr. Darcy."

The colonel looked at them in complete puzzlement, and as soon as the doctor's short visit ended, Darcy gave him details regarding the new addition to their household.

"If not for Elizabeth, most likely the girl would have frozen to death," Darcy concluded.

"Yes, it was quite fortunate. Sadly, such situations are not rare. The master and mistress have complete power over the lives of their servants. God knows what stupid error this girl had done, and she was thrown out with no mercy. You know, I do not think anyone else living in this part of Town would take the trouble to even speak to someone lost on a bench in the park."

"I am sure anyone would have done the same, Colonel. Or at least, you and William would," Elizabeth said warmly.

"Yes, well—perhaps. Now, I feel I have stayed too long. My mother is waiting for me at dinner, and she allows no delay. She will be happy to hear you will join us tomorrow."

"So are we. I am sure it will be at least four very entertaining hours."

"My servant will bring some wine. I always prefer to have my own in such cases," the colonel said.

Colonel Fitzwilliam left after a visit that lasted an hour and a half, promising to convey their warm greetings to Georgiana and his parents.

Mr. and Mrs. Darcy informed the staff they would have dinner in their apartment, and in the privacy of their rooms, they continued the celebration of their first "anniversary."

The next morning found Elizabeth sleeping soundly in her husband's tight embrace, wearing nothing but the jewels he gave her and a trace of their shared passion.

IMMEDIATELY AFTER BREAKFAST, MRS. HAMILTON INQUIRED WHETHER they had reached a decision about Maud. The young woman had asked to be given more tasks—to be helpful to the house.

"Please bring her here. We will talk to her, then Mrs. Darcy will decide the best course of action," Darcy said, and the housekeeper exited to comply with his request. Elizabeth smiled at her husband.

"I understand her family is lacking the means to support themselves. And her aunt works as a servant at that inn. I doubt she can be of much help. Could we offer her an assignment in the house?"

"We could...but I want to know where she stayed before and the reason for her leaving. I have always avoided hiring people we cannot trust, even if their situation is pitiful."

"I understand...I find your reasoning very wise."

"However, I will accept any decision you make. You are the mistress of the house," he said, briefly kissing her hand.

The young woman entered behind Mrs. Hamilton as if she were trying to hide.

"I am pleased that you look better," Elizabeth said kindly, noticing the girl's unusual pallor.

"I thank you for your generous help, ma'am. I am truly grateful."

"Maud is your name?" Darcy asked, watching her carefully.

"Yes, sir."

"Maud, where is your family from?"

"A small village near Oxford."

"Do you have parents? Siblings?"

"My father passed away five years ago. I have two brothers and two sisters."

"I see. So you came to Town to work, I imagine. Can you tell me what you did for a living?"

"I was a maid, sir." The answer finally came with a trembling voice.

"And do you intend to find a place in another household? Or do you have other plans?"

"Yes…I mean…I am not sure if I can…I have no plans, sir." The woman's face turned paler, and she could barely whisper. Darcy glanced at Elizabeth, who continued in a softer tone.

"Maud, you can work here if you wish. You shall have a trial period, and if Mrs. Hamilton is content with your performance, we expect a long-time commitment. Would you like that?"

Astonishment made the young woman silent and tearful, and she could barely nod in gratitude. Then Darcy stepped forward again.

"However, Maud, I must know why you were in the middle of the park on a very cold evening. Why did you leave your previous position? I cannot admit a stranger into this house without knowing more details."

The woman's knees seemed to betray her, and she clasped her hands together to stop their tremor.

"The mistress dismissed me two days ago. She was very upset and asked me to leave the house at once. Then I went to talk to my aunt, but she was not at the inn, and I did not know what to do. I slept the first night at the inn in the hall, but I had no money to pay, so I had to leave. I sat on the bench to rest…and then you found me. I thank you so much…I did not expect. Forgive me…"

"Maud, I see you are distressed, but I need you to answer me directly: why was the mistress so upset with you that she threw you out of the house? And with no proper payment? It seems a rather harsh measure. You must have done something dreadful."

She was ghostly pale. "I broke the rules of the house, sir. That is all I can say."

"Did you steal anything?"

"Oh no—no—I would never do that. No sir…"

Darcy paused a moment, watching her carefully.

"I see. So, Maud—if Mrs. Darcy decides to hire you, how can we be confident you will not break the rules of this house too?"

"I will never do that, sir. It will never happen again—never."

"Very well—we shall see."

"Maud, you will remain with us. Our expectation is that you will accomplish your duties acceptably. You will work with a worthy staff, and I trust you will quickly find your place. Mrs. Hamilton, please take care of everything," Elizabeth said warmly, and the housekeeper approved then showed the young woman out.

When they were alone, Darcy poured himself a glass of wine while Elizabeth filled her cup of tea.

"What do you think, William? Is she guilty of some sort of crime? Otherwise, why would they throw her out to freeze to death? She refused to say more, and she is reluctant to speak against her former employer. She seems polite and modest—she surely does not deserve such treatment."

Darcy took a few moments to search for the proper words. He looked at Elizabeth, slightly embarrassed, then took her hand.

"My suspicion is that she became involved on a personal level with someone in the house and the mistress did not accept it."

"I see...you must be right. But still—that is hardly a reason for such cruel measures!"

"Except if he was a gentleman...if she was involved with the master or the master's son."

"Oh...yes, that is very likely. But—the gentlemen himself who was the subject of this—how could he allow the girl to be thrown out to her possible death? And speaking of this—he surely cannot be called a gentleman. He is just a horrible human being. Even worse than the mistress herself! I hope it was not a respectable family, or I would be very disappointed. People in possession of means, education, and connections are even more horrible when they take advantage of those below them. Surely, this girl was just a victim."

Elizabeth grew angrier as she spoke, and Darcy smiled then kissed her hair.

"My love, you are right, of course. It was wrong, and this young woman was apparently saved from death. But we cannot know the entire situation. I mean—she might have been smitten with the young son who can easily be still a boy. From her behaviour, she seems to feel guilty and not at all indifferent to the people behind all this. It is not unusual for a young man to fall for a lovely maid. In this case, he can hardly make any decision—he might not even have been at home when she was asked to leave."

"Yes, that could be. Perhaps someone is looking for her as we speak and wishes to help her."

"My dear, I do not want you to entertain too much hope as I dread to see you disappointed. There can be many other circumstances that we cannot even guess now. I know it sounds horrible, but it frequently happens within marriages of convenience that a respectable gentleman prefers to spend his nights with a young maid than with his wife, who is very pleased with such arrangements."

"Yes, I know. I am not naive," Elizabeth replied, turning from pale to red. "But this is just horrible. I know for some it can be acceptable, but I find it appalling. And it cannot be the case here; if it had been, Maud would not have been sent away. Or would she? Perhaps that so-called gentleman became bored with the arrangement and searched for someone new. Oh—this is too ugly to even speak of!"

He smiled and kissed her hand again. "It gives me so much pleasure to hear your decided opinion. I know you find it horrible—which is why you did not make a marriage of convenience." He teased her, but she became even more serious and distressed.

"This is why I said so many times that I feel blessed. Marrying for love is for many women only a dream."

"And for many men also, my love. I feel blessed too. And no matter what may have happened to Maud, she will be safe now that she has met you. I told you a long time ago that you have the power to bring joy into people's lives."

She laughed, and tears glittered in her eyes.

"You spoil me with undeserved compliments, dear husband. But please continue to do so."

IN THE AFTERNOON, ELIZABETH STARTED TO PREPARE FOR THE THEATRE. Mrs. Hamilton came to assist Molly in arranging the mistress's hair, and more than an hour was needed before all of them declared themselves content with the result.

Elizabeth knew her appearance would be carefully observed and harshly judged. She wished to be the Mrs. Darcy that her husband deserved on his arm.

She chose a pale green dress, and complemented it with the set of jewels she received the previous day. For a moment, she was tempted to wear another set of ornaments from those given to her after the marriage but she was too fond of her new and more meaningful gift.

A last glance in the mirror showed an image she was pleased to display when Darcy knocked on the door, and his expression of deep admiration was her best reward and confirmation.

"You look beautiful, my love. Any dress, any jewel, any colour suits you so well. Your eyes are simply glowing."

"I thank you, my love. My eyes are glowing not from the dress or jewels but from my love for you," she replied with a tender smile, and he touched her lips with his.

"Let us be careful. I cannot afford to ruin my appearance," she said teasingly. "I am forced to look my best since so many gazes will be fixed on me only to find fault. I feel obliged to prove your good taste in choosing your wife, Mr. Darcy."

"I hope you are only mocking me, my dear. You cannot possibly give any consideration to such criticisms that, I must warn you, will come anyway, no matter how perfect you are."

He helped her enter the carriage then sat in front of her and took her hands in his.

"You are so beautiful," Darcy repeated. This time his voice was hoarse, and his eyes gazed deeply into hers. A chill ran along her spine, and Elizabeth unconsciously bit her lips. His eyes lowered toward her mouth, then he suddenly stole a kiss—a very brief one as he reluctantly separated from her only a moment later.

"I shall not risk ruining your perfect appearance, Mrs. Darcy, do not worry. For now. However, on the way home, I cannot promise the same decorum in my behaviour."

"I once considered you the most proper of men. But, as it happened with my other judgements of you, in time I gained a better understanding of your true nature," she teased him, her voice carrying a sweetness he found impossible to resist. She caressed his face and continued more seriously. "You are like deep, dark water. One must have courage to dive into it and search carefully to discover all the beauty and kindness and generosity you are hiding."

He kissed her hands, the emotion apparent on his face.

"And you, my beloved, are like a fresh, lively summer breeze. You stirred my soul and warmed my heart—and now I can barely breathe when I am not with you.

Their entwined hands and locked gazes spoke the rest. The steps of the horses were the only sounds that broke the silence, filled with so much tenderness that even their hearts forgot to beat.

"Here, I have another small gift for you," he finally said, releasing her hands reluctantly to place a small box in her palm. She opened it with surprise and curiosity to find, against a background of black velvet, an exquisite golden opera glass.

"It belonged to my mother. I thought you would like it. We may also order a new one if you prefer."

"This is exquisite. I am happy and honoured to have it. Thank you."

They only needed a few more minutes to reach their destination. In front of the impressive building, there was a large gathering, and the carriages kept arriving.

As soon as they entered arm in arm, Colonel Fitzwilliam hurried to them.

"I am very pleased to see you. We arrived a little earlier. Lady Ellen does not enjoy throngs and disorder. She is already in our box with the other ladies in our party. My father and Thomas are greeting some acquaintances."

The colonel politely pulled aside the thick curtain that covered the entrance to the box where Lady Matlock, Georgiana, Lady Beatrice, and four other ladies were carrying on a rather cold conversation.

Three of the ladies Elizabeth remembered seeing at Lady Matlock's private ball; the fourth was a young girl of Georgiana's age—Sophia.

Greetings were exchanged, and Lady Matlock invited Elizabeth to sit near her and her niece. Elizabeth thanked her aunt then embraced Georgiana affectionately.

Darcy took the chair right behind his wife then tenderly kissed his sister's hands.

"My dear, you look lovely."

"I am happy to see you, Brother; I missed you both so much."

"We missed you too. I believe we should speak of your return home sometime soon," Darcy whispered to Georgiana, whose eyes shone with delight.

"I think congratulations are in order for your marriage. It was very surprising to hear of your engagement and then of your rather hasty wedding, Mr. Darcy. Quite unexpected."

"I thank you, Lady Pemberton. It is true that our marriage might be considered surprising, but that makes it even more happy," Darcy answered.

"Mrs. Darcy, may I ask you how you met Mr. Darcy? We are all curious. I understand it happened somewhere in the country?" asked Lady Marianne.

Elizabeth glanced at her husband, wondering how she should respond to such a daring question. She was uncertain how close friends the ladies were, and what tone was proper to use with them.

"It is hardly appropriate for a young lady with high education to ask such direct questions," Lady Matlock intervened sternly. "And very appalling in gentlemen's eyes, I assure you."

"Lady Matlock is right, Marianne. You are not sufficiently acquainted with Mrs. Darcy to make such an inquiry," Lady Pemberton censured her daughter.

"I was only curious, Mama!"

"Indeed, I see no harm in such a question, and I am sure Mrs. Darcy has nothing to hide from us." Lady Beatrice entered the conversation, and Lady Matlock favoured her with a cold glance.

"I was taught that a young lady of genteel breeding must always know when to speak and what to say. I am proud to say that, although so young, Sophia's manners are beyond reproach," interjected the Countess of Wellford. "When she comes out, I am confident she will be much admired."

"I can testify to this. And so will my niece Georgiana," Lady Matlock added.

Sophia and Georgiana both blushed and thanked them for the praise, not daring to form a reply.

Elizabeth could hardly conceal her amusement. The conversation, which was first directed to her, turned into a fierce argument among the ladies in the group. It reminded her of discussions between her mother and Mrs. Philips or Lady Lucas—and her smile widened.

"So—will we be allowed to ask Mrs. Darcy any question at all? It would be awkward not to since we will spend an entire evening together. And I heard the first play is a silly comedy. I am sure I will not enjoy it at all." Lady Beatrice's question was addressed to no one in particular, but the three elder ladies threw her displeased looks.

"You might ask some, but naturally this will give Mrs. Darcy the privilege of doing the same and inquiring about subjects of a personal nature too,"

Lady Matlock concluded, and the countess approved.

Darcy followed the exchange carefully, tempted to intervene if his wife should be placed in an uncomfortable situation. Then he reconsidered: Elizabeth's expression, her eyebrow slightly raised and her lips twisted in a smile, showed him that she was perfectly capable of handling the situation by herself. But again—she had showed him that long before, even when they were in Hertfordshire. She was not the kind of woman who needed her husband's continuous protection. Her wit was as bright as her sparkling eyes, and he was as enchanted by her cleverness as he was by her beauty.

"Please ask me anything you wish," Elizabeth replied. "Although we are not closely acquainted, your familiarity with Lady Matlock—whose opinion I much value and admire—is enough reason for me not to mind any questions at all. Although, I might be unwilling to answer some of them. And yes, I met Mr. Darcy in Hertfordshire in a small town called Meryton."

"You live in that town Meryton? Is your father in trade?" Lady Marianne quickly inquired.

"My father is a gentleman; he owns a modest estate near Meryton. However, my uncle Mr. Gardiner—who lives in London—is in trade, and I am proud to say he is very successful."

She raised her chin forward with determined pride as she spoke about her family.

"One of the finest gentlemen I have met in a long time. Lord Matlock was quite impressed by Mr. Gardiner's knowledge in business. As for Mrs. Darcy's father, I have rarely met anyone with a more profound love for books and understanding of literature. In this, I dare say Mrs. Darcy resembles him." Colonel Fitzwilliam settled things without any doubt left regarding the Bennet family.

A short pause followed, and then Lady Pemberton addressed Darcy.

"You must understand our curiosity—we had come to believe that you would never marry since, for several years, you showed little interest in the social events in Town. Then we suddenly heard news that you are engaged and now already wedded. Many people wondered how Mrs. Darcy managed to persuade you."

"I hope your curiosity will soon pass, Lady Pemberton; please believe me, there is nothing worth your preoccupation. And it was not Mrs. Darcy who persuaded me, but the other way around. She quickly engaged my heart and my mind—and I saw no reason to waste any time in beginning to share my life with her. That would be all."

He noticed Elizabeth's bright eyes watching him, and their smiles spoke to each other. Silence fell over the group, quite strange among all the other crowded and noisy boxes.

Then Lady Beatrice turned to Elizabeth again.

"Mrs. Darcy, have you ever been to the theatre before? Do you know the subject of the play that will be performed tonight?"

Georgiana turned pale at such an offence and Lady Matlock's cheeks coloured discreetly. Darcy's expression darkened, but Elizabeth smiled as charmingly as she used to do with Caroline Bingley.

"Yes, I have been to the theatre many times. It was our favourite way of spending the evenings with my uncle and aunt. And *Hamlet* is one of my preferred plays."

"Oh, I see…well, this time, you will surely see the performance much better. I am sure your uncle does not own a box."

"Oh, one cannot attend a spectacle if one does not own a box," Lady Marianne said animatedly. "I wonder if those people"   she pointed toward the balcony and the stalls, where the majority of the spectators were crowded—"can see anything at all."

"Well, I doubt they understand much, anyway," Lady Beatrice added.

Elizabeth breathed deeply to keep her control.

"No, my uncle does not own a box, and we used to purchase tickets as close to the stage as possible. But I assure you there is no reason for concern; the view is reasonably good from everywhere, especially if there is a true love of theatre. And I am confident that people who need to pay for the tickets out of their limited incomes are doing it precisely because they understand the spectacle and love it."

"Mrs. Darcy possesses an impressive knowledge of literature and theatre—and much more. I am sure she will be happy to expound on any subject with you during the intervals. I confess she put me in a difficulty with her judgement more than once, but I am happy and proud to face such a challenge," Darcy said, kissing his wife's hand.

Many pairs of eyes stared at such an intimate gesture, and both Lady Beatrice and Lady Marianne remained pale and silent.

"I doubt Elizabeth will have a female partner to debate tonight on any subject besides lace, bonnets, and reticules. And perhaps the latest gossip in town," Lady Matlock concluded sharply.

That moment, the curtain was pulled aside, and the viscount and Lord Matlock entered together with the Earl of Wellford and Lord Pemberton.

A new round of introductions was performed, then the first play of the evening began and the party remained in their seats.

Elizabeth noticed the coldness between Lady Matlock and her daughter-in-law, Lady Beatrice, and she recollected the colonel's comments from the previous day. It seemed neither of them made any effort for a true reconciliation, and she wondered about the reasons behind such a deep family conflict.

During the comedy, Elizabeth only exchanged a few whispers with Georgiana. From time to time, she felt Darcy lean towards her or felt his hand gently touch hers with small caresses.

Once the comedy ended, there was another long break before the main performance. The gentlemen left the box to take a much-needed stroll in the lobby and to enjoy some drinks. The ladies began another conversation, moving from the subject of Almacks's balls to the fashion plates in the latest edition of *Ackermann's Repository*.

Elizabeth made a comment regarding a poem she read and very much enjoyed in *Lady's Monthly Museum*, but none of the other ladies had seen it, and the topic was quickly abandoned.

Lady Matlock—as well as Sophia and Georgiana—intervened very little in the conversation. Her ladyship seemed deep in her own thoughts, and at length, she addressed her nieces.

"I would like to take a few steps to stretch my legs. Would you keep me company?" Both Elizabeth and Georgiana were happy to oblige her. The countess and Sophia also joined them, and the party of five stepped out into the crowded hall. A servant was sent to bring tea and refreshments while they looked around for familiar faces.

"I am a little cold. I should have brought my shawl," Lady Matlock said.

"Let us send a servant to fetch it," the countess replied.

"Lady Ellen, I will get it for you in an instant." Elizabeth smiled and hurried back, her eyes eagerly searching for a sign of her husband.

She was about to pull aside the curtain to their box when she heard animated voices and a few words that made her wait and listen.

"I cannot imagine what was in Darcy's mind to marry her. Surely, she has nothing to recommend her over so many accomplished young ladies with far better situations and wealth. And I find it even harder to believe that Lady Matlock seems to approve of her."

"My mother-in-law must have her reasons. She always acts according to her interests. As for Darcy's reasons for marrying her, it is rather easy to guess. No doubt, he wished to bring some new blood into the family to perpetuate their name. Certainly, you know that his mother died from weakness, and his sister and Cousin Anne do not seem too strong either."

"Yes, that might be…I never thought of that…"

Elizabeth's heart raced with anger while she struggled to breathe calmly. She finally entered the box and noticed the three surprised faces.

"I have come to retrieve Lady Matlock's shawl," she said briefly and attempted to retire. She had no wish for further discussion.

"Have you? I would think a servant could have been sent for that," Lady Beatrice said coldly.

Elizabeth took another deep breath and turned to her. "It was my pleasure to assist Lady Ellen since she was so generous and kind to me without having any ulterior motives, I am sure. Amiability and mutual support within the family are what strengthen it."

She took a few steps then turned back, a large smile on her face.

"Oh, and I doubt Mr. Darcy married me only to bring new blood into his family. If that were his intention, he could have proposed to any of you a long time ago. However, I promise I will ask him directly and will come back to you with the answer."

With no little satisfaction, she noticed the two younger ladies' faces colouring then turning white, their wide-open eyes staring at her. Only then did she leave the box graciously, barely stifling her laughter and wondering whether the two would have other questions for her later in the evening.

It proved later that they had none.

The performance of *Hamlet* was a most powerful one, rising to the audience's high expectations. At its end, a storm of applause and praise rewarded the actors.

On their way toward the carriage, the entire party was finally in complete agreement regarding the worthiness of the evening.

Elizabeth and Darcy took a warm farewell from the others, embracing Georgiana while they promised to visit her again the next day.

The countess told Elizabeth to expect an invitation to her ball for the next week; Lady Marianne and Lady Beatrice said nothing but a proper farewell.

It was rather late when the Darcys entered their carriage and slowly rode back toward their privacy. He closed his arms to entrap her, and she sighed in delight.

"I am so happy to be alone with you," she whispered.

He kissed her temples. "I was in the midst of so many people, many of whom I have known for a lifetime, and yet I felt lonely all the time when you were not by my side. You are my world now, Elizabeth."

She lifted her face, her eyes glowing at him, and he gently claimed her lips, slowly satiating his thirst.

By the time the carriage arrived home, their thirst, however, had only increased then turned into an overwhelming hunger that needed the entire night to be soothed.

Chapter 6

Elizabeth related to her husband the sharp argument she had the previous night with the two ladies. She kept a humorous tone and chose her words carefully, omitting the cruel reference to his mother and sister's health. Regardless, Darcy was upset at the offense bestowed upon Elizabeth, but her laughter and tender kisses dissipated part of his distress.

Both of them were aware that their marriage was not readily accepted. And while they gave little importance to malicious gossips, Darcy could not easily ignore anything that harmed Elizabeth. Her spirit, however, would not allow anything to ruin her felicity or to shadow the light in her eyes.

The incident at the theatre, however, made her sad on Lady Matlock's behalf. To have her only daughter-in-law speak of Elizabeth so bitterly, so offensively, must have been painful for the lady whom Elizabeth so admired. It also explained Colonel Fitzwilliam's sharp remarks and his disapproval of his sister-in-law. Elizabeth could only hope that things would improve in time and the family would find the peace and harmony they deserved.

The next couple of days, the Darcys balanced their privacy with visiting their relatives again. Further, Elizabeth attended the modiste with Lady Matlock and Mrs. Gardiner. She ordered several new gowns for herself as well as two new dresses and two elegant nightgowns for the soon-to-be-married Jane.

They had agreed that Georgiana would stay another two weeks with the Matlocks then return home. However, Lady Matlock argued that, since the couple would shortly return to Hertfordshire for Jane and Bingley's wedding,

Georgiana should remain with them until after this event. Miss Darcy saw the wisdom in that suggestion and accepted it. Elizabeth and Darcy were truly missing Georgiana, but they did not insist on her earlier return.

The Matlocks invited the Darcys and the Gardiners for tea one day, and for dinner two days later. With the colonel's departure from Town—and the tense relationship with their eldest son and daughter-in-law—Lord Matlock found Mr. Gardiner's presence a welcome addition. As proof, the earl invited the gentleman to keep him company at his exclusive club, an honour to which neither the Gardiners nor Elizabeth remained unaffected.

Lady Matlock had undoubtedly grown attached to the Gardiner girls; both her ladyship and Georgiana were also pleased with Mrs. Gardiner's company. On her side, Elizabeth's aunt was as surprised as she was grateful for the attention bestowed upon her by one of the most illustrious members of the ton.

Elizabeth could not have been happier with the Matlocks' treatment of her uncle and aunt from Cheapside or more proud of the way Mr. and Mrs. Gardiner adapted to such exquisite company.

Although they were pleased to spend time with their relatives, the Darcys declined any other invitations to dinner. They preferred to return to their home and their apartments, which were the sanctuary of their love.

Almost a fortnight after their marriage, their desire for each other was relentless. It was not just their lovemaking but also every touch, kiss, glance, and smile meant for their loved one. Their feelings grew and intensified as their mutual passion was enhanced by the slow discovery of each other's most secret wishes.

Both were content to have the other's company and nothing else. They were sufficient for each other—completed each other. It was never just him and her but them together.

He offered her fresh roses, knowledge of politics, art, and business and stories about his childhood, his parents, and Pemberley. And passionate love.

She gave him joy, liveliness, laughter, and decided opinions. And passionate love.

He bought a small piano for their apartment, and she played for him any time he wished.

When he spent time with his business papers, she kept him company, reading by his side.

Their passion knew no day or night; they shared love and desire whenever they wished, just as they shared everything else. The only rule with which Darcy was even more preoccupied than Elizabeth was to ensure their perfect privacy and always to avoid being caught in uncomfortable situations. He still remembered Caroline Bingley barging into the library and finding him kissing Elizabeth most passionately—an image that Caroline likely had not quickly forgotten. Consequently, the library—the room where they spent most of the time outside their suites—often had a locked door.

However, the servants never bothered them except Miles, Molly, or Mrs. Hamilton and only when urgency required it, so any impromptu disturbance was entirely avoided.

Their two-week anniversary matched the beginning of March with warmer weather and a bright sun. Spring was slowly melting winter away.

Darcy struggled to find a way to make the day special. He knew she needed nothing, nor did she want any particular gift. She had repeatedly told him so, and he had no reason for disbelief.

"My love, I have done something that might upset you," he informed her solemnly during their late breakfast.

Her eyebrow rose in surprise. "I find that hard to believe."

"I have purchased a horse for you...for Longbourn. A mare. It will be delivered in a couple of days. I already sent an express to Mr. Bennet."

Her surprise opened her eyes wide. "A mare? At Longbourn? What for?"

"Since we will spend some time in Hertfordshire for the wedding, I thought you might enjoy taking riding lessons. I selfishly hope you will allow me to teach you. And I remember that, when Jane came to Netherfield, she said your father had only one riding horse, which was also used on the farm. So it might be useful for them too. I hope you do not disapprove."

She looked at him in wonder. "I cannot believe you still remember what Jane said four months ago."

He moved near her, embraced her, and then caressed her face. "I never forget anything even remotely connected to you. So—shall we ride through the Hertfordshire woods together?"

"We shall—but most likely at a very slow pace. You will have to temper your horse, sir."

"The pace does not matter, only the pleasure of sharing the enjoyment with you. I vividly recollect that time we rode together—on my horse."

He whispered between light kisses spread over her face. "On second thought, perhaps improving your riding skills might not be such a good idea."

She laughed and turned to meet his lips. "It was an excellent idea; as Lady Ellen implied, it is one of my duties as I cannot see Pemberley by foot. However, that feeling of riding in your arms through Longbourn Grove I will never forget, and I will gladly enjoy it again anytime."

IN THE AFTERNOON, THE SKY SUDDENLY DARKENED, AND IT BEGAN TO RAIN steadily. Elizabeth was reading on the couch while Darcy studied some papers from Pemberley's steward.

She put the book away to listen to the rain then moved toward the window, looking outside through the thick curtain of drops falling rapidly to the ground.

"Elizabeth? Is anything wrong?"

She turned to him with a bright smile and sparkling eyes. "No. I was just thinking of the rain...Not this one but that on the 23rd of November. How angry and distressed I was to meet you and to be forced to spend time alone with you. My feelings were so bitter and my opinion of you so poor...I was such a simpleton! Do you know that, when I took off my wet clothes, for a little while I was worried that you might take advantage of the situation? Of me?"

He put his arms around her.

"I am glad it was only for a moment. Despite your poor opinion of me, you must have known I could not harm you," he teased her.

She laughed and caressed his face. "It crossed my mind that you did not seem to need to ensure ladies' attention by attacking them. Besides, I knew you found me not tolerable enough to dance with, let alone to have other improper thoughts."

His laugh matched hers as his embrace tightened.

"In that, you were very wrong. I found you more than tolerable. In fact, I found you the most attractive woman I had ever met, and I had to struggle mightily to control my urge to kiss you. It is fortunate I am a man of great self-control. Those few hours spent alone with you were the first steps toward this complete bliss."

"True...and it gave me the chance to see you in such a different light. By the time we left the cottage, my opinion of you had already started to change. And when you held my hand for the first time…I cannot describe what I felt. I was so disappointed when you let go…"

"Nor can I describe what I felt when I touched your hand for the first time. Such overwhelming delight could not compare with anything else in my life before you. My heart and my mind were already full of you when we met on that rainy day. But I changed, too, once I realised your true opinion of me and that my future felicity was tightly bound to you."

"I agree so much what you just said: 'my life before you.' I can also split my life into before and after I met you. My heart and my mind are 'now' full of you, my love, and have been from the day we spent in the cottage—even before I realised it."

She leant closer and rose on her toes to reach his ear; then she whispered, her lips touching his skin, "My soul and my body are yearning for you… every inch of my skin craves your touch, your kiss, your scent, your strength, your tenderness, your passion known only by me…"

His silent stare betrayed the depth of his reaction to her powerful profession of love. It was not that he did not know it; it was not that she had never confessed her love to him before. But every time, her words revealed new meanings just as their affection grew in different ways every day.

"My love, my tenderness, my passion are meant only for you. I had never felt nor behaved this way until you charmed me with your fine eyes and your lovely face. Can you imagine how besotted I was since I did not hesitate to confess it to Caroline Bingley?"

Her laughter tickled his heart. "That was not really a surprise since Miss Bingley always pretended you were intimate friends."

"Dearest, please never use the word 'intimate' when you refer to me and Caroline Bingley under any circumstances."

"I might have to since we will all be family now, you know. I only hope Caroline's manners will improve in time, or at least that she and Louisa will come to love Jane as she deserves."

"I share your hope, but I am afraid it will be difficult to accomplish. However, I trust Bingley will succeed in making Jane as happy as she deserves; it is his duty and his responsibility."

"I wish nothing more than to see Jane as happy as I am."

He covered her face with tantalising kisses; then his lips brushed over hers. "That, my beautiful wife, would hardly be possible. I take it as *my* duty and responsibility to make you the happiest woman in the world."

"And you have already succeeded, my love," she said a moment before her words were lost in a passionate kiss.

The Countess of Wellford's ball took place on a Friday night. As Lady Matlock mentioned, it was one of the most important events of its kind. Among the attendants were distinguished members of the ton, including the noble patronesses of Almack's Assembly Rooms. Even Colonel Fitzwilliam—who had returned to Town for only a day—declared he looked forward to the evening.

Although Darcy treated the entire situation with mild amusement, Lady Matlock was quite determined to secure Elizabeth's entrance into the most exclusive circles of London society as she insisted it was for the benefit of the Darcy name and for Georgiana's future coming out. Despite her usual tendency to support her husband's opinion, Elizabeth could easily see the wisdom in Lady Matlock's argument, and she behaved accordingly.

For this ball, she wore a most fashionable and elegant dress of pale green satin overlaid with pellucid, hand-embroidered lace to which she matched a jewellery set of gold, diamonds, and pearls. The gown came with a stunning new pair of shoes, which Elizabeth admitted to being more beautiful than comfortable.

Darcy's gaze the moment he laid eyes upon his wife showed his surprise, his approval, and his admiration, and Elizabeth needed nothing more.

As she walked to the carriage on his arm, she proudly wondered whether there could be another gentleman as handsome as her beloved husband.

The countess's residence was only around the corner from the Matlocks', but the building looked even more impressive. The entire first floor was tastefully decorated, and the main hall and ballroom were already crowded when the Darcys and Matlocks entered.

Lady Matlock complimented Elizabeth's appearance, and so did the Countess of Wellford when she greeted their party. Inside, Elizabeth recognised many persons she had already met at Lady Matlock's private ball, and she elegantly curtseyed to each of them while Darcy whispered to her any names she could not remember.

To the Viscountess Castlereagh, the Countess of Sefton, and the Countess of Jersey—three of the Lady Patronesses of Almack's—Elizabeth and Darcy, under Lady Matlock's careful supervision, dedicated a special greeting and several minutes to answer their inquiries. When the Countess of Sefton ended the conversation, congratulating the newly wedded couple and expressing her wish that she would see them often during the Season, Elizabeth could see Lady Matlock breathe in relief.

Before the music started, they met with Lord Buxton and Lady Beatrice. Lady Pemberton, her husband, and Lady Marianne were also present. The latter smiled charmingly at the colonel, who responded only with a proper bow.

Since the colonel was her only close male acquaintance and etiquette frowned on her dancing with her husband, Elizabeth anticipated an evening spent in light conversation and the chance to know better some of those in attendance.

Colonel Fitzwilliam asked her for the first set, during which her partner mostly joked about Darcy's apparently poor mood and his constant gaze at them. Elizabeth remembered Darcy's lack of interest in dancing, which was confirmed once again. At Lady Matlock's private ball a month earlier, he had danced only because he could do so with her. Now, he seemed to return to his old ways. Only his eyes, caressing her from afar, reminded her of the man with whom she was deeply in love.

To Elizabeth's surprise, after the first set she received four other invitations, which she could not refuse. Lady Matlock said it was an excellent sign of appreciation. Elizabeth, however, was convinced that most gentlemen asked her to dance out of curiosity, for the chance to speak with her, and to find fault with her behaviour. Darcy, on the other hand, had no doubt that the invitations were a result of Elizabeth's beauty being widely admired, a fact he found rather disturbing. Colonel Fitzwilliam, a witness to all these speculations, was amused and inclined to support his cousin's opinion.

Before the fifth set, Darcy was engaged in conversation with his uncle, Lord Pemberton, and several other gentlemen as little inclined to dance as he was.

Elizabeth was in a group of Lady Matlock's friends, exchanging impressions about the ball, when she was stunned to see Lord Felton approach her and ask for the favour of the next set.

The mere presence of the man irritated her, and she noticed Lady Matlock's darkened countenance. She glanced toward her husband, but he seemed involved in his own discussion. The other ladies in her group appeared to be on friendly terms with Lord Felton, and although she attempted to find an excuse to deny his request, she could think of no reason for an elegant refusal. Therefore, she had to accept, and as the music began, she took his arm and accompanied him to the set.

She had just taken the first steps when she observed Darcy's angry stare. He looked determined to move toward her, but Lord Matlock caught his arm to stop him. Elizabeth paled for a moment then smiled as lightly as she could to calm him down.

"Mrs. Darcy, it is such a pleasure to have your company for half an hour. I thank you for this favour. I imagine your husband is not very pleased with our dancing together."

"Lord Felton, I trust you did not ask me to dance in such a large company only to ensure I could not refuse you and to upset my husband. That would be rather childish behaviour and not at all worthy of a gentleman of your position."

She smiled, but her eyes were as sharp as her voice, and her partner appeared disconcerted by her words.

"You are a very self-confident woman, Mrs. Darcy, and that adds even more to your charm. I assure you that my invitation only reflected my desire to know you better."

"I see…well, I doubt a set would be enough for closer acquaintance, but fortunately, both of us know ample details about the other to have already formed an opinion."

"I am afraid I am at a disadvantage here, Mrs. Darcy. I barely know anything about you. And I am afraid your opinion about me is biased since you certainly have only unfavourable accounts about me. I am sure neither Darcy nor the Matlocks have anything positive to say about me."

When the dance steps brought them closer, Elizabeth spoke in a tone that admitted no debate.

"Lord Felton, I beg you not to go any further with this conversation as I would be sad to have to respond rudely. Please trust my word that I know all the relevant details about your history with my husband, Lady Hothfield, and the events that occurred. I would kindly suggest that, for the rest of the dance, you choose only subjects that would be approved by both my husband and your wife. So—what do you think of this lovely weather?"

The remaining time, Lord Felton said little else. He complimented Elizabeth a few times, expressed his surprise to see Darcy married in such haste and so far from his usual circle of friends, and mentioned that he was closely acquainted with Mr. Wickham, who—such a coincidence—had recently married one of her sisters.

She answered briefly, keeping her smile wide, and glancing frequently at her husband to show him that she was well and he had no reason to worry. Darcy's expression, though, remained dark and preoccupied.

When the music stopped, Felton directed Elizabeth to her chair, but Darcy was beside them in an instant.

"Darcy, I congratulate you for your wife; we had a lovely time together. Oh, do not be so distressed. You look ridiculous, honestly. Do not worry; we did not discuss Miss Alton at all—pardon, I mean Lady Hothfield," Felton said insolently.

Elizabeth became angry, astonished by the man's impudence. She felt herself gently pushed away, and Darcy stepped closer to Felton, replying in a low voice.

"Do not ever dare approach my wife again under any circumstances. This is the first and last warning I shall give you."

"Or what? Will you call me out?" Felton laughed with spirit.

"Not at all; Lord Hothfield already defeated you and made you look the fool. But if you ever bother my family again, I will injure you with my bare hands such that you will pray for the shot of a bullet or the cut of a sword."

Lord Felton was about to answer, but Darcy ended the conversation.

"Do not make the mistake of taking my words lightly. I would do anything for my family's comfort, and please meditate carefully on the word 'anything.' Now excuse us; we have no more time to waste on this matter."

Darcy took Elizabeth's arm and showed her to a corner of the room. The awkward incident went mostly unnoticed as the general noise made normal conversation impossible to hear.

Lord Felton remained still for a few moments, gazing after them, then returned to a group of loudly speaking gentlemen and took up a glass. Darcy glared at him once again then returned his attention to Elizabeth. She smiled at him, and he briefly kissed her hand.

"Are you well, my love? Did he say anything to upset you?"

"I am perfectly fine; you have no reason for concern. His offenses were all directed toward you, not me. I really cannot understand what is in his mind. What does he hope to accomplish? But he is a good dancer; I will give him that," she added in jest, trying to dissipate Darcy's anger.

He remained serious and frowned, so she smiled again, a different smile that both of them knew well. "My love, please do not allow him to distress you. He is truly more ridiculous than anything else. I will never take his words seriously, and he cannot possibly affect me in any way. Let us forget about him."

He raised her hand to his lips again. "You are correct as always, my dearest. Come – let us go to supper."

As the guests moved toward the supper-room, Lady Matlock slowly separated from her husband and firmly took the arm of a man she had been following with her eyes for some time. He stopped and gazed at her in disbelief.

"Lord Felton, may I have a private moment with you?"

"Lady Matlock…" With his arm held by the lady, Felton stepped away from the crowd then decidedly pulled his arm free.

"How may I help you, madam? I hope you have not also come to threaten me to stay away from the newest addition to your family. Darcy already did that," he said impertinently.

"Not at all—I just want to say I understand your distress perfectly."

"My distress? I do not know your ladyship's meaning."

"Come now, my meaning is very clear. You tried to gain Lady Hothfield's favours when she was a famous actress, but you failed. You maintained the impression that she chose Darcy over you, which is as silly as it is untrue. She did not reject you because she preferred Darcy but simply because you were not the kind of man to gain her interest. So you have no reason to envy Darcy and continuously provoke him to compensate for your frustration."

"I fail to follow your reasoning," he interrupted her, self-confidently wearing the same impudent smile. "And please do not presume you know the nature of my relationship with Miss Alton—or Lady Hothfield—nor what kind of man I am. As for Darcy, I am not provoking him at all."

"I think you are insincere. We both know the actual reason for your jealousy, and I feel for you. It must be hard to accept that you are so poorly gifted precisely in the area that is most important for a man."

Lady Matlock's voice was so low that nobody could hear her, but she never blinked as she spoke the infamous words. Lord Felton stared at her in complete shock.

"Lady Matlock, how dare you say that? This conversation has become ridiculous, and I will end it instantly." He turned pale and looked around in panic.

"I agree, we should conclude this entire conversation, and you should try to forget it. It is the only thing to do. Even if rumours say your 'manly qualities' are far from impressive and that might be the reason that your wife has not provided you with an heir after four years of marriage, I am sure you have other things to recommend you. Just focus on those and avoid any useless conflicts."

"But that is…that is outrageous! It is not true! I am not—that is a horrible falsehood!"

"Is it? Well, that is what I heard, but I have not repeated such gossip to anyone—yet. I do not like to harm a person's reputation unless I am forced to do so. Oh, and that rumour that you always try to take advantage of any maid that crosses paths with you—so very un-gentlemanlike! Several servants in my house spoke of it, but I still hope—for the sake of your mother and wife—that it is not true."

"It is not true! Who said that? What servant? What maid?"

"Keep your voice down. You should avoid by any means having such words spread further. People are quickly catching them, and the damage will be impossible to control."

Lord Felton seemed lost, and a grimace hardened his features. Lady Matlock continued.

"I have not had the chance of speaking to you lately, but I am on the edge of my patience with you, young man. I have known you since you were a boy, but that will not stop me from giving you a proper correction if needed. I can ruin your reputation in a heartbeat."

"That is nonsense – you would not dare. Nobody will believe you."

"Do not *duel* with me, Gilmore Felton, as you have no chance to win. I have never lost a battle in my entire life, and I will certainly not start with you. Even your mother would believe my word over yours. Let this be the first and last time we speak on this matter. Be wise and turn your attention to the people who are pleased with your company if you wish to have a social life in this Town," Lady Matlock concluded coldly, then majestically stretched her hand for Lord Felton to kiss as a gesture of truce. He looked at it, dumbfounded, and then finally, unwillingly took it to his lips.

Lady Matlock walked toward the supper table and took her seat among other ladies of the ton, including his mother. Lord Felton stood in the middle of the empty ballroom another moment, then he turned away and left the house, forgetting to fetch his own wife.

THE REST OF THE NIGHT WAS PLEASANT WITH ELIZABETH DANCING ALMOST every set and Darcy none. She was amused at Lady Marianne's attempt to catch Colonel Fitzwilliam's attention and the gentleman's struggle to escape her insistent admiration.

During supper—and often afterward since they were again separated—Elizabeth felt her husband's eyes on her, and his gaze warmed her. She knew quite well the meaning of such looks and the silent promise deeply hidden within them.

For Darcy, the ball was equally boring and distressing. Not fond of large gatherings, he found few moments of entertainment. He managed to avoid dancing, as there were enough young gentlemen willing to enjoy the music and the ladies' company.

The notion that Elizabeth was asked for almost every set he accepted with petulance.

The custom not to dance with one's own wife yet allow other men to dance with another's wife he found ridiculous and unacceptable. He briefly decided to reject that idea at any future balls—if they ever attended again.

Then he remembered Lady Matlock's insistence on introducing Elizabeth at Almack's, and he realised any attempt to ruin his aunt's plans would start a war worse than Napoleon's, and he did not have the least chance of winning it. He then admitted himself defeated and found solace in admiring his wife: her beauty, her dancing skills, her smiles, her eyes searching for him around the room, her most becoming blushes, and the small gesture of biting her lower lip when she was distressed by something. He could easily see that many other men were gazing at her, yet he knew she hardly saw anyone but him—just as her image was the only thing in his mind and heart.

A gripping longing for her—for touching her, kissing her, caressing her, loving her—slowly grew inside him, and he was painfully counting every moment until the ball was over and he would have her in his arms.

When the last set began, Darcy glanced around the impressive room; most of the guests appeared engaged in finishing their conversations, and only a few couples occupied the dance floor.

He took his wife's hand and caressed it briefly.

"I cannot waste the chance of dancing the last set with you, my love. I am starting a tradition which I intend to carry out at every possible occasion."

Her face showed disbelief, quickly overcome by genuine delight.

"As Lady Matlock has repeated many times, dancing with one's own wife is very unfashionable. Surely, you do not consider breaching propriety in public," she whispered, and he could not keep his eyes away from her lips.

"Between the rules of decorum and the pleasure of having you in my arms, my choice is easily made. Would you do me the pleasure of dancing the last set with me, Mrs. Darcy?"

"I would by no means suspend any pleasure of yours, Mr. Darcy."

Many pairs of eyes and even more disapproving whispers and frowning faces watched the aloof and haughty man holding his wife's hands and eyes in the rhythm of the music.

For the couple, however, nothing mattered except each other. Just as happened at the Netherfield ball, they felt alone in the room full of people, paying attention to nothing and no one and surrounded only by their love.

From her seat, Lady Matlock observed the couple with mixed feelings; her amusement over her nephew's changed behaviour matched her disapproval for his decision to dance the last set with his wife, especially as he had not danced at all the entire night. His manners could easily be considered offensive toward the other ladies and the hostess herself and threaten future invitations from influential persons of the ton.

The Countess of Wellford looked rather well humoured—perhaps due to the third glass of wine she was enjoying.

"Upon my word, Darcy does not cease to surprise me; he seems a completely different man since he married," Lady Beatrice whispered to her friend Lady Marianne, and the latter nodded with obvious disdain.

Lord Matlock, his sons, Lord Pemberton, and Lord Wellford only drank their brandy in silence, glancing at the dance floor from time to time.

"That is true," the countess admitted. "Some men do change after they marry for love, and most of the time it is exceedingly pleasant."

"I agree," Lady Matlock intervened with a restrained smile. "However, marriage for love is a subject barely known to most of the people here, and that makes Darcy's behaviour even more difficult to understand and accept."

"Not that Darcy would care much about the acceptance of anyone outside his close family," the colonel whispered with a grin, snatching another full glass as he watched his cousin lost in his wife's bright eyes. Indeed, why would he care about anyone else besides the beautiful woman who obviously adores him and with whom he will go home soon? Darcy had always been a smart and decided man; nobody could deny that. And that night he had proved it once again.

Before dawn, the ball ended, and the Darcys eventually were able to take their leave. After a warm farewell from the Matlocks and their hosts, they were finally alone in the carriage. To Elizabeth's surprise, Darcy sat on the opposite bench and only watched her without any other gesture. She held his eyes for a few moments, trying to hide her amusement.

"You are staring, sir."

"Am I?"

"Indeed, you are."

"You must be right. Does it trouble you?"

Elizabeth could see how he struggled to conceal the smile that was twisting his lips and to appear solemn.

"A little. Unless you reveal the reason for your stare."

"Can you not guess it?"

"Hardly."

"I doubt it. Had you been oblivious of my interest, you would not have blushed so becomingly."

She laughed heartily. "You have been staring most of the night. I hope you were not displeased with my manners during the ball."

"Not with *your* manners but with the others'. Since I did not dance with anyone's wife, I would expect the same courtesy in return."

She laughed again. "Come, sir, everybody knows your dislike of dancing, but fortunately, it is not a common trait. Balls would be sad and boring if all gentlemen shared the same repugnance for such activities. Most ladies enjoy dancing."

"I enjoy dancing too—with you." His voice was solemn, and his eyes darkened.

"I know that, as I enjoy dancing with you too," she whispered, moving to his side.

He leant towards her. "I was staring because I missed you so much. And because you are so very beautiful."

"You are partial to me, but I love your lack of objectivity."

"Not at all— I am always honest. And it just crossed my mind that I would like to have your portrait painted—just as you are now. I shall arrange for a painter to come before we leave for Hertfordshire."

She gently touched his lips with hers. Her hand caressed his face, and she daringly deepened the kiss while he barely moved. She then placed herself on his lap, and her arms encircled his neck.

With delight, he received her conscious attempt of seduction, caressing her warm body through the fabric of her gown.

"I missed kissing you…and touching you…" he moaned through the kisses. "I could think of little else the whole night…but of this moment when we would be alone in the carriage."

"I thought more of what will follow later…once we arrive home," she replied daringly, and he withdrew a moment to look at her laughing, teasing eyes; then his hands cupped her face to savour the smile of her red lips.

Neither of them noticed when the carriage stopped in front of the house. The footman had to call Darcy several times until he finally regained some composure and helped his wife to leave the vehicle.

MOLLY AND MILES WERE WAITING AND IMMEDIATELY ATTENDED THEIR duties, helping their master and mistress prepare for the night.

Washed and changed into her nightgown, her hair loose on her shoulders, Elizabeth finally realised how tired she was and that her feet—tortured in the exquisite new shoes from dancing the entire night—were swollen and painful. She cuddled in the bed, covering herself with the thick, soft blankets, and dismissed Molly. The steadily burning fire gave her a sense of complete peace and comfort. It had been a pleasant, animated night, but she was happy to be in the silence of their rooms with only the company of the man who mattered most to her.

Darcy appeared shortly and sat on the bed. He slowly caressed her face, arranged the dark locks of hair falling over her temples, and then leant down and gently tasted her lips.

"Are you tired?"

"A little—it is not like I did any hard work," she said laughing. "Only my feet hurt. My new beautiful shoes are nothing like my comfortable ones that allowed me to walk five miles from Longbourn to Netherfield."

"Let me see if I can help," he said, slowly exposing her feet. They did not seem swollen to him but charming, and her delicate ankles allured him. His fingers touched her toes and her heels, rubbing them gently.

He continued his ministrations for some time while she closed her eyes and allowed herself to be spoiled by the most delightful sensations. His touches burned her skin and spread cold shivers inside her body. Then his palms cupped her heels, slowly pressing against them. A moan escaped her lips while his caresses shifted to her ankles.

"Is it better now?" he asked hoarsely.

She nodded and licked her lips. He put her feet in his lap and continued to caress them while he leant to claim her lips. Elizabeth's hands encircled his neck, and she pulled him toward her.

"Much better," she whispered. "Everything is much better with you..."

"I am glad, my beloved wife. I miss your closeness, your warmth, your softness...I want to feel you completely. I yearn to be with you...inside you..."

His words were interrupted by eager attempts to satiate their desires. With hasty movements as she tried to help his efforts, he completely removed his nightclothes and hers then slowly leant over her—skin to skin and heart to heart, hands meeting hands and lips meeting lips, passion matching passion.

Chapter 7

In the middle of March, Darcy and Elizabeth prepared to travel to Hertfordshire for the wedding of Miss Bennet to Mr. Bingley.

The week before their departure, they mostly spent time at home. As he intended, Darcy hired a painter to have Elizabeth's portrait drawn and also one of them as a couple. That kept all their mornings busy, but it brought them great enjoyment.

During the afternoons, Elizabeth finished the shopping for Jane, and Darcy encouraged her to purchase some gifts for the rest of the family. During their last day in Town, they visited the Matlocks and took their farewell of Georgiana, promising to convey her warmest wishes to Jane and Bingley.

Darcy suggested the Gardiners travel with them in their largest carriage. The Gardiner boys were old enough to realise that the time spent in preparing a wedding in a crowded house like Longbourn meant nothing but boredom, strict rules, and severe restrictions, so they happily agreed to remain in Town with their governess, Mrs. Burton.

The eldest girl, Margaret, held the opposite view: she was happy to see her elder cousins again and to be part of all the preparations, and she showed great interest in everything regarding new gowns, lace, and bonnets. As for the youngest child, it was unthinkable that Becky would be allowed any distance from her mother's keen supervision.

Therefore, on a cold early morning, a party formed of two carriages headed toward Longbourn. In the smaller one there were two footmen, Molly and Miles. Inside the larger one the Gardiners sat on one bench, and Darcy and Elizabeth on the other. Young Margaret Gardiner, impeccably dressed and exceedingly polite, sat between her parents while Becky sneaked next to Elizabeth, who quickly wrapped her in a warm blanket.

"Lizzy, why have you not come to see me for so long?"

"I am very sorry, sweetie. We were extremely busy."

"But did not you not miss seeing my lovely face?" the girl asked in earnest, and Elizabeth laughed, kissing her cheeks.

"Of course I did, my dearest. I promise to spend more time with you while we are at Longbourn."

"May I sleep with you? I always sleep with you when I am at Longbourn."

"Well, I…" Elizabeth glanced at her husband then at her aunt, uncertain how to answer.

"Becky, Lizzy and Mr. Darcy will stay at Netherfield, and we will stay at Longbourn."

"But why?"

"Because this is what they decided, young lady! Let us change the subject," her mother intervened.

"But you promised that you will spend more time with me! I can see you will spend time with Mr. Darcy; I know it."

"Dearest, married people must spend time together. Just like your mama and papa. And you will sleep with Margaret in my old room. Would you like that?"

"Yes, I suppose…" The girl pulled an upset face to show her displeasure.

"Becky, when we return to London, I will ask your mother to allow you and Margaret to visit us. You will spend plenty of time with Elizabeth and with Georgiana," Darcy attempted in consolation.

"Oh, really? I like Miss Georgiana very much. She is as beautiful as a fairy. Even my brothers think so. Will Lady Ellen come too? I like Lady Ellen. Mama, can we go, please? Oh, but can we still go to Pemberley?"

The storm of questions was difficult to handle, and Becky became increasingly animated while the others could do little else except laugh and allow themselves to be caught up in her game.

"Lizzy, since you and Mr. Darcy are like mama and papa, will you have children too?"

"I hope so. Will you enjoy playing with them?"

"I am not sure. But will you love them more than you love me?"

"I will love them very much—just as I love all four of you."

"Will you have girls or boys?"

"I am not sure. It will be God's will."

"I hope God will give you girls. They are much better than boys. Boys are mean and loud," she said as she climbed into Darcy's arms, covered in the blanket.

"I doubt any girl or boy is louder than you, young lady," Mrs. Gardiner said. "And please come stay with us, dear. You are bothering Mr. Darcy."

Darcy signed with a gesture that it was no trouble while the girl continued.

"Yes but I am not mean, and I never push anyone. I am very cute. I heard when Mrs. Burton told you that, Mama."

Mrs. Gardiner rolled her eyes in exasperation.

"No matter whether you have girls or boys, I hope you will not make the same mistake of spoiling them excessively as we did with a *certain* child of ours."

"She speaks about me, you know," Becky whispered to Darcy and then continued as if telling him a secret. "I am already spoiled, so you can do it again if you want," she said in complete seriousness.

"I will consider your invitation," Darcy replied with great amusement.

"Lizzy spoils me, too, because I am so pretty, and she loves me. Do you think I am pretty?"

"Indeed, you are the prettiest, funniest, sweetest girl I have met in a very long time."

"What about Margaret?"

"She is a beautiful, elegant, and very proper young miss."

"You know, you are very good at making compliments, Mr. Darcy. I think you got it from me."

"I think you may be right, my dear."

"My Aunt Bennet will be very happy to see you. She is very fond of you. She speaks of you all the time. She said it was a miracle that you married Lizzy. Are you a wizard?"

"No...not at all."

Elizabeth glanced at her husband with worry, and Mrs. Gardiner was ready to intervene again. Darcy could hardly restrain his laughter.

"Good—here is the Inn where we will stop for refreshments," Mr. Gardiner said and ended the conversation with great relief.

After a brief break of hot tea and biscuits, the party continued their journey. Happily, Becky was rather tired, and she slept in Elizabeth's arms until they reached their destination.

MRS. BENNET'S EXCITEMENT AT SEEING THEM WAS BEYOND WORDS. IN truth, she was more enchanted by Darcy's presence than by anyone else's, and he was the first one to notice it.

Bingley was also present, overwhelming them with his joy while Jane's tearful eyes proved her happiness at seeing her sister again.

Mr. Bennet quickly embraced his favourite daughter, and Elizabeth could see the emotion on his face. Then he invited the gentlemen to his library for a glass of brandy, and they happily accepted.

The first two hours were a pandemonium. Elizabeth offered her sisters and her mother their gifts then showed Jane what she purchased as a wedding present. Jane was beside herself with gratitude and blushed violently at seeing the exquisite nightgowns.

Mrs. Bennet asked every five minutes how life was in London, Kitty was in awe to hear about the balls and jewels, and Mary forgot to breathe when Elizabeth described their impressive collection of books.

It was late in the afternoon, and since everybody was tired after the journey, Elizabeth and Darcy, together with Bingley, prepared to remove to Netherfield.

Before that, the eldest sisters barely succeeded in securing a few private minutes, hiding in Jane's bedchamber.

"Oh, Lizzy, I am so glad you are here! I cannot bear so much happiness. It is too much. And we changed the date of the wedding—Charles proposed to do it. I am so pleased! And the gowns you bought for me—please thank Mr. Darcy on my part. Lizzy, I am so happy!"

"I can see you are, dearest." Elizabeth embraced her tearfully. "I think it was an excellent idea to move up the wedding date. I am certain you will be even happier after the wedding." Elizabeth smiled, and Jane blushed again.

"I know I shall be. I just hope to be the wife Charles deserves. He is the best of men.

"I have no doubt that you will be perfect for each other," Elizabeth replied while she silently considered that Charles Bingley might be the best of *some* men but surely could not compete with her husband.

"Oh, Lizzy, I am so grateful that you are here. I missed you so much, my dear. You look beautiful! It is obvious how happy you are!"

"I am, indeed, more than I ever dreamt. And so will you be. Now I have to leave. We shall see each other again tomorrow. I am very sorry to exchange your lovely company for Caroline and Louisa's, but I have no choice. Longbourn is very crowded, and we will be more at peace at Netherfield. Besides, Mr. Bingley seems to have missed William's company."

"Yes, he did. And I agree that it would be much better for you to stay at Netherfield. Dearest Lizzy, please remember that Caroline and Louisa are Charles's sisters. I know they are not the kindest persons, but I beg you to be patient with them—for my sake and his."

"I promise I shall try."

"I really cannot understand why you are leaving before dinner," Mrs. Bennet wondered with distress as they prepared to depart. "You will be very much missed. Hill prepared some special dishes for you, Mr. Darcy."

"I am deeply sorry to refuse you, madam, but we are tired after the journey and certainly not properly dressed for dinner. I could not accept your invitation without wearing attire that would do justice to your excellent dishes and company," Darcy answered with a bow, and Elizabeth could hardly conceal her laughter while Mr. Bennet raised his eyebrow in surprise at such a speech.

"Oh…I see…of course, you must be tired. It is very kind of you, sir. Oh, but do not worry about your attire, you could very well wear only a potato sack or no clothes at all and would still be the most handsome gentleman in several counties."

Everybody remained speechless and with eyes wide open at that statement, so Mrs. Bennet continued, conciliatory.

"Do not be upset, Mr. Bingley, you are very handsome too, only not quite as much as Mr. Darcy."

Mr. Bingley was not upset but tried to see whether Jane shared the same opinion. Pleased with his betrothed's adoring smile, he silently agreed with Mrs. Bennet; he always knew that he could not compare with his elder friend, and not even attempted to.

On their way toward Netherfield, Bingley rode while the Darcys followed in their carriage.

Once alone with her husband, Elizabeth struggled against her embarrassment.

"I do not even know what to say; my mother is always a little too..."

Darcy laughed loudly.

"I am sorry for poor Bingley. It seems both Mrs. Bennet and Becky favour me over him. I must ask: Did you ever imagine how I would look dressed in a potato sack?"

Elizabeth watched him in astonishment but had no time to reply as he captured her lips in a kiss that both longed for.

Their reception at Netherfield was as cold as Elizabeth expected. Miss Bingley and Mrs. Hurst welcomed them properly and inquired about the weather in London and about Georgiana. Mr. Hurst said nothing.

"Come, Darcy, we will take your luggage upstairs, and while Miss Bennet—forgive me, Mrs. Darcy—prepares for dinner, we can have a drink. I have many things to tell you."

"Mr. Darcy will have his usual room," Caroline said as the mistress of the house. "For Eliza we prepared the largest guest room. I trust it will be at least as comfortable as the rooms at Longbourn."

Elizabeth smiled as charmingly as possible while Darcy replied sternly. "You are very attentive, but that will not be necessary. Elizabeth and I will be happy to share the room. We always do."

Caroline Bingley froze in disbelief. Louisa stared with eyes and mouth wide open, and Mr. Hurst held his glass, forgetting to drink.

Darcy offered his arm to his wife and took the well-known direction to his former room.

Inside, Elizabeth laughed loudly while looking around. "It is a very handsome room. Poor Caroline and Louisa were shocked by your statement."

"I tried very hard to ignore Miss Bingley's rudeness, but I will not allow her to ruin my mood. I have long dreamt of sharing this room with you, my love. You cannot imagine how many times I dreamt of you during my days and nights spent here."

They sat on the bed, and he kissed her hands tenderly. "Do you think we can claim fatigue and retire for the night? Or do we have to bear the dinner?"

Elizabeth rewarded him with a quick kiss. "Mr. Bingley seemed eager to speak to you. You cannot disappoint him. I think we should behave properly, at least for the first day."

He returned the kiss more passionately. "You are right—we should behave properly at least for the first day."

DARCY AND BINGLEY HAD A LONG CONVERSATION BEFORE DINNER. THE younger gentleman was barely coherent as he mentioned Jane's name every other sentence. He was equally joyful and distressed by the prospect of the approaching wedding and wondered whether he could be as good a husband as a true angel like Jane deserved.

"Oh, and I look forward to living with Jane. I visit Longbourn daily, but there is so much activity. I hardly can spend more than a few minutes with her."

"I perfectly understand that. How about your sisters? What is your plan?"

Bingley was puzzled. "What do you mean?"

"Bingley, you must offer your wife the best possible life. And that does not mean pin money and luxurious rooms but comfort, peace, and the trust that she can be the mistress of her home. I doubt your sisters will give up their role easily, and Jane Bennet is not the kind of person to fight for her advantage. She will have your sisters on one side and her own family on the other side—all much too close. She will try to be kind and generous and will accept anything to ensure the well-being of the entire family, but I fear she will not be completely happy. And believe me: you *want* to make your wife happy. This should be your main purpose—your only purpose."

Bingley stared at him, astonished to hear the longest speech ever from his friend. Then he started pacing the room.

"You are right. Yes, you are always right. I must do something. You saw Caroline and Louisa—they are too much to bear even for me. Darcy, I am so relieved that you are here. Yes, I must think of something."

"Calm down, Bingley. You will find a solution. For now, finish your glass and let us go eat. I am rather tired, and I need to retire soon."

"Yes, of course. We will talk more tomorrow. Is your room acceptable? Do you want another one? I am not certain whether any other is larger but—"

"The room is fine, Bingley. I used it before, and I am rather fond of it."

Dinner went reasonably well with Bingley and Elizabeth carrying most of the conversation. He asked about their life in town then said he and Jane might go to London after the wedding.

Caroline immediately added that she would like to return to town too, and the Hursts also approved of that decision.

After the last course was served, Darcy declared they were very tired and apologised for retiring early. No attempt to prolong the evening met with any success.

The Darcys returned upstairs while Miss Bingley and Mrs. Hurst commented about how ill Eliza looked and how less pleasant Mr. Darcy had become since his wedding.

DESPITE THE STRONG FIRE, THE CHAMBER WAS STILL COLD AS IT HAD NOT been used for a long time. Darcy opened the curtains so they could admire the stars while embracing in the bed that had held his secret dreams, struggles, and fears.

Elizabeth nestled her head on his chest, finding warmth and comfort.

"This is so lovely...all this peace and silence, and the stars. I am so glad to be in Hertfordshire again," she said.

"So am I because I am with you."

"It was a difficult day, and I am afraid many others will follow before the wedding. My family is a little tiresome even when there are no special events. But I have missed them dearly. I can understand why you preferred to stay at Netherfield instead of Longbourn, though."

"My darling wife, if you think I chose Netherfield over Longbourn because of your family, you could not be further from the truth. I would have been perfectly content to share any room with you, if only—"

"If only?" she inquired. He remained serious, and she insisted on his satisfying her curiosity.

"One of the reasons was, as I said, my attachment to this chamber and what it represented for me. And the second..."

"Yes?"

"Well, I have the deepest respect for Mr. Bennet. I have grown very fond of him, and I could not possibly...you are his favourite daughter, and I would not dare...being in his house..."

He looked so uneasy that she started to laugh heartily until he silenced her with a deep, long kiss. She somehow managed to escape, and she laughed again.

"But, Mr. Darcy, what will we do when my family stays with us at Pemberley for the entire summer? My father will be in the same house with us for four months. Do you plan to move to the Lambton Inn? Or purchase another property?"

He rolled her onto her back and covered her with his warm weight, trapping her hands with his and covering her face with small kisses.

"That would be different, madam. I will be in my own home. Pemberley is an extremely large house, and the guests' wings are quite far away from our bedchamber."

"I am relieved to hear that. I began to grow really worried," she replied, but her last words could not be heard.

During his first stay at Netherfield, Darcy had carried on a most difficult struggle—one of his mind against his heart, his duty against his wishes, his reason against his felicity. He had known many sleepless nights, painful dreams, and distressing thoughts.

But he never found so little sleep and so little rest in that room as during the first night he shared it with his wife—nor had he ever fallen asleep so deeply and peacefully by the time the dawn almost broke.

Chapter 8

The next morning, Darcy and Elizabeth, followed by Bingley, returned to Longbourn soon after breakfast. Neither Louisa nor Caroline expressed any desire to keep them company and showed that quite clearly.

Even before she entered her parents' house, Elizabeth wished to see the horse her husband had purchased for her.

Her gasp of delight was more heartfelt than her loudly expressed gratitude. She was awed by the appearance of the mare—a stunning red with white spots—from the moment she laid eyes on her.

Elizabeth had never had a horse of her own—nor had she ever wanted one—but the moment she touched the magnificent animal, she was charmed. The filly seemed a bit shy amongst the other horses in the stable, but she readily accepted the apple Elizabeth offered and appeared to enjoy being petted.

"William, I am lost for words! What a beautiful surprise! I already love her. She seems so gentle and patient!"

"I am glad you approve. Her name is Summer, but you may change it if you wish."

"Oh no, I think it fits her very well. She is like a bright, summer day."

He smiled approvingly and put his hands on Elizabeth's shoulders. "I will ride her later today to check her traits and behaviour. I want to be sure she is safe for you," Darcy said.

"I am sure she is," Elizabeth replied, caressing the horse's beautiful neck.

"She is a beauty."

"I am glad you like her, but I still need to assess her carefully. However, I purchased her from a most trustworthy source, so I hope there will be no problems."

They were interrupted by the impromptu arrival of Becky, who hurried to embrace Elizabeth.

"Lizzy, I saw Mr. Bingley, and I knew you had come too. Oh, is this the horse Mr. Darcy bought? My Aunt Bennet said Mr. Darcy would better purchase a phaeton too, so she could use the horse to go to Meryton. And Lizzy, you should send some money to Lydia, aunt said. She is very poor, but she is such a lovely, joyful girl, aunt said."

Becky was proud of herself as she provided such firsthand information. Elizabeth turned pale from embarrassment at the new lack of decorum showed by her mother. She glanced at her husband but did not dare to hold his look, so she turned to pet the mare while she whispered an excuse.

"Oh, and Papa told Aunt Bennet that she always demands more and more, just like me. I do not think this was something good because Papa was solemn and Aunt Bennet was angry."

Elizabeth's cheeks changed from white to crimson. Although she trusted Darcy's affection and his good opinion of her, she could not avoid wondering how much more rudeness he would be willing to accept from her family.

They entered the main door, Darcy carrying Becky in his arms, and were surprised to see a house more crowded than they expected. There were Sir William, Lady Lucas, and Mr. and Mrs. Philips—who all hurried to greet Darcy.

Elizabeth was speechless. She attempted to interfere but met with no success.

Defeated, she took a seat near Jane while Darcy chose a chair. Mr. Philips and Sir William remained standing only to be close to him.

For the next half hour, Sir William continually asked when Elizabeth would be presented at court. Lady Lucas inquired about the number of balls she attended during her stay in London, and Mrs. Philips was curious about the quantity of jewellery Elizabeth had received.

Not even during the Netherfield ball had Elizabeth been so embarrassed. She felt an urge to run from the house and pull Darcy with her, but she remained frozen and constantly glanced at him with regret and silent apologies.

His eyes often met hers, but his expression was rather stern, and he seemed content to offer short answers and enjoy his brandy.

Elizabeth also glared at her aunt Gardiner and her father, silently asking for help, but there was nothing to be done against Mrs. Bennet and her friends.

Finally, after more than an hour, Mr. Bennet found a moment of silence to intervene.

"Well, well, look how the weather is changing. The sky has turned cloudy. It will inevitably start raining very soon. Spring rain can be very cold and dangerous. I am glad to be home."

"My dear Mr. Bennet, I thank you for noticing it. Indeed, it seems it will rain soon. My dear, we must leave. Mr. Darcy, we apologise for not staying longer, but—"

"Sir, any wise man would hurry to return home before the storm starts. I heartily encourage you not to delay another moment," Darcy said in earnest, offering a strong handshake that caused Sir William to admire his firm grip.

Mr. Bennet hid his amusement behind his glass, and as soon as the guests left, he invited the gentlemen to his library and headed there without waiting for them.

Elizabeth wanted to speak to Darcy, but she hesitated to go after him. She chose, instead, to let him relax after the last trying hour while she took a seat near her aunt.

"What is it, Lizzy?" Mrs. Gardiner asked in a low voice. "You seem upset."

"I am—a little. I wonder what to do with Mama. She puts William in a very unpleasant situation, and I am afraid she will continue to do so every day we stay here. And if I talk to her, I am afraid I will only make things worse."

"Oh, do not distress yourself, my dear. Mr. Darcy seemed to bear the situation well," said Mrs. Gardiner, attempting to lighten the mood.

"He tries to be patient for my sake, but I know his real feelings. He is a private man. He cannot be an exhibition for the amusement of the Meryton inhabitants—not to mention Mama's assumption that he should buy a phaeton or that I should send money to Lydia. That is equally rude and unfair."

"Dearest, I believe you are taking this too hard. I shall speak to your mother—but tomorrow. She already had a harsh discussion with your uncle today on the same subject."

"Yes, I know, and as a result, we had a houseful of unexpected guests at the most unsuitable hour. That is exactly what worries me: Mama always wants to have her way. Nothing will change her mind."

Mrs. Gardiner smiled conciliatorily. "Come, my dear, let us all have a cup of tea and calm ourselves. We must be patient—for Jane's sake. She is rather distressed anyway. Let us not begin another argument."

"You are right, of course. Poor Jane, she is trapped between mama's enthusiasm and Caroline's rudeness, and she is too kind to argue with any of them. I am going to speak to her."

Elizabeth improved her disposition as she talked to her sisters. She hoped her husband was comfortable enough in his present company and that his day was not completely ruined. She missed her family dearly and was happy to be in their company, but she was not blind to her mother's lack of decorum. Yet, there was little she could do about it.

Another half hour passed, and then Mr. Bingley entered the drawing room and walked directly toward Jane, wearing a large smile.

"You seem very pleased with yourself," Jane said, blushing charmingly.

"I am," Bingley replied. "I spoke to Darcy, and he made me think of something. I will tell you later—after the wedding."

"Oh..." Jane needed nothing more than her betrothed's adoring gaze. Anything else could wait.

Elizabeth smiled at the lovely couple. "I wonder whether I can go the library and speak to William. I hope I would not disturb them," she addressed Bingley.

"Not at all. But Darcy is not there. He left some time ago."

"He left?" Elizabeth was so surprised that she could hardly gather herself. "Where?"

"He said something about riding—on your horse, I think. I am not certain. I am sure Mr. Bennet knows better. I confess I did not pay much attention."

"Oh..." She was puzzled and slightly distressed. She knew about his intention, but leaving so suddenly was certainly another sign of his being troubled by the morning's events.

She still went to the library, though, and she was welcomed by her father. Mr. Gardiner excused himself to allow them privacy.

"Please take a seat, Lizzy. I am very glad to see you in my library. I truly missed you, child."

She smiled and embraced him. "I missed this library, Papa. And talking to you."

"So, how is London life? Quite exciting, I understand. A lot of lace and jewels and balls. Your mother speaks of little else since you married. Thank God she is now preoccupied with Jane's wedding, but she still does not neglect to praise your husband daily."

Elizabeth laughed. "I noticed, Papa. My life is not quite so glamorous, you know. William and I preferred to attend only a few events. We also spend quite a lot of time in the library," she said then suddenly blushed with shame at the hidden implication of her words.

"Yes, Darcy told me you have a 'keen interest and a bright mind' to discuss his business. The poor fellow seems foolishly in love with you. Quite ridiculous at times—it is very entertaining to see such an impressive man acting like a schoolboy."

"Acting like a schoolboy? What do you mean, Papa? And please do not mock him. He is having a hard enough time handling Mama and her unexpected guests."

Mr. Bennet dismissed her concerns with a gesture. "Do not worry, Lizzy. Mr. Darcy and I are good friends now. I can mock him whenever I want. He owes me as much for taking you from me. Oh well, he is a good enough fellow. Not as good as my cousin Mr. Collins, but he will do. You may compete with your friend Charlotte about your felicity in marriage."

"Papa!"

"Come, Lizzy, laugh with me. You know, your husband asked me if I wanted him to have a look through Longbourn finances and find ways to improve our income. I have always been a poor manager. You know that."

"Oh—that sounds like a good idea. I hope you accepted."

"Not at all. You see, my dear, I will tell you what I also said to him. Since my two eldest daughters made such excellent matches, I have less reason for worry. I am certain that neither you nor Jane would allow your mother and two unmarried sisters to be thrown into poverty if I happen to die. Even more, Darcy violently refused any attempt to pay him back what he wasted to make my unworthy son-in-law marry my silly youngest girl. Therefore, I confess I shamelessly plan to be even lazier than before. I see no reason to put any particular efforts into improving Longbourn's income and leaving a successful estate to Mr. Collins. I am fine just as I am now. But I do appreciate Darcy's offer."

"Papa! You are just...I do not know what to tell you, really. I am not certain whether I should laugh or be upset with you."

"Oh well, you may do either. Darcy agreed that I will have more time to spend at Pemberley, fishing in his lakes and taking advantage of his library."

"That is an excellent plan, and I heartily approve of it." She embraced him lovingly, and he kissed her forehead. "And, of course, you have nothing to worry about. Besides, I am sure Longbourn will be in our family for at least another twenty years. Mr. Collins is very well where he is—by Lady Catherine's side."

"Well, well, I hope to be so. I really want to take advantage of my present favourable situation for as long as possible. Now let me finish my reading, child. I have had enough disruptions for one day."

"As you wish, Papa, but it is not nice to throw out your favourite daughter," she teased.

Elizabeth made to leave then turned to her father again. "Papa, did William say something when he left?"

"What was to be said? He was not off to fight Napoleon, only to take a ride. He will be back soon. Do not be so missish, Lizzy."

Elizabeth closed the library door and took a deep breath. Her father was right: she was behaving ridiculously.

DARCY RETURNED MORE THAN AN HOUR LATER WITH A LARGE SMILE ON his face. He tenderly kissed his wife's hand and greeted everyone in an obviously good humour.

"How was Summer?" she inquired while Mr. Gardiner poured him a glass of wine.

"Excellent—just as I hoped. I believe we should start the riding lessons this afternoon if you agree."

"Yes, of course. But is she not too tired after such a long ride?"

"Tired? Well...no, I do not believe she is. It is splendid weather."

She was puzzled by his disposition but found nothing more to say.

Later that day in the Longbourn stable yard, Elizabeth slowly became acquainted with the beautiful mare Summer under the careful assistance of Darcy, Margaret, and Becky—and Mr. Gardiner supervising his daughters. Jane and Bingley were also nearby, but they stole as many private moments as they could and were mostly oblivious to anything else.

Elizabeth already possessed the basic skills of riding, but she had always lacked confidence and pleasure in doing so. However, she quickly bonded with the new horse, and when she sat in the saddle for the first time, her eager excitement was clear.

Although she did not leave the back garden, Elizabeth rode for more than an hour. After walking beside the horse and holding the reins for half of the time, Darcy slowly allowed her to take control; even more, he rode by her side on his own horse, taking several tours of the garden together.

With each step, Elizabeth's confidence increased as well as her delight. From time to time, she glanced at her husband with gratitude and infinite love.

Again, he had known her heart and her desire better than she knew it herself. He offered her one of the few things she did not have: the joy of bonding with a stunning horse, the pleasure of riding, and a new type of independence.

And she could easily imagine the happiness of riding with him through the grounds of Netherfield and enjoying together the beauties of Pemberley. Everything that she missed in her life before meeting him he was now generously offering her—complete, overwhelming bliss.

A WEEK PASSED, AND LESS THAN ONE REMAINED UNTIL THE WEDDING.

The Darcys spent most of their time at Longbourn except for sleeping and having breakfast at Netherfield.

In the first days, they returned in the afternoon, changed for dinner, then returned to Longbourn again. Then Elizabeth decided to move several changes of clothing for both of them to her parents' house to solve the problem.

In the evenings, they usually retired early, so there were few opportunities to be in the company of the Hursts and Caroline. It was enough, though, for Elizabeth to notice Caroline's and Louisa's disapproving looks at every gesture of tenderness between Darcy and her, and that number was not insignificant.

One evening they played cards for half an hour, then Darcy abandoned the table and declared he intended to write to Georgiana. Elizabeth almost chuckled behind her teacup, waiting for Miss Bingley to offer to mend his pen again. Yet, she did not do that, but she did not miss the occasion to praise Georgiana's qualities, which—she declared—only a few women possessed.

During breakfasts, Caroline took every opportunity to make Elizabeth uncomfortable, often commenting about the faults of her family.

"In truth, I never would have imagined that things would progress in such a way, Mr. Darcy. Less than six months ago I heard you expressing your disapproval of Meryton society, and now you seem rather comfortable in the midst of it."

As much as she struggled to keep her patience and amusement, Elizabeth lacked the generous kindness that Jane possessed, so she struggled to reply calmly.

"It is fortunate that Mr. Darcy changed his opinion about Meryton society, just as people from Meryton changed their opinion about him. I would say it was a mutual development. It is a proof of wisdom and wit for one to admit one's errors and remedy them."

"The entire situation is strange, that cannot be denied. I have never heard of someone from the ton becoming a brother-in-law to the son of his former steward."

Darcy paled with anger, and Elizabeth was speechless with embarrassment while Bingley attempted to intervene and stop his sister. However, Darcy was the first to reply.

"It might be considered a strange situation; however, everything that brought Elizabeth and me together I can only consider a blessing, even if that involves some persons of whom I am not very fond. It is similar to having a good friend whom you deeply care for. One agrees to accept his family too, even if one disapproves of some of them and would be happy to avoid them."

Elizabeth could hardly believe her ears. That Caroline had been rude was without doubt. But for Darcy to answer her so coarsely in her own house was hard to believe. Caroline's and Louisa's faces coloured as they glared at each other with fury.

"I see your point, sir, but you must understand my surprise. There was a time when you were not so easily pleased. I can still remember your harsh judgment of both Miss Eliza Bennet, her mother, and her sisters when you first met them and also later when you happened to be in their company again. You were not very favourable towards either her beauty or her wit," Caroline replied, her smile barely compensating for her spiteful words.

"Ah, but you must not be surprised, Miss Bingley, since you were the first to whom I confessed my admiration for Elizabeth's handsome face and her enchanting eyes. I hope you remember that too."

"Oh, come now, Caroline, this discussion is ridiculous," Bingley intervened decidedly, already bored by a conversation that seemed endless. "You cannot question Darcy's change of mind! I, for one, am the happiest man since he married Elizabeth. We will be brothers now although he might not be so happy to have you as his sister-in-law!"

Both sisters stared at him with wide eyes.

"Charles!" Louisa cried, but he was preoccupied with a piece of cold meat.

"Forgive me, I shall retire to my room," Caroline suddenly said and left the table, leaving her plate half-full.

Elizabeth and Darcy glanced at each other. Neither of them felt satisfied with the small victory against Miss Bingley, and such sharp, unkind exchanges only threatened to ruin their mood. Fortunately, they always lifted their spirits with long, passionate kisses in the privacy of their room, which they did most diligently as soon as they found a spare moment.

BY THE FIFTH DAY OF RIDING LESSONS, ELIZABETH FOUND THE COURAGE to travel between Longbourn and Netherfield on horseback. At a very slow pace, accompanied by both Darcy and Bingley—but she did it nevertheless, bringing her a sense of accomplishment that added even more to her present felicity.

After two more days, Summer's pacing increased to a trot. Elizabeth relaxed more and could pay attention not only to the road in front of her but also to the beauties around her. Her husband remained close to her, always careful and protective. She felt that, if anything went wrong, he would be there to help her in an instant.

"William, do you think we could take the path through the wood? I would love to see the cottage again," Elizabeth pleaded.

"Well, maybe another day. The roads must be wet and muddy. We shall see…"

She had asked him to visit the cottage many times, and his answer was always the same. He seemed uninterested in doing it and always found reasons to delay, which left Elizabeth puzzled and a little sad. She had vivid memories of the day that changed her life, and although she felt the power of his love every moment of every day, she was heavyhearted knowing he appeared detached from that place. Every time she attempted to open a discussion about it, he would close it with a kiss and a change of subject.

At Longbourn, Darcy spent most of the time with the gentlemen, but whenever he had a chance, he would secure a few private moments with Elizabeth. He declared she was his peace and comfort, and only holding her hands or embracing her or stealing a kiss would dispel his distress. And there was plenty of distress as Longbourn was full of people most of the time. It seemed Mrs. Bennet daily invited some of those four-and-twenty families with whom she was on familiar terms.

There were still occasions when Darcy left everyone for a ride by himself. At her question, he only replied that he needed some time for calm and reflection, and she could not argue with that. His lonely departures were balanced with the times when the entire party went for peaceful rides around the estate: Jane, Bingley, the Gardiners, and the Darcys. Mr. Gardiner would take Margaret with him in the saddle while Becky preferred Darcy and was beyond herself with happiness when he allowed her to take the reins in her small hands. Elizabeth still struggled to maintain the pace of the others, but she was increasingly successful.

FOUR DAYS BEFORE THE WEDDING, THE ENTIRE LONGBOURN HOUSEHOLD became a maddening din.

Later in the afternoon, the sky became dark with clouds, and Darcy, Elizabeth, and Bingley decided to return to Netherfield before the rain started. None of the ladies opposed that plan—Mrs. Bennet because she was too busy establishing the dishes for the wedding breakfast, and Miss Bennet because she would not expose her beloveds to the danger of riding in the storm.

After mounting their horses and while Elizabeth gently petted Summer, Darcy suddenly said, "Perhaps we should take the road through the wood. It is shorter."

Bingley readily agreed while Elizabeth looked at him in disbelief. This was a day completely unsuited for a ride through the woods.

Darcy kept his horse close to hers, asking frequently whether she was well. The path was steeper, but Summer seemed comfortable with it.

Shortly, Elizabeth's surprise increased as she noticed the horses were directed toward the old cottage—the place she had so long wanted to see again. She gazed at her husband, intrigued but very pleased, and he seemed content with her reaction.

Unexpectedly, he stopped and dismounted then took the reins and halted Summer, stretching his arms to help Elizabeth down.

"We should walk further. Bingley, please take care of the horses."

The two gentlemen apparently had a previous understanding, so Elizabeth could do nothing but take her husband's hand and follow him.

"William, are we going to the cottage?"

"Yes, my love."

He said no more, and she chose not to inquire. In a few minutes, as the wind started blowing and a few single drops of rain began to fall, they spied the cottage through the green trees.

"Oh, it is beautiful! And the wood is so fresh, so full of life. Spring is so lovely!"

"Yes, it is," Darcy answered, kissing her hand, then both took a moment in front of the cottage. He put his hands on her shoulders and kissed her cheeks.

"Shall we enter?"

He opened the door, and before she had time to recover, he lifted her in his arms and stepped in. Elizabeth gasped in surprise and put her arms around his neck, their eyes locked. Without a word, he slowly put her down, and she finally took her eyes from his and looked around.

She gasped in astonishment as her eyes sparkled with tears.

"Oh, William, this is…"

"I have been waiting for this day…for a rainy day…to bring you here again."

"Oh, William" were the only words she kept repeating.

Everything looked as she remembered yet entirely different. The wooden furniture, the floor, the windows, the closet—even the small bed in the adjoining room—were clean and tidy. On a small table, there was a kettle and some cups of tea.

"Let me start the fire." He smiled, brushing his lips on hers. "It should be warm enough soon."

Speechless and tearful, Elizabeth watched her husband's every move. He pulled a small package from his inner pocket, knelt in front of the fireplace, and a moment later, a bright, red flame lit the chamber. Afterward, he unfolded the package he had carried and put some cold meat, fruits, cheese, and bread on a plate.

Only then did he turn to meet Elizabeth's eyes, where she remained motionless in the middle of the cottage. Her expression—breathless, tearful, biting her lower lip with emotions matching her happiness—melted his heart. He had thought of that moment from the day they had last been there. He wished—and planned—to return together someday soon to complete their wonderful memories with new ones even more unforgettable.

Once they arrived in Hertfordshire, he had hired two men to restore the cottage to a liveable condition, and he went daily to supervise the project. He was sorry to have to deceive Elizabeth, but it was his strongest desire to make her a surprise she would never forget. And there she was—more beautiful than ever—and he took his reward as he had so many times before from her bright eyes that enveloped him in an adoring gaze. That was what he had hoped.

They stepped toward each other and their arms entwined in a tender embrace.

"William, sometimes I fear my heart will break in pieces from so much happiness. No words can express how I feel now. This is…I cannot imagine anything more wonderful. And I thought you did not care to see this place again. I am such a simpleton! I thank you so much, my love!"

"It was my fault that I concealed my intentions from you. But I hope you forgive me. The delight on your face was worth any effort."

"You should forgive me for doubting your intention, my beloved husband." She leant her head against his chest, and he gently removed her bonnet then kissed her temple.

Outside, the rain intensified, and hasty drops were falling on the roof like a drumbeat.

"I am so happy it is raining," she whispered. "I hope it will not stop soon."

"I planned to spend the night here if you agree. It should be comfortable enough, I hope."

She rose on her toes and teased his lips with her fingers. "You and I and the solitude of this magical place—how could I possibly wish for more? And you waited all these days just for the rain? I did not know you were such a patient man, sir."

His lips searched her, tasting and tantalising them playfully.

"I hoped it would…just as when we met. I can be patient when necessary, madam."

"It seems the sky has plotted with you, my dear husband."

"Yes, it is quite fortunate. And I confess I also colluded with Bingley and your father, so they both know where we are. Nobody will worry about us. And I brought some food, so we can make tea and—"

"I am not even surprised anymore. You always think of everything. But I am not hungry at all…and I can hardly think of anyone or anything else," she whispered, kissing him passionately. Then, still tightly embraced, she pushed him into the armchair by the fireplace and sat on his lap. Their words were crushed between hungry lips as they both recollected her in that same armchair four months before—wet, scared, frozen, and wrapped in dirty blankets.

She stopped for a moment, her eyes meeting his. "I remember how cold I was. My body felt trapped in a cage of ice; then I slowly started to warm—by the fire you made but also by your care and kindness and by the new sides of your character that I began to discover. And I have been warming ever since. Your arms, your love, your care never allowed me to be cold again."

"My beautiful, dearest Elizabeth…" he replied, covering her face with sweet, tender small kisses, like a warm, sunny rain.

The rest of the day and the entire night, their lovemaking was only interrupted by shared memories, confessions of past feelings, and professions of their present life.

Every word, every recollection, every image from the past enhanced their passion, and their growing desire was hardly satiated until dawn. And the fire burning steadily in the fireplace had little to do with the warmth that indulged their bodies and their hearts.

Chapter 9

The sun shone through the windows, tickling his face, and Darcy woke, observing that the rain had finally stopped after falling savagely the entire night. The cottage was warmed by the strong fire that he struggled to keep alive through the night. The bed was rather small and not very comfortable, but he would gladly sleep anywhere if she were by his side.

He breathed deeply, intoxicated by the scent of the woman who was sleeping soundly in his arms. His heart was so full of love for her that it became heavy. He took a moment to admire her although he knew too well the feeling and the taste of every inch of her silky skin. Her beauty seemed to grow every day, as did his love for her. She belonged to him just as he belonged to her. Her place was within his arms, in his mind, and in his soul as he had told her the day he proposed.

As with other mornings, he was tempted to awaken her only to meet her eyes, enjoy her smiles, and hear her voice teasing him. And, just like other mornings—he did not do it. No matter how much he wished one thing, her wants and needs were more important to him. And if he had to admire her peaceful sleep in silence for another few hours—so be it. There was no rush to leave unlike the first time they were there.

Darcy was pleased with the idea of arranging the cottage and returning to spend a night remembering sweet yesterdays and the passionate present. His reward had been even more delightful than he hoped—like every moment he had spent with her since falling in love with her fine eyes.

He gazed steadily at her, marvelling once again at the happiness she had brought to his life. With a smile, he noticed goose bumps on her arms, and he knew it was because of his intense stare. Her body was so accustomed to his adoration that he did not even have to touch her to arouse a response.

Her head rested on his torso, her hair caressing their bare skin. With a shiver, he felt her lips upon his heart and her warm fingers travelling along his arm. He tightened his arms around her then stroked her dark, loose locks. Her eyes lifted to meet his.

"Good morning, my love."

"Good morning, my beautiful wife."

"The rain has stopped, hasn't it? It seems a lovely day," she said, placing another kiss on his chest. Then she suddenly rose, and her eyes widened in surprise. "Oh William, look—a rainbow! It looks so close that I feel I could touch it!"

She abandoned his protective embrace, and pulling the blanket around her naked body, she hurried to the window. He followed and closed his arms around her again.

Indeed, a stunning rainbow fell upon the creek through the blooming trees. She stretched her hand along the window, and said merrily, teasing him while her eyes sparkled with tears of happiness, "Look—it is as if the rainbow is my bracelet. Is this another gift for me? Did you buy this rainbow, Mr. Darcy? Is this another part of your surprise?"

"I would gladly give you the rainbow, the sun, the rain, and the entire world, my beloved Elizabeth," he answered, cupping her face with tender hands.

"I know you would, my darling husband. But I need nothing except your love...and your entire being, and I know I already have it. I shall leave this rainbow where it is, but you must promise me another one—at Pemberley. Soon."

"I promise. Very soon!"

He sealed his promise with another passionate kiss, which turned into many more and delayed their stay in the cottage until late afternoon.

It was almost dinnertime when Elizabeth and Darcy finally returned to Netherfield after a long and nostalgic walk. They departed from the place so dear to their hearts with sadness mixed with joy and with the hope of returning someday. They knew, though, that in the next months—and probably the next years—they would likely spend little time if any in

Hertfordshire. It was perhaps time to say a tender goodbye to the past and step trustingly toward the future.

THE NEXT TWO DAYS FLEW WITH THE EXPECTED AGITATION. EVEN BECKY declared she had had "enough of this marriage business" and preferred to play outside or seek the company of Darcy, who was usually in the most peaceful parts of the house.

The day before the wedding, it was impossible to carry on a normal conversation at Longbourn. Therefore, Bingley did not call on them—for the first time in more than six weeks. He remained at Netherfield to prepare for the next day's event.

Mr. Bennet took the opportunity to tease his wife, suggesting that the gentleman might have changed his mind and run away while he still had time to do so. Mrs. Bennet was about to faint, but she postponed it since she was too busy supervising the food for the wedding breakfast. However, she did complain for more than an hour about Mr. Bennet having no compassion for her poor nerves.

Jane Bennet forced herself to take a distressing farewell from her old room in which she was about to sleep for the last time. She carefully arranged her luggage, brushing with shy fingers the exquisite nightgown she planned to wear on her wedding night. She turned to her sister with a restrained smile.

"Lizzy, this is so beautiful…"

"I am glad you like it, dearest. May I help you with anything?"

"No…I was only thinking that…can you stay with me a little longer?"

"Of course, I would love to. Is anything troubling you?"

"Nothing especially…I just wish to talk to you, as we used to…away from the others. I am ashamed to admit it, but I am a little tired. I am glad everything will calm down starting tomorrow."

"I imagine, my dear. But it was worth it, was it not? Just imagine how happy you will be with the man you love."

"Oh, I know, Lizzy. Sometimes I wonder how I will be able to bear such bliss."

Elizabeth laughed and kissed her cheeks. "I ask myself the same thing every single day! And my felicity will now be completed by yours. It is so fortunate that you decided to wed earlier. It would be much worse if you had to wait another six weeks."

"It is Charles's merit entirely; he convinced me. He anticipated all the bustle and restlessness that would precede the wedding day, and he believed it would be easier for me to shorten it. Besides, he made the point that you and Mr. Darcy fell in love much later than we did and married much sooner."

Elizabeth laughed again. "He is right, but do not believe he did so out of generosity. He surely is eager to have you as his wife as soon as possible and to spend every day and every night with you."

"I know...and so am I."

"Do you remember when we used to talk about marrying someone we could respect and care for? And here we are—having much more than that. I always hoped to marry for love, but I confess I completely understood what love truly meant only after I wedded William. You will see for yourself, dearest."

"I am so grateful, Lizzy, that I cannot stop praising the Lord for everything that happened to us. I only hope that I will be the wife Charles deserves. And that he will not be disappointed—"

"Jane, that is silly. How could he be disappointed?"

"It is just that...I am thinking of tomorrow...you know what I mean..."

"Oh, I see. Your wedding day—or rather your wedding night—worries you."

"It does. It is not that I do not know. Aunt Gardiner spoke with both of us a long time ago. But I still wonder how things will truly be. I know Charles is so anxious, and I am afraid I will not be as he expects. You must think I am silly..."

"I was nervous too. But there is nothing to worry about, believe me. You must trust your husband and be honest with him. You should let him know what you wish, what you desire."

Elizabeth paused a moment, felt her cheeks burning, but continued daringly. "Jane, I cannot find the words to describe how wonderful love can be. How much joy and delight and pleasure you will feel in your husband's arms. More than you imagine. And you have nothing else to do but allow him to prove his affection. His eagerness will soon be matched by yours, I am sure."

"Lizzy, you are teasing me." Jane smiled tearfully, her cheeks crimson. "Please do not make fun of me."

"I am not. Pray tell me, have you and Mr. Bingley—I mean Charles—shared any affection? I would imagine so, considering what I saw when he proposed to you."

"Lizzy!" Jane cried, shocked and embarrassed, which only made Elizabeth laugh.

"Do not answer if you do not wish to, but keep in mind that everything you feel when you are in his intimate company will be ten times better."

"Lizzy!" Elizabeth saw her beloved sister staring at her, eyes wide open, incredulous and distressed. Then Jane lowered her eyes, breathed deeply, and looked at her sister again.

"What do you mean 'ten times better'? Surely, you are exaggerating."
Elizabeth laughed harder.

"Not at all. You may consider me the most wanton woman alive, but I admit that I look forward to every evening when I can be alone with my husband. And when we are at our home alone, we do not even need to wait for the evening to come. It is more difficult while we are at Netherfield."

"Lizzy! Surely, this is not—you mean that you and Mr. Darcy...William... share a bed every night? Are you not teasing me?"

"I am telling the truth. Let us speak again in a few days. You will not be equally surprised by then."

"Oh, Lizzy..." Jane remained silent and puzzled, glancing at her sister then at the fireplace. "We did break propriety several times. We kissed while we walked in the garden but nothing more. It would not have been possible with so many people around us. But it was so pleasant! I dreamt of it many times, and I wondered...and now that you tell me..."

Elizabeth embraced her affectionately. "My dearest, everything will be fine. More than fine! I am glad you decided to come to London. Even if you will have Charles's sisters around, it will still be less crowded than at Longbourn. You do deserve some peaceful time for yourself."

"Charles said he will ask Caroline to stay with Louisa, at least for a few weeks. I hope she will not mind."

"I like Charles more and more. It was the right thing to do. You should think of nothing else but your and your husband's happiness for now. It is time for you to be a little selfish."

"Dear Lizzy, I will try to follow your advice, if not for my sake, for Charles's. Yet, I cannot help worrying for our families; you know me too well. I thank you for your patience and advice. You have always been the comfort of my heart."

"I am confident that this place will be occupied by someone else starting tomorrow. And that is how it should be, my dear Jane."

AT NETHERFIELD, BINGLEY AND DARCY WERE HIDING IN THE LIBRARY, seeking privacy, both of them restless and impatient to carry on a logical conversation or at least to sit down for more than several minutes. Darcy was distressed that Elizabeth had remained at Longbourn and counted the hours until he could fetch her. Bingley seemed distressed by everything.

They filled their glasses a couple of times, but it did not help them calm down.

Bingley paced the room several times, stopped in front of Darcy, opened his mouth to speak, then abandoned his intention and started walking around again. When he did this for the fourth time, Darcy could bear it no longer.

"Bingley, what is wrong? You have been acting strangely for the last few days."

"Nothing is wrong. Yes it is, it is just that—"

"Yes? For heaven's sake man, take a seat. You make me dizzy with your irrational pacing."

"I am sorry. I am just nervous."

"Is there any problem that I might help you with?"

"No, it is just...no problem at all, only the wedding."

"Are you nervous about the wedding?"

"Yes...I mean...you know..."

"No, I most certainly do not know."

"I still cannot believe that I will marry Jane...that she will be my wife. I am afraid of disappointing her. She is so beautiful and so perfect and..."

"Yes, she is. And you should be happy. You will be married in a day."

"I am happy. Very happy." He gulped another glass of brandy.

"Yet, you are still distressed it seems. Am I wrong?"

"You are not wrong; you know me well enough."

"Well, if there is nothing I can do, I would suggest you retire and rest a little. Later I will go to Longbourn to fetch Elizabeth."

"Will you not have another glass?"

"Very well—one more. It will help both of us to sleep better."

Bingley paced the room again, stopping from time to time as if he were tempted to say more, then he resumed.

"Bingley, you are behaving strangely. If I did not know better, I would say that you look like a young, unexperienced boy who is distressed about his wedding night. However, that cannot be the reason since I know very well that you were intimately favoured by quite a few ladies before you became attached to Jane."

"Yes, well…it is not the same. You cannot compare Jane to any other woman. Things will be different. Were you not nervous when you married?"

"Not at all. However, I was happy and content and relieved that I could finally have Elizabeth by my side without anyone interfering with or disturbing us."

"I should have imagined that…you are never nervous or distressed about anything. So—do you have any advice for me? You have been only recently wed."

Darcy patted his arm. "Let us not speak more about nervousness. From tomorrow on, you will be happier than ever before. And if you are resolved to make your wife happy, your felicity will be enhanced every day. This is the only advice I can offer: make sure you attend your wife's desires first, and yours will be easily fulfilled afterward. Think of what she prefers before considering what you want. Even now—you keep talking about your nervousness, but just imagine how she must feel. You must be confident to earn her trust. She is offering herself to you, and you must be strong enough to hold her and protect her."

"You are right, of course. That is true. I am being selfish, am I not? You are right. Yes, let us sleep a little—please forgive me for being such poor company. I will see you later at dinner."

Darcy shook his hand with a sympathetic smile. "There is no need for apologies, but please do me a favour: restrain yourself from drinking more than usual today and especially tomorrow. That will not calm you down and will certainly not prepare you for your first day and night with your wife—quite the contrary."

"I will do that—of course. Do not worry, I will do just that."

THE DAY JANE BENNET MARRIED MR. CHARLES BINGLEY WAS, FOR MERYton's inhabitants as well as for Mrs. Bennet, almost as exciting as the wedding of Elizabeth to Mr. Darcy—almost.

While the bride was much praised for her beauty, the gentleman was also universally admired for his appearance and amiability. However, everybody agreed that he was not as tall, nor quite as handsome as Mr. Darcy. And it was generally admitted that ten thousand a year was beyond comparison with half that sum.

Four and twenty families were invited to Longbourn for the wedding breakfast and remained until late in the afternoon. Except for Caroline and Louisa, who barely spoke a few words to anyone, and Mr. Hurst, who only paid attention to his drink, the guests declared they had a lovely time and that Mrs. Bennet's selection of dishes was perfect. The mother of the bride took the opportunity to mention that, at her second daughter's marriage to Mr. Darcy, Lady Matlock herself complimented her arrangements and that she was already experienced in this matter. With such a statement, even Lady Lucas had to agree. After all, she had only married off one daughter—to the clergyman of Mr. Darcy's aunt—as Mrs. Bennet reminded her constantly.

The newly wedded couple barely separated at all during the entire day. Elizabeth smiled affectionately, noticing their brief touches, stolen glances, blushes, and whispers—so well known to her too. She had no doubt that her sister would be happy and that Charles was worthy of his wife. Their mutual adoration was enough to compensate for anything else and an excellent premise for their future.

IT WAS ALMOST DARK WHEN THE RESIDENTS OF NETHERFIELD LEFT LONGbourn. Mrs. Bingley's unease was apparent and seemed to increase as the carriage approached her new home. She kept her gloved hands in her lap, rubbing them together while her eyes were mostly fixed upon the window. Her smile was as serene as ever, but Elizabeth could easily guess her distress.

Once at their destination, Caroline and the Hursts retired to their rooms. Charles and Jane, together with the Darcys, remained in the main hall as if they did not know how to proceed. The host seemed even more nervous than his shy wife. Elizabeth eventually took the lead.

"Jane, do you need me to help you with anything?"

"Help me? Oh, yes, that would be very kind of you. If you could…" Jane glanced at her husband, her cheeks coloured.

"Bingley, would you have another glass of wine with me?" Darcy asked, gazing at his wife. His friend seemed exceedingly happy with the proposal.

"Yes, of course...I shall...let us go to the library..."

Elizabeth could not conceal her amusement as she took Jane's arm and accompanied her to her apartment. Once inside, Jane sat on the bed, struggling to breathe.

"Oh, Lizzy, I am so silly...Forgive me..."

"Jane, dearest, calm yourself. Look around—you are in a beautiful chamber where your husband will join you soon. I know it can be a little distressing, but all will be well. There—here is your lovely nightgown. You should wash and then change for the night. I shall ring for the maid to bring you hot water."

Slowly, Elizabeth managed to calm her sister. When the maid came to help her, Jane finally kissed her sister, thanked her, and asked her to return to her own husband. The new Mrs. Bingley was ready to take her place.

Elizabeth hurried downstairs and found Darcy and Bingley in the library, talking animatedly. At her entrance, they stopped, and Bingley stared at her as if waiting for news. Elizabeth smiled.

"Is Jane well?"

"Of course she is. I left her with her maid."

"Oh, well—I should go too."

"Yes, you should," Darcy said. "And I would suggest leaving the glass here."

"Yes, I will do that," Bingley said, but he left the room holding the glass tightly.

Elizabeth laughed and was about to make a comment when her husband silenced her with a kiss.

"I missed you so much, my love. I cannot believe that a whole day passed without my holding you."

"I missed you too. I am so glad everything is finally done. It was much more tiresome than our own wedding."

"It was—because I was smart enough to take you away right after the ceremony. If you remember, a couple of hours later we were in the carriage on our way to London."

"I do remember—quite vividly," she answered, pressing herself to him and returning the kiss.

"I believe it is time for us to retire too, Mrs. Darcy. Although it is very rarely used, it would not do to behave wantonly in Bingley's library."

Chapter 10

The morning after the wedding seemed strangely quiet and peaceful after the past two weeks of pandemonium. When Elizabeth and Darcy appeared, the Hursts and Caroline were already gathered for breakfast. The ladies greeted them politely yet coldly; Mr. Hurst only nodded.

Fortunately for everyone involved, it was the last day they were to spend together at Netherfield, and Darcy had already thought of a way to invite only Bingley and Jane to Pemberley for the summer.

Elizabeth could not hide her smiles when Charles finally appeared. She waited to see her sister too, but the gentleman was alone and his expression stern. He greeted them briefly then asked for a cup of coffee.

"You are late," Louisa said. "We did not wait for you since we were quite hungry."

"Good." Bingley seemed to answer with difficulty.

"Will Jane come down soon? We are not accustomed to being late for breakfast."

"No, she said she would rather not have breakfast. She had a slight headache."

No other conversation followed. Elizabeth exchanged concerned glances with her husband, both of them equally puzzled. Darcy looked at his old friend several times, but Bingley refused to meet his eyes.

Eventually, breakfast came to an end, and Bingley rose in haste. "I will go for a ride," he announced.

"Do you wish me to keep you company?" Darcy inquired.

"If you want to, I would not mind," Bingley replied after a brief hesitation.

The two gentlemen left the house. Caroline and the Hursts moved toward the drawing room while Elizabeth hurried upstairs to check on her sister.

DARCY FOLLOWED BINGLEY IN HIS GALLOP THROUGH THE FIELDS. THEY rode, forcing the horses almost too much, for about an hour until Bingley suddenly stopped on a hill that offered a perfect view of Netherfield and dismounted.

"I am a poor excuse for a man. If I say I am ashamed of myself, it would be too little. And any embarrassment and distress I might suffer means nothing compared to Jane's hurt expression. I failed her, and she is disappointed with me. I am a poor man and an even poorer husband."

He stared toward the horizon. Darcy paced around as if he feared to approach closer.

"I do not dare ask what happened. You seem more distressed than I have seen you in a long time. I hope nobody suffered any harm."

"They did—my pride is hurt. And Jane's tender heart."

"I really hope you are overreacting. I pray things are less distressing than you let me believe. You are not the kind of man to hurt your wife, so anything else can be easily repaired, I am sure."

"This cannot ever be repaired. I am a ridiculous and pitiful man who deserves no respect."

"Oh, for heaven's sake, I shall lose both my patience and my reason if you continue in this way. So I must ask: What on earth did you do?"

"Nothing."

"Nothing? Nice to see that you can mock me. Let us end this silly conversation, and I shall return home now before I go mad."

"I do not mock you. I did nothing. I remember knocking on Jane's door, and she looked as beautiful as a fairy. She said she would be ready in a half an hour, and I left her with the maid. I changed for the night, poured a glass of wine, and…the next thing I remember, it was morning. I fell asleep."

"What? You fell asleep? You got drunk and fell asleep on your wedding night? Did I not warn you not to drink more than usual? You are an idiot indeed," Darcy admitted, suddenly realising the justice of Bingley's agitated struggle.

"I told you so. I am so ashamed of myself that I could stab my leg, and the pain would not be as sharp. And Jane's face...I knocked on her door this morning, but she seemed to have been crying, and she said she was tired and wished to rest, and she refused to talk to me. She turned her back to me and...how can I ever make amends for such shameful behaviour? Obviously, I am not the man she deserves."

"Well, I shall not argue with you about that. Did you explain to her what happened?"

"No...it seemed she wished to sleep, and I did not dare trouble her more."

"So you left? You had breakfast and then went for a ride?"

"Yes—you know I did."

"How could you do that? You hurt your wife then you left her alone? This is not to be borne! You cannot leave until you are certain your wife understands and forgives you—not ever in your life and certainly not on the first day of your marriage. Have you lost your mind?"

"But...should I have stayed? Even if she said she wanted to sleep?"

"Of course! You cannot imagine what is in a hurt woman's mind, but you must try to discover it and compensate for your error. You should have stayed with her!"

"I did not...I thought..."

Darcy suddenly grabbed his friend's arms. "Bingley, listen carefully, as I will only have this conversation with you once and will then forget it and never admit it took place. Elizabeth and I barely left our apartment in the first days of our marriage. I did nothing but make sure she was as happy as I was. We even had breakfast and dinner in our rooms. Do you understand my meaning?"

Bingley listened to him, puzzled and shocked, nodding.

"I am certain that Elizabeth talked to Jane about what she should expect in her own marriage. Instead, Jane spent her wedding night alone with her husband never coming to her. Surely, she must believe she was not desired—that you preferred sleeping alone to her company. How do you think she must feel right now? She must be as embarrassed and ashamed as you are. And even worse since you left, which means you also prefer riding to her company."

"What are you saying, Darcy? That is madness; I would give up anything in my life for Jane's company."

"Well, nobody can be certain of that, and Jane less than anyone. At least, not before you return home and prove it to her."

"But I am sure she…she could not possibly…oh, I must return home. I have not a moment to waste."

He mounted and whipped his horse while Darcy hurried to catch him, barely able to conceal his laughter.

In front of Netherfield, Bingley released his horse and ran towards the door. Darcy barely had time to grab his arm.

"Bingley, wait a moment. Breathe deeply, and do not rush things again. Go to your room and refresh yourself then change your clothes. You look rather savage. And only afterward go to your wife and resolve this misunderstanding. And send us word later if you want something to eat. You do not need to leave your apartment today."

Bingley's jaws dropped. "You mean…? Now? But…it is daylight. I do not think Jane would…do you think she would…?"

"Bingley, you are impossible, man! How should I know that? It is your duty to discover exactly what your wife's wishes are. Just do not presume and worry again for no reason. Go and make your wife happy. And for heaven's sake, draw the curtains closed if needed; that will be dark enough."

Bingley remained still and silent a few moments as if trying to comprehend his friend's words, then he entered the house hastily and ran upstairs.

Darcy went directly to the library, asking for a glass of brandy.

ELIZABETH KNOCKED ON HER SISTER'S DOOR. NO ANSWER CAME, SO SHE opened it hesitantly.

"Jane, how are, dearest? Charles told me you were unwell. Should I bring you something?"

"It is nothing, Lizzy. Please do not worry for me. Where is Charles?" Jane inquired with obvious distress.

"He went for a ride. William is with him."

Elizabeth took her sister's hands and was astonished to see her pale face wearing the trace of tears.

"Oh, my dear, what is wrong? What happened? Are you hurt?"

Elizabeth caressed Jane's face then embraced her. Jane started sobbing while Elizabeth's anger increased. She was certain Bingley was to blame for her sister's distress, and she hastily considered several ways to murder him in his own house.

"Will you tell me what happened? Are you in pain? How may I help you?"

"Nothing happened."

"Jane, please do not deceive me. Something terrible happened—that is clear. And I shall find out about it, one way or another."

"No, no…please believe me. *Nothing* happened. I spoke to Charles last night, and he said he would come to meet me later after I was finished preparing myself. But…he did not come. I waited and waited. I did not know what happened, so I opened his door, and he was sound asleep…and…"

As Jane's sobbing increased, Elizabeth breathed in relief. She gently embraced her sister again, caressing her hair, while she bit her lips to cover her mirth. How could she possibly believe that Bingley would have hurt her sister? Poor fellow! She remembered his filling his glass many times during the day at Longbourn and later in the library, apparently to conquer his nervousness, then her husband's warning to put down the glass.

Now she easily understood Bingley's pallor and his attempt to avoid their company. He was certainly as distressed as Jane. Fortunately, despite its being a most embarrassing situation, it was easy to remedy.

"I am sure Charles does not find me desirable enough. I was such a simpleton. I hoped that…and I do not know what to do. I was wearing the nightgown you purchased for me—it was so beautiful—but…"

"Oh, come now, my dear—wipe your eyes. Jane, look at me. I am sure you are wrong, completely wrong. I think Charles found you too desirable, and he was just nervous about the prospect of your wedding night. I am certain he had one too many glasses of wine and, most likely having not slept well lately, he was overcome by fatigue. Things will be much better soon."

"If I could only know what I did wrong…"

"Jane, you are being silly. Your husband will return soon. Wash your face and refresh your appearance. You do not look very desirable at the moment; I can tell you that."

"Lizzy! Please do not tease me, I am—"

The new Mrs. Bingley gasped when they heard the door to Charles's rooms slam and his voice talking to the servant. She gazed at her sister in panic, but Elizabeth smiled and kissed her cheeks then arranged her hair and offered her a handkerchief to clean her face. Jane moved to the mirror then sat back on the edge of the bed.

Even if it was expected, the knock on the door startled Jane, and a new expression of panic widened her eyes. Elizabeth asked Bingley to enter; in another moment, he appeared and stopped in the doorway, looking from one lady to the other.

"Did my husband return too?" Elizabeth asked.

Bingley nodded in agreement, his eyes and full attention focused on his wife.

"Well then, I shall leave you now. I must find him. One of the greatest joys of marriage is that one can be with one's own spouse whenever one wishes."

Bingley and Jane glanced at her, but by the time she closed the door, they were staring into each other's eyes, and Elizabeth heard them struggling to apologise and to take upon themselves an unwarranted blame. She hastened her pace in search of her husband, eager to be in the arms of the man who never failed her. She easily found him in the billiard room, and only a moment later she enjoyed the comfort and delight of his kisses. Without separating from her, he suddenly lifted her to sit on the billiard table, his lips never abandoning hers.

"Did Charles benefit from your advice to solve this delicate matter?" Elizabeth murmured between tantalising kisses.

"Let us just say that I hope not to see him again for the rest of the day. Was Jane upset?" He barely spoke, and it was even harder for her to reply.

"She was…but I trust she will be fine now. Will you not teach me to play? I would like to keep you company," she said, holding her arms tightly around his waist.

"I would be happy to," he whispered, his warm breath tickling her ear. "And I will certainly put a lock on the door and a couch in our billiard room at Pemberley."

THE NEXT MORNING, THE ENTIRE PARTY DEPARTED FOR LONDON AFTER A short but emotional farewell from the Bennets. Elizabeth was sad to leave her mare Summer behind, so they decided to take her with them. Darcy promised to purchase another horse for Longbourn, but Mr. Bennet advised him otherwise: with Jane moving to Netherfield, there was nobody left who enjoyed riding.

In one carriage were the Hursts and Caroline Bingley; another carried the servants. Darcy's carriage would not accommodate eight people, so the gentlemen decided to separate from the ladies.

Mr. Charles Bingley—more handsome and joyful than usual—was reluctant to separate from the beautiful, blushing, and exceedingly happy Mrs. Jane Bingley, but he could not find a better arrangement. Travelling with his sisters appeared to be an even less desirable option.

Therefore, he joined Mr. Darcy and Mr. Gardiner in a smaller carriage while the three ladies, together with the Gardiners' girls, entered the large one.

"Mama, why can I not go with Papa and Mr. Darcy?" Becky asked. "I like speaking to him."

"Because we made some decisions and everybody must respect them. The ladies will travel in this carriage. And you have bothered Mr. Darcy enough for several months."

"But I am not a lady; I am a little girl! And I did not bother Mr. Darcy enough. That is why he invited me to Pemberley!"

"Becky, please come and stay by the window," her sister Margaret whispered, taking her little hand. Becky obeyed for a few minutes then turned to her cousins and took a place on Elizabeth's lap.

"Jane, will you come to our house in London? I have several new dolls to show you!"

"Unfortunately, I cannot, dearest. I have a new home now with Mr. Bingley. I will live with him," Jane answered, her face and neck suddenly crimson.

"Jane, why is your face so red? Are you ill?" the girl inquired, touching her cheeks.

Jane blushed even more. "I am well, my dear, do not worry. It is just that… as I said, I cannot stay with you since I am married now."

"So you will live with Mr. Bingley all the time?"

"Yes. But he is a very kind man, and we will both visit you often."

"Lizzy and Mr. Darcy said the same, but they only visited me a few times. I do not like that. It was much better when you and Lizzy stayed with us."

"You should be pleased that Jane and Lizzy married such good gentlemen," Mrs. Gardiner interjected. "It is every girl's dream—to meet a handsome, honourable man, fall in love, and marry him."

Becky shook her head in disapproval, breathed deeply, and crossed her small arms over her chest.

"It is surely not my dream. I find marriage to be a very distressing business. I am quite sure I do not like it at all."

"It can be disturbing at times, but I do like it." Elizabeth laughed, kissing her young cousin.

"So do I," Jane admitted, her cheeks turning crimson again.

Becky just sighed and rolled her eyes, puzzled to see such a complete lack of understanding in her beloved elder cousins. Half an hour later, rocked by the carriage's motion, she fell asleep in Elizabeth's arms, having decided never to marry.

Chapter 11

It was late in the evening when the Darcys finally reached their house in London.

Dinner was brought to their room and hot water was prepared for bathing.

Darcy allowed Miles to shave him while he eagerly anticipated the delight of having Elizabeth in his arms after two exhausting weeks in Hertfordshire and a long day on the road.

He barely stifled his laughter, recollecting Bingley's animated chatter during the journey and his constant confessions about being the happiest man on earth. Without a doubt, any difficulty his younger friend and his new wife might have had on their wedding night was overcome quickly and most satisfactorily.

Darcy was about to dismiss Miles when he was pleasantly surprised by Elizabeth entering his room, ready for the night, her long hair falling on her shoulders and covering her arousing cleavage.

His eyes caressed her adoringly, and he could see her blushing under his stare. She was as beautiful as ever, yet something was different. She stepped further, the fabric of the nightgown moving along her tempting curves. He suddenly felt hot and wondered whether he should open a window.

Elizabeth approached the bed, her gaze locked with her husband's while she addressed the valet.

"Miles, you may leave now. I am certain Mr. Darcy does not need you any longer tonight."

The servant appeared puzzled and slightly embarrassed; he would not question the mistress's request, yet he could not leave without the master's permission. The approval came an instant later with a brief wave of Darcy's hand, and Miles exited the room discreetly.

Darcy looked at his wife, mesmerised, his entire body tensing in anticipation. Elizabeth sat on the edge of the bed, and he stretched his hand toward her. She smiled and leant until her lips gently touched his then withdrew, looking at him intently. His curiosity increased, as well as his yearning for her.

Only then did he notice the small box she held in her right hand and the mischievous smile that twisted her red lips.

"What are you trying to hide from me, Mrs. Darcy?"

"On the contrary, I only waited for the proper moment for disclosure."

"Truly? Then I beg you to let me know what it is."

"Please have a little patience, sir. All in good time."

Her flirtatious tone stirred him. He tried to claim a kiss, but she withdrew again.

"Patience is a virtue I still need to learn how to master. It is good that I have enough self-control to keep myself under good regulation," he answered hoarsely.

"Then you will have to carry on a difficult struggle tonight, sir, as I request that you do nothing but wait...and accept...and receive. Will you promise me?"

"I would promise you anything as you well know, my beloved wife, but I am growing very intrigued."

"But you must keep your promise, sir. And I feel your strong self-control will be much needed. Please humour me."

"I would not wish to suspend any pleasure of yours, madam."

She rewarded him with a tender kiss then offered him the black velvet box.

"Since we wed, you have made each of our celebrations unforgettable. From the first week, I have thought of what I could offer you. And since we have now reached six weeks of marriage, here it is. I hope you will enjoy my little gift although I am ashamed to admit it was purchased from my pin money, which is actually still yours." She laughed, attempting to conceal her emotions.

Darcy looked at her adoringly and kissed her hand, which was still holding the present. He took the box with the eagerness of a schoolboy and opened it, his expression showing his pleasure. Inside, there was an exquisite golden pocket watch. He turned it over, and on the back he read: "To my love."

"This is beautiful…you have made me very happy, my dearest Elizabeth," he said, caressing her face with infinite tenderness. She smiled.

"Oh, but there is more. Please open it."

He found himself uncertain of his fingers as he opened the lid; the image made him gasp.

Inside were two miniatures of the painting he ordered for their one-month anniversary: a portrait of the couple and one of her alone. Emotion overwhelmed him.

"This is beyond words. How did you…? When? We were in Hertford-shire together. How did you manage to do this? This surprise is…such a wonderful, thoughtful gift…and I have nothing for you…"

"My love, almost from the beginning of our acquaintance, I have been the recipient of your kindness and generosity and tenderness. I do not need another gift. You have offered me your love, your home, your care, your passion, your heart…and I have not even mentioned the jewels." She smiled as he took her hands to his heart, and their gazes held. "I have so few occasions to give you anything at all, so I asked my uncle to help me. I conspired with him, and one day when you were out, we went to choose the watch. Then I spoke with the painter, and he agreed to do the miniatures even before the paintings are ready. I left him the watch when we departed for Longbourn, and he delivered it to me just in time. It was an easy plan, perfectly executed."

He pulled her to his chest, kissing her hair. "Thank you so much, my beloved wife. I am touched by all the trouble you took." Her eyes moistened with tears, and his own emotions were no less affected.

"I confess I am also a little frightened that you did all this without my noticing. You are a dangerous woman, Mrs. Darcy."

"I hope you are not disappointed, sir," she teased him.

"Do I look disappointed? I hope not, as I am as proud of your tenacity as I am charmed by your beauty. And eager to show you how delighted I am with your gift," he whispered while his arms trapped her.

"I am afraid you will have to wait a little longer, sir," she whispered against his ear then decidedly freed herself from him. "You made me a promise, and I expect you to keep it. You must not forget that this is the evening you must do nothing but receive what I have prepared to offer you…"

He looked at her, surprised and intrigued, trying to guess the meaning behind her words.

She slowly abandoned her robe then walked around the room, blowing out the candles until the only light came from the fire and the moon shining outside.

He followed her with his eyes, enchanted by her arousing features and even more so by her confident attitude. The fabric of her nightgown slid around her curves, and his body started to burn.

Elizabeth returned to him and gently pushed him onto the pillows, just as he had done with her in the past.

Her mouth engaged his for a passionate yet short kiss then tantalised his face, the line of his jaws, his neck. A moment later, she withdrew enough for their eyes to meet, and her fingers touched and stroked his lips. He parted them and captured her fingers, his tongue playing with them briefly, before she pulled them out slowly to continue her exploration.

Darcy struggled to keep his hands still while she untied his shirt, exposing his bare torso to her curious eyes and warm caresses. She had touched him before and had seen him without clothes every night, but this time, it was different, and both knew it.

Her gestures grew more and more daring while he felt every spot of his skin burning. He easily recognised that she tried to mirror the way he had offered her pleasure, so he knew what would follow, and his entire being trembled in anticipation, wondering how far she intended to go.

Small kisses teased his chest while her hair tickled him like the softest silk. Her hands lingered around his waist then lowered to his hips and stroked along his thighs, between them, resting on the place that had long burned him painfully. He moaned so that she stopped for a moment. He begged her to continue, and the caresses renewed as he groaned and called her name. She suddenly stopped again and pushed her gown down from her shoulders. Her warmth brushed against him, and he wondered how he possibly could keep his promise when he wished nothing more than to return the caresses and the pleasure and to feel her skin shivering under his touch.

His mind burst into countless pieces when her hand glided hesitantly inside his trousers and he gasped as she felt his hardness. He could no longer control his hands, which entwined in her hair while his pleasure became so intense that it hurt.

The newly discovered sensation shattered them both. She stopped; their hearts beat wildly, and both struggled to breathe.

"My love, please," he whispered.

Elizabeth was still hesitant, but an instant later, her hands and her lips continued to discover and explore every inch of his body, touching, kissing, and tasting—just as he was doing with her. His moans gave her more courage and confidence. Everything she had learnt from him she was now returning.

Time elapsed and his strength, his control, and his reason evaded him while he wondered whether one could die of too much pleasure. He felt almost relieved when the sweet, maddening torture ended and her body glided along his until their faces met again. Their eyes locked, and he gasped when she finally allowed their bodies to join. She was as warm and soft inside as she was outside, and his hands eventually lost control, trapping her against him, stroking her back and lingering on her hips while he helped her find the perfect rhythm of their lustful dance.

He sensed his body quivering against hers—inside hers—then heard her cries and felt her biting his shoulder as she took her pleasure. Only then did his body and mind shatter in complete fulfilment.

"I am so happy to be back home," she murmured sometime later, still trapped in his arms and with no desire to free herself.

"So am I, my dearest love. But I am even happier for the joy of holding you in my arms. And for your most astonishing gifts—most astonishing, indeed. I must think of something to repay you as you deserve."

She giggled and cuddled to his chest, her eyelids growing heavy. "I trust you will find a way. You always do."

THE SUNNY MORNING WOKE THEM EARLY, BUT THEY LINGERED IN BED FOR another hour, embraced, and held hands, their bodies still wearing the warmth of their passionate night.

Being home alone again was a comfort they had deeply missed.

However, they were also eager to visit Lady Matlock and to finally be reunited with Georgiana. Despite the delight of spending the first weeks of their marriage by themselves, they both looked forward to having their small family complete.

Even more, Elizabeth made plans to host a large dinner in a week's time for all their relatives in London. Darcy encouraged her yet demanded to know what "all the relatives" meant as he professed being frightened by Lady Ellen's influence in that area. Elizabeth laughed and placed a kiss on his cheek, and he knew he would not be able to refuse her—even if she intended to invite four and twenty families as Mrs. Bennet did at Longbourn.

With teasing and smiles, they went to breakfast. Before they could fill their plates, their joyful chatting was interrupted by Mrs. Hamilton, who entered hesitantly, apologising at each step.

The housekeeper looked more distressed than usual, and she was rubbing her hands together as she tried to speak.

"Mrs. Darcy, forgive me for intruding; there is something I wished to talk to you about. I did not want to disturb you last night as you were already tired from your journey."

"Do not worry, Mrs. Hamilton. Tell me what worries you."

"Maud. She is unwell—has been unwell for more than a week. She fell in the kitchen. I fetched the doctor, and she confessed to him that she had been feeling ill all this time but concealed it from us because of shame. Since you put me in charge, I took the liberty of seeking assistance for her. Many other mistresses would have thrown her out, but I knew you would not do so."

"Throw her out? Why would anyone do such a thing? You said she is working hard and that you were pleased with her."

"I am indeed, ma'am, but the doctor discovered Maud is with child... has been for about five months. It seems the days spent in the cold affected her. The doctor said the child might have died...inside...she...we are not certain what will happen. The doctor is giving her herbs, and he bled her, but she is not well."

"She is with child? What do you mean 'died'? This is so unexpected. I thought she had improved before we left London. Oh, dear Lord! What can be done? Poor girl..."

Elizabeth glanced at her husband, astonished, worried, and pale.

"The doctor will come to speak to you if you approve."

"Of course."

The housekeeper left the room, and Elizabeth's pallor increased.

He caressed her hand then brought it to his lips. "My love, I am sorry to see you so distressed."

"There is no need to be sorry for me, my dear. I am just...I did not expect.

But it seems you were right again: that was the reason for her being thrown out in the first place. What a terrible fate she has to bear."

"True…I confess I am uneasy about the entire situation too. I know it is a common situation—a maid being left with child then abandoned. But I never met with such a case in our family or with anyone in my immediate acquaintance. I do not know anyone who would do such a horrible thing, except—"

The doctor entered and interrupted their conversation. Darcy invited him to sit and asked for a report.

"I understand Mrs. Hamilton briefly described the situation to you. For now, we can do little except palliate her pain and reduce the fever. She is well enough to eat a little, drink tea, and take her medicine. She even wished to perform her duties, which, of course, was a silly request."

"Can we not do something more? I shall go and talk to her. She will be forced to keep to her bed until you advise us otherwise," Elizabeth added, and the doctor shook his head.

"If there were another solution, my dear Mrs. Darcy, I would have used it by now. We do not know for certain either her situation or that of her unborn infant. Please rest assured that I am doing everything possible. And I confess I find your interest and your generosity in saving this girl quite astonishing and unusual. It is indeed remarkable."

"We only do what we consider to be our duty," Elizabeth replied.

"We will expect you again tomorrow, doctor," Darcy added as the doctor took his leave.

"Of course, sir."

A few minutes later, when they were alone again, neither had any interest left in the meal.

"William, I would like to check on Maud if you do not mind."

"As you wish, my dear. I shall be in the library. Elizabeth, the doctor was right. You are remarkable, indeed."

Elizabeth smiled with sadness while she hurried downstairs, thinking it was easy to be remarkable when she had everything and others had so little.

LATE IN THE AFTERNOON, THEY WENT TO GREET THE MATLOCKS AND TO retrieve Georgiana. Their reunion was affectionate and enthusiastic. Miss Darcy had all her belongings prepared and was eager to return home and begin life with her brother and new sister.

Contrary to the Darcys' joy, Lady Matlock was truly sad to separate from her niece. It was the first time she had a young lady's company for so long, and she had greatly enjoyed the experience. They separated with the promise of meeting again in a couple of days, and Elizabeth conveyed an invitation for dinner, which Lady Matlock gladly accepted.

"And Elizabeth, please mark your calendar: on the fourth Wednesday of April, you will attend your first ball at Almack's. You will be my guest, but hopefully we will soon secure you a voucher. I was assured that your admittance would be approved. It is one of the first steps toward full acceptance within the ton. That will make a tremendous difference for your children's future and even for Georgiana's position once she comes out. I am not struggling without reason," Lady Matlock said, speaking mostly to Darcy, whose face showed his lack of enthusiasm.

"Thank you, Lady Ellen, I look forward to it. I confess I have heard many things about it, but nobody in my acquaintance has ever been invited. I understand its importance, and I am very grateful for your support," Elizabeth answered.

"I am glad you appreciate it. Unfortunately, the attendance of the Gardiners or the Bingleys at Almack's is out of the question, at least for the time being. We will see whether anything can be done in the future."

"I am aware of that; as much as I love my relatives, I know that at times they will not be able to join me. We are all aware of the differences attached to our present situation, and we try to cope with them as well as we can. Again, I thank your ladyship for being so thoughtful."

"Your efforts are greatly appreciated, Aunt," Darcy added.

"Very well, I shall fix some appointments with the modiste; you need some new and appropriate outfits to make a well-deserved impression."

Elizabeth hid a smile, considering that her mother would have said exactly the same. She noticed her husband rolling his eyes behind her ladyship and Georgiana covering her lips with her gloved hand to hide her giggles, so she hurried to take their farewell before Lady Matlock could observe their lack of consideration.

THE FIRST DINNER TOGETHER WAS PLEASANT BUT ALSO DISTRESSING. THE entire staff appeared genuinely happy with Miss Darcy's return, and the housekeeper even took the liberty of embracing the young mistress.

It was Elizabeth's daunting task to inform Georgiana about Maud's sad story and to share their concerns. As Elizabeth feared, her sister was deeply impressed, and she struggled with her tears the whole time and kept asking what could be done to save Maud.

Elizabeth went downstairs regularly to check on the maid herself, but she did not allow Georgiana to accompany her, as the situation was too difficult for a girl of such a young age and with such an emotional disposition.

Maud, fighting the high fever and intense pain, kept apologising to Elizabeth for all the trouble she had caused and constantly thanked her for the care they bestowed upon her until Elizabeth demanded she not say another word about it. Another maid was assigned to watch Maud during the night, and Mrs. Hamilton declared she would stay nearby to supervise her.

Over the night, the patient's state worsened, and Dr. Harris was fetched again.

Elizabeth went to bed very late, and she could find little rest in the caring arms of her husband. They spoke more than slept, and for the first time since they married, they were kept awake not by passion and desire but by worry for a stranger wholly unconnected to either of them.

The next day brought little relief, and the tension within the house increased. The entire household, as well as the master and the mistress, were affected by the distress. Dr. Harris declared himself less and less confident of a positive conclusion to the tragic situation.

Darcy was troubled by his wife's obvious distress more than anything else and knew not how to comfort her. It was one of the few circumstances in which he felt helpless. He was well aware that their emotional involvement was unusual. The best thing any other mistress would do for a servant in need would be to provide some medical assistance. But Elizabeth's kind heart could not remain unaffected, and her generosity led her to do more than others. And he could not argue with that as it was one of the reasons he loved her so profoundly.

On the second day, Darcy was surprised to receive Lady Matlock and Colonel Fitzwilliam for an impromptu visit. Her ladyship declared that she made a call in the neighbourhood and took the opportunity to have a cup of tea with Elizabeth and Georgiana.

"We are always happy to see you, Aunt. Please join me in the drawing room, and I shall send for Elizabeth and Georgiana at once."

"Are they not at home?"

"Yes, they are, but…please take a seat and allow me to call for some tea and refreshments. We…have a rather distressing situation here. One of the servants is very ill…Elizabeth is downstairs with Mrs. Hamilton. Georgiana is resting as she did not sleep well last night."

"Oh, please, do not disturb Georgiana. And if Elizabeth is busy, we shall leave. I should not have intruded in the first place. But what can Elizabeth do for an ill servant? Did you not fetch Dr. Harris? Surely, this is not a task for the mistress of the house."

"Dr. Harris is with them too. But Elizabeth…she is quite affected. It is a tragic story, truly."

"Well, if you think we should stay and keep you company, please share the story with us."

"Is it the same woman you found in the park a month ago?" Colonel Fitzwilliam intervened.

"Yes, the same…"

Darcy started to explain, at first reluctant and uneasy about having such a conversation with his aunt then somehow relieved that he had someone to trust and to understand his concerns. When he finished, Lady Matlock appeared equally appalled and angry.

"It is easy to imagine that the silly, naïve girl was tricked into a sordid relationship, and she now has to suffer the consequences. It was surely either the son or the master himself. I have always considered men who share a bed with one of their servants to be pathetic beyond words. In this case, it seems it was also very cruel. Such a shame."

As they spoke, Elizabeth entered and greeted the guests while she forced a smile. Lady Matlock and the colonel glanced at each other, surprised by her pallor and the darkness around her eyes. Darcy helped his wife sit, and he poured her a cup of tea.

The visit ended very shortly afterward. Elizabeth apologised for being poor company while Lady Matlock insisted it was her fault for coming unexpectedly.

Once they were alone, Elizabeth's eyes filled with tears. Darcy's heart broke, and he put his arms around her, wishing he could take her distress upon himself.

"I shall accompany you to your room this very moment. You cannot go any further without resting a little while. I shall not allow you to fall ill from exhaustion."

"I cannot rest now, William; I am so angry and sad and helpless...all this suffering...Dr. Harris fears she would not pass overnight...the child has died inside, and that caused all her pain and fever. She is almost a child herself..."

"Elizabeth, please..." There was little distance between them, and he took her hands in his, bringing them to his chest.

"My love, I beg you, let me check on her...one way or another, it will not last long..."

"Be it as you wish, my dearest; it is just that...tell me how I may help you. What can I do?"

"You have done everything by being my husband. There is nothing else I want."

To his disbelief, Elizabeth pressed her lips to his hands with a tenderness that warmed his soul. She needed to say no more, as her feelings perfectly matched his.

Against his will, he gazed at her as she departed from him and stared at the closed door. He understood she felt she had a duty to accomplish, and nothing would deter her from it.

SEVERAL HOURS PASSED, AND DARCY STRUGGLED TO READ WHILE GEOR-giana played for him in the music room. Neither of them paid attention to what they were doing, but it was a way to keep their minds occupied. Elizabeth joined them part of the time until she excused herself and went downstairs again.

An hour later, Darcy's patience was exhausted, and he left in search of his wife. As he walked down the stairs, he could hear alarmed voices and cries from afar. He approached carefully, walking down the hall of the servants' chambers. As he got closer, the cries became stronger and more disturbing. He observed the room where several people were crowded, including Molly and Miles who stayed in the hall a short distance from the door. He could also spot Elizabeth standing against in the doorway, gazing inside, her hand covering her mouth.

Darcy halted in deep shock, staring at the traces of blood that could be seen on the floor, on the bed, and on the doctor's clothes. He could not see Maud, but he heard her screams, which pierced him like a sharp blade. Several other servants were waiting in the hall; at seeing the master, they left in a hurry to return to their duties.

"We are almost done here; thank God, we are done. Mrs. Darcy, are you unwell? You should not be here. Mrs. Hamilton, send the servants away with these bloody sheets and bring clean ones. We are almost done. We need more towels and warm water!"

Dr. Harris made requests and gave orders with a determined and severe voice, and Darcy had a difficult time understanding what was truly happening.

And then again—Maud's grieved voice.

"Please do not throw my child away...please bury him...in the Lord's name...please," Maud cried, her words barely audible.

Darcy leant against the wall then clenched his jaws and fists in a helpless gesture.

"Do not worry. I promise we will take care of him. I shall speak to the master. Do not cry... " Mrs. Hamilton tearfully replied.

"We will take care of him," Elizabeth repeated, her voice weak with tears.

Darcy almost lost his balance when he stepped further and had a full view of the most disturbing picture: a woman at the edge between life and death. His eyes were captured by a white sheet covering a form like a doll.

Only then did the others notice him, including Maud, who threw him a glance that burned him inside.

"We shall take care of everything," he managed to whisper then stepped back as in a nightmare. His mind blurred, but he managed to reach the kitchen and take a seat, trying to breathe regularly. A sense of fury and a compelling need to make someone suffer as much as Maud did overcame his reason.

He felt Elizabeth's gentle touch on his shoulder, and he turned, meeting her tearful eyes.

"I will take care of everything," he repeated in a weak and unsuccessful attempt to bring her a little comfort.

"I know you will. The doctor said we should leave now...he will come to tell us more when he is done..."

"Yes. Where is Miles? He must go to the church. I will write a note for the vicar..."

Suddenly, Darcy seemed more troubled and insecure than Elizabeth; he rose and looked around then glanced at his wife again. She took his arm.

"William, let us go to Georgiana now. She must be frightened. There is nothing we can do for Maud now."

"Is she…Maud I mean…will she too…?"

"No, no…the doctor gave her two spoons of laudanum, because she needs to rest…to sleep. Now we can only wait. It was…oh, William…come, let us go. The doctor will come later."

"Forgive me for being so weak. I do not know what to do…there is nothing one can do against death. I hoped I could keep it away from this house for many years, but this shows me once again how insignificant and helpless we are."

She took his cold hands in hers, her heart aching for the sadness on his face.

"We can pray…and keep hope alive. There will always be problems you cannot solve, but you are not weak. And we are together now."

He lifted her hand to his lips briefly and absentmindedly, barely hearing her encouragement.

They walked arm in arm, hesitantly as if their feet might not support them. Darcy then put one arm around her shoulders, and he kissed the top of her head then her hands several times until they entered the main hall of the house and met a pale and trembling Georgiana.

Together they retired to the library, and Darcy closed the door behind him, a deep, painful silence surrounding them.

"Elizabeth, please tell me what happened. How is Maud? I know something tragic is happening. I can sense it."

"My dear, with the Lord's mercy, there is a chance that Maud will recover. The child had passed away as we feared. Now we must pray for her…it is all that we can do now."

Georgiana dared not ask for more details. Elizabeth tried to calm her younger sister and to convince her to stay in her room, far from the tragic events happening elsewhere in the house. Reluctantly, Georgiana agreed, knowing that her brother and sister only wished to protect her sensibilities. She would like to have stayed and been more involved, but she admitted to herself that she did not feel strong enough. She was not Elizabeth.

Alone again, Elizabeth and Darcy moved to the settee, comforting each other with tender and chaste caresses, silent and deep in their own thoughts, which neither dared to share with the other.

Around dinnertime, Dr. Harris finally appeared. Darcy quickly offered him a glass of brandy, which the doctor immediately emptied, and a second one was filled.

"Doctor, what is your report?"

Two pairs of eyes watched him with obvious distress while the doctor spoke calmly.

"Fortunately—and quite unexpectedly—nature followed its course. The child was born...as I anticipated, he was not alive...he had not been for several weeks, I suspect. It was a boy...he must have been about six months when the tragedy occurred. It is a shame...the poor girl wants him to be buried. I have seen so many situations like this, and yet I am still deeply troubled each time. Oh well...we cannot defeat fate, I suppose."

"We will take care of the child. Mr. Darcy will take care of everything. And Maud? Will she live?"

"She is young; now that her body is free of its burden, she might recover. I have seen it before, so we can expect either possibility. However, I must repeat myself: if not for Mrs. Darcy's generosity, the girl would not be alive today...she would not have had any chance."

"Dr. Harris, we thank you for your dedication to this poor young woman."

"Well, well, I did nothing but my duty. Now, if you have room to spare, I would rather stay overnight in the house. And if Mrs. Darcy would be so kind as to order me something to eat..."

Slowly, both Elizabeth and Darcy remembered their duties as hosts and behaved accordingly.

Elizabeth made certain the doctor was properly accommodated while Darcy sent Miles to settle everything for the next day's funeral of the lost child.

Sadness and concerns for future developments still burdened their minds, but they struggled to accomplish their responsibilities while praying for the night to pass and the next day to bring some alleviation and new hopes for Maud.

Sleep had fallen upon most of the household when dawn broke—the exception being the master, who found not a single moment of rest.

TWO MORE DAYS PASSED, AND THEIR PRAYERS SEEMED TO HAVE BEEN

ANSwered. Maud was still unconscious most of the time as the doctor kept her under laudanum, but she was no longer bleeding, and her fever was diminished. One of the maids stayed with her all the time, and Doctor Harris checked on the patient twice a day, declaring he grew increasingly optimistic about the outcome.

Life in the house slowly returned to its usual routine. Elizabeth decided to postpone the dinner she intended to host for her relatives but did not have time for the announcement. Therefore, she proposed that she, Darcy, and Georgiana should pay brief calls to the Fitzwilliams, the Gardiners, and the Bingleys to inform them of the change in plans. Only then did she realise that she had been so caught up in the painful events of the last three days that she completely forgot about her newly wedded sister, who had just started her happy life in Town.

To their pleasant surprise, they found the Gardiners also visiting Mr. and Mrs. Bingley. This fortunate coincidence was the perfect opportunity to spend more than an hour in the warm comfort of their extended family, and it was a chance for Elizabeth to witness once again the felicity and the glow on her sister's face. At least in that regard, she had no reason for concern.

Afterwards, they stopped at the Matlocks' residence, where they only planned to stay for a cup of tea.

Lady Matlock was delighted to see them, and she immediately invited Elizabeth and Georgiana to the drawing room while Darcy, the earl, and the colonel retired to the library for a drink.

"You still look pale and tired, my dear," Lady Matlock addressed Elizabeth. "I hope you are not unwell."

"I thank you for your concern, but I am quite well. I confess I was a little tired, but hopefully things will improve soon."

"So, what happened with that maid?" Lady Matlock inquired to start the conversation.

"She is recovering...at least we pray that she will recover. We cannot be certain yet, but we have hopes. Sadly, she gave birth to a dead child...a boy. It was heartbreaking."

"Oh, we should not speak such things in front of Georgiana. She is too young for this. If I knew such things would occur, I would have kept her with us a little longer. She has had her share of distress and illness and danger in the last months," Lady Matlock said, slightly reproachful.

The girl intervened animatedly.

"Do not worry for me, Aunt. I am happy I was home and I could offer Elizabeth a little help and comfort, although not much. I am ashamed to admit how weak I am. And when I think that poor Maud is almost my age, and she had to go through so many things...it is good that she will be safe from now on due to Elizabeth's care."

"Maud? Who is Maud?" Lady Matlock asked with limited interest, paying more attention to her cup of tea."

Elizabeth smiled politely.

"Maud is the maid we were speaking about. Forgive me; I did not mention her name before."

"I see...this is quite strange as it is not a common name."

"That is true, I suppose; I did not think of that," Elizabeth admitted politely.

"Well, I hardly think of the servants' names. But my daughter-in-law also has a maid called Maud, and she used to complain all the time about how low-class people possess particular names but have no desire to work hard for their pay. But then again, Beatrice always complains about something, so I rarely give any importance to her whining. The coincidence is amusing though."

"Whose whining? And what coincidence?" the earl asked as the three gentlemen joined the ladies.

"I was just telling Elizabeth how strange it is that both she and Beatrice have a servant called Maud. If only my son's wife possessed further resemblance to you, I would be very happy, my dear."

"It is a rather strange coincidence but I confess I find little reason for amusement, considering the tragic events we had to handle lately. In our case, we speak of a young woman left to die in the freezing weather, whose child was just buried without even seeing the light of this world," Darcy replied with a severity that turned all eyes toward him.

Lady Matlock paled and attempted to reply, but her words were interrupted by Colonel Fitzwilliam dropping his glass on the floor.

Chapter 12

"I am sorry; I was distracted," the colonel said, ringing for a servant to clean the broken shards.

"It seems we are all distracted," Lady Matlock answered. "Elizabeth, I apologise if I sounded insensitive regarding the disturbing situation you went through. I do sympathise with that poor girl's suffering, and I admire your personal involvement in helping her. It is yet another proof of your excellent character."

"I thank you, Lady Ellen. Your kindness is much appreciated. Now I am afraid we must leave. As always, it was a pleasure seeing you all."

The farewell was rather hasty and slightly awkward. Despite Elizabeth's warm politeness, Darcy's harsh scolding of his aunt did not go unnoticed, particularly as it had rarely happened before.

Inside the carriage, there was a heavy silence. Elizabeth and Darcy kept glancing at each other but no one spoke a single word. Georgiana preferred to look outside.

At home, they asked for a report on Maud and were informed her state was the same. She was sleeping soundly—just as Dr. Harris recommended.

Content, they retired to their apartments to change for dinner, and still no word was spoken. Darcy dismissed both Molly and Miles, and when the couple were finally alone, he took Elizabeth's hands and sat next to her on the edge of the bed. She moved closer, and his arms embraced her.

"You were very harsh to Lady Ellen. But I cannot blame you; the last days have affected us all," she said compassionately.

"I regret that I upset my aunt, but I could not bear her detached amusement after all of the trouble you have suffered. And yet, I have to admit that my reaction would have been the same as hers a few months ago. I never would have given more than a brief thought to any story involving those outside my close family. Even worse, whenever someone from my staff had a problem, I instructed either Mrs. Hamilton or Mrs. Reynolds to handle it, but I never gave it further attention. I never asked how the problem ended. I only presumed that, if nobody complained, it was solved correctly. Since my infancy, I was taught to provide help, but I was not a helpful man. I was taught to apply generosity, but I was never generous. Every day spent with you proves to me your worthiness and shows me how much I still have to improve myself."

"Please allow me to disagree. You are truly the best man I have ever known, and I shall not become tired of repeating it. You were only accustomed to doing things differently. It does not mean you showed less generosity or kindness."

Darcy gently kissed her lips with more tenderness than passion. Elizabeth put her hands around his neck and pressed herself against him, but only a moment later he pulled away.

"We should go to dinner now; Georgiana is certainly expecting us."

She was reluctant to separate but responded with a smile.

"You are right. I will ring for Molly and will be ready in a few minutes."

While the maid helped her change, Elizabeth's thoughts distracted her again. She suddenly recollected Lady Matlock's mentioning the coincidence of the two Mauds, Darcy censuring his aunt, and the colonel dropping his glass of brandy in the middle of a conversation that should not have affected him at all. It was obviously an extraordinary situation for everyone.

So deep was she in her thoughts, that she did not hear Darcy enter, so she startled when she felt his fingers caressing her nape then sighed when his lips pressed against her neck. She turned to search for a real kiss, but he gently touched her face and took her hands, helping her out of the room.

On their way to the dining room, Elizabeth held his arm tightly while his hand covered hers. He kissed her temple and the top of her head several times, and a shiver ran down her spine. His gestures seemed to be more of concern than of the passion she had learnt to expect from him.

Dinner passed calmly with little conversation. Afterward, Elizabeth briefly visited Maud; she found her still asleep with another maid by her side. Her fever had apparently lowered, and her features were less marked by suffering although she was still pale and looked very thin. Elizabeth stood by the bed a few minutes, heavyhearted, praying for the girl's health and wondering whether any woman could recover from such a tragedy.

When she lifted her eyes, she saw her husband waiting for her in the hall. As always, he had felt her sadness and come to offer her comfort and safety. She stepped toward him, and he opened his arms for her—where she belonged.

The Darcys' evening ended with Georgiana playing for them about half an hour. Her playing was as flawless as ever, yet less joyful, less sparkling. Elizabeth admired once again her young sister's discretion, understanding, and compassion, and her obvious efforts to bear her grief without burdening the others.

Darcy's expression was haughty and distant, and it appeared to darken with each passing moment. He barely spoke with either of them and paced the room from the window to the fireplace until his sister ended her performance and everyone retired for the night.

Elizabeth's worry increased when, exhausted from tiredness and concerns, she finally nestled in her bed, waiting for him to join her. Instead, he sat on the bed, then rose again and sat once more.

"William, what is it? You frighten me."

He hastily kissed her hand. "Forgive me, my love, it is just that…there is a maddening thought that keeps tormenting me. I was wondering…I am afraid that…but no, that cannot be."

"What is troubling you? Please let me know. Perhaps I can help you find the answer."

"Not now—we will speak more tomorrow. After some rest, I will be able to think more rationally."

"Yes, I believe you are right. Come—I have missed you so much."

He finally lay by her side beneath the blanket, and pulled her against him. Elizabeth tried to calm herself and forced herself not to inquire further, wrapping her arms around his waist. Her head rested on his chest, and she gently moved against him; her right hand slowly caressed his arm, then his torso. He kissed her temples then her eyes, and his hand captured and stopped hers.

"My dearest, we should sleep now. You are very tired, and your pallor worries me. You need as much rest as possible."

"I do need rest...but I need you too. Your arms spoil me with so much warmth and tenderness..." Her voice became lower until it turned into a whisper.

"I will be here...watching you. And I will never let you out of my arms," he whispered back, his lips barely touching her ear.

Several minutes later, Elizabeth fell deeply asleep while Darcy continued to caress her hair absentmindedly, his head spinning with questions he dared not ask.

He impatiently counted the hours until dawn. He had decided to pay a visit first thing in the morning—even before Elizabeth woke up—and to clarify a coincidence in which he did not believe.

BEING QUITE UNUSUAL COMPARED TO OTHER OCCASIONS, THE DARCYS' visit left Lady Matlock dissatisfied—even irritated. One cause was her nephew's impertinent comment, but there were other reasons she could sense but not understand.

Lady Ellen Fitzwilliam, Countess of Matlock, paced her large and elegant apartment in a state of restlessness she had rarely experienced. Always self-confident, calm, and decided, and accustomed to having her wishes fulfilled, that sort of emotion troubled her.

There was still time before dinner, so she decided to search for her younger son and inquire about his own strange behaviour. She could not recall his dropping a glass since he was four years old or being so silent and solemn at a family gathering.

To her surprise, she met him fully dressed to leave the house.

"Robert, are you going out? I was not aware that you had any engagements tonight. We are almost ready for dinner."

"Yes...no...I do not have an engagement. In fact, I do have, but it was entirely unexpected. I shall return rather soon, I suspect."

"Son, why are you so inarticulate? I have not seen you like this in many years. It pains me to admit that we all behaved strangely today."

"I am not...I must solve an urgent problem, but it will not last long. I will return soon..."

Lady Matlock moved closer, watching her son with interest. He was never nervous about his plans, nor did he ever struggle to explain his decisions about spending evenings—or nights—outside the house. His rambling excuses increased the lady's puzzlement.

"As you wish; I am in no position to question your plans. However, you should be careful, Robert. You were not yourself today. I hope you are not unwell."

"No—I am very well, thank you. It has been a rather disturbing day. As you witnessed yourself, not even Darcy and Elizabeth were their usual selves."

Lady Matlock took another step toward the colonel. Her eyebrow rose in contemplation, and she gazed at him as she spoke in a low voice.

"Elizabeth and Darcy had the excuse of being personally involved in a tormenting situation, which is not the case with either of us. Is it not so?"

The colonel averted his eyes, and Lady Matlock's gaze grew more severe.

"Robert, I did not miss your dropping the glass precisely when Elizabeth mentioned that maid. And I am not easy to deceive. There is something that troubles you greatly, and I suspect it is the reason for your suddenly urgent engagement. Am I wrong?"

"Mother, I am not comfortable debating this subject with you. And please excuse me; I am in a hurry."

"Robert!" Lady Matlock grabbed her son's arm tightly. "If I only had some suspicions before, now I am beyond doubt. I am asking you to tell me the truth. I want to know in what way you are connected with that poor girl."

"In no way, ma'am. I have never seen her, and I am pained to see your ladyship's readiness to accuse me."

"I made no accusation—only asked for some explanation. I know quite well how such things occur. And your answer proved to me I was correct in my assumption."

"Quite the contrary. And I wonder that you think so poorly of me. Surely, I am better than to take advantage of a young maid and abandon her to despair. You should have guessed that, if not my honour, my personal taste would lead me elsewhere."

"Then…" Lady Matlock easily recognised the justice of her son's harsh words. Her heart was heavy with regret for hurting him while her mind insisted on discovering the truth. Could he be so deceptive? Could she have been so wrong in trusting her son? He had always been a little too… inclined toward the pleasures of life, but she had believed him to be a man of honour and surely not someone to take advantage of those in need—men or women. And yet… how was it possible that he had a relationship with a servant from another house?

The silence was so tense, so overwhelming, that she felt the need to sit. She raised her eyes to meet her son's hurt gaze and suddenly felt all the blood drain from her face.

"There is no other "Maud," is there? There is only one, and she was thrown out of your brother's house. I wrongly blamed you. How long have you known? Was she…? Oh dear Lord."

Lady Matlock attempted to rise, but she fell to the floor as her knees failed to support her. The colonel helped her to the settee and hurried to get her a glass of water.

"Did you know from the beginning? Does your father know too? Am I the only fool here? Myself and poor Elizabeth who had to remedy the outrageous outcome of my son's reckless behaviour?"

"Mother, please let us be calm and speak rationally; it would not do if you fell ill from distress. I did not know—I did not even suspect anything—until today. Thomas mentioned to me some time ago that Beatrice had severely dismissed a servant, but I had no interest in hearing more on the subject. I did observe his interest in the maid; he called her by name quite often when he spoke of her. But—forgive me—I took it as the usual inclination of a gentleman toward a handsome young female servant. As you said, it is very usual. I would say it happens in most houses among the ton."

Lady Matlock did not answer; she finished the water and asked for more.

"About a month ago, while visiting Darcy, they told me about the young woman they found in the park, but not for a moment did I connect the two accounts. Again, I confess I listened only to half of it, and they never mentioned any name. Only today, when you and Elizabeth discussed the coincidence, did the connection strike me. I did not want to say anything although I imagined either you or Darcy would guess the truth soon enough. It was my intention to discuss it with Thomas immediately."

"So that is where you planned to go."

"Yes."

"Forgive me for offending you, Robert. I have no excuse for my unfair accusation."

"It does not matter now. I will call on Thomas briefly, and hopefully he will come to discuss it with you. I am not certain he would agree, though."

"I am coming with you."

"Pardon? Mother, you cannot seriously consider—"

"Robert, I am going to talk to Thomas right away—with or without you. Your father is resting. Should I wake him?"

"This is...very well, I have learnt by now that one cannot ever change your mind. Do not awake father yet. There will be enough scandal even without him."

For half the ride, there was complete silence in the carriage. The colonel continued to glance at his mother, uncertain how to proceed. The situation could almost be more dangerous than a battle with Napoleon's army.

"Mother, forgive me for being so blunt, but what exactly do you hope to accomplish by talking to Thomas? You cannot possibly reproach him for anything. He is a man in his thirties and the future earl of Matlock. It is truly his business where he spends his nights and with whom."

Lady Matlock threw him a stern glare. "He is my son—just as you are. I can well reproach him for anything I consider proper, and I most certainly can censure his behaviour if it is improper, no matter how old he is, especially when he affects innocent people or the honour of our family."

"Mother—"

"No 'mother'! Tell me, Robert, do you believe it was his child—that the unborn infant who died was my grandson?"

"Mother, you cannot torture yourself like this. We cannot be sure of anything. Besides, you know too well that such accidents occur. It is not the first child to pass away before being born—and sadly not the last."

"Without doubt your point is correct. Yet, I fail to see how this might make me feel better."

The appearance of Lady Matlock and Colonel Fitzwilliam at such an improper hour was an obvious surprise even for the butler. They asked for the Viscount, and they were shown into the drawing room to wait for him.

When Lord Buxton entered, his smile betrayed his pleasure in seeing them. A moment later, however, as he tried to read their sharp expressions, he became concerned and mixed politeness with worry.

"Mother, I am so happy to see you. I believe it is the first time you have come unannounced."

"True—and I apologise for the intrusion. We came to trouble you with a simple request. May I speak with your servant Maud, please? Or should I ask your wife?"

The young lord held his breath while his face turned pale then crimson.

"I do not understand your request. What business might you have with one of our servants?"

"Is she still your servant? Is she still in the house? If so, I shall be happy to see her and not bother you further."

"She…is not here any longer…she left…some time ago…"

Lord Buxton glanced often at his brother as if asking for support, but the colonel stepped back and leant against the window as he had confirmation that his worst suspicions were correct.

"Did she? Of her own will? About a month ago, you would say?"

"Perhaps. I have no memory for such things."

"How unfortunate. Does your brain always desert you when you use other…personal attributes?"

"Mother!" cried both men, but Lady Matlock stood, her back straight, her eyes casting poisoned arrows. She never raised her voice, but her tone had the chill of a blizzard and the edge of a sword.

"Mother, I am astonished by your inquiries. Why are we speaking of Maud? Why would you be interested in such a matter? There are countless servants who have left over the years, and you have never asked about them."

"That was because I was perfectly aware of the circumstances of each servant that left my house—even those who were dismissed. I wonder whether you know where Maud might be and whether you are aware of the *particular circumstances* she was in at the time of her dismissal."

From the doorway, Lady Beatrice yelled angrily, hastening to them. "Why would your ladyship care about a horrible servant who betrayed our trust and disrespected our house? She was thrown out and rightfully so. She deserved even worse!" Fury twisted her beautiful features, but Lady Matlock responded with a cold smile.

"What a strangely powerful reaction for a lady regarding a member of her staff. It is our duty to be wiser than to become involved in emotional fights with our servants. It is very unbecoming for a woman of character and education."

"Let us not argue over this any longer, Mother. Beatrice is the mistress of the house, and she is entitled to hire or dismiss anyone she wishes, just as your ladyship does in your own home. As I said, I confess I find it difficult to understand your discontent and to follow your reasoning in starting this debate."

"Then I shall speak more clearly and slowly, so you can comprehend my words, Lord Buxton. Maud was found in the middle of Hyde Park, freezing to death. She had no means, as it seems she had been dismissed without any payment for her services. Strangely, it appears that the maid possessed character and honour, as she never blamed her former employers for their unfair treatment. Had she betrayed more details, it would have affected the good name of that employer."

Lady Beatrice was unmoved. "She said nothing because she knew she was guilty. She was a shameless, low woman who did everything to gain the favours of the men. Did you know she was with child when I asked her to leave? I am glad she took her bastard and disappeared."

"Beatrice, that is uncivil. Keep your voice down; we do not need the servants to hear our conversation. I have no doubt that they already know all the details of this story, though."

"Lady Matlock! This is my house, and I have every right to speak as I please and to decide what my husband and I say to you!"

Lady Matlock's expression hardly concealed her anger; then she addressed her daughter-in-law sharply.

"First, this is the house that was given to your husband by his family; second, I have every right to speak to my son in whatever manner I choose. If you prefer, you may leave. I am sure we all will be more reasonable. Afterward, should your husband choose to share this conversation with you, he may do so."

"This is outrageous! I have never been so offended! How dare you put the entire blame on me? What about your son? Are you proud that he shared a bed with a servant behind my back? How do you think I felt? What would you have done in my place, Lady Matlock? Would you have allowed your husband to raise his child with a servant in your house? Admit it: you would have done just as I did."

"I agree that the situation was unacceptable, but a true lady would have demanded that her husband solve it discreetly. You reasonably did not allow the outrageous relationship to continue, but that does not justify your selfishness and cruelty. You are neither kind nor generous, Beatrice, and I wonder whether you know what love and affection mean. But again, this does not diminish your husband's share of the blame. It pains me to observe your marriage, but until today, I had not realised how harmful it could be not only for you but also for others around you. You have everything in life—both of you—and yet you completely fail to be happy. This is heartbreaking."

"I am not unhappy. I am like any proper lady should be in her marriage," Lady Beatrice responded contemptuously. "You will excuse me now; I cannot listen to this any longer. Thomas, I shall await you impatiently in the dining room!"

She left furiously, slamming the door and shouting something at a servant. Lady Matlock rolled her eyes then turned her attention to her eldest son.

"Mother, why do you bring up this story now? And how did you learn of it? I mean—it is more than a month since it happened. And yes, I am not proud of myself, but Maud was…we had a relationship of a particular nature. Beatrice found out, and she dismissed her immediately. I could not argue with my wife over a maid; certainly, you must see that."

"Of course not; after all, there are plenty of other maids in your house, and if necessary, you may borrow a few from your neighbours," Lady Matlock said sarcastically.

The offense made both men pale, but the colonel still tried not to interfere. It was his brother's duty to take responsibility for his behaviour.

"You are unfair and unreasonable, mother. Surely, you cannot blame me for something that every man does."

"Every man? They might—but surely not any *gentleman*. And will you pretend—like your wife—that she was the one who tried to gain your favours? I have heard she was very young, almost half your age. And she was with child—did you know that?"

The viscount averted his eyes. Lady Matlock put her hand on her chest to calm her heart.

"So you did know. And it was your child?"

"I believe so…I have no reason to think otherwise."

"And you still would let her freeze to death? With no money and nowhere to go? While carrying your child? What kind of man are you?"

"Mother, listen to me. Beatrice demanded she leave while I was at the club. She was very angry when she discovered Maud was with child, and she likely waited for a moment when I was not at home. When I found…I knew she had an aunt at an inn, and I imagined she would go there. The next morning, I went to look for her, but I was told she had left. I tried to find her whereabouts for a few days but with no success. I am not a monster. I know I should have been more careful but…how did you find out about her?"

"Darcy and Elizabeth found her in Hyde Park, took her into their home, and had her taken care of! Elizabeth—who is everything your wife is not! The generous, kind, warm, caring Elizabeth saved a life that you carelessly threw away."

"Oh, please, let us not be so dramatic. Can we please stop praising Darcy and his wife? For heaven's sake, he married a country nobody! You never would have accepted that I marry a woman so far below us! You were content when I chose Beatrice! Elizabeth's custom of taking home people she finds in the park is not praiseworthy but another proof of her low breeding. I understand you are upset. I know I should have made arrangements to handle the situation better. I was wrong, and it will never happen again. But you cannot despise me for doing something any man in London would do and commend Darcy for neglecting his duty and marrying against his family's will—and to a woman whose only merits are her charms, her beauty, and probably her delightful company in the marriage bed!"

"You are an idiot," the colonel finally interfered, struggling to control his voice. "Stop repeating that this is something every man does, and take responsibility for your stupid error. It was no accident or mistake: you had your way with a young maid, got her with child, and then left her to freeze to death! That is the truth! You are irresponsible and selfish and cruel—very well suited to your wife who, by the way, chased Darcy around Town for two years and married you only when she realised she had no chance with him."

"Robert, you forget yourself! You cannot speak to me in such a manner in my own home. Are you out of your mind?"

"Of course I can! How dare *you* speak of Elizabeth in such a manner? Darcy would call you out for a single offensive thought against his wife! Let us admit it: he was the only one of us who had the daring, the wisdom, and the tenacity to obtain the woman he not only desired but the one who would make him happy. He will never have to trick a servant girl into his bed! Not all of us have the fortune to marry for love, but we can have enough honour and dignity to praise his character and strength. Of course, we could choose to be like Wickham: take advantage of Darcy's help when it was needed and trash his name behind his back the rest of the time."

"That is outrageous! I only now discover your true opinion of me, Robert. I have never been so offended! This cannot easily be forgotten."

"I agree, Brother—and it will certainly not be. Mother, may we leave now? I need some fresh air."

"Yes, let us leave."

"Mother, please…" the viscount attempted to intervene.

She stopped and turned to him, a sad smile on her face.

"Thomas, I have always been proud of you, and I have loved you with all my heart. My affection for you will never change, no matter how powerful my disappointment in you might be. My heart is in pain now, and I cannot continue to ignore the traits of your character that I refused to accept before. Because you are my son, I will try to forget and to forgive your recklessness and will pray to see you struggle to improve yourself. But I am afraid I will never have the strength to forgive and forget that you and your wife caused the death of my grandson—of your own son. Let us go, Robert. I have nothing more to say."

The colonel offered his arm to his mother, still tormented by the horrible argument. He was worried for the lady who seemed to have lost all her powers and could barely walk. The colonel could easily understand his mother's torment. He had also deeply cared for his brother since they were infants, and telling him such terrible words was equally burdening for all of them.

As they moved to the main door, Beatrice appeared and stood near her husband, crossing her arms over her chest and glaring defiantly at them while Lord Buxton leant against the wall to avoid falling to the floor.

Chapter 13

The Matlocks had no dinner that evening.

Colonel Fitzwilliam brought his mother home safely then hurried to his club. He needed company and entertainment to expel the memory of the horrible fight between his brother and his mother.

He blamed his elder brother entirely as much as he loathed his sister-in-law. It was hard to believe that Thomas Fitzwilliam was such a weak man. On further consideration, the colonel observed that his brother seemed not insensible regarding the young maid. It was easy to guess that, finding so little warmth and passion inside his marriage, he turned his attention elsewhere. Even more so, the colonel remembered hearing his brother mention Maud's name several times during the last months. Even then, he suspected his brother's interest for a young, lovely maid but never opened the subject; he had been rather amused by it. It was far from being a rare situation: most men with means, bound in a marriage of convenience, kept a mistress—or more than one.

Few men had Darcy's good fortune to marry for love. It was also true that few had Darcy's courage—to follow their heart instead of the demands of family. And yes, he was certain that his own parents would object strongly if any of them chose a wife below their position and connections. In Darcy's case, the earl expressed his disagreement but had little to say on the matter. Darcy did not once beg for their approval, and nobody could deter him from marrying Elizabeth. His mother had been more diplomatic—as always—and her affection for Elizabeth had grown, but that also happened because she had no choice. Darcy would have preferred to cut the connection with them if they continued to disapprove of his wife, and that forced Lady Matlock to give Elizabeth the attention and respect she deserved.

If Darcy were a weaker man, the Matlocks never would have accepted Elizabeth; he was certain of that. Therefore, the colonel could sympathise with Thomas's reproach toward his mother. Yes, everyone had approved of Beatrice and encouraged him to marry her. She was no better and no worse than the majority of ladies in her position.

What the colonel could neither forgive nor find excuses for was his negligence and lack of responsibility in finding an arrangement that would have avoided such tragic events. He also blamed his elder brother for his impertinence in handling the discussion with their mother, as well as his offensive comments regarding Elizabeth. It was a very ungentlemanlike strategy, which would turn Darcy into his enemy if it were ever discovered.

Colonel Fitzwilliam was relieved when he reached the club; inside, there was a gathering of the most distinguished gentlemen of the ton, most of them appearing happy and carefree. And without a doubt, most of them had a similar situation in their lives but probably gave it little thought.

LADY MATLOCK BEGAN TO FEEL ILL EVEN BEFORE SHE LEFT HER ELDER son's house. She barely managed to walk from the main gate to her room on the arm of her younger son. Once inside her apartment, she rang for her maid, changed into a nightgown, and fell against the pillows, sending word to her husband that she would not dine that evening. She felt unable to have any conversation and only needed silence to think through everything that had occurred. Her pain was as heavy as her sorrow and disappointment.

With equal surprise and concern, Lord Matlock received the information that his wife would not join him for dinner. She had always been the strongest supporter of rules and decorum, and she always behaved with the same manners she demanded of others.

He knocked on her door and waited to be invited in—as he had done for the five and thirty years they had been married. He found his wife pale, her eyes betraying a trace of tears, her beautiful features twisted by obvious suffering.

"What is it, my dear? Ellen, you are frightening me; you look truly ill. I will send for Dr. Harris at once."

"Please stay with me, husband. I do not need Dr. Harris. I am as fine as can be expected under the present circumstances."

"What circumstances?"

"Did Robert tell you anything?"

"No—he left for his club as soon as you arrived home. Is he the reason for your distress?"

"We must cease blaming him so readily. I did the same and most unjustifiably. It is Thomas about whom we must worry."

"Thomas? What on earth do you mean?"

For almost an hour, Lady Matlock shared with her husband the knowledge she had acquired that day—a day that painfully changed many of her beliefs and deprived her of her pride in her son and the hope of a grandson. If only a few days before the prospect of Thomas having an heir by a servant would have been horrifying and unacceptable for Ellen Fitzwilliam, Countess of Matlock, the realisation that the child existed and was tragically lost forever brought her unbearable pain and a sense of guilt that she could not overcome.

The earl, however, listened to the story with much interest and great preoccupation for his wife, but his feelings were different. The subject was not at all strange to him. He even remembered his brother-in-law Sir Lewis de Bourgh having an inclination for his wife's maid. The difference was that Catherine de Bourgh pretended to be oblivious to her husband's weakness, and the named maid left the household to "take care of her old mother," and they barely heard of her again. At the gentleman's death, the woman was left with a fair amount of money and a modest house in town, where she likely was still living. To avoid scandal and gossip, Catherine had never opposed her late husband's will.

Lord Matlock gently kissed his wife's hand.

"I am very sorry for your sorrow, my dear. I can understand your pain, and I will make sure Thomas hears my opinion on the subject. What a strange twist of fate, though, that the maid was found by, of all people, Darcy and his wife. I wonder whether anyone else would even consider taking a strange woman into their house. Darcy has indeed changed since he met his new wife."

"I am not certain whether he has changed or has always been a superior sort of man, and his wife only brought his excellent traits to the surface. It appears to be quite different in our son's case."

"Come now, Ellen, you cannot be so harsh on your own son for a mistake. Yes, he has been weak, but these sorts of *accidents* are rather frequent among the gentlemen of the ton."

Lady Matlock's eyes were lit with fire.

"Accidents? Leaving a servant with child then throwing her out into the cold? Throwing out your own child to die in the dead of winter? Letting my grandson die? He was a boy—did you know that? Is that an accident?"

"Ellen, please...you will make yourself ill if you do not calm yourself. I can understand how much you suffer, but it will soon pass. We cannot change what happened. And Thomas is no worse than any other of his peers. He is like any other gentlemen we know."

"I am calm, husband. I just wonder whether you have lost your mind too. You keep repeating that it is a common situation. Does that make it better, or does it prove our failure as parents? Can you imagine Darcy behaving in such a way?"

"Let us not make such a comparison. We do not know how Darcy would have behaved if he had married as his duty required, nor do we know how his marriage will end. That he disregarded reason and failed to fulfil everyone's expectations in his marriage is not necessarily praiseworthy."

"Well, you should be content that your son followed *reason* and our *expectations* in his marriage. We were all delighted when Thomas chose Beatrice and so upset when Darcy decided to marry Elizabeth. We wholly approved of the first and rejected the second. And now we can all contemplate the outcome in both cases. Again, this proves what *excellent* advice and principles we provided for him and what good judges of characters we both are."

"Ellen! That is grossly unfair!"

"We had the absurd arrogance to disapprove of Darcy's choice of a wife! Can you dare to compare Elizabeth with your daughter-in-law? What kind of choice did your son make with our support and encouragement? A woman who stands for nothing but vain appearance, useless education, and an unkind, selfish character! You called Elizabeth a country nobody, but observe how much joy, happiness, and love she has brought to Darcy and Georgiana! Watch her smiling countenance with the servants! Then go and see your daughter-in-law's treatment of her staff! It is our fault as much as Thomas's! But this will not remain as it is! I shall not allow it!"

"Lady Matlock! You should calm yourself before you do something unreasonable! We should better rest now and continue this conversation tomorrow."

"Lord Matlock! Tomorrow will bring no improvement. Let us at least take responsibility for our wrongs! Can you not see how foolish are all our pretensions to superiority? We are no better than any others! We failed in raising our firstborn child as the honourable gentleman he should be."

"Ellen, how can you say that?"

"How can I not? I had the arrogance to believe that my children would be better, not as bad as others! I foolishly believed that each would become a good example, not a shameful one! Can you not see how wrong we have been?"

"I strongly disagree with you. I have always been proud of my sons!"

"So have I, and it seems we were wrong! How is possible that Darcy grew up almost by himself and turned out to be such an excellent man, and our son is so deficient in character and generosity? Do you not see that this proves how little we mean as parents? We taught him nothing of consequence!"

"Surely, you cannot believe that!"

"But I do! Give me reason to think otherwise! He should take care of his family and those in his care, not take advantage of his power and bring pain and despair to those around him!"

Emotions almost overcame the powerful countess, and her husband ceased arguing with her, pained by her suffering. The earl gently took his wife's hands and caressed them in silence in a poor attempt to calm her.

"I shall bring you some tea, and I will have a drink to keep you company. Let me see what can be done. I will talk to Thomas first thing in the morning, and we will find a way to make amends. We will find the best resolution for this."

She said nothing, only leant against the pillows and asked to be left alone to rest. In five and thirty years, it was the first time she had refused tea and her husband's company in a time of sorrow.

ELIZABETH WOKE TO AN EMPTY BED. SHE HAD SLEPT MANY HOURS, YET she did not feel as rested as she expected. She knocked on Darcy's door then entered. The room was empty and the bed tidy—a clear sign that nobody had disturbed it.

Elizabeth rang for Molly, and she inquired after Maud immediately. Apparently, the young woman had passed the night as well as could be expected.

While she dressed and had her hair arranged, the maid informed her that the master went out and left word that he would return before breakfast.

Elizabeth wondered about the reason for his leaving the house so early and hoped no other unpleasant event had occurred during the night. Then she asked the maid about breakfast, and suddenly the mere thought of food made her nauseous. She had not felt that way in years, and she understood she must be very tired. It was a relief that her husband was not there, or else he would certainly be worried. The last thing they needed was another reason for concern.

She spent a few more minutes in her apartment, glancing out the window to spot his carriage, but her impatience was not rewarded. At almost ten o'clock in the morning, there was still no sign of Darcy.

As Georgiana had not left her room either, Elizabeth decided to check on Maud personally. Mrs. Hamilton was there and Dr. Harris.

The young woman's state was stable; there was no fever or bleeding, but she was still unconscious due to the laudanum. The doctor decided it was better for the patient to sleep as much as possible and allow her body to recover through rest. He expressed his hope that, starting that evening, she would drink some tea and perhaps eat a little soup.

In the middle of the conversation, Elizabeth was informed that Lord Matlock was upstairs, asking to talk to the master. Puzzled, she went to meet the earl, wondering whether it was a habit of the London ton to pay unannounced visits before breakfast. What could be the explanation for both her husband and his uncle wandering around Town at such an hour?

Her surprise increased when, in the main hall, there was not only the earl but also his elder son, Lord Buxton.

She greeted them properly and asked with genuine concern whether anything had happened.

"Mrs. Darcy, please forgive our intrusion. We apologise for disturbing you. We only wish to speak with my nephew for a few moments. Is he not home?"

"There is no reason for apologies within the family; we are always pleased to see you. Please come to the library. We will wait for William together. He is not at home, but we expect him to return any minute."

They followed her reluctantly, and Elizabeth could easily guess that something was amiss and that their visit had no pleasant reason behind it. She invited them to take a seat and offered drinks and refreshments, but they refused any. She chose a chair in front of them, making a polite inquiry after Lady Matlock and the colonel.

Minutes passed, and the conversation faded.

"I hope everything is well here too, Mrs. Darcy," the viscount said. "When we arrived, we were informed that you were in the company of Dr. Harris."

"Oh, yes—everything is fine with the family. Unfortunately, we have a delicate situation with one of our maids, and Dr. Harris is taking care of her."

Elizabeth was surprised to see the earl glaring at his son.

The viscount pretended to be oblivious to his father's silent reproach. "Is she the one that lost her child? My mother told me about her."

Elizabeth's astonishment grew, and she continued in a reserved tone. "Yes, the one named Maud. Lady Ellen told me you have a maid with the same name. Quite a coincidence."

The earl's expression turned more severe while the viscount averted his eyes and went to pour himself a drink. Elizabeth's eyebrow rose with curiosity.

"Yes, well…things are rather delicate. In fact, I confess we…I have come here to see Maud. Would you please call for a servant to show me the way?"

"Thomas!" the earl shouted. "It is not a subject with which to bother the lady of the house! We will wait for Darcy! Or even better, we will return later. We thank you for your kindness, and we apologise for any inconvenience…"

Elizabeth's head became heavy. She stared from one to the other, countless thoughts spinning in her mind. What was happening? What was she to understand? Had the viscount come to see Maud? He said that things were "rather delicate." What things?

"Why would you want to see Maud?" she asked, her voice sounding harsh even to herself. "Surely, you cannot be acquainted with her. She is but a poor servant who was left to die in the cold."

"I know…there was a very unfortunate circumstance. Maud worked in our house for almost a year, and her unexpected departure…"

Elizabeth struggled to maintain the appearance of calm while the revelation struck her and her anger became overwhelming. There was no coincidence. There were not two Mauds but only one. She vividly recollected the horrifying moments from the previous day: Maud's suffering, her pain, her cries, the blood, the poor child…

"Lord Buxton, forgive my boldness, but this situation must be drawn correctly. All the evidence shows that her departure was not unexpected, but she was rather dismissed and, for reasons which are incomprehensible to me, thrown out and denied even what was her due."

"Yes, I know that. I also found that you have generously taken care of her. This is why I would like to talk to her and perhaps find another arrangement that would not trouble you anymore," the viscount responded slightly embarrassed while the earl seemed undecided about whether to intervene again or not.

Elizabeth frowned as she struggled to understand his meaning. She took a few steps then resumed her place.

"Did I understand you correctly that it is your intention to remove Maud from this house? Surely, you cannot consider taking her back to the household from which your wife banished her."

"Yes, this is my decision. As I said, I believe it is better for you not to be burdened with her care any longer. And no, she will not return to that house."

She forced a smile, fighting the impulse to answer with the severity the man deserved. He was her husband's cousin, yet that could hardly compensate for his wrongs.

"I see. Your thoughtfulness for my comfort is much appreciated, sir. I believe we should talk more on the subject in a few days. However, Maud is in no condition to be moved now—in fact, she is not even conscious. Her state is very delicate and the doctor instructed us to provide her with rest, silence, and constant supervision."

"She shall be provided with all these things."

"Perhaps. But I must question your right to make any decisions regarding Maud, sir. As far as I know, her only relative in London is her aunt, from whom Maud begged us to keep complete secrecy. As I see it, for the time being, the only one who can decide anything regarding her is Dr. Harris. Once she is fully recovered, she will be able to choose her own path for the future."

The viscount looked at Elizabeth with surprise and obvious displeasure at her strong contradiction and harsh reproaches. While Elizabeth's voice grew sharper and decided, the gentleman's countenance betrayed his restlessness. Obviously, he had not anticipated having such an argument with his cousin's wife.

Lord Matlock rose and bowed to Elizabeth. "Mrs. Darcy, you are correct. As I said, we shall return when Darcy is home."

"That might be a wise decision, although I trust my husband will agree with me on this subject."

The young lord ignored his father and continued to address Elizabeth.

"Mrs. Darcy, I understand your point of view. However, I insist. I doubt seeing her and talking to her briefly would do any harm."

"Talking to her? I am not confident you understand the gravity of her situation. She has just lost her child, and it is a miracle that she survived; her life is still uncertain. As I said, she is not even conscious."

"Forgive me, but I feel you are doing this on purpose just to disregard my request," the young lord replied impertinently to his father's astonishment.

"Thomas!" the earl cried.

Elizabeth took a step forward, watching intently the two powerful men in front of her—the closest relatives of her husband. She knew that neither of them had accepted the idea of their marriage, and if she had reached a truce with the earl after Lady Catherine's visit, the viscount had never spoken more than several polite words to her. And suddenly he came into her house, attempting a poor remedy for his previously outrageous behaviour and had the audacity to question her fairness.

"Lord Buxton, I am sorry if I left you with the impression that this matter might be a subject for debate. It is not. As the mistress of this house and the one who has offered Maud shelter and care, my decision is made, and it will suffer no alteration. I understand your concern, and I applaud it; therefore, William will keep you informed about Maud's improvement. Also, as soon as she regains her strength, I shall let her know of your visit. From that point on, my involvement will end. Until then, I am asking you to change the conversation toward the weather. It would also be my pleasure to offer you some refreshments since obviously neither of us has had breakfast."

The viscount and the earl listened to her in silence, eyes widened in disbelief. Her tone, her straight shoulders, her chin daringly pushed forward, and her eyes casting sharp arrows left no doubt about the strength of Mrs. Darcy's character. Neither found anything to reply to a speech that allowed no contradiction.

They exchanged several glances then bowed to her briefly, bade her farewell, and prepared to leave while repeating that they would return when Darcy was home.

To their mutual surprise, the door opened, and the master himself entered, his presence bringing relief to everyone.

Darcy needed only a moment to notice the tension in the room: his wife's troubled expression, his uncle's embarrassment, and his cousin's barely concealed anger.

He took Elizabeth's hands and kissed them, asking how she was feeling. She assured him she was fine then excused herself and declared she must talk to Georgiana. There were many unsaid words between them and many questions, but both felt it was not the time for them. Darcy followed her with his eyes, tempted to go after her but forcing himself to remain and settle things with his relatives.

Once alone, Darcy closed the door and turned to his cousin.

"What a strange coincidence to find you here, Thomas. I planned to call on you first thing in the morning, to clarify *another* coincidence, but I was told you were already out. I also checked at uncle's house, but you were not there either—only to find you both here."

The earl nodded. "It seems we all were of the same mind—to talk together and find a solution to the mess Thomas has produced. This has never happened before in our family. I cannot believe that one of my sons has been such a weak fool. It is no wonder my wife was so angry. I have not seen her in such a state of distress for more than thirty years."

"Offending me will not solve anything, Father. We are all men and know how the world works. I never would have imagined that Maud was in your house, Darcy. When my mother told me yesterday, I immediately decided to come and see her. I have been a fool to let this grow to such proportions. Now I know what I must do."

Darcy stared at his cousin, astonished to see his apparent calm. He found it difficult to believe that the person responsible for these tragic events—the one he had despised and blamed since they found Maud in the park—was part of his close family, a man he had considered his friend for a lifetime. The night before, he was struggling with suspicions, and now each of them had turned into a most disturbing certainty.

He paused a moment then breathed deeply. "For heaven's sake, Thomas, I expected to carry out such a conversation with Wickham, not with you. Have you lost your mind?"

"I asked him the same," the earl intervened. "This situation is very unpleasant, and we must solve it somehow. I completely disapprove of Thomas's behaviour, but on one point, he is correct. Let us not be hypocritical. Most of the gentlemen of our acquaintance are in similar situations. I believe it is precisely the fact that Thomas is not accustomed to such circumstances that he did not know to handle them in a better and more discreet way. A careful resolution is needed as we must avoid making our family the laughingstock of the ton."

Darcy brushed his fingers through his hair. "I agree. Let us talk calmly. First, I want to know what you told my wife."

"We did not need to say much. She understood the truth the moment Thomas asked to see that woman."

Darcy was displeased and grew impatient. "My wife seemed troubled and upset. She must have had a reason for that."

Thomas agreed. "We had a rather serious argument. To be honest, I find Mrs. Darcy to be unreasonable and stubborn. I wished only to talk to Maud. I have already arranged to move her to a very comfortable house five miles outside London. She will have all the care she needs to recover. Your wife, however, refused to indulge me or hear any argument. I say, Darcy, you must take measures; she cannot impose her will on a matter she clearly does not understand. A woman cannot command a man."

The viscount spoke more and more animatedly with no restraint in show-ing his discontent, and he paid little attention to Darcy, whose countenance expressed his displeasure.

The master of the house rose from the chair and thundered to his cousin. "Thomas, I am afraid I did not hear you correctly; I was under the impression that you just offended my wife and that you just offered me advice regarding my marriage. Surely, I must have misunderstood you."

The viscount looked disconcerted. "Yes, well…I was just mentioning…I know your wife is not accustomed to the particulars of life among the ton. I was surprised that she answered my request so unreasonably. And you must believe that I am not a scoundrel. I treated Maud very well before she left, and I intend to take responsibility for her from now on. I shall provide her all the comfort she deserves."

"You surely know your Uncle Lewis de Bourgh did the same," the earl intervened calmly, but Darcy's face turned even darker, and he took one step toward his cousin, his voice so deep and powerful that it almost struck the other gentleman.

"You may not be a scoundrel, but you are a fool if you dare say another word against my wife! How dare you! You should thank her and apologise for all the distress you caused her! You find her to be unreasonable? Truly? And you pretend she cannot command a man in her own house? You want me to take measures against my wife, whose behaviour and character are beyond reproach? Did you take measures against yours?"

Both guests watched him in disbelief, astounded by a fury they had never seen before in Darcy. The viscount attempted to answer, but his father grabbed his arm to stop him, and he addressed Darcy politely.

"Nephew, we apologise for our behaviour, and you must believe that we are grateful to Mrs. Darcy for her gracious involvement. Thomas has spoken much nonsense since we arrived. I can only give him the benefit of being worried. Would you not allow him to see the young woman? I understand Mrs. Darcy meant well, but perhaps you would indulge your cousin."

Darcy breathed deeply several times, paced the room, poured himself a glass of brandy, and emptied it in one gulp. Only then did he return to face his relatives.

"Uncle, Elizabeth is never unfair or ungenerous. If there were a proper way of allowing Thomas to see Maud, she would have found it. But she has been unconscious since yesterday, and she might not recover. I have witnessed what she went through for only a few moments, but Elizabeth was by her side most of the time. So much blood, so much suffering…all I could do was to ask for the vicar's approval to bury the child in the churchyard. If you trouble her now, it might take her life away. Besides, just imagine the other servants' reactions: How will you justify visiting her? What are you to her? They already know or guess the truth behind her situation, but they do not know the names of the persons involved. Do you wish to expose yourself to that? This might cause her to be subject to fresh gossip since she tried so hard to keep the secret. You will have to wait and see how things progress."

His arguments accomplished their purpose, and the others could slowly see the correctness of his reasoning. Not much was said, only awkward silence and embarrassed glances. When they were about to leave, Elizabeth unexpectedly entered. She stepped hesitantly, and her husband hurried to take her hand. She smiled at him, and their hands entwined, then she turned to Lord Buxton and spoke kindly.

"Sir, if you wish to see Maud for a moment, I might make it possible.

Perhaps I have been too harsh. I can only imagine how hard it might be to fear for the life of someone dear to you. Despite the wrongs of the past, feelings cannot be repressed."

The viscount paled while the earl glanced at her with surprise and an interest newly found.

"I...it is very generous of you, Mrs. Darcy, but I have decided it would be better to wait. Please accept my deepest apologies for disturbing you."

The two gentlemen bowed to Elizabeth and left the library.

Darcy silently put his arms around his wife and pulled her close to his chest, wanting to take her sadness upon himself and wrap her in all the love he held for her.

At the Matlocks' residence, the earl diligently related to his wife the meeting with the Darcys. She addressed specific questions, asked for more details, and demanded explanations.

In the end, Lady Matlock took some time to think and analyse everything she was told then addressed her husband with great solemnity.

"Lord Matlock, Mrs. Elizabeth Darcy just proved to you and your son what superiority of character truly means, and your nephew showed you the face of love and devotion. You should be grateful and humble for this lesson and learn from it."

Chapter 14

I am very sorry for all the distress my cousin caused you, Elizabeth. Are you well? Would you rather go and rest a little? I can find no proper words to apologise…"

Darcy held his wife in his arms on the couch in the library, caressing her hair.

"You must not apologise for his faults. And do not worry about me—I am perfectly fine. But I confess I am rather troubled. I still find it hard to believe that your cousin is the one responsible for Maud's situation. I wonder how they found out."

"It appears that, after our visit yesterday, my aunt and Robert slowly realised the truth, and they went to confront Thomas. I can only imagine the fight. My aunt is very upset."

"And you? How did you discover it?"

"I began to think of the coincidence of names, and my suspicions were aroused last night. I decided to speak to Thomas first thing in the morning, and the rest you already know."

"Yes—how shocking. The only positive thing is that your cousin seems to be interested in Maud's well-being. Although his fault cannot be diminished, at least he did not purposely abandon her. I almost regret that I have been so harsh with him. I wonder whether he suffers…"

"You are too kind and too generous. I cannot be so indulgent with my cousin. I have no doubt that you have been anything but fair to him. As for his suffering—he kept repeating that most gentlemen are in similar situations, and he made this his excuse. Well, if other gentlemen survive their suffering, I am confident he will do so too. Let us not pity him."

"What will come of this? Could there be a positive ending to such a story? I am quite positive that she possesses a deep affection for the viscount, and he declares he is not indifferent to her. Can he truly take care of her? If his feelings fade in time, what will become of her?"

"Elizabeth, I must draw some limits to this. I feel this story affects you in a way that might harm you, and I cannot allow it. Maud will receive the proper care until her full recovery, but there is nothing more we can do. Once her health allows it, she must decide what she wishes to do. For the present, my primary concern is your well-being. I shall have it no other way, and I must insist that you obey me, just as you vowed in church."

His voice sounded half mocking, but his expression was severe enough. Elizabeth could easily see the correctness of his reasoning, and she knew she was to blame for not showing enough attention to her own husband.

She gently caressed his face.

"Forgive me, my dear; I am aware that my reactions were exaggerated, and I thank you for your patience. I allowed this situation to affect me more than it should, but I will correct that. It is just that I have not been myself lately."

"You must not apologise for being caring and kind. That is just one reason why I love you so deeply. But we must return to our usual schedule. And we shall start by riding our horses in the park after breakfast. Would you like that?"

"Yes, very much."

As they walked toward the dining room, Elizabeth turned to her husband. "William, did you ever think about what would have happened had Mr. Bingley never leased Netherfield? What if you had married your cousin Anne, perhaps, and Charlotte married Mr. Collins? We might have met while we visited Rosings. Would we still have fallen in love? And if so, what would have become of us?"

Darcy stared at her as though struggling to understand the meaning of her words. He frowned and then seemed to search for the right words.

"No, I have not thought of that. And I thank the Lord that I do not have to. I am sure of one thing: that I would have done everything for the privilege of earning your love and keeping it."

THE NEXT THREE DAYS PASSED UNEVENTFULLY. TO EVERYONE'S RELIEF, Maud's improvement continued, and the signs of her recovery were beyond doubt.

Darcy kept his word and dedicated most of his time to his wife. They walked or rode in Hyde Park, listened to Georgiana play, or read in the library. And he filled her room with fresh, spring flowers.

When he attended meetings at his club, Elizabeth—with Georgiana, Jane, and Mrs. Gardiner—visited the modiste. Lady Matlock did not keep them company. The colonel called on them once to inform them his mother was in no disposition for visits, and nobody insisted on further details. However, every second day, Lady Matlock sent Elizabeth a note inquiring about Maud's health, a fact that Elizabeth found both surprising and admirable.

The Gardiners and the Bingleys spent an entire afternoon at Darcy House. As the master had promised, a large, comfortable room was arranged for Becky and Margaret when they would spend the night there. The girls were overjoyed, and Becky declared Darcy to be her favourite gentleman—except for her papa—and she forgave him for stealing her dear Lizzy.

Elizabeth needed only a few minutes of private conversation with her sister to be convinced of Mrs. Bingley's growing happiness. The newly wedded couple was still alone in their home, and they had only dined once with Miss Bingley and the Hursts—which was further proof of Mr. Bingley's improved determination. He seemed perfectly capable of ensuring his wife's peace and felicity.

Strangely even to herself, all the pleasant activities made Elizabeth tired quite often. She felt the need to rest in the afternoon and went to bed rather early in the evening—a rare occurrence.

Darcy was there all the time, watching her. He held her in his arms before she fell asleep, and his eyes were the first thing she noticed when she woke up.

On the fourth evening after the terrible confrontation with the Matlock gentlemen, Elizabeth was ready for sleep, covered in soft sheets and admiring her husband's features as he read at the table by the window. He said he wished to allow her sleep without disturbing her.

With a shiver, she suddenly realised they had spent almost every minute together but had not loved each other for a whole week—from the first night of their return to London. Was it possible? Had it been so long? Had she neglected her husband so completely that she had become indifferent to him? And he made no attempt at closeness either. He held her in his arms many times, and she had slept in his embrace often, but nothing more. Yes, he had generously offered her the peace she needed to rest, but she had told him many times that his love was the best palliation for any distress.

And that evening—how was it possible that he had not joined her in their bed? Reading while she fell asleep—why would he do that?

"William, will you not come to bed, please? I cannot sleep without you."

He smiled and put down the book.

"Of course, I will."

He lay near her, and she cuddled into his chest.

"This is much better. I missed you—I miss you every minute when you are not near me. And I longed to feel you near me. I missed the feel of your hands, your warmth, your passion…"

"I have missed you too, my beloved wife. I miss you every day, every hour, every moment. I have never desired anything as much as I desire your closeness, your warmth, your sweet passion. Never doubt that."

He started to kiss her neck while his hands stroked her body through the silk of her gown. She sighed with pleasure, abandoning herself to his caresses, which soon conquered her. He hastily removed her clothes, making her naked body shiver from the cold of the room and the warmth of his kisses. His strong yet tender hands fondled every spot of her skin, arousing inside her a yearning for more. As pleasure slowly overwhelmed her, her body opened to him while her arms and legs pulled him closer. Her moans proved how much she craved to feel him closer to her, above her, inside her.

He removed his shirt and she daringly caressed his torso, then her fingers stroked along his spine. His kisses silenced her and took her breath away, but instead of joining with her as she expected and desired, he gently moved out of her grasp while he continued the exploration of her body: touching, caressing, kissing, tasting. Unable to speak or to think, she allowed herself to be spoiled by him, abandoning herself to him, greedily accepting the pleasure he wished to offer her—different than before, more times than before.

At midnight, exhausted by delight and spent by her unleashed passion, she lay in her husband's arms. He gently caressed her hair, kissing her temple while she struggled to understand what he wished and why he purposely avoided loving her in the most complete way as they had done so many times before. The pleasure she had experienced, almost too powerful to bear, was lacking something, and both her body and her mind were left wanting.

She wished to ask him but did not find the right words for such a question, nor did she dare to move. He stroked her arms, and she shivered, which he immediately noticed. He helped her put on her nightgown, then his arms tightened around her and he wrapped them both in two heavy blankets.

"Is it comfortable enough? Are you still cold?" he whispered in her ear, his lips fondling her earlobe.

She shivered ever harder. "I am not cold—I never was. I am perfectly comfortable. William, I—"

"I am pleased to hear that. My love, we should sleep now. It is very late."

Elizabeth was not oblivious to the interruption but found nothing to say except, "You are right of course; let us sleep."

Sometime later, Elizabeth was almost asleep when she heard him whispering through the dark silence.

"I love you so much, Elizabeth…so very much."

THE FOLLOWING MORNING, ELIZABETH WOKE WITH A FEELING OF REST-lessness. She was alone and hurried to knock on her husband's door, but he was not there. While she rang for Molly, Elizabeth's thoughts of the previous night invaded her mind again. She could sense that something was amiss and feared that some problem might have troubled her husband and he did not want to share it with her. And not knowing what it was only increased her uneasiness.

When she entered the library, she met Darcy's tender gaze, which dispelled her worries. He came to her and held her hands, then kissed her palms.

"Good morning, my love, did you sleep well?"

"Yes…and you? Did you wake early? I see you have business to attend."

"I read some documents for a brief meeting with my uncle and my solicitor. I will be at the club at noon but will return very soon."

"I see…very well then."

"I was also informed that Maud rose from her bed today. Dr. Harris was kind enough to keep me company for a while."

"That is wonderful news."

"It is. Now—shall we have breakfast? Georgiana is already in the music room, waiting for us."

Darcy's behaviour was everything Elizabeth could hope for, and his warm voice, loving glances, and small touches during breakfast put her mind at ease. It was a lovely day, and the sun shone through the open curtains, brightening the room and Elizabeth's disposition.

Darcy left the house for a couple of hours, and Elizabeth spent the afternoon with Georgiana. It was the first day that they had some time alone, and both enjoyed it exceedingly. They played together and made plans for attending the theatre and for the much-expected journey to Pemberley.

Elizabeth shared her intention to finally host a dinner for their common relatives, and Georgiana gladly approved.

"I remember the first time we had dinner together with your family, Elizabeth. I was very ill and kept to my bed. And you were so kind to visit me. And you tricked me to eat. From the very beginning, I hoped you would someday become my sister. I knew of William's affection for you, and I prayed that you returned it."

"Thank you, my dear Georgiana. My happiness with William is complete having you as my sister."

Elizabeth smiled with no little emotion. She vividly recollected that dinner. It was the evening she and Georgiana met. And when Darcy kissed her palm and her wrist for the first time—and told her she had the power of bringing joy into their lives and asked for permission to call the next day—it was the moment her dreams of an arrangement with Darcy first came to life.

She shivered just remembering those sweet moments but also the painful, heart-rending hours that followed when they learned of Lydia's elopement, and she was certain her happiness was gone forever.

"Elizabeth?" She startled at her sister's voice, and a glance was enough to see that Georgiana's thoughts were not far from her own.

"Do you have news from your sister Lydia? How is she?"

Elizabeth caressed the girl's hand.

"I do have news, dearest. She is well—or so she wrote us. She seems happy with the balls and the parties. As you can well imagine, she asked for some monetary help to purchase a few new gowns—both from me and from Jane. I will talk to William about that and see what he thinks. I would like to help my sister, but I cannot possibly allow her to take advantage of us."

"I am glad she is well. If I may suggest something: perhaps you could help by purchasing her some gowns and bonnets and reticules—everything she needs—instead of sending her money."

"This is wise advice, my dear, very wise indeed. I am very glad we had the chance to talk. So, what would you recommend as a main course for the dinner?"

Their conversation continued until Darcy returned and joined them. He seemed in excellent spirits, and after a short greeting, he invited them both for a walk in the park to take advantage of the beautiful weather.

Arm in arm, the ladies informed him about their recent decisions. He approved everything they said, content to see them as close as two real sisters could be.

"So, whom do you wish to invite to dinner? The Gardiners, Bingley and his wife—and who else?"

"Well, your uncle and aunt and the colonel. And Mr. Bingley's sisters of course. It would be impolite to do otherwise."

"Oh…" said both Darcy siblings at the same time.

Elizabeth laughed. "Do not make me feel guilty for inviting them. After all, they were a regular presence in your houses for years. Surely, it cannot be worse this time."

"Probably not. But my tolerance and self-control appear to have diminished lately," Darcy admitted.

"Besides, Miss Bingley admires you both very much. I am the one she hates, but I am already accustomed to it, and I dare say I bear it quite well," Elizabeth concluded.

"Miss Bingley always admired William; she only befriended me by extension." Georgiana chuckled, glancing at Elizabeth.

Her brother rewarded her with a stern and disapproving glare, contrasting with the smile that twisted his lips; then he addressed his wife.

"Well, you will be responsible for entertaining and abiding the ladies. I shall be accountable only for the gentlemen, so my mission will be rather easy."

"Yes, but I always count on your support, sir," Elizabeth teased him. "I am sure you would not abandon me to Miss Bingley and Mrs. Hurst's censure."

"Madam, I trust you will succeed in handling the situation properly by yourself. You always did before."

"Such a cowardly response, Mr. Darcy," Elizabeth mocked him while Darcy stared at her lips, wondering what would happen if he kissed her there in the middle of the park.

AFTER DINNER, ELIZABETH FELT TIRED RATHER EARLY, BUT SHE DID HER best to remain awake long enough to hear Georgiana play for half an hour. Afterwards, she excused herself and declared she wanted to retire. Georgiana followed her, but to Elizabeth's surprise, Darcy wished them good night and told his wife that he would join her soon as he still had something to finish.

Elizabeth's distress returned, but she refrained from saying anything in the presence of Georgiana. Once in her room, she rang for Molly, changed for the night, then dismissed the maid and knocked on Darcy's door. He was not there, so she returned to her bed for a few moments then hurriedly left the chamber.

She found her husband reading in the library. At her entrance, he rose and came to her.

"What happened, my love? I thought you would be asleep by now."

"Nothing happened to *me*. Is there anything happening to *you*, William?"

"Not at all. I was just looking through some notes."

"In the middle of the night? Is there an urgent situation?"

"No...not really."

"Then would you finish your reading tomorrow, please? I would like to go to bed together."

He hesitated only a moment then put his arm around her shoulders.

"Of course, I will. Come, let us go to sleep, my dear."

Inside their apartment, he gently helped her to the bed and briefly kissed her lips while he wrapped the covers around her.

"I will change and return in no time," he said, and she followed him with her eyes while he entered his own chamber.

A few long minutes passed, and he did not return. Elizabeth impatiently left the bed and entered his room unceremoniously. He was having a glass of wine, staring out the window.

"William, this will not do! Please let me know what is happening, and I beg you not to tell me it is nothing. Why do you avoid my company?"

"I do not avoid your company, quite the contrary. Have we not been together most of the day?"

"You do avoid my company when we are alone. You cannot deny that you purposely avoid me. You wait for me to fall asleep, and in the morning, you leave me before I wake up. We have not made love in many days—and I know it is my fault because I spent so much time with Maud, and then I was tired all the time. Now I feel that a distance is growing between us, and I wish to change that. I want things to be as they were. How can I do that?"

Her emotions intensified as she spoke, and he swiftly embraced her as tightly as he could.

"My dearest, you have done nothing wrong, and surely there is no distance between us. You have my heart, and I can hardly breathe at all when I am not close to you."

He attempted to keep a light tone while he pulled her into his arms and carried her to her bed. This time, he laid her against the pillows and joined her. She cuddled to his chest, and he kissed her hair again.

"William, we have always been honest with each other. Please do not keep your distress from me. I sense your tension, and it greatly troubles me."

Elizabeth gently caressed him through the thick fabric of his shirt then untied it and placed warm kisses along his chest. She brushed her body against his and almost lay atop of him. He turned her on her back and kissed her face then captured her lips in a deep, passionate kiss while his caresses matched hers. He removed the gown from her shoulders, then his lips lowered along her neck toward the softness of her breasts.

She groaned, and her body arched toward him while her hands entwined around his neck and she whispered in his ear. "My love, please…please do not make me wait any longer…I missed you so much…"

He needed no more begging, and their moans of delight combined as his body finally joined hers. Her hands and legs tightened around him, and they moved together, slowly sharing the overwhelming pleasure until the rhythm increased and Elizabeth shattered in anticipation of what she knew would come. Her body reached its completion first, and she continued to move against him, expecting to sense his warmth release inside her.

She held her breath when he unexpectedly pulled away from her, and only his moans tickled her neck. Elizabeth's heart raced as Darcy embraced her and placed small kisses on her shoulder while he struggled to breathe regularly.

There was silence for some time, and Elizabeth tried to understand what had just happened. He continued to stroke her hair then took her hands to his lips.

"William…please tell me what is wrong," she repeated. "We have made love so many times; I know you and I know myself so well that you cannot deceive me. Things are different. *You* are different, and I am pained that you do not trust me enough to tell me the truth."

A deep silence fell and lasted for some time. He kissed her hands again then finally spoke.

"It is something that…" He was in obvious distress, struggling for words. "I am frightened. I cannot escape the tremendous fear that I might put you in danger. I cannot allow that. I will do everything in my power to keep you safe, even if it means that I must stay away from you."

She raised her head to meet his eyes, completely astounded. "How could you put me in danger? And why would you need to keep me safe? William, I am totally lost…"

He lay back against the pillow, facing her for a few moments, then averted his eyes.

"I saw Maud that day…when she almost died. All that blood, that suffering, the child that I held…Doctor Harris said that could happen to any woman. That he had seen cases before and there was not much he could do. I finally understood that men are selfish—they never consider what their wives must go through to give birth to a child. I realised that, every time I indulge my passion for you, I put you in danger. I have thought of that every day and every night since then. If I risked my own life, I would not worry, but I cannot jeopardise yours. I will love you in any possible way that will not threaten your safety. I know there are ways to do that. I have always hoped to have children, but now I wonder…"

With each word, distress twisted his handsome features, and Elizabeth listened to him in complete disbelief. His struggle was obvious, and he caressed her hands while he continued his confession.

"Forgive me for worrying you. I tried to keep my thoughts private, but it seems I did a poor job of it. I only troubled you even more with my strange behaviour."

Elizabeth gently cupped his face, and he turned his head to kiss her palm.

"My darling husband, please do not keep secrets from me. Just as you wish to protect me, I want the same. Your distress is also mine, and I cannot be happy or even content when you are not."

"I know, my love—forgive me."

He tenderly kissed her lips, stroking her hair.

She allowed herself to engage in the sweet, delightful comfort then withdrew a few inches.

"William, let us speak more of your fear. I confess that, as distressed as I was by Maud's condition, I never considered that it might happen to me. But I cannot deny the rightness of your concern. However, my dear husband, we can only pray and hope that everything will be fine. Thousands of women have children every day. Some of them go through a terrible ordeal, but many others—most—do not."

"I love you more than my own life. You must know that I shall never take chances with you. I might sound unreasonable, but this is how I have been feeling for days."

She did find him unreasonable, and she hoped it was only the result of everything they had faced in the last week. But her heart ached for his pain; it was his deepest love for her that made him think that way. She was certain it would all pass soon, so she only needed to be patient.

Elizabeth felt his eyes scrutinising her, and she knew he could read her thoughts again.

"Elizabeth, I know you must think that I am being silly. And I do know that most married people have children. But I also know that very few men love their wives as I love you. Every fibre of my body desires you and craves you, but every thought in my mind fears what might happen."

She held his hands tightly and leant to kiss him. "I do not think you are silly, my dear sir. I feel proud and grateful for your love and passion. But..."

She paused and looked at him lovingly, wondering how it was possible that she had gained the complete love and devotion of such a man.

"Have you ever feared anything about yourself? I would say you have not."

"Of course not, but that is different. Men are different; they are not delicate creatures. Men are those who carry out wars. It is their duty to protect their country and their families."

He sounded quite solemn as if he were surprised that she could not understand something so obvious.

Elizabeth laughed with all her heart—and all her love.

"Very well, then let us speak of women—let us speak of me. If you were to worry about me, I should never ride: what if the horse threw me to the ground. We should never travel: what if we were to be attacked by villains. Would you like me to go on?" she inquired teasingly. "You cannot protect me by locking me in a cage of fear. I shall be well and safe and protected as long as I have you. You cannot cage our love and passion for each other, and we should await our children with eagerness and joy, not fear."

She looked into his eyes, determined but tearful, struggling to find the best way to convince him. She could see that he had not changed his mind. There was still worry on his countenance. But he forced a smile and kissed her hands again.

"Very well, my dear. Let us sleep now. We will talk more tomorrow and in the next days."

She decided not to push the argument any further and only glided into his arms. She was relieved to discover the reason for his changed behaviour. Yes, his distress, his worry was indeed something grave, and it troubled her too. But she knew he had no true reason for it. She only had to give him time to overcome his own restraints.

After some time of peaceful silence, Elizabeth released a small laugh.

"My mother has five children. My aunt Gardiner has four. Does either of them appear harmed in any way? Would you say that giving birth to their children affected their health?" Elizabeth inquired teasingly, attempting to dissipate the tension.

He breathed deeply and replied cautiously. "Only your mother's nerves.

Elizabeth burst out in laughter until he silenced her with a deep passionate kiss that—to her disappointment—stopped too soon. She continued to caress him, but he decidedly held her hands and kissed them briefly.

"We must absolutely sleep now, my dearest Mrs. Darcy."

It was her duty as a wife to obey—at least for the time being.

Chapter 15

The next morning, Elizabeth and Darcy woke up together. They both felt lighthearted after the awkward conversation from the previous evening and remained in bed a little longer, tightly embracing and making plans for the near future.

If it were a few weeks before, they would have spent the time making love, but Elizabeth observed that Darcy's uneasiness about the delicate subject was not completely dispelled. She could not blame his stubborn concern since it was all meant to protect her from a danger that became overwhelming in his mind.

"My dear, would you like to leave for Pemberley at the end of the month? After the Almack's ball?"

Elizabeth's eyes brightened. "That would be wonderful! You know I have long waited for this moment."

"So have I. We will take Georgiana with us as I feel more at peace to have her under my supervision, considering the health problems of the last months. But I will warn her that she might spend quite some time alone before the others arrive. I wish to show you Pemberley with all its beauty and secrets—only the two of us."

She smiled with delight, whispering back, "I would be thrilled to discover Pemberley with you…only the two of us."

He rolled her on her back and leant atop of her, his weight almost taking her breath away.

They gazed into each other's eyes; then his lips captured hers. Their bodies brushed against each other, and Elizabeth sighed as her hands glided through his hair.

"Do you think we could be a little late for breakfast?" he whispered.

"I believe so…besides, it seems you already decided we will," she teased him, and he tasted her lips, laying kisses down her throat.

"May I hope your fears are gone?" she asked, shivering as her gown slid from her shoulders.

"They are not. But now that we spoke of it, at least my distress has vanished. I love you so much, and I want to prove it to you in many, many ways."

She chuckled then pushed him away a little to meet his eyes.

"And may I ask, sir, where and how you acquired such extended knowledge and skills in that area?

Her tone was only half-serious, but the curiosity in her eyes was undeniable. His answer came in a hoarse voice while his hands eagerly fondled the perfect roundness of her breasts.

"You may ask, but it is unlikely that I will answer. Or you could just fully benefit from my experience. You must understand, Elizabeth, that everything I did in the past, was only meant to prepare me for cherishing you for our whole lives."

"Then I shall not ask more," she murmured, her curiosity quickly overwhelmed by a storm of sensations.

THE DINNER AT THE DARCYS FINALLY TOOK PLACE ON A THURSDAY EVENING.

Elizabeth was a little sad that Lord and Lady Matlock declined the invitation, but she had sympathy for her ladyship's not feeling the inclination for large parties.

Except for regular notes exchanged with Lady Matlock, the only one in the family that Elizabeth met was the colonel. She knew she would see the others again soon, though: Maud was steadily recovering, and it was expected that the viscount would come to talk to her. Besides, it was likely they would all meet the following week at Almack's.

Although it was just a family dinner, Elizabeth prepared herself with care. She chose an evening dress of creamy satin, garnished with dark blue lace on the sleeves, neckline, and along the bottom. As jewels, she selected a cameo and matched earrings.

She was pleasantly surprised to see Georgiana wearing a pale blue dress and a necklace with small blue sapphires and pearls. They smiled at each other, noticing the coincidence of their matched colours.

Darcy's contentment at seeing them was clearly expressed by compliments and even more so by his affectionate gaze when he offered one arm to each of them while accompanying them to the drawing room.

The guests arrived at the perfect time. The first to come was the colonel, then the Gardiners, and finally, the Bingleys and the Hursts.

Jane, in her elegant gown, looked even more beautiful than usual on the arm of her husband. She and Bingley embraced their hosts warmly while Caroline and Louisa showed a polite coldness toward Elizabeth but animatedly greeted Georgiana.

"My dear Georgiana, I am so delighted to see you again! You look as lovely as always. I understand from my brother that you lived with Lady Matlock until recently."

"I am pleased to see you too. Yes, I had the pleasure of staying with my aunt for a couple of weeks, but I am happy to be home."

"Well, I am still living with my sister. I am not certain whether I shall ever return home," Caroline said sharply. "I find it hard to understand why such an arrangement was needed. When Louisa got married, she did not push anyone from the house."

Bingley helped his wife to enter the drawing room then, perfectly serene, turned to his sister.

"Caroline, when Louisa married, she moved in with her husband, and you remained with me—so the situation was different. And you must understand that newly wedded couples need some private time. You may not understand that; it is something peculiar to those who marry for love."

Darcy appreciated his friend's wit and his proper answer to Caroline's rudeness. He considered adding something, but the conversation was interrupted by the servant announcing that dinner was served.

They took their seats, with Darcy and Elizabeth at each end of the table. The arrangements were elegant and tasteful, and Mrs. Gardiner complimented Elizabeth.

"Indeed, Mrs. Darcy, everything looks exactly as a regular dinner table should be," Louisa Hurst said with condescension.

"Lizzy, you were very kind to invite us," Jane quickly intervened. "We hope to meet again often; we will return the invitation soon."

"We will certainly meet regularly. We have had a very busy week since we returned to town, but hopefully things will turn for the better," Darcy answered. "It is our pleasure to have you all here tonight."

"I say, Darcy, we have dined at your house many times, but somehow it looks even more handsome than before," Bingley said, gulping some wine.

"Of course it is—since there are now two beautiful ladies in it," Darcy replied, glancing at the two more important women in his life. "Speaking of regular meetings—we plan to leave for Pemberley at the end of the month and hope you will all join us soon. We would be delighted to spend the summer together as a large family."

The Gardiners, the Bingleys, and even the colonel expressed their delight at such a generous invitation.

"Spending summers at Pemberley was always an enjoyable experience. However, I never remember its being crowded. Mr. Darcy has always been a private man and very strict with his choice of friends," Louisa Hurst commented as if addressing no one in particular.

Darcy lost his patience and replied with cold sharpness. "I would say that summers at Pemberley have been rather boring in the last few years. And it is true that I used to be strict in my choice of friends, but it appears strictness does not always guarantee quality."

"Shall we eat now?" Elizabeth invited the guests, undecided whether she should laugh or be angry at Bingley's sisters' lack of civility.

For a few minutes, there was silence, then Caroline Bingley addressed Elizabeth.

"I understood Lord and Lady Matlock were to be present too. Did they decline? I imagine they had more important engagements."

Her boorishness was not even concealed, and Miss Bingley's jeering smile only strengthened it. The colonel was the first to answer, allowing Darcy time to calm himself.

"My parents declined because my mother has been unwell in the last few days. However, they regretted their absence tonight. Lady Matlock is very fond of Mrs. Darcy and takes every opportunity to enjoy her company. She often says she is now happy to have two nieces."

Caroline paled slightly, but the colonel had even more to say.

"My mother wishes to rest so that she will be in her usual spirits by next week when we attend the ball at Almack's. She is very pleased to have

Elizabeth as her guest."

Both Caroline and Louisa turned red, glancing at each other in disbelief.

"Oh, my dear Lizzy, you are going to Almack's?" Mrs. Gardiner inquired with the enthusiasm of a young girl. "What an honour! The only thing better than that is to be introduced at the palace! I am so proud of you, my dear!"

"Lizzy, that is wonderful indeed," Jane repeated.

"You seem more excited than I am." Elizabeth laughed. "I have no merit in this; I owe everything to Lady Matlock, who rightfully insisted that Mrs. Darcy must have her position among London's ton. I do everything in my power to rise to her expectations."

"In truth, one must be very lucky to be admitted to such places only due to suitable connections," commented Miss Bingley.

His sister's scurrility made Bingley glare at her.

Elizabeth, however, smiled with a charm that concealed the arrows cast by her eyes.

"You are right of course, Miss Bingley. I do consider myself very fortunate. However, being admitted to Almack's is only one of the minor sources of happiness attached to my situation as Mr. Darcy's wife. There are many other things much more important that do not require us to be out in public."

All the ladies—either favouring or opposed to Elizabeth—were astonished at such a statement and did not know how to take her meaning. Darcy laughed.

"If it were my choice, I confess I would rarely seek any other company except Elizabeth's. My sister and our close friends, with whom we share a mutual regard, are of course the exceptions."

"I sympathise with you, Darcy," Bingley admitted. "I congratulate myself every day for coming to London right after my wedding. I thank God that we are not obliged to fulfil as many obligations as you are."

Jane blushed and silently nodded in approval of her husband's words.

Happily, the second course was served, and everybody's attention was drawn to the elegant plates.

"How are the children, Mrs. Gardiner? I really miss Becky and Margaret," Georgiana said some time later, willing to introduce a pleasant and neutral subject of conversation.

"They are very well, Miss Darcy, although quite upset that we did not bring them with us. They missed you too. I believe Mr. Darcy and Lizzy are spoiling them—especially Becky—a little too much. But then again, we all do," Mrs. Gardiner answered with a warm smile.

"I confess myself guilty of the charge," Darcy admitted. "I have rarely been as comfortable in the presence of children as I am with yours. They are not only very pleasant but also excellently educated."

"Darcy was always awkward with children," the colonel intervened. "In fact, he was rather awkward with adults too. I am glad that marriage has changed his manners. He is a much more pleasant fellow now."

Darcy cast a cold glance—half-serious, half-mocking—at his cousin, who only laughed. Georgiana supported her brother while Elizabeth smiled reproachfully at the colonel.

"Oh, I would rather disagree," Mrs. Hurst said. "I preferred Mr. Darcy's previous seriousness. I have always known him as a gentleman with high expectations and impeccable behaviour. In such situations, change is rarely a good thing."

The hidden meaning of Louisa Hurst's statement did not go unnoticed— with the exception of Mr. Bingley, who paid attention to little else but his lovely wife.

Georgiana lowered her eyes to her plate. Elizabeth glanced at her husband, observing his frown. She would not allow either of Bingley's sisters to ruin their evening, so before Darcy had time to reply, Elizabeth addressed the colonel teasingly.

"I also disagree, sir. I do not think marriage improved anything in regard to Mr. Darcy as he has always been the best of men. I hope you gentlemen do not take offence for my being biased."

The colonel laughed again.

"Of course not; it is a lady's duty to praise her husband. I am certain Mrs. Bingley would say the same about hers. I wonder whether I should marry to benefit from the same treatment."

"Oh, you must ponder that carefully, Colonel," Caroline Bingley intervened. "Marrying for the wrong reasons or with the wrong person is an error that cannot be easily remedied."

Several pairs of eyes turned to her, some embarrassed or quite angry. Elizabeth breathed deeply, trying to keep her calm.

"True," Darcy said gravely. "However, marrying for the right reason and with the right person is a lifetime of gratification. I am happy I am only at the beginning of enjoying my reward," he concluded.

"I say, only watching you and Bingley here gives me an inducement to consider matrimony," the colonel said then turned to Caroline. "But I appreciate your concern for my future felicity, and I thank you for warning me."

Caroline did not reply but cast a disgruntled glance to her sister.

The colonel continued, keeping his good mood.

"If we are to speak of marriage, I would say it suits very well both Mrs. Bingley and Mrs. Darcy. You ladies look more beautiful than ever, and I am honoured to have you both among my acquaintances."

Jane's face coloured while she thanked the colonel for his kindness. Elizabeth smiled with gratitude, not so much for the colonel's praise of her but for his amiability toward Jane. A colonel in his majesty's army and the son of an earl complimenting the new Mrs. Bingley was very helpful for her self-confidence. As for Elizabeth, as much as she admired the colonel, the only opinion that mattered to her was that of her husband.

"I am sure marriage would suit any woman who marries a man with a situation in life significantly above hers," Caroline Bingley said, and Darcy' face became severe, his eyes narrowing in anger. He almost rose from his seat, but Elizabeth's glance convinced him to allow her to respond.

"That may be true, Miss Bingley. I cannot speak for Jane, but in my case, it is less about my husband's situation in life than his love and devotion for me that makes this marriage suit me so well."

"As for our situations in life, I am a gentleman and Elizabeth is a gentleman's daughter. I would rather say we are equal," Darcy declared with solemnity. "Except that Elizabeth is a much better person than I am, and I am grateful for every moment I spend with her."

"Yes, well…I am sure Caroline did not mean—" Mrs. Hurst intervened, but Bingley interrupted her.

"Well, I would rather say I was lucky to secure Jane's affection. She is not only the most beautiful woman I have ever met, and with a most excellent character, but while her father is a gentleman, most of my fortune was made in trade. I still wonder that she chose me when she surely could have made a much better match."

"Charles!" Louisa interrupted him with reproach, appalled by the reference to trade.

"Oh, Charles, never say such a thing again," Jane objected, her adoring gaze tearful. "I could not dream of a better match."

"As I said, I am very lucky," Bingley concluded as he and his wife gazed at each other.

The Gardiners and the colonel exchanged smiles. Georgiana spoke in a low voice, crimson from the courage of own words.

"I know that many ladies would have been happy to marry my brother, and I thank the Lord every day for his choice. Having Elizabeth as my sister is the most wonderful thing I could imagine."

The target of her statement was obvious, and Miss Darcy felt uncomfortable for being so harsh to Miss Bingley; yet, she could not bear having her new sister offended without supporting her. And her brother's smile of approval showed that her gesture was correct.

"Dear Georgiana, you have always been exceedingly kind and willing to think the best of all the people around you," Miss Bingley answered with forced amiability. "Quite unlike Mr. Darcy who used to be a sharp and fastidious judge of character. When we first arrived in Hertfordshire, he could hardly bear the company and would rather not speak with anyone except us. At that time, nobody would have imagined that someday he would be related to those whom he so loathed. Time changes many things it appears. I am anxious to see what Mrs. Bennet will say of Pemberley. "

For a moment, silence fell over the room, the guests' embarrassment mixing with the hosts' anger. Darcy started to speak, but Elizabeth's voice—at once clear, determined, cold, and calm—dominated the room.

"Miss Bingley, before the third course is served, please allow me to be blunt about a matter to which I have paid attention for some time. I have great affection for Mr. Bingley, and I consider his family as my own. Therefore, I have generously pretended to be oblivious to your rudeness, which I date almost from the beginning of our acquaintance, and I see that it continues even when you are a guest in my home. From this moment on, I shall no longer tolerate any lack of propriety with my family or me. I understand you consider me responsible for ruining your unrealistic dreams of marrying Mr. Darcy. Your suffering is pitiful, but it cannot excuse bad manners. If it is so unpleasant for you to be in our company, please let me know, and I will gladly refrain from extending an invitation to you in the future, either in London or Derbyshire."

A polite smile twisted Elizabeth's lips, sweetening her harsh words. Her expression admitted no opposition, and neither Jane's blushing and obvious panic nor Miss Bingley's astonishment and barely concealed fury made any impression on her.

"It is an excellent time to discuss this since we will soon leave for Pemberley, and it would be good to know the number of people in our party," Darcy intervened with perfect composure as if discussing a business matter. "After all, our family has grown lately, and Pemberley might become too crowded. Since Bingley and the Bennets will join us, Netherfield would be a better option for you to spend a peaceful, undisturbed summer in the countryside."

Elizabeth offered her husband a barely perceptible smile.

Caroline turned even paler, obviously struggling to keep her calm, and gazed at Louisa who seemed suddenly preoccupied with her plate, ignoring her sister's signs of distress.

The dinner lasted for another four courses, and afterwards, Miss Darcy was glad to indulge her brother's request for music. Elizabeth joined her in a duet; then the colonel amused them by performing a short song at the pianoforte.

Until the evening ended, neither Caroline Bingley nor Louisa Hurst spoke another word. It was also true that nobody attempted to involve them in conversation, nor did anyone try to stop them when they declared they intended to retire very early.

Chapter 16

L ife below stairs returned to its usual routine.

Ten days after the tragic burial of her unborn child, Maud had regained her strength enough to rise from her bed and visit her son's grave. She was still not allowed to do any work, but her life was no longer in danger. However, her pallor, the weight she lost, her drooping shoulders, and her eyes looking mostly at the floor or staring at the wall showed clearly that her recovery was not complete.

The involvement of the Matlock family remained unknown to everyone except Elizabeth and Darcy. Not even Georgiana, Jane, or Mrs. Gardiner was informed about the story behind Maud's accident.

Two days later, Elizabeth went to talk to Maud privately. She was embarrassed by the subject she was about to bring up, while the young woman looked frightened by the mistress's presence in her room and the request for a private conversation.

Maud expressed her gratitude one more time and declared that not even ten lives would be enough to repay the master and mistress's kindness.

"Please do not worry about that, Maud. There is something important and delicate that I must talk to you about."

"With me, ma'am? What could possibly be so important for you to take the trouble of coming downstairs? Please just ring for me, Mrs. Darcy, and I would come in no time."

"The thing I am about to tell you will shatter you, I am afraid. You will not have to do anything for the time being, only to know what to expect and to think of a possible solution for the future."

"For the future? Oh…am I dismissed, ma'am?"

"No—no, not at all. What I wish to tell you is that, about a week ago, the viscount—Lord Buxton—came to inquire after you."

The young woman released a cry and fell to the edge of the bed, struggling to avoid Elizabeth's eyes.

"How…I do not understand? Why…I never told everyone…I would never…"

"Maud, calm yourself. I know it is very distressing news, but you have nothing to fear. Let us speak calmly. We found the truth by mere coincidence. Are you aware that the viscount is Mr. Darcy's cousin?"

"No…I did not know. Does the master know too? Dear Lord, what a shame! I beg your forgiveness. I never imagined that—"

"Maud, please stop for a moment and hear me. Yes, Mr. Darcy knows and so do the viscount's brother and his parents—but nobody else."

The maid was pale, her hands clasped together in her lap, her lips trembling as she fought tears.

"Mrs. Darcy, I shall leave at once. I am sorry that I repaid your kindness with even more trouble…"

"Oh, hush, girl," Elizabeth scolded her in a light voice, trying to put her at ease. "I ask you to stop and let me finish. We do not want you to leave. We were quite pleased with your work in the house, and Mrs. Hamilton was impressed by your talent as a seamstress. We will surely need your help in the future if you decide to stay."

"Ma'am, I would never want to leave if you allow me to stay."

"Yes, but…the viscount has asked to talk to you. He seemed very interested in your fate. He wished to take care of you, he said. We told him everything that you suffered, and he took the blame for what occurred."

"He did? Is this possible?" The woman's astonishment coloured her cheeks, and her lips and hands trembled even more.

"In fact, he intended to take you with him immediately, but you were in such a state that we feared for your life, so I could not allow you to be disturbed. But I promised him I would inform you when you were healthy enough—so you could decide whether you wish to talk to him or not."

"Oh…Mrs. Darcy, I never imagined that…"

Before Elizabeth had time to react, the girl knelt and humbly kissed

Elizabeth's hand.

She pulled it away gently but decidedly.

"Maud, you must rest now. Just consider things properly, and when the moment comes, you can tell me whether you wish to talk to him. Just keep in mind that you do have the choice to remain in our house. You already know the entire household and are familiar with Mrs. Hamilton's requirements. We expect your loyalty and diligent work, and we will offer you in exchange a suitable payment and fair treatment for a long-time commitment. If you decide, however, to follow another path, nobody will hold it against you."

"Thank you, ma'am. Thank you. Please forgive me and…thank you."

Later on, Elizabeth shared with her husband the brief yet painful conversation with the young maid. As happened before, Elizabeth empathised with Maud's obvious affection for her former employer and worried about the possible conclusion to her unfortunate story.

Darcy attempted to ponder her emotions and insisted there was nothing more that she could—or had the right to—do. Neither of them was certain that the viscount was steady in his decision regarding Maud: What might he propose? How would she judge the entire prospect? What would she decide for her future well-being?

"My dear, you must promise me that you will distance yourself enough to remain untouched, no matter what Maud does. It is not unlikely that she will choose the comfort of a house where she will be served and have the company of a gentleman she is fond of instead of remaining to serve others for an income that, no matter how fair, would be likely insufficient to support her entire family."

"I understand your reasoning, and I can easily understand her temptation, especially if she holds the viscount in high esteem. But what if, in a year or two or five, he loses his interest in her?"

"Sadly, this is the risk that any woman in a similar position accepts in exchange for the benefit of a luxurious yet illicit life."

"Yes…I am aware that you are right. And I must follow your advice and detach myself from this now that Maud's life is no longer threatened. Would you please walk with me? I think your company is the incentive I need."

"Your wish is always my command, my dear wife. And everything you need I am happy to offer—now and forever."

She smiled at his impetuous confession, confident that his affection and interest would remain unchanged. Now and forever.

The following morning, Lord Buxton arrived before breakfast, alone, asking for a private conference with Darcy. He requested to speak with Maud, and the young woman, pale and overwhelmed by emotion, agreed.

The meeting took place in the library, and Darcy remained present, but he took a book and diligently read it in the opposite corner of the large room. He tried not to hear anything. What he did notice was the young earl speaking most of the time while his partner barely voiced a few words.

The discussion lasted about half an hour. Afterwards, Maud silently returned to her duties while Lord Buxton addressed Darcy in an apparent state of distress.

"I thank you for your considerate support, Cousin. It is likely that I shall remove Maud from here in a couple of days."

"She chose to take your offer, I understand?"

"She has not given me a definite answer yet, but I suspect she was ashamed by your presence. I have no reason to doubt her decision. Surely, she can see how generous and convenient my arrangement is for her."

"I am sure she does," Darcy answered sternly.

After a glass of brandy, the viscount left, and Darcy went in search of his wife. He found her in the drawing room, looking through the window. They exchanged a glance before he put his arms around her and she leant her back against him.

He kissed her cheeks just near her earlobe and said, "It seems he made her a very advantageous offer—he said—and it is likely she will accept it."

She entwined her hands with his. "As you said: the decision belongs to her. Let us go and search for Georgiana; she must be waiting for us."

The following morning after breakfast, the three Darcys were in the library when Molly discreetly entered and whispered to her mistress that Maud was waiting outside and asked for a few minutes of their time.

"Please send her in," Elizabeth said, slightly uneasy at the prospect of having the conversation in the presence of Georgiana.

The young woman stepped in hesitantly, stopping at a respectful distance from them, keeping her eyes down and her hands clenched in front of her. She looked even thinner than before, her unusual paleness showing her distress and lack of sleep.

"I beg your forgiveness for disturbing you. I wished to thank you again for your kindness and to tell you that I have decided to leave. I cannot say how grateful I am; I will pray for you all my entire life."

"You want to leave?" Georgiana asked in complete surprise. "But why?"

"Georgiana, we knew that Maud might make this decision; we respect it and wish her all the best," Elizabeth answered gently. "Maud, when do you expect to move? I will make arrangements to have your services repaid."

"Oh no, ma'am—you need not pay me; I am already in debt to you and the master."

"But Maud, did you find another situation? Where will you go? You are barely recovered," Georgiana asked with genuine concern.

"I did not, Miss Darcy; I will return home to my mother—in Oxfordshire."

Elizabeth and Darcy glanced at each other in disbelief then stared at the young woman.

"You return to your village?" Elizabeth could not refrain from inquiring. "We were under the impression that— Oh, please forgive me, I did not mean to intrude."

"I believe it is best, ma'am. I do not want to cause any more trouble to you or to your *family*. I would like to stay and repay you for your kindness with all my power if things were different. But as it is, I am afraid nothing good would come from my staying."

"Oh…this is entirely unexpected—very surprising," Elizabeth continued, and her husband's countenance showed he was of the same opinion.

"So…" Darcy rose from his armchair and took a few steps toward the young woman, watching her carefully. "You wish to travel such a great distance in your present state, but you refuse the payment Mrs. Darcy offers you. May I ask how you plan to do that?" Darcy's voice, although kind, startled the young woman who glanced at him with apparent fear.

"I will go talk to my aunt. Perhaps she can help me find a way…"

"I see…and do you think you will find employment in your village? I suspect it will not be easy, or otherwise, you would not have left before."

"I am not certain, sir…but we will try…"

"Do your mother or siblings have jobs? Do you have other family there? Other relatives?"

"No—only the aunt who works here in London. My eldest brother—he is fourteen—works for anybody who might need him. He is very hardworking. My mother works too: she used to sew and stitch and even make dresses for the ladies in the neighbourhood. She still does so, but her fingers are weak, and she is a little slow now…and there are few ladies left. The village is very small."

"Your mother knows how to make gowns? Then, did she teach you to sew? Mrs. Hamilton told me you are very talented," Elizabeth asked, growing more curious. The notion that a young servant who had suffered so much—with no means and no certain future—had the strength and dignity to refuse the proposal of a viscount was equally astonishing and impressive. It was evident that Darcy's thoughts matched hers. His preoccupation made his features severe and impossible to read.

"Yes, ma'am; when she was young, my mother spent a few years in Paris, working for a modiste. She knows how to create all sorts of dresses and bonnets and reticules. She was very good at it…then she married my father and returned to Oxfordshire until he passed away five years ago. He had poor lungs."

All three Darcys looked at the young woman as if they had just begun to see her clearly. The maid's sadness quickly overwhelmed both Elizabeth and Georgiana. Darcy continued to watch her then spoke solemnly.

"Maud, you said you feel indebted to Mrs. Darcy and wish to repay her kindness. There might be a way for you to do that if you still wish to."

The woman's eyes widened in disbelief, and then she turned to Elizabeth, searching for help. However, both Elizabeth and Georgiana were puzzled and astounded by Darcy's unexpected demand.

"Of course, master. If I can do anything at all…"

"I imagine you do not know it, but we own an estate in Derbyshire named Pemberley. It is actually very large. Only five miles away, there is a little town—Lambton—that is closely connected to Pemberley. Mrs. Darcy's aunt also lived in Lambton years ago."

There was complete silence, everybody waiting eagerly for the master to reveal his intentions.

"Lambton has not had a good seamstress in years. There is a shop where a Mr. Martin sells clothing for ladies and gentlemen, but there is nobody to repair or to alter them. Mr. Martin is in his late sixties, and he takes care of the shop by himself. There is only so much he can do. Having a gown restored may take weeks to be sent to London and back, and it can be very expensive. And since we all plan to spend most of our time at Pemberley and we also expect a large party of visitors for the entire summer, I can foresee a significant waste of time and money for us."

Maud looked still completely lost, but Elizabeth smiled graciously at her husband while Georgiana's eyes suddenly widened in understanding.

"Oh, that is true! Mr. Martin is a very nice man, but he brings the gowns from London, and they are often unsuitable. I remember that last year Mrs. Annesley and I needed some bonnets, and we had to order them by mail—and we received them only in the autumn."

"So, Maud, here is my request: What would you say to a move to Lambton, together with your family? You would be in charge of the daily clothing needs for Pemberley's inhabitants, and you would also serve the people of Lambton. You may work for Mr. Martin first; I am sure he will be pleased to expand his business. And we would also need extra help at Pemberley if your brother would be interested in working for us."

Maud stopped breathing and lowered herself to the nearest chair; then she rose to her feet in a hurry, apologising and hardly capable of speaking coherently.

"Oh, master, this is…could it be true? This is…would it be possible?"

Her distress grew, and the tears rolled down her cheeks while she continued to mumble her gratitude and disbelief. Darcy only dismissed her with a severe gesture, which could barely conceal his own emotions.

"Do I understand that you agree?"

The maid nodded, still tearful.

"Very well, I shall send Miles to you later so that you can provide him all the details regarding the location of your family. If your mother agrees, you will all be residing in Lambton by the end of next month. You may retire now; we will ring for you if you are needed again."

Maud kept nodding at his every word, took a few steps, then returned to them again, and said, her lips trembling, "If I gave my life for you, it would still not be enough to repay you."

Elizabeth smiled at her warmly, but Darcy dismissed her again with all seriousness.

"Maud, you have every reason to be grateful to Mrs. Darcy, but for my part, I am not doing you any favour. I only demand you provide the services we lacked until now, and you will be paid for it accordingly. I do the same with everyone who works for me."

"Of course, Mr. Darcy, please forgive my foolishness. I will do everything to rise to your expectations," she answered, struggling to control her tears when she understood the master would accept no sign of gratitude.

Maud left, and from outside the door, her sobbing could be clearly heard.

"Oh, brother, you are the kindest man that ever lived," Georgiana said, embracing him.

"I am hardly that, dearest. Now that we are done with this, let us change and go for a ride; the weather is beautiful."

When they went to change clothes, the solitude of their apartment allowed Elizabeth to kiss her husband and say, "You are indeed the best and kindest man who ever lived, my love. And very poor at receiving thanks and gratitude."

He embraced her tightly, caressing her tenderly.

"My beloved, I am honestly telling you there is no need for gratitude. I have done everything out of the most selfish reasons. It is my intention to spend a lot of time outside showing you the beauties of Pemberley, and I suspect I will ruin many of your gowns. So you will need frequent and affordable replacements."

Elizabeth remained speechless at that shameless assertion then burst out in laughter until her lips were captured in a passionate kiss—a promise of his previous statement.

THE SAME EVENING, JUST BEFORE DINNER, LORD BUXTON RETURNED, AND another meeting took place in the library. His astonishment at receiving Maud's response angered him, and he was only calmed by Darcy's presence. Maud could barely stand, yet her determination remained unmoved.

Eventually, the young woman excused herself and left. Rejected, the viscount expressed his displeasure and contrived several reproaches regarding Maud's ingratitude, speculating about who might have intervened to change her mind.

Darcy lost his patience. "Cousin, for heaven's sake, would you cease being ridiculous? Can you not see that this poor girl is more dignified than many other women you have met? She reasonably refused to be the cause for ruining your family."

"My family would never know, even less so being ruined. I had everything arranged."

"You are out of your mind. Your family is already ruined. Can you not see that? We tend to blame Beatrice, but are you any better?"

"Darcy, it is not for you to speak so."

"You may be right, but this girl is under our protection. She wished to return to her village, alone, without means and ready to jeopardise her life and her family's, just to separate from you. Have some pride, man! She had the strength to reject you despite the fact that she seems to be fond of you. Surely, you can recognise her worthiness. She has more wisdom and more honour than many people with important wealth and connections. She deserves a peaceful life and perhaps a good man to take care of her, although he would by no means be an earl."

"I cannot speak more of this; I will leave you now," the viscount said, trying to control his temper.

Darcy's voice remained sharp. "The feeling is mutual. Let this be the last time you call on me regarding this subject. You are always welcome to our house as long as your motive is a reasonable one. And please make sure your calls follow the rules of decorum. I will not receive any more visits before breakfast or at dinner time unless it is for something of the greatest urgency."

The viscount was stunned for a moment then lifted his chin and answered with a superior air. "I will remember that. Good evening, *Mr. Darcy*."

"Good evening, *Lord Buxton*."

THREE DAYS BEFORE THE ALMACK'S BALL, ELIZABETH WAS CAUGHT BY A sense of uneasiness. She talked about it so much that Darcy teased her mercilessly and declared he would write Mr. Bennet about his favourite daughter's shocking transformation.

Georgiana—happy that she was by no means directly involved in the event—heartily supported Elizabeth and spent time in endless discussions with her.

At noon, Darcy planned to meet his uncle and cousins at the club, leaving the two ladies by themselves.

To their surprise and delight, Lady Matlock unexpectedly called at a rather unsuitable hour, which she had never done before.

Lady Matlock's appearance was as flawless as ever, but her countenance was different. She was paler and thinner, and Elizabeth worried for her. She kindly accepted the offer of tea and spent half an hour talking to her two nieces.

She then approved the dress Elizabeth had chosen for the ball, and offered more details that someone attending the event for the first time should know.

Sometime later, as Elizabeth expected, Lady Matlock changed the subject.

"Elizabeth, I was wondering what news you have about the young maid who has been ill?"

"Oh, she is well now," Georgiana answered animatedly. "Fortunately, she made a full recovery. And we have a surprise: we discovered that she is very skilful with the needle and that her mother worked for a modiste in Paris. Maud seems very nice and hardworking, and William suggested she move to Lambton with her family and work as a seamstress. Isn't it lovely?"

Lady Matlock's surprise matched her disbelief. "Move to Lambton?"

"Yes…for some reason, she wished to return home to her village, but it is unlikely they would be able to support themselves there. She said she did not want to cause more trouble to our family, but we could not possibly understand what she meant."

Her ladyship cast a quick glance at Elizabeth then turned to her young niece again.

"My dear, Elizabeth will explain to you later what Maud meant. I believe you are old enough for us to choose the truth over a tendency to protect you." She smiled at Georgiana's astonished expression and addressed Elizabeth.

"Would you mind if I talk to Maud a few moments?"

"Talk to her? I would not mind, but she might be too distressed to handle such a discussion. She is only a young and modest girl. I expect she has little experience conversing with someone of your ladyship's position, and her prior discussions with Lady Beatrice likely will make her uneasy."

"Please do not worry. I do not intend to reproach her for anything—quite the contrary. It will not be a difficult discussion, and you may witness it if you like. Georgiana dearest, would you please excuse us for a little while? As I said, Elizabeth will talk to you later. I would be grateful for your discretion."

Georgiana was astounded, and she only nodded as she left the drawing room with a last glance to her sister-in-law. Elizabeth, heavy-hearted and concerned for what would follow, sent for Maud.

"I imagine my son visited Maud. I expected him to make a convenient proposal. He seemed determined to…preserve this connection. I do not approve of his behaviour, but he is my son, and I will become accustomed to what he decides. I have little choice."

"Lady Ellen…" Elizabeth tried to interrupt her, but the lady continued in her impressive voice.

"This is precisely what I want to talk to Maud about—to tell her we do not condemn her. Although I could never show my acceptance in public or have any kind of relationship with her when in company, I do not intend to disturb her tranquillity in any way. And if she had my son's child, I would have happily supported him. But what is this story that she will move to Lambton? Did my son purchase a house there?'"

"Lady Ellen, the viscount did come with a proposal for her…and she refused him. As Georgiana already told you, she declared a wish to avoid further scandal and decided to return home. She also refused any payment from me as she considered herself already in my debt. She was ready to walk all the way back to Oxfordshire. We have rarely seen such courage and dignity. That is why William proposed she move to Lambton."

Lady Matlock frowned, and then her eyebrows rose in disbelief. She dropped to the settee, looking inquiringly at Elizabeth for further details.

"She refused Thomas? So she has no affection for him? I was certain she would accept him. I do not intend to be insensitive, but very few girls in her position would reject an easy way of living. I can hardly believe she did it."

"We first suspected that she would readily accept his offer because she does seem to hold him in regard. And in truth, it would have been an easy and advantageous option. Many girls in her position would have accepted it. I cannot say what influenced her decision, but she refused him and remained unmoved. I believe it mattered that our families are related, and she did not want to disappoint us."

"This is quite astonishing," Lady Matlock whispered.

A knock on the door made Elizabeth open it to meet a shy and apparently frightened Maud. Elizabeth smiled encouragingly.

"Maud, I invited you here because there is someone who would like to talk to you. I promise you have no cause for concern. This is Lady Matlock; she is our aunt and—"

"Oh, dear Lord!" Maud exclaimed, all the blood draining from her face. It was clear that she recognised her ladyship, and the shock made her nearly faint.

Elizabeth was not surprised by the reaction; even when she smiled, Lady Matlock was an impressive and intimidating presence, not only for a young maid but for everybody who knew her.

"I am sorry," Maud said, meeting the lady's gaze for only an instant.

Lady Matlock stepped closer until she could observe Maud carefully. The young woman—looking almost like a child—was thin and pale, and her brown eyes seemed too large for her small face.

Her ladyship spoke kindly. "Maud, I do not wish to disturb you. I only came to see you and to speak to you for a moment—to apologise for all the suffering you had to endure from our family and for the tragic loss, which I can well understand."

"Oh..." Maud's face coloured instantly, and she appeared even more frightened. "I beg you not to say that...you cannot apologise to me..."

"I can and I need to, Maud. I know everything that you went through, and I regret it. Is there anything I can do for you? May I help you in any way?"

"Your ladyship must not show me so much kindness because I do not deserve it. Everything that happened was my fault. I broke the rules, and I was punished for that. I am sorry that I caused so much trouble..." She was obviously fighting her tears, so Lady Matlock took a step back, for the first time in her life not knowing how to answer.

"I did not want to make you cry, Maud. I do not know what to do to help. I understand you decided to move to Derbyshire?"

Maud only nodded in silence.

"Would you allow me to offer you some monetary compensation to make your move easier? It must have been difficult for you and your family since you have been ill for so long. Perhaps three hundred pounds? Or more?"

Both the maid and Elizabeth startled at such an offer. Lady Matlock looked uncomfortable and glanced from one to the other. Maud lowered her head again.

"Your ladyship is very generous, but I cannot possibly accept it. I am grateful for your help, but I am well now. God has been good to me. Mrs. Darcy has been my saviour; I owe her my life. And the master has now saved my family. All is well."

"I see. So there is nothing I can do for you? Are you certain?"

Maud kept her eyes on the floor while she dared to answer. "If your ladyship is ever in Derbyshire and happens to need anything sewed or mended, I would be happy to serve you."

A small, restrained smile lifted Lady Matlock's lips.

"Matlock Manor is only twenty miles from Pemberley. I am certain I will have many gowns to repair—and so will all my acquaintances in that part of the country."

Maud's pale face lit slightly and she held Lady Matlock's gaze for a moment.

"I thank you, your ladyship."

Lady Matlock prepared to leave, and she offered her hand to Maud, who briefly took it with disbelief.

"Please do not thank me, Maud; I have truly done nothing. We are only fortunate that our faults have been remedied by the generous hearts of my niece and nephew. I trust everything will be well for you and your family now. You could not be anywhere better than under Mrs. Darcy's care."

WHEN DARCY RETURNED HOME LATER IN THE AFTERNOON, HE FOUND HIS wife and sister speaking solemnly in Elizabeth's apartment. He worried at their apparent seriousness and inquired about the subject of their conversation.

Elizabeth answered with a smile.

"Lady Matlock was here earlier. She spoke with Maud; she was very kind and considerate. And I thought I should tell Georgiana the details of the story she did not know yet."

"I am glad you did, and I thank you for trusting me, Elizabeth," Miss Darcy whispered.

Darcy frowned, searching his young sister's face for a sign of distress.

Elizabeth continued. "I was reluctant to do it too, but I believe Lady Matlock was correct in her opinion. Georgiana is wise and old enough for us to choose the truth over the tendency to protect her."

Darcy kissed his wife's hand and smiled at his sister.

"I will always protect you both—always. But I agree with you: my dear sister has grown very wise. I may say that Maud's story has changed us all in a certain way. We have all grown older and wiser."

Chapter 17

On the afternoon of the Almack's ball, the Darcys received a visit from the Gardiners—with Becky and Margaret—as well as Mr. and Mrs. Bingley. Nearer to the hour of departure, the colonel made his appearance.

Darcy, already dressed for the event, invited the gentlemen to join him in the drawing room while the ladies vanished into Elizabeth's apartment as soon as they arrived. Even Becky showed less attention to Darcy than at any other time, explaining to him in a hurry that she could not talk to him because she must "go help Lizzy be more beautiful than ever."

Darcy laughed and rolled his eyes toward his companions. "I find it difficult to understand women in general and my wife in particular. She has always been amused by the stiffness of society rules regarding balls and the season. And suddenly, she is nervous and worried about this ball as if it were an event to change our lives. She has tried on three dresses and changed her mind about which to wear. In my opinion, any of the three would be perfect. They are spectacular gowns and fit her wonderfully. In truth, I firmly believe she looks lovely in any dress."

"Of course, you do; that is why you married her," the colonel said with a laugh.

Darcy continued, mostly joking. "And even stranger, she seems displeased if I tease her—she, who has always been a master of teasing. Not to mention my own sister is equally preoccupied though she is not even attending the ball. And she is also displeased about my teasing."

"Well, Jane has also spoken about this ball for more than a week although she will not attend either. She woke up this morning so anxious to come here that she was counting the hours."

"Yes, my wife is the same," Mr. Gardiner admitted. "However, I can easily understand it. We never could have imagined that someone from our family would ever be admitted to Almack's. It is truly something that—in some ways—has changed our lives. And she is already talking about Lizzy's presentation at court. It is not about the event itself, but its meaning. It is also a responsibility for Lizzy to appear at her best and to rise to the expectations of her position. My wife says that the impression Lizzy makes among the members of the ton may affect the success of Miss Darcy's coming out, as well as of your children in the future. But of course, we might be wrong as we are very far removed from this."

"Both you and Mrs. Gardiner are correct, sir," the colonel intervened. "My mother has always insisted upon the rules and about what society demands from its members. For Mrs. Darcy, the stress must be enormous. It will be her first appearance at Almack's at my mother's invitation. She will be observed, judged, criticised. Every detail must be perfect, from her appearance to her introduction to the seven patronesses. I have always mocked these details, precisely because I have been part of it my entire life, but I understand Mrs. Darcy's nervousness."

Darcy nodded, offering his guests more brandy. "Do not consider me insensitive to my wife's concerns. I know how she feels, and I have tried to support and protect her. I even considered opposing my aunt's insistences—no matter how genuine they were. But I know Elizabeth is brave and determined. She would succeed at anything she wishes to accomplish."

"I believe the same," Mr. Gardiner answered. "I dare say Lizzy must be left to handle everything that comes with her new title. She will have equal advantages and responsibilities as Mrs. Darcy, and she has to honour them accordingly."

"I have no doubt she will; she already does," Darcy added. "I imagine this is what preoccupies Elizabeth the most—the legacy and expectations she has to meet in her new position. I have no doubt that Miss Elizabeth Bennet would have been more relaxed than Mrs. Elizabeth Darcy is."

"Miss Elizabeth Bennet would have never been admitted to Almack's," said Mr. Gardiner. "We must accept the truth: none of us will ever be, not even Jane and Mr. Bingley. It is not about the expensive fees for admission and for the ticket to each ball; I would have gladly made this sacrifice for my wife. What makes it prohibitive are the rigid and sometimes absurd rules of approval. Forgive me for being so blunt. Some of my business partners who are respectable gentlemen of good breeding complain about the same thing."

The colonel laughed. "Please do not apologise, I completely agree with you, and I know that Darcy does as well. The noble patronesses are more powerful and more severe than politicians or generals. I wonder whether they are the same in their private lives. I would be frightened to be the husband of any of them."

"Caroline and Louisa have tried to secure a voucher for years with no success," Bingley said. "But I am rather relieved. I can well live without it. And I hope Jane is not too disappointed either."

"I am sure Jane will live very well without it too," Mr. Gardiner assured him.

"My sisters, however, I am afraid will never forgive Mrs. Darcy for being accepted," Bingley continued. "I believe we will have to spend this summer without them."

They were interrupted by Becky barging in, red-faced, her curls dancing on her temples.

"Lizzy is ready, and she will come right away. Mama says she is so beautiful that you will all faint when you see her. I did not faint, but you had better sit down," the girl informed them solemnly.

Darcy caressed her hair and attempted to ask more, but the girl was overwhelmed by excitement, so she hurried to open the door widely.

A gasp of surprise escaped the gentlemen in four different voices when Mrs. Darcy—blushing with nervousness and smiling somehow awkwardly—entered the drawing room.

She wore a dress of pale gold lace gliding over a white slip satin fabric, trimmed in gold and white cording. The bottom of the dress was garnished with a row of pale gold roses that moved elegantly with every step, allowing a lovely view of her ball slippers.

For jewellery, she chose a set of elegant pearls with matching earrings and a bracelet over her white satin gloves. Her dark hair was arranged in perfect curls, ornamented with delicate white flowers.

She stopped, looking at her husband, her smile widening. He said nothing, only stared at her, mesmerised.

"I considered wearing the ruby set that you offered me on our engagement, but I thought it would be too strong a colour," she whispered.

"You look so beautiful…you completely bewitch me. You are just perfect." Darcy stepped closer, taking her hand and briefly touching it to his lips. "Just perfect."

Mrs. Gardiner, Jane, Georgiana, Becky, and Margaret looked happy and content that they had been part of such a special evening and contributed to Elizabeth's preparations. Outside in the hall, Darcy spotted Mrs. Hamilton and Molly looking at their mistress with pride and gratification.

Becky pulled on Darcy's coat. "Mr. Darcy, will you faint? Should you not sit?"

He laughed and kissed the top of the girl's head. "I almost did, my dear. Thank you for your care."

Mr. Gardiner gently embraced his niece. "I am so proud of you, Lizzy," he whispered.

Bingley struggled to form a compliment, yet he seemed overwhelmed by the moment. The colonel intervened, bowing to Elizabeth.

"Mrs. Darcy, you look astonishing. May I take advantage of this opportunity and ask you for the first set? I am sure that, once you enter the ballroom, your card will be full in no time."

Elizabeth released a small laugh, glancing at her husband.

"I would gladly accept your invitation, Colonel. Since dancing together is unfashionable for spouses, there will be no other gentleman in all of Almack's with whom I would like more to dance," she answered.

She held her husband's arm tightly and continued. "But I very much doubt anyone will be interested in my dance card. I am sure there will be so many unmarried, young, beautiful ladies that the gentlemen will barely have time to dance with them all. I confess I am quite curious about this evening. I have received such different reports and I have read so many things in magazines that I hardly know what to expect."

"You should not have too high expectations, Mrs. Darcy. It will be crowded and noisy and not at all luxurious—quite different from the private balls you have already attended. There are no truly elegant arrangements, the food is average at best, and there are no real drinks—*men's* drinks I mean. Who can go through an entire night without any brandy or wine?"

"I would say my cousin's description is entirely accurate," Darcy concluded, caressing his wife's hand.

Elizabeth's eyes brightened with amusement. "It sounds rather unpleasant. I wonder why so many people are desperate to be admitted there. Why is it a mark of accomplishment?"

"I have been wondering about that for almost fifteen years since I first attended," the colonel replied. "I cannot understand how these balls have gained such high importance and how the ladies who patronise it have grown so powerful."

"It is said that one is not considered truly important if one has not been admitted to Almack's," Mrs. Gardiner intervened. "I, too, wonder who the first was to say it, but it has become a truth universally acknowledged."

"True; but I would say it is rather a hunting ground for prospective spouses," Darcy said, glancing at his wife and pleased to see her more soothed.

Becky moved near Elizabeth and gently touched her gown. "Lizzy, will you keep this dress to give to Margaret when she goes to the balls? She says she likes it very much."

"Becky!" young Margaret cried to her sister, blushing in embarrassment at such a daring request.

Elizabeth addressed both girls. "When you are old enough to attend balls and parties, you will have new dresses as beautiful as this one. Your mother and I will take care of it."

Margaret's eyes widened in delight while Becky waved her small hand to dismiss the proposal.

"I do not care much for balls and parties, and such a dress looks very uncomfortable. How could I walk in it? May I have the pony Mr. Darcy promised me instead?"

Elizabeth kissed her cheeks. "Of course, my dearest. But I hope you will change your opinion about dresses."

"I will not. But some biscuits would be lovely. All these arrangements make me hungry," Becky said decidedly to general amusement.

"Georgiana will give you everything you need, my dear, but we must leave now," Elizabeth said. "We cannot afford to be a single minute late, or else we will not be allowed inside. The doors close at a precise hour."

"If that happens, we will gladly return home to have dinner with you," Darcy added with mockery while Elizabeth threw him a scolding glare.

Arm in arm, they finally left the house with a last glance and warm farewell from their relatives. The colonel followed them, and the carriage departed at a steady pace.

The Bingleys and Gardiners remained to have dinner with Miss Darcy, sharing questions and speculations about what would happen at the ball.

Becky enjoyed her biscuits while young Margaret Gardiner dreamed of the day when she would finally attend her first ball.

ONCE AT THEIR DESTINATION, THE CARRIAGE BARELY FOUND A PLACE TO stop among so many others. The gentlemen exited first, and Darcy helped his wife to step out.

Secure in her footing, Elizabeth glanced around. Her eyes widened at the large gathering of people and carriages. There must have been over five hundred participants, she guessed.

Most of those in attendance were walking toward the large door while others were waiting in front of the building.

Darcy noticed the direction of her gaze and whispered, "The people over there were invited as guests but have not been fully accepted by the patronesses. They still await the final decision."

Elizabeth's eyes widened in surprise. "So they just stay there to find out whether or not they will be allowed to enter? It must be very unpleasant. They all seem to be people of consequence."

"They are; otherwise, they would not have been here in the first place. I warned you there were some peculiar rules at this institution."

Darcy put her hand on his arm and covered it with his own. Elizabeth could feel his tender reassurance and protection while they continued to walk toward the entrance.

She tried to remember the persons she had met before and their names so as to be prepared to greet them.

It was easy to notice that some looked at her with curiosity. However, the advantage of such a crowded event was that each had their own interest, and many were completely oblivious to her presence, so she felt more at ease.

Before the entrance, they met Lord and Lady Matlock, and a little distance away Lord Buxton and Lady Beatrice were waiting. All seven walked together as a small party.

"Your appearance is flawless," Lady Matlock addressed Elizabeth.

"You look very charming, indeed," Lord Matlock confirmed.

"Thank you." Elizabeth smiled warmly.

Lady Matlock continued. "Darcy, please do me a favour and do not even consider dancing with your own wife tonight. I would not want there to be any gossip on this subject."

"Very well, Aunt," he replied seriously then leant to his wife, whispering, "I will impatiently wait to return home and dance with you there—at least two sets."

Elizabeth's cheeks coloured, and her eyes sparkled with amusement while a chill ran down her spine.

A few steps forward, at the main entrance, were all seven patronesses, sharply scrutinising every person who attempted to enter while two doormen carefully checked the tickets.

Elizabeth recognised Viscountess Castlereagh, the Countess of Sefton, and the Countess of Jersey—to whom she had been introduced at the Countess of Wellford's ball—but they looked at her as if they were seeing her for the first time.

Lord Buxton and Lady Beatrice greeted the ladies, showed their tickets, and moved forward.

Lord Matlock, the colonel, and Darcy—who still touched his wife's hand—bowed most properly and were rewarded with a smile of acknowledgement.

Lady Matlock introduced Elizabeth to the seven patronesses as being her niece, Mrs. Elizabeth Darcy, the wife of Lady Anne Darcy's son.

Elizabeth curtseyed with elegance, suddenly amused by the severity of the ladies in front of her. If only her father could see them! However, she showed perfect composure and thanked them with genuine pleasure when she received a positive comment about her choice of gown.

As they finally passed over the most challenging step, Elizabeth took her husband's arm again. She was surprised to observe Lady Matlock a little behind, speaking privately with the Countess of Jersey for a few moments. When she joined them in the main hall, Lady Matlock's face was lit by a wide smile.

She addressed Elizabeth and Darcy in a low voice to avoid being heard by the others.

"Their ladyships were amused—in a positive way—as they watched you two before you entered. It seems Darcy whispered something to you, and you blushed. They presumed that you were very nervous about meeting them and Darcy tried to encourage you. They found that quite lovely."

Elizabeth and Darcy looked at each other, wondering what made her blush. Then she remembered his comment about dancing with her at home "at least two sets," and her face and neck coloured again.

Darcy narrowed his lips to stifle his laughter and answered his aunt in all seriousness.

"Their ladyships were perfectly right. How kind of them to find that lovely."

Lady Matlock's eyebrow rose in wonder. She knew her nephew too well to miss the hidden meaning behind his words but wisely decided to end the conversation.

From the hall, they ascended by a handsome stone staircase to the ballroom of impressive dimensions, able to accommodate three times the people that were inside. The room had a brilliant appearance, being illuminated by an impressive number of candles that astonished Elizabeth. Near the ballroom, there was a tearoom and a card room.

Inside, they met Lord and Lady Pemberton and their daughter, Lady Marianne, as well as the Earl and Countess of Wellford. Lady Beatrice spoke privately with Lady Marianne while Lord Buxton preferred the company of the gentlemen.

Half an hour after their arrival, at the exact time, the music started, and the colonel stood up with Elizabeth for the first set. With enough young gentlemen in attendance, Darcy kept to his usual habit, standing by the wall and watching his wife's winsome moves. The dance steps made the gown glide around her graceful figure, and her face was brightened by a friendly smile toward the colonel.

He knew he was biased, but he was certain that she was the most beautiful woman in the entire gathering. It was not that her features were perfect, but her whole image was perfect. She seemed to have a certain glow that not even he had noticed before, and he wondered whether the dress and the jewels could have such power.

For the second set, Elizabeth had no partner, a fact that pleased Darcy exceedingly. They spent the time in discreet, private discussions, joined by the Matlocks. Occasionally, some other guests came to greet them and remained involved in the conversation. Lord and Lady Buxton still kept a distance from the rest of the family.

By the third set, Elizabeth's ball card had four more entries, information that annoyed Darcy and amused her exceedingly. Moment by moment, her spirits rose, and she felt more and more at ease among the large gathering.

For the fifth set, Elizabeth was astonished to be invited by Lord Buxton. She had not seen him since the day Maud rejected his proposal. The invitation surprised her even more as he had not addressed a single word to her since they arrived at the ball.

The first minutes passed in silence.

"It is lovely to see you here, Mrs. Darcy. I am glad we have the chance to dance—and to speak a few words," he eventually said.

"Likewise, sir."

"I hope everything is well with you?"

"Yes, sir, thank you."

"Would you tell me: How is she feeling?"

Elizabeth could not hide her surprise. She searched the gentleman's face and noticed his concern.

"Very well. Everything is as we hoped."

"I am glad to hear it. I am sure you have a poor opinion of me, Mrs. Darcy. And so does Darcy, I am sure."

"Lord Buxton, you are my husband's cousin, and I know he is fond of you. As Mr. Darcy said—we all had something to learn from this story. Some mistakes will never be remedied; others will vanish in time. We must learn to live with both of them."

"Yes…we must learn to live with our mistakes and choices…"

"And hopefully not repeat them in the future," she whispered daringly.

Lord Buxton stared at her for a moment then said nothing again until the end of the set.

Elizabeth's dancing with Lord Buxton drew the attention of Darcy, as well as of Lady Matlock and Lady Buxton. Though Darcy was slightly intrigued but easily guessed the reason behind his cousin's invitation, the two ladies showed obvious concern.

Lady Matlock moved toward her daughter-in-law.

"Are you alone? Will you not join us?"

"I thank you, but no. I am alone as Lady Marianne was invited to dance, but she will return soon. Married women rarely dance when there are unmarried women in the party."

She then turned to her mother-in-law and continued sharply. "Therefore,

I am surprised to see Mrs. Darcy's card so full. In truth, I find it strange to see Mrs. Darcy here at all. I could not have imagined that she would be admitted."

Lady Matlock's eyes narrowed with displeasure. "Mrs. Darcy is my guest. Her presence was approved by all seven patronesses, and she made a good impression on them."

"That is because your ladyship took so much trouble to support her. You hosted a ball for her when she was barely engaged to Darcy, and now you have used your power and connections to bring her here when so many other people, with much more wealth and better connections, are unable to obtain a ticket."

"Elizabeth Darcy is rightfully here. Anne Darcy was one of the most admired personages at Almack's. Her elegance, her beauty, her perfect manners are still remembered. And her private balls were always highly sought. She was one of the best-known members of the ton, much appreciated by her peers. The wife of her son must step into her shoes, and I am certain Elizabeth will do that flawlessly."

"I doubt that, and I cannot understand why your ladyship is so partial to her. A few months ago, she never would have imagined entering the yard of this building. Anyone can see her place is not here. She behaves awkwardly, and she keeps looking at her husband every other moment She barely knows how to act without him."

"That is completely unfair, Beatrice. Elizabeth's manners have been beyond reproach so far—and have been since I first met her. She is pleasant, lively, and charming; everybody can see that. As you yourself said: she already has many entries on her dance card. And her dancing is exquisite. I am confident your husband appreciates it."

"I have no doubt that Thomas invited her only to annoy me. If we are to speak of manners and behaviour, you must admit that your sons are far from being without reproach. It seems he shows more attention to Mrs. Darcy than to his own wife—just as your ladyship does. Everybody notices your entire family's unfair treatment of me. And still, I am the one blamed and accused of being cruel and inconsiderate."

Lady Matlock frowned, her face pale at the storm of accusations. She looked around, worried that somebody might hear the outrageous discussion. Fortunately, there was no one near them, so she said in a barely audible voice, "Beatrice, please keep your tone down and guard your countenance. Surely, you are aware that you, too, are observed and judged. As you know, neither your wealth, position, nor title is enough to ensure you a voucher next season if your presence is considered undesirable."

"I am certain you would make no effort to take my side if that were the case."

"And what side do you mean? Do not believe me oblivious to the real reason for your unreasonable anger against Elizabeth. Your attitude is rather childish. I expected more wisdom and decorum from you."

"Should my husband—your son—not show more wisdom and decorum too?"

"Yes, he should. But all men should, and quite a few actually do when it comes to a certain subject. And I admit my share of blame too. I always take responsibility for my acts. I accept my faults, and I try to remedy them when possible—that is a trait all of us should have our entire lives. Not admitting one's wrongs shows a lack of both maturity and character. Persisting in our own errors is foolish and leads to ridicule."

The younger lady averted her eyes; her lips were tight, attempting to conceal her anger.

Lady Matlock continued. "You have been wrong in dealing with a certain situation. You are wrong in your behaviour towards Elizabeth. You have been wrong in your attitude towards us since the moment you married Thomas. Will you not accept any of these errors?"

"I will not. I have done nothing wrong. Your ladyship has always been cold and distant to me."

Lady Matlock appeared surprised. "I was certain that was the kind of relationship you preferred. As you might remember, from the first day of your marriage, you have often reminded us that your father is a marquess and that your grandfather was a duke, and that placed you above us. And indeed, he was—God rest him in peace—and we remember him quite vividly as a very pleasant and generous man with questionable passions, which left his family close to ruin. I entertained no hopes that you married my son for love."

Lady Buxton blushed slightly then responded sharply. "We all know it was a marriage advantageous for us both—as all marriages should be among respectable members of the ton. People of our position do not neglect their duties by marrying someone below them. I heard your ladyship say that many times."

"So it was. And I remember everything I said. But I hoped you would come to grow affectionate toward each other. You are both handsome, educated, and accomplished—yet you appear even more distant to each other than at the beginning of your life together."

"It is not my fault; I have done everything that was my duty. I cannot imagine what more you can expect from me. What do you want from our marriage that would please you?"

"I do not expect anything, Beatrice, nor is it my right to want anything. Only...come, take a look at Elizabeth—just for a moment, although I know that gives you little pleasure. As you see, she is not by any means more handsome than you, but she is all liveliness and genuine smiles. Therefore, she raises the admiration of those around her. And she is glowing every time she glances at her husband. Now look at Darcy. We all knew him to be a severe, aloof man. Watch his expression when he gazes at his wife. Read the love on his face. I would say this is a marriage advantageous for both."

Lady Beatrice grimaced with restrained anger. "Surely, your ladyship cannot believe that. I am certain you never would have approved your son marrying someone of such a low situation in life."

"Most likely, I would have not. But I feel compelled to admit my errors and to admire Darcy's excellent judgement."

Lady Beatrice averted her eyes in disapproval, her anger mixed with obvious distress. Lady Matlock breathed deeply and spoke more warmly. "Beatrice, let us not argue anymore. I do not wish to upset you further. We may continue this conversation on another day if you like. I am willing to search for a way to improve our relations if you wish to. But we have been separated from the others for too long, and this is neither the time nor the place for such a delicate discussion. Let us return to our group."

The younger lady seemed surprised, and for a moment, she seemed to not know how to reply.

"You are correct, of course. We should return. I should not have started an argument here. I would not be opposed to talking. We might have tea one day..."

"That would be lovely..." Lady Matlock said conciliatorily.

They took a few steps when, unexpectedly, the Countess of Sefton approached them. They were both surprised and even more so when her ladyship started to talk.

"Lady Matlock, Lady Beatrice. I must say it is a pleasure to see such a strong bond between a mother and a daughter-in-law. We observed you for several minutes. It is quite unusual that, even in such large company, you found a few moments for a private conversation. I am sure that you, Lady Buxton, may learn from your mother-in-law."

She waited for no answer before she turned toward Lady Matlock.

"As for your guest, Mrs. Darcy, we have no reason to regret our approval. She seems a pleasant young woman with proper manners—and quite skilful at dancing. Although we cannot approve Darcy's choice—and I am certain he would have found at least equal felicity with someone from his own circle—it is rather amusing to see him smitten with his wife. Quite unusual but diverting nevertheless. I wonder what Lady Anne Darcy would have said about his marriage. I doubt she would have approved of it either."

"I believe she would have, my lady. After all, she too married for love, and her marriage was a very affectionate one."

"My dear Lady Matlock, as far as I know, you too married for love, but both you and Lady Anne fell in love with someone more close to your own position. I would say Darcy was less wise."

"Perhaps, but my nephew fell in love with a young lady who is the daughter of a gentleman, which makes her an honourable choice. And what she lacks in fortune, she surely compensates for in wit, charm, and excellence of character. Although many might disagree, I strongly believe Darcy made a decision that is the perfect choice for him."

"Well, well, we shall see. In the meantime, you may encourage Mrs. Darcy to apply for a voucher. We will take her application into consideration."

"Thank you. Your generosity is much appreciated."

The countess moved away to express her opinions to another group while the two ladies returned to their family, both keeping an awkward silence, both preoccupied with their previous harsh conversation.

The music stopped, and Lord Buxton accompanied Elizabeth back to her husband. He thanked her for the dance, briefly glanced at his own wife, then moved to the tearoom to talk to Lord Pemberton.

The rest of the night passed pleasantly.

Lady Beatrice still did not speak more than a few words to either Elizabeth or Darcy, nor did Lord Buxton make another attempt to approach them.

Lady Matlock declared that the evening had been a success and told Elizabeth that she was proud of her. Elizabeth, on her side, could easily see that her ladyship was still not her usual self and that she was still greatly preoccupied and distressed, but she did not dare broach the subject. She only thanked her ladyship once more for the generous care she bestowed upon her.

"There is no need to thank me, my dear. I am glad we went through this together and it turned out so well. If only everything else would go so easily in our family, I would want nothing more."

THE DAWN BROKE AS THE GUESTS FINALLY LEFT ALMACK'S. INSIDE THE carriage, Elizabeth felt tired, and she put her head on her husband's shoulder. He embraced her and caressed her hair.

"How are you, my love? You look very tired."

"I am tired but pleased—and relieved. As Lady Matlock said, I am glad it turned out well."

"Lady Matlock said you were invited to apply for a voucher. That is quite an honour from what my aunt said."

"Yes, I imagine...I am quite grateful for it. Now I am thinking..."

"Yes?"

"I look forward to going to Pemberley—only the two of us."

He pulled her closer to his chest and kissed her temple. "So am I, my love."

The Darcy house—like all the others along the street—was as silent as a quiet, dark giant, yet Elizabeth felt it to be the warmest and brightest place she knew. It was their home—the shelter of their love away from everyone and everything, away from rules and judgments and demands.

"I am so content finally to be home. I will never be comfortable in such large gatherings; besides, I need no one else but you," Darcy said, showing her once again that they think alike.

"So am I, my love," she repeated his words from a little earlier.

They entered then Darcy dismissed the footman. They were not expecting to receive any visitors for the next several hours. From below the stairs, a few voices could be heard; part of the household was already awake and attending to their duties.

Inside their suite, Molly and Miles were waiting, but Darcy told them they were not needed. Dawn was claiming its right over the night, shyly lighting the room through the half-parted curtains.

Once alone, they removed their coats and gloves; then Elizabeth glided her hands around her husband's waist.

"Will you dance with me now, Mr. Darcy?"

"I have been counting the minutes until I could do so, Mrs. Darcy."

His arms encircled her back and their bodies brushed against each other while their eyes were locked and their faces glowed in anticipation.

"And what dance will you choose, sir?"

"It does not matter. Holding you as I do now is more gratifying than any dance."

He took a step to the right, then another to the left, without allowing a single inch of distance between them. Their eyes never left each other.

"This is a wonderful dance, Mr. Darcy—lovelier than any other that might require us to separate."

"Perhaps we could try the waltz?" He smiled, and his hands stroked her arms, her nape, then lowered down her spine and stopped on her hips.

"The waltz?" She licked her lips, suddenly dry from the intensity of his stare.

"You surely have heard of it. Do you want me to teach you?"

"I did hear; I also read about it in some ladies' magazines. It appears to be rather scandalous. May I ask where you learnt it? It is well known that you are not fond of dancing—not even of the traditional, proper dances."

"Robert has friends who learnt it from some French ladies. It has been popular in other countries for some time now. I attended several parties with them last year, and I even danced a few times, but I found it rather daunting. And I enjoyed it just as little as I enjoy other kinds of dances. But now, it suddenly has grown much more appealing to me."

"It is a pity we do not have music."

"I am confident we will manage without it if you only follow my lead."

His steps changed to the rhythm of the waltz, and she tried to mirror his—first tentatively, even a little clumsily—but in a few minutes, their movements became consonant while their lips joined in a kiss.

"I suspect this is not the way the waltz is usually danced," Elizabeth murmured. "Surely, you did not hold another lady so close in your arms on a dance floor—not even at a private party."

He stole another brief kiss. "I have never held anyone else so close in my arms, my love—not on a dance floor or anywhere else. And no, this is not how the waltz is danced, but the steps are the correct ones. I am pleased to see how proficient you have become in such a short while."

"I am a very quick study of anything you teach me, my dear sir."

"So you are, my beloved wife."

Their teasing became tender whispers, the dancing steps slowed, the touches turned into caresses, and kisses silenced any whispers.

Gently, his fingers removed her hairpins and the small flowers, allowing her locks to fall freely down her back. A deep kiss intoxicated her, and, as in a dream, she felt her dress unfastened and slowly pushed down from her shoulders. Her skin first shivered from the coldness then suddenly burned under his warm hands.

Her fingers stroked his shoulders and chest then loosened his neckcloth. Their clothing fell piece by piece to the floor. Then the dance stopped, and he lifted her in his arms and carefully placed her on the bed. Light kisses, tender strokes, and passionate whispers aroused the passion inside her, and his groans betrayed his eager desire.

Then Elizabeth called his name, and he stopped, looking at her in wonder. She entwined her hands around his neck, then her legs wrapped around him.

"William, enough with restraints and worries and fears. I will have none of it. I want you to love me with all your heart and all your body. I want to feel you beside me...upon me...inside me...this very night and not a moment later."

"Elizabeth...my love..."

"Please look at me...I am fine—all will be well. I need nothing but your love, so please love me...please."

Her body slowly moved beneath his, against him, while her lips joined his to stop his whispers of weak opposition.

He struggled to stay in control for a while, then her pleas, her caresses, her warmth, her softness, and his own thirst and unleashed desire became impossible to oppose. So he surrendered, and they allowed themselves to start and end another dance together —in perfect harmony, with only the music of their hearts—which reached its completion at the same time as the daylight that flooded the room.

Chapter 18

The week following the Almack's ball was more animated than ever in Darcy's house. The long-awaited journey to Pemberley was carefully prepared by Darcy, and Elizabeth's enthusiasm grew with every day, happily shared with Georgiana.

Elizabeth was sad to separate from her relatives, but it was a comfort to know they would all reunite at Pemberley in six weeks. She knew she had no reason to worry: her sister Jane was as happy as one could hope for and she seemed more in love with her husband than ever. Her aunt, uncle, and cousins were all in excellent health, and Mr. Gardiner's business had improved due to his connections with Darcy and the Matlocks.

Her only reason for slight concern was Lady Matlock, whose strength and spirits still seemed lower than usual. It was clear that her ladyship was affected by the last week's events more than the other members of her family were. Elizabeth's suspicions were strengthened when, one morning very early, Maud returned from church in a great disturbance; at her mistress's insistent inquiry, the maid confessed that she had happened upon Lady Matlock at her son's grave. Maud and Elizabeth found this so astonishing that they did not even dare to discuss it.

Elizabeth shared her thoughts with Darcy, and both felt helpless about how to proceed further. There was nothing they could do except wait for time to heal the wounds that had proved to be deeper than they seemed.

Lady Matlock appeared to find great comfort in the presence of the two Gardiner girls. Margaret's elegant beauty and perfect manners delighted her ladyship, and Becky's wit and boldness raised her spirits and made her smile constantly. Therefore, she was quite frequently in the company of the Gardiners, even more so since Lord Matlock and the colonel also approved of Mr. Gardiner.

Elizabeth was exceedingly content and proud to see the growing relationship between her different relatives. The notion that such illustrious and fastidious people as the Fitzwilliams admitted a close connection to the family of a gentleman who was in trade was astonishing and could only be explained by the Gardiners' worthiness.

For the summer, Lord and Lady Matlock decided to retire to the Matlock estate in the last week of May. It was expected that the colonel would join them for a short while, and since Matlock was only twenty miles from Pemberley, regular visits between the two estates were eagerly anticipated.

The Gardiners, together with the Bennets and the Bingleys, planned to travel to Derbyshire at the beginning of June.

Becky promised Lady Matlock that she would visit her from Pemberley "on the pony Mr. Darcy will give me as soon as I learn to ride." Lady Matlock suggested that, in the meantime, she should come by carriage; after a short consideration, Becky accepted the wise proposal.

Among the joyful plans for the journey, Elizabeth had two reasons for uneasiness. The first was her rather frequent bouts of illness and lack of appetite. Almost daily, she felt dizzy and tired, and food made her nauseous. As she did not remember ever having felt that way in her life, she was certain it would soon pass. She was not so preoccupied with the sickness itself but rather with the distress and worry her husband would feel if he discovered it, so she decided to keep it secret. Surely, all would be fine once they arrived at Pemberley.

The second concern was her sister Lydia, who was writing her weekly, complaining that "her dear Wickham was not earning enough to cover all their expenses," and that life in a town full of soldiers was not as entertaining as she expected. Lydia even dared to suggest that Elizabeth should make her husband find Mr. Wickham a less demanding and more generously paid living. Elizabeth did not even consider opening the subject with Darcy, but she asked his opinion about ordering some gowns and having them delivered to Lydia.

"Georgiana suggested I should send my sister what she needs rather than providing her any monetary help."

"I agree, it is a wise idea. I thank you for informing me, but please do not forget that the pin money is yours to use as you want."

"I know that, William, but I could not possibly waste it carelessly. You already offered Mr. Wickham much more than he deserves, and you saved my sister's tranquillity."

Darcy gently kissed her. "Let us not talk about the past. I only did what needed to be done at the time. The only thing of which I will never approve is Wickham's presence at Pemberley. Besides, I was informed that his colonel is diligent in supervising Wickham carefully. It is likely that he will have several important responsibilities to keep him in his regiment for at least half a year. If your sister wishes to visit us alone, she would be welcome."

Elizabeth returned the kiss, caressing her husband's hand, and he needed nothing more to feel her gratitude. On the day of Lydia's marriage to Wickham, he had promised Elizabeth that he would continue to oversee Wickham even from afar and to protect Lydia as needed. And there he was—keeping his promise just as he always did.

After further consideration and a private council with her aunt and elder sister, Elizabeth decided not to suggest that Lydia visit them at Pemberley. After all, she was newly married, and she needed to spend at least one year at her husband's side and learn what marriage truly means. However, a large box with five dresses and matching bonnets was sent to Mrs. Wickham before summer began.

Three days before their departure, the Darcys hosted an informal dinner for the Bingleys and the Gardiners—a joyful time spent in the family with no distress or special arrangements. All four Gardiner children attended, bringing a breeze of joy to an already delightful evening.

"Mr. Darcy, we thank you again for your kind invitation. I still cannot believe that we will spend the summer at Pemberley. It sounds like a dream," Mrs. Gardiner said.

"And I am afraid you will change your mind in future years once you have to bear the Bennet and Gardiner families for three entire months," Mr. Gardiner said, attempting to joke.

"I am sure we will have a wonderful time together and repeat it as often as possible," Darcy answered, and Elizabeth rewarded him with a warm smile.

"Oh, I am sure it will be a lovely summer," Georgiana intervened.

"Pemberley has not hosted such a large party in a long time. I believe I was very young because I can hardly remember it. I know my mother was still with us. I must have been Becky's age."

Miss Darcy's eyes moistened from sorrow, and she smiled to conceal her sadness.

"I will be five years old in August," Becky said enthusiastically.

"And I just turned eight," Henry Gardiner added.

"Truly? My birthday will be in June," Miss Darcy said.

"Well, well—it looks as though we will have many reasons to celebrate. And we must prepare many gifts, I imagine," Darcy concluded.

"I believe being at Pemberley is enough of a gift," Mrs. Gardiner intervened.

"But can I still have a pony?" Becky inquired, her eyes full of hope.

Darcy laughed. "Of course. A promise is a promise. Have any of you ridden before?" Darcy addressed the four children.

"Yes, I have," Thomas answered in haste, pleased that he found something to single him out from his siblings.

"And I rode with Papa," Henry said.

"Very well, I am sure you will all be excellent riders by the end of the summer. And you can also swim or fish if you like."

"I am very good at fishing too," Thomas replied, and Becky looked at her elder brother with apparent envy.

"I would be very good at fishing if Papa ever took me with him," Becky said.

"You will have a chance at Pemberley," Elizabeth intervened. "And I am sure Thomas will help you. Mr. Darcy will certainly be very pleased to see you all well behaved, kind, and helpful to each other. That is what brothers and sisters do. Mr. Darcy is an exemplary elder brother for Miss Darcy."

All four children glanced at Darcy then at each other. Except for Margaret, none of them could say they behaved in an "exemplary" manner, and they suddenly worried about what the gentleman might say of their behaviour. Their concern increased when Miss Darcy related some past stories from her childhood, praising her brother's kindness. Both Thomas and Henry admitted to themselves that they needed to improve their manners toward their sisters if they ever wanted to be like Mr. Darcy.

"Well, I remember being rather naughty when I was a young boy," Bingley confessed. "I used to upset my sisters quite often."

Becky looked at him, shook her head in disapproval, then looked from him to her brothers.

"I could tell that all the boys with blond hair are nasty. This is why I like Mr. Darcy better."

Her mother almost choked on her food, red with embarrassment, and she attempted to scold her younger daughter; however, Bingley started to laugh.

"Well, Becky, I am pleased to tell you that things changed when I grew up. I rarely upset anyone now."

"I know you do not; otherwise, Jane would not marry you," Becky replied wisely.

Bingley glanced with adoration toward his wife. "That is true—so very true."

After dinner, the gentlemen retired to the library for a drink and further discussion about their travel arrangements. Although Charles Bingley had taken that trip at least four times in the past, he did not even remember the names of the inns where they were supposed to change horses or to rest for the night. So Darcy insisted on writing down all the necessary details, counting more on the attention of Mr. Gardiner than that of his friend.

In the drawing room, the ladies and the children remained to amuse themselves, the main subject still being Pemberley and the journey toward it.

"But, Lizzy, why can I not come with *you*? I am very small, and I will stay quietly in a corner. I promise I will not even speak," Becky pleaded with her cousin.

Her mother frowned and sent her a sharp gaze. "Miss Rebecca Gardiner, have we not spoken about this many times? You will travel with your parents and siblings in six weeks—and only if you all behave until then. Did we not agree on this?"

The girl shook her head energetically. "No, we did not agree. You decided alone, Mama. I hoped you would change your mind by now. I will go and ask Mr. Darcy himself."

"You will do no such a thing! We will proceed as we discussed, and I will have not another word about this," Mrs. Gardiner concluded severely. Then she softened her voice and took the girl onto her lap. "My dear, please remember what I told you. Mr. Darcy, as well as Lord and Lady Matlock, are among the most illustrious families in the country."

"Mama, is 'illustrious' good?"

"Yes, Becky, it is very good. And it is quite an honour for us to be their guests. Therefore, all of us must behave accordingly. We do not want to upset them with unreasonable requests."

"Very well, Mama, but I am heartbroken, you know."

The girl sat beside her sister Margaret, who took her hand to comfort her.

Becky continued solemnly. "I am sure Mr. Darcy will never be upset with me. He is always kind to me. I will have a pony at Pemberley. I am his favourite!"

"I think you are Mr. Darcy's *third* favourite after Lizzy and Miss Darcy," Thomas corrected her. "And he is always kind to all of us because that is how a gentleman behaves. I know because I am a gentleman too."

Becky frowned in displeasure at her brother's contradiction, but she found no good reason to contradict him. Eventually, she had a reply.

"If you are a gentleman, why are you here with us and not in the library? Men should stay with men and girls with girls."

"Because mama did not allow it."

"That is because you are not a gentleman but a boy," Becky crowed triumphantly.

Young Thomas remained disconcerted for a few minutes, looking at his sister and searching for a sharp reply. He then felt the ladies' gaze upon him—especially the lovely eyes of the beautiful Miss Darcy—and he straightened his back, answering with dignity.

"But I am a gentleman even if I am boy. And someday, I will be just like Mr. Darcy. You will see."

Becky shrugged her shoulders, not quite impressed with her brother's statement. "And I will be just like Lizzy. Only I will not marry you because you are my brother. And anyway, I will not marry anyone—ever. And you have blond hair like Mr. Bingley not like Mr. Darcy."

"Mr. Bingley is a most excellent man. I would like for you to grow up like him," Jane intervened.

Elizabeth laughed. "I am very pleased to have two young gentlemen and two young ladies as my cousins. As for the matter of marriage, let us talk again in about fifteen years or so. In the meantime, you should finish your biscuits because we will all go to sleep very soon. Even the strongest gentlemen and the most courageous ladies need rest."

ON THE LAST DAY OF APRIL WITH DAWN BARELY UPON THE TOWN, TWO carriages filled with people and luggage left London and headed north. One held the Darcys and the other Molly, Miles, Maud, and two other servants.

Elizabeth decided to take Summer—the beautiful mare bought by her husband—to Pemberley. Secretly, she hoped they would not return to Town for the rest of the year, and she could not bear to be separated for so long from the beautiful horse that helped her improve her riding skills. Darcy told her that they had other horses at Pemberley, but he supported her decision and made the travel arrangements accordingly.

The journey to Pemberley was as beautiful as it was difficult for Elizabeth. Her joy and eagerness to reach her new home was overshadowed by her illness, which turned worse from spending so many hours in the carriage. Even more distressing for her was the attempt to keep her condition secret from Darcy—the man with whom she used to share every thought and feeling.

Their first stop was Oxfordshire where Maud reunited with her family. It was unlikely that Maud confessed the whole truth to her mother except that her present employers offered them the chance to move to Derbyshire and make a living from tailoring.

The flood of gratitude and tears bestowed upon them by Maud's mother and four siblings was overwhelming. Darcy announced that in three weeks' time a carriage would fetch them with all their belongings and move them to Lambton where a house would await them. He tried to avoid their thanks, insisting once again that it was a decision made to favour all the parties involved, especially Mrs. and Miss Darcy, who would be the main beneficiaries of the alliance. However, Maud repeated that they had saved her life and now were saving her family's too, and the emotions became difficult to bear.

Eventually, they took their farewell and continued the journey, spending the night at an inn in Oxford.

Despite Elizabeth's efforts, Darcy noticed that she was unwell and lacked an appetite. She insisted she was only tired and fell asleep very early. Most of the night, he watched her sleeping, and from time to time he touched her forehead to be certain she was not feverish. He blamed himself for not worrying more about the small things he observed when they were in London and for not asking Dr. Harris's opinion on the matter.

The second day, they travelled through Warwickshire. Elizabeth felt better, and she was delighted to admire all the beauties that passed before them. They stopped every two hours for rest, tea, and refreshments and took a longer break to visit the Castle of Kenilworth then remained overnight in an inn on the border of Derbyshire.

The third day started at dawn, and Elizabeth's spirits rose with every minute that brought her closer to Pemberley. Darcy and Georgiana also grew more animated, sharing memories of their past journeys and stories from bygone years, to which Elizabeth listened with interest and delight.

On the way, they passed by Chatsworth and the Matlock estate—of which Elizabeth grew fond immediately. She was in awe at seeing Matlock Manor—one of the most beautiful places she ever beheld—where the elegance of the building matched the natural beauty that surrounded it.

"It is so perfectly fit to Lady Matlock," Elizabeth said. "Just beautiful."

"True," Darcy agreed. "Besides Pemberley, I believe it is the property I admire the most. Of course, I might be biased because Chatsworth—and several others—are also remarkable. As soon as the Matlocks are settled for the summer, we will visit them."

"Oh, yes—the entire trip from Pemberley to Matlock is a delight," Georgiana said.

Elizabeth smiled. "My soul is already so full of beauty and joy that I wonder how I can bear more."

"Just wait a little longer until we reach Pemberley," answered Georgiana. "I still wonder at its beauties every time I return to it. As Becky said, I might seriously consider never marrying and never being forced to leave Pemberley."

Darcy frowned then answered in earnest.

"I cannot be opposed to that idea. Having you married and leaving Pemberley is not something I am pleased to consider."

Elizabeth laughed and took her husband's arm. "As I told Becky, let us discuss this matter of marriage in a few years. First, we must organise Miss Darcy's coming out. I am sure it will be an event to remember among the ton."

"My coming out?" Miss Darcy panicked at the mere prospect of being the centre of attention in London, and Elizabeth laughed again.

"I wonder how it is possible that both of you are so reluctant to attend balls and parties. From what I have heard, Lady Anne Darcy was one of the most admired ladies of her time and a perfect hostess for exquisite entertainments."

"She was indeed," Darcy agreed in a light tone. "And Georgiana resembles her very much. But certain traits we surely took more from our father."

"I would wish to have learnt more things from our mother, but I was not old enough. I barely remember her at all," Georgiana whispered.

Elizabeth's heart ached, and she gently took her sister's hands in hers. "I am sorry if I saddened you, my dear. I should not have brought up this subject."

"Please do not apologise, Elizabeth. It was not your fault. I am always a little sad when I speak of my parents."

Darcy covered their joined hands with his.

"I believe we should talk about our parents as often as we can—and with no sadness but with love and gratitude. Let us bring joy back to Pemberley. There were so many things our mother wished to do, and she had not the time for them. I know she left a book with all her notes. If you agree, I believe you should read it together. She would certainly be proud to see you both following in her footsteps—including the balls and parties."

Elizabeth and Georgiana were both tearful while they struggled to smile.

"William, I think Mama and Papa would be happy to meet Elizabeth."

"I believe the same, dearest. And they would certainly be happy to see you only one month before your sixteenth birthday."

A short pause helped him regain his composure, and he suddenly changed his tone.

"I hope you are prepared for an enthusiastic reception from Mrs. Reynolds because we have just entered the Pemberley grounds."

Georgiana sighed, Elizabeth gasped, and both leant toward the small windows. Darcy asked the coachman to slow the pace of their carriage while the other one continued on its way.

Elizabeth looked out, mesmerised, her heart racing while she waited for the first appearance of Pemberley. She felt her husband's arm encircling her shoulders, and she enjoyed his comforting presence.

As if guessing her eagerness, he whispered, "Pemberley Manor is still far away; we have about half an hour of travel yet."

"Oh...I never imagined the estate to be quite so vast."

Georgiana chuckled. "Now you see why we told you that it would not possible to know it by walking."

"True...I begin to understand many things better," Elizabeth answered, her attention focused to admire every remarkable beauty before her eyes.

It was full spring, and every tree, thread of grass, and flower was alive, blossoming in a harmony of green with colours that took Elizabeth's breath away.

The carriage drove for some time through a beautiful wood stretching over a wide extent. They gradually ascended for a while until they arrived at the top of the hill. There was a grove where the sunshine glittered through the trees' leaves to light and warm a carpet of wild flowers.

"Stop the carriage," Darcy demanded then opened the door and allowed Elizabeth out.

"There is something I want to show you, my love."

She released a cry of surprise and rapture when she stepped onto the high grass that caressed her ankles. Careful not to harm the flowers, she held her husband's hand and followed him while Darcy pulled her forward.

"Here. This is the highest point of the estate. And there is our home."

Elizabeth remained still as if she had fallen under a spell.

Her eyes, widened in astonishment, were instantly caught by Pemberley House, situated in a valley in the midst of an impressive park backed by a ridge of woody hills. The green of the land perfectly complemented the serene blue of the sky, and in front of the handsome building was a majestic lake of natural splendour.

"Oh, William…this is…I have no words…"

Elizabeth pressed her hands over her chest to quiet her racing heart as she marvelled at her future home. She felt her husband's palms on her shoulders and his gentle whisper.

"We should go now; we are expected. But I promise we will return soon. I have so many places to show you, my love."

"Only a moment longer, please," she pleaded, reluctant to take her eyes from the sight before her. Eventually, she followed Darcy back to the carriage while a cold shiver ran down her spine as she slowly began to understand the meaning of being the mistress of Pemberley.

Georgiana was waiting with a smile. "What do you think, Elizabeth? Do you approve of our home?"

"Do I approve? I have never seen a place more charming. It is equally as impressive as it is astonishing in its beauty. I still cannot believe that I will live here."

"You will—for the rest of our lives. And I hope you will love it as much as we do," Darcy said, holding her hand.

"I already do…" She felt her eyes burning with tears, and she forced herself to laugh to hide her emotions. "My dear Georgiana, now I fully understand why you prefer not to marry rather than leave Pemberley."

Miss Darcy laughed too. "And you have not even seen the inside of the house."

The carriage followed the road down the hill through the woods, and slowly approached the house.

When they stopped in front of the main door, Elizabeth remained still, astounded, gazing at the remarkable stone building. She hesitantly left the carriage, glancing around, and took Darcy's arm as her feet seemed unable to obey her will.

Darcy kissed her hand and entwined his fingers with hers. "We are finally home, my love."

Georgiana almost ran inside, and in front of the elegant stairs, a lady of middle age hurried to embrace the young mistress, wishing her welcome home.

"Oh, dear Lord! Miss Darcy, you are so beautiful! And so grown up! And here is the master! We are so happy that you came home earlier this year! Oh, forgive me, Mrs. Darcy; we are honoured to receive you at Pemberley. Oh, I am such a fool—I am standing in the way. I heartily apologise…"

"Mrs. Reynolds, we are happy to see you too. Elizabeth, allow me to introduce Mrs. Reynolds. She has been with us since I was four, and she is in charge of Pemberley's management. Things are going so well here because of her efforts and competence."

Elizabeth greeted the lady with a warm smile, and Mrs. Reynolds answered in a trembling voice, equally pleased and embarrassed by the praise bestowed upon her.

Finally, inside the house, Elizabeth's rapture increased at each step. She felt enchanted, awestruck, and humbled by the exquisite elegance that surrounded her. It was not only a house beautifully furnished but also a home whose beauty was equalled by its warmth and character.

Darcy briefly showed her the main rooms while Georgiana retired to her apartment.

"Sir, will Mrs. Darcy want to meet the staff today?" Mrs. Reynolds asked when they were visiting the drawing room.

"Yes, I would, thank you," Elizabeth answered. "I am quite anxious to meet them. Perhaps in an hour or so?"

"Oh, thank you, ma'am, that is so kind of you."

"Mrs. Reynolds, I will show Mrs. Darcy her suite, and we will refresh ourselves after the journey. We will have dinner very early tonight—around six o'clock. I believe it would be best if Mrs. Darcy meets the staff right before dinner. Miss Darcy and I will also assist."

"That would be perfect. Please excuse me; I will retire now. If you need anything just ring."

Darcy kissed Elizabeth's temple. "I have never seen Mrs. Reynolds so unsettled. I believe she is worried about you. She surely wants to make a good impression."

"Oh, I hope I am not so frightening. I confess I am rather unsettled too. This is so much more than I expected...such grandeur! Now I understand why people worried I might be a fortune hunter. I am quite certain any woman would put up with a great deal to be the mistress of all this," she said, her voice mixing seriousness with teasing.

"Should I be content then that you accepted me before you saw the true extent of my fortune? Can I put my mind at ease about your not marrying me for my fortune?" he teased her back, placing small kisses on her hands.

"Sir, I fell in love with you in a cottage when you were all wet and dirty. Do you need further proof? But I *do* understand why Lady Catherine and Lord Matlock accused me of trapping you in this marriage. If we had a son, I would share the same worry! Anyone he intends to marry, I shall put through many tests to be certain of her real affection."

Darcy laughed out loud. "I am slightly frightened. I hope you will not turn into Lady Catherine…"

"I am afraid I shall in regard to this point," she said with such seriousness that he laughed again then trapped her with his strong arms and her mouth with his eager lips.

She rejoiced in the tender interlude a few minutes then gently pushed him away.

"Sir, let us not risk being caught in improper situations on the first day of my arrival here."

"Have no worries—nobody would enter this room unannounced. But you are right: we should go upstairs. I will show you our chambers now and perhaps you will rest a little. You have plenty of time to become accustomed to the house."

"Very well—but tomorrow I must visit the library. My father asked me to send him a detailed report of it," she said with a laugh while clinging to Darcy's arm. He laughed again in the main hall and stole another hasty kiss.

The discovery of the master suite brought Elizabeth new reasons for delight and enchantment. It was warm and welcoming but elegant. The furniture of dark wood showed exquisite taste—similar to that in their London house. On a small table near the window, there was a rich bouquet of fresh, red roses.

Darcy did not allow her much time to admire her surroundings but invited her to the windows. Only then did she notice that her apartment—consisting of a chamber with a cabinet, a smaller room, and the bedroom—was situated on the corner of the wing. The generous windows offered a magnificent panoramic view of both the front yard and the back gardens. The trees and flowers were blossoming under the soft sun of mid-spring, and delicate, white clouds were mirrored in the clear blue lake.

Elizabeth hurried from one window to another, spellbound, glancing to her husband, then outside, and back to him again. He trapped her in his arms.

"Your eyes tell me how happy you are, my beautiful wife."

"I do not think my eyes are enough, William. Only if you could see deep into my soul would you perhaps have a glimpse of my felicity. But I cannot stop wondering whether I truly deserve to be here—whether I fit here."

He cupped her face and gently kissed her lips. "Nothing makes me happier than your happiness, my beloved. And never doubt that your place is right here—in our home and in my arms. There was never a better fit."

THE INTRODUCTION OF THE STAFF WAS SUCCESSFUL. ELIZABETH GRACIOUSLY greeted each member—assisted by Darcy and Georgiana—asked for their names and responsibilities in the house, and promised to spend the time to know everyone.

Each of them studied the new mistress with interest and curiosity, and Elizabeth could feel their scrutiny.

She knew she still had to prove herself to them, especially to those who could compare her with Lady Anne, and she was ready for the challenge. The complexity of her new duties was revealed to her step by step. The staff members were more numerous than she anticipated, which was only natural since Pemberley was so much larger than the house in London. Besides these individuals, there were the tenants and their families—not to mention Mrs. Darcy's involvement within Derbyshire's society—and many others she could not even guess at the time.

She was not worried about her capacity to live up to the demands of her position—not anymore. Her husband showed his complete trust in her so many times that she had no doubts remaining. She would have to learn, to discover, and to acquire all the information and skills she was lacking, but she was certain she would succeed. The Darcy name, the Darcy legacy, and the Darcys' love were at stake. And failing any of them was unthinkable.

Their first dinner at Pemberley was prepared with extra care, and the richness of the courses matched the elegance of the dinner table.

Elizabeth observed that the servants who brought the various plates were mostly watching her. It was only natural; they were already accustomed to Mr. and Miss Darcy's tastes in food and were now eager to please the new mistress. Mrs. Reynolds herself entered a couple of times to inquire whether everything was to their liking.

Therefore, Elizabeth was careful to taste and praise each dish, sending her appreciation to the cook. Her words brought a trace of relief to the servants' faces and a little smile of approval to her husband's lips.

During dinner, both Darcy and Georgiana amused Elizabeth with stories and vivid descriptions of the beauties she would soon discover.

With great amusement, Georgiana related to Elizabeth a story from three years before when the Bingleys were invited to spend the summer with them.

"So, William, Mr. Bingley, and I went for a ride. Miss Bingley and the Hursts refused to join us because the weather was too hot. When we returned, William stopped his horse, took off his coat and his vest, and jumped into the pond to cool himself after the ride. He always did that when we were children. Now, please imagine us approaching the main entrance: Mr. Bingley and I on the horses, William walking all wet; suddenly, we found ourselves face to face with Miss Bingley and Mrs. Hurst. They just stood there, dumbstruck. Miss Bingley asked what happened, and William said with his usual gravity: 'Forgive me; I am not properly attired to carry on a conversation.' Then he entered the house while they remained there, staring at him."

Georgiana could barely finish the story because of her laughter, and Elizabeth listened with curiosity until the last word, then lost all composure and joined Georgiana in her amusement.

Darcy attempted to contradict his sister, but he could not intervene to make them listen to him.

Finally, he managed to reply, causing even more laughter. "I must stipulate that, as soon as I came out of the water, I put my vest back on. I could not risk being seen only in my wet shirt."

Then he gulped some wine, keeping a perfectly serious countenance, while Elizabeth and Georgiana's faces were crimson and their eyes tearful from uproarious laughter.

With similar retellings and recollections, the evening progressed.

Excellent food, a glass of wine, and the fatigue of the journey soon overcame the joy of being home. There was nothing more inviting than the prospect of resting in one's own bed, so they retired for the night, and silence fell upon Pemberley together with the dark. There was no rush; many happy days and evenings were ahead of them, and their life as a family sharing both sadness and joy had just started.

Molly helped Elizabeth prepare for the night, and in a half hour, the maid repeated several times that she had never seen a more beautiful place than Pemberley.

"I thank you, Molly, all is well now. Please go and rest; these have been exhausting days for all of us. I will ring for you when I need you tomorrow morning."

"Yes ma'am—good night." Molly moved toward the door then returned.

"Mrs. Darcy, forgive my boldness, but I must tell you that you look even more beautiful than usual. There is something different; I cannot say what it is…"

Elizabeth smiled. "Thank you. It must be the charm of Pemberley, for sure."

When she was alone, Elizabeth pulled the robe around her and went close to the large window. In the room there was only a single lit candle and the light of the fire; outside, however, a row of torches lit the front the house. A full, shining moon and countless stars brightened the sky and the lake that guarded Pemberley.

She shivered from a chill as she admired a new side of the beauty lying before her. She did not turn when she sensed her husband approaching and wrapping her in his arms.

"I cannot believe you are here, my love. I dreamt about you—about your laughter and liveliness warming Pemberley's cold rooms—for so many days and nights that I still wonder whether it is true."

"I cannot believe I am here, either. I was just thinking: Pemberley is so handsome—and powerful and majestic—just like its master."

His lips fondled her neck while his hands slowly untied her robe. "I cannot claim any merit in this. Pemberley has been the same for two generations now. I only try to keep and to enhance what my ancestors built."

"Perhaps...then I should rather say that you grew handsome and strong like Pemberley."

She turned in his arms, facing him. The robe fell to the floor, and he stroked her bare hands, lingering on her waist, then caressed her long, loose hair.

"I have waited so long to love you here at Pemberley," he said hoarsely then carried her to the large, elegant bed and laid her down against the soft, silky pillows.

Only a few moments later, the fatigue of three days of travel vanished under eager passion and impetuous desire. It was their first night at Pemberley, and neither of them wished to spend it sleeping. So they did not.

But they both missed the sunrise in the next morning as they were deeply asleep in each other's arms. Yet, there was no rush; there were many other sunrises waiting for them. Their life at Pemberley had just begun.

THE FOLLOWING MORNING, DARCY WOKE UP RATHER EARLY, RESTED AND lighthearted. He slowly removed himself from the bed, careful to not disturb Elizabeth, and returned to his room to dress.

Nothing could shadow his felicity, not even the rain that started to fall. He would have liked to take Elizabeth on a tour of the estate, but he had plenty of time to do so. She still needed to become accustomed to the house, and he had so many things to show her inside and out.

He entered the library, breathing deeply; he had truly missed the scent of it. He ordered some coffee while musing what his father-in-law would have to say about the room they both favoured.

Half an hour later, Mrs. Reynolds entered, inquiring whether he had any special orders.

"No, thank you. Mrs. Darcy will speak to you later. For now, I am just pleased to be home."

"And we are happy to have you here, sir. Breakfast will be ready in about an hour if you approve."

"Let it be an hour and a half, Mrs. Reynolds. The ladies are still tired from the road," he said, averting his eyes as he knew very well that it was not the only reason for Elizabeth's late sleep.

"As you wish." Mrs. Reynolds excused herself to leave, then returned and stepped closer to the master.

"Sir…"

"Yes? Is there anything else?"

"Forgive me for being so bold but…yesterday, when you were in the drawing room and later at dinner…I heard you and Miss Georgiana laughing, sir. I have not heard you laugh as loudly or joyfully in more than ten years. Just before Lady Anne fell ill," the lady said tearfully.

Darcy startled at her words then rose from his chair and embraced her affectionately.

"With God's will, there will be much laughter at Pemberley from now on, Mrs. Reynolds. Mrs. Darcy has brought happiness to our lives—both to me and to Georgiana."

"That is enough reason for me to love Mrs. Darcy already. Forgive my boldness; I know it is not for me to judge any of your decisions but—"

"Do not worry; I perfectly understand your meaning, and your care is greatly appreciated. I count on you to share the love you carry for Georgiana and me to Mrs. Darcy too. I trust you will be greatly rewarded. She is truly my blessing…our blessing."

"So she seems, sir."

As Mrs. Reynolds left the library, Darcy resumed his place, leaning his head on the back of the armchair and closing his eyes. He truly could not remember the last time he had laughed aloud in the past nor whether Georgiana had ever done so as she had the previous evening.

Joy and laughter had entered the cold halls of Pemberley at the same time as Elizabeth.

Chapter 19

The first week at Pemberley was the happiest time of Elizabeth's life. Every day, every hour, every moment her heart nearly burst with felicity.

As she promised, the first thing she did the second day after her arrival was to write and send by express four short letters to announce their safe arrival: to Jane, her aunt Gardiner, Lady Matlock, and her father, his including a detailed description of the library.

Her time was split between getting familiar with the details of the household, meeting the tenants, meeting the people of Lambton, and spending sweet, tender moments with her husband in the slow discovery and exploration of her new home.

One by one, every room of Pemberley was visited and admired, sometimes with her husband, other times with Georgiana and Mrs. Reynolds. If in the first days Elizabeth walked through the large halls and chambers with shyness and restraint, every passing day made her part of Pemberley, and Pemberley part of herself.

Her favourite places in the house—besides the master suites—were the library, the gallery, and the small office used by Lady Anne Darcy, which now belonged to her.

The moments she shared with Georgiana were even more intimate than in London. As Darcy suggested, they spent hours looking through the papers Lady Anne had left as a legacy. Sadness and sorrow combined with a desire to complete the projects started by Lady Anne—some of them unknown even to Darcy.

Mrs. Reynolds often joined the Darcy ladies, offering her share of memories about the past years of the family, proving her genuine affection for the family.

Elizabeth tried to learn the details regarding the household and to be involved in the decisions about running the house without interfering with Mrs. Reynolds's responsibilities. She had every reason to be pleased with Mrs. Reynolds, and there was nothing she wished to change about Pemberley.

Many hours of every day were spent by Elizabeth and Darcy together in privacy. Georgiana wisely chose not to join them in their long rides around the property.

Darcy's pleasure in revealing the secrets and beauties of his home to Elizabeth was compounded by her vivid interest and genuine delight in knowing Pemberley and its tenants as well as the lovely people of Lambton.

Their bond strengthened until words were barely needed for them to communicate. It was enough to exchange glances and smiles to understand each other's wishes, pleasure, or displeasure.

She avoided worrying him unnecessarily with her occasional states of sickness; fortunately, those were rare and occurred early in the morning. If she kept to her bed until later, nobody would notice. During the daytime, she was full of energy and liveliness, enjoying every moment of her new life.

Her past preference for walking was mostly replaced by the joy of riding Summer. Together with Darcy and Georgiana, she still took strolls around the house or near the edge of the lake, but to go further was impossible by foot. Besides, the mare herself had grown fond of Elizabeth, and the attachment was mutual.

Elizabeth's skills in riding improved much more quickly than Darcy's confidence in her experience as well as in the horse, which was not yet familiar with Pemberley's grounds. Therefore, he always rode side-by-side with his wife and only on easy paths, his heart aching when Elizabeth pushed her horse to a gallop. He was pleased and proud to observe her daily progress in riding and all her accomplishments in filling her role as mistress of the estate, but his concern had not yet vanished.

After their serious argument in London following Maud's illness, Darcy struggled to control both his mind and his heart and to behave rationally. He admitted that Elizabeth's point of view was valid: no matter how much he wished to protect her, he could not avoid having children only for the fear that he might put her in danger. His restlessness remained, but he decided to behave as she wished because it was the most reasonable way.

Then her lack of appetite, the unusual fatigue, and her pallor distressed him greatly, but he was relieved to have rarely observed them since they arrived in Derbyshire. Everything appeared to be fine, and she certainly looked happier and more beautiful than ever. He was careful to protect her from any possible risk as best as he could without betraying his anxiety to her.

Darcy had always felt happy at Pemberley, but the word had new meanings lately. He kept wondering about his fortune, and every day when he marvelled at his felicity, he felt a cold, irrational fear of losing it.

He helped her sleep with his kisses and caresses then remained to watch her rest until late at night. He woke in the morning eager to see her face and hear her voice. His days and nights were filled with her, and he could feel her presence even when she was away from him. She was completely his in every possible way. She meant his life; she was his life.

He was old enough to remember his parents' life before his mother fell ill—and afterwards. Their joy had turned into despair, the music into lament, and their smiles into tears.

He knew there was nothing he could do to oppose fate, nor did he have any reason to believe that Elizabeth's health was in danger. But the fear remained, and he had to fight against it. Fortunately, she proved to him daily that he had no reason for it.

On the first Sunday at church, Elizabeth was already acquainted with the tenants' families and with several families in Lambton. She was pleased to finally meet Mr. Martin—the gentleman who owned the shop where Maud and her mother were planning to work—and Dr. Baring, who had taken care of the Darcys at Pemberley for twenty years.

People's curiosity over the new Mrs. Darcy was combined with their surprise in witnessing the new mistress's warm manners and amiable smiles. And those who had known the family for a long time could testify that they had never seen Miss Darcy so animated nor the master smiling so much.

After the church service, they returned at Pemberley, and when they were close to the house, the rain started, lasting for the rest of Sunday and most of the next day.

Miss Darcy used the opportunity to play her pianoforte several hours a day; she was preoccupied with improving her performance, but even more so she wished to offer privacy to her brother and sister.

In the library, Darcy studied some papers while Elizabeth read the letters received in response to hers. Outside, the rain fell vigorously, drumming in a rhythm of its own.

"Pemberley is as beautiful in the rain as it is in the sun," Elizabeth whispered, walking toward the window.

"It is indeed." He moved behind her, placing his arms around her.

"Is there any news in your letters?" Darcy inquired.

"Nothing particular. Jane wrote me two pages about her felicity in marriage and their plans to return to Netherfield next week. And my aunt says Becky asks about us several time a day."

"I am pleased to hear that—about Jane and Bingley, I mean. I wonder if it is wise to return to Hertfordshire so soon, though. As for the Gardiners, you may assure them we are eager to have them here."

"I will, my dear. The Matlocks and my parents seem all in excellent health."

"Lovely to know that," he said then gently pulled Elizabeth to join him on the settee. "My love, I need you to be my ally in finishing a most secret plan."

Elizabeth's face was filled with curiosity. "Of course—how may I help you? What plan?"

"As you know, Georgiana will be sixteen soon. I have a present for her that I expect to arrive soon. I ordered her a new pianoforte—an exquisite instrument, very appropriate for her talent."

"What a wonderful idea," Elizabeth exclaimed. "Dearest Georgiana, she will be so happy!"

"I believe the same. I expect it to arrive in a few days. You will have to take Georgiana on a long ride, perhaps visiting Lambton for several hours, so I will have time to place it in the music room."

Elizabeth's eyes twinkled as she laughed. "Excellent plan, sir. You are very good at surprises, as Becky would say."

He stole a kiss. "I have had the chance of practising more lately, so I feel I have improved myself."

She circled her arms around his neck. "Indeed, you have. You are quite close to Miss Bingley's description: a man without faults."

The kiss silenced their shared laughter, and then Elizabeth withdrew a few inches, glaring at her husband.

"I am tempted to believe that Miss Bingley's admiration for you and her desire to mend your pen started the day she saw you all wet and informally attired."

He pulled her into his lap and trapped her in his arms. "I would rather say Miss Bingley's admiration started much sooner, but it might have increased accordingly the day of my swimming adventure."

"Do I detect a tendency to present yourself wet in front of young ladies, Mr. Darcy?"

"Not at all, Mrs. Darcy; I only had two such accidents in my life: one was one of the most awkward moments I have ever borne, and the other was the start of my happiness."

"I am glad to have been a part of the second one, my dearest Mr. Darcy," she answered. Then any words became useless, and they were completely abandoned.

The rain continued to fall for another two days and nights. On the dawn of the third day, it finally stopped, and the silence was only broken by birdsong. Elizabeth was deep in a restful sleep when she startled under her husband's insistence on awakening her.

"My love, wake up," he whispered, fondling her neck while he pushed the sheets away from her. She sighed and turned on her other side, but he continued his attempt—tenderly but decidedly—to accomplish his goal.

"If you wake up for only a moment, you may return to sleep again. I only wish to show you the rainbow, my love—the first rainbow we shall see together at Pemberley."

Elizabeth opened her eyes and met his joy-filled gaze. She smiled at him, and he pulled her into his arms, carrying her toward the small balcony. There, he sat on the floor, still holding her tightly, and she cuddled to his chest, admiring the sight before them.

Above the hills and the woods, opposite the sun, a magnificent rainbow shone seven shades of colour over the Pemberley grounds.

Elizabeth turned in her husband's arms to have a better view, her eyes widened in delight as if she were waking from sleep only to fall into a beautiful dream.

"Forgive me for disturbing you, but I could not permit you to miss the rainbow," he said.

She leant against him, entwining her hands with his.

"We have been here for only a fortnight, and you have already given me the rainbow—and so much more, my dear husband. So much joy and so much beauty…and please feel free to wake me whenever you want. I much prefer daydreaming to sleep."

"I will keep that in mind, my dear wife."

IN THE FOLLOWING DAYS, THE WEATHER IMPROVED, AND THE SUN, WARM and bright, reminded everyone that summer was expected soon.

Georgiana's piano arrived as scheduled, and the plan worked flawlessly. Elizabeth asked her sister to join her in Lambton to check two houses that might be suited to host Maud and her family and to speak with Mr. Martin. Once in the small village, they were invited for tea by Mrs. Martin; then Dr. Baring conversed with them about London.

They returned to Pemberley after more than three hours, and they were welcomed by Darcy. To Georgiana's surprise, her brother insisted she play something for him. Astonished and slightly tired, she indulged him, following him to the music room.

The girl's cries of joy and tears of gratitude, the pure delight on her face, and the gentleness of her touch on the instrument brought Darcy and Elizabeth to the edge of their own tears.

"This is our present for your sixteenth anniversary, dearest," Darcy said.

"William, I cannot believe it…this is so beautiful…a pure work of art. How could I thank you? There is nothing I would have liked more…"

"Will you not try it?" Elizabeth encouraged her.

"Of course I will…but my fingers are still shaking…such a surprise. And what a devious scheme—to keep me away from the house. I should have guessed something. William would never agree to be away from you for so many hours," Georgiana teased them through her tears.

She then sat at the piano, and her hands masterfully touched the keys, filling the room with enchanting music, which slowly drifted outside through the open window.

Pemberley echoed with Miss Darcy's playing, and everyone in the house and nearby paused in their duties for several minutes to listen to the brilliant performance.

Georgiana continued to play for another hour then returned to the instrument before dinner and again after it, when she played for her brother and sister until late in the evening.

As Darcy had hoped, the instrument was exquisite in every aspect and quality—a perfect companion for Miss Georgiana Darcy's talent.

THE NEXT DAY, IT WAS ELIZABETH'S TURN TO BE SURPRISED. THE DAY WAS lovely and warm, and at first, she found nothing curious when her husband told her, "My dear, please dress for the outside. We will take a longer ride in the phaeton."

The surprise appeared when she discovered that the ride was planned for late in the afternoon and that Georgiana would not join them.

"Will we return in time for dinner?" she inquired.

"No," he answered briefly. "Please take a thicker coat; it might get colder later."

He was obviously reluctant to offer more details, so she did not insist. When Darcy helped her enter the phaeton, Elizabeth noticed a large basket and some blankets.

He noticed the direction of her gaze and smiled.

"We will have dinner outside. Do you remember the grove where we stopped on our first day? I promised you we would return there, and I thought today would be a proper occasion."

"I know it is our three-month anniversary; surely, you did not expect me to forget," she said.

He kissed her hand. "Of course not."

The day was still bright, and the road was in excellent condition. The horse took them at a steady trot to the top of the hill. Darcy was holding the reins, and Elizabeth's hand glided under his arm as she recollected the emotions she experienced the first day she arrived at Pemberley.

He stopped the phaeton away from the main path, helped Elizabeth down, took the blankets and the basket, and then tied the horse to a tree.

Elizabeth walked through the high grass, touching the trees' leaves and the flower blossoms while Darcy put the blankets on the ground.

The place was secluded behind trees and bushes on one side but opened widely on the other side toward Pemberley House. From that height, the entire estate displayed its greatness and beauty.

Darcy invited his wife to sit on the blankets as he revealed the secrets of the basket: cold meat, cheese, vegetables, biscuits, and sweets. He took

Elizabeth's hand in his.

"I would like to have dinner here. It is one of the most remarkable places on the entire estate, and the view is unique, particularly at sunset."

"What a lovely idea." She caressed his face then leant to touch his lips. "You have spoiled me so much that I expected another surprise for our anniversary. What does this say about me?"

"It says you are starting to know your husband quite well." He laughed, stroking her arms and placing small kisses on her face.

She sighed, rejoicing in his attentions. "Is this grove private enough to allow me to kiss my husband without being caught?"

He cupped her face and claimed her lips. "It is very private. I am quite positive it cannot be seen either from the main road or from the valley."

"I am relieved to hear that..."

"Besides, nobody uses this road unless I am informed about it. We do not expect visitors at this time."

As he spoke, their bodies touched, as did their mouths and hands, every gesture turning into a passionate caress.

"Look, the sun is going down!" Elizabeth broke the embrace, as elated as a child, marvelling at the sight. "The sky seems to be on fire—such an astonishing view!"

"I enjoy seeing your eyes sparkle with delight," he said, staring at her while she gazed at their surroundings. "Elizabeth, there is something I want to give you while it is still light."

"Another gift? I should be dishonest not to admit that I like your surprises, but I truly have everything I want. Everything."

"Allow me to doubt that. You certainly do not have this."

He offered her a package, and by its size, she thought it was a large, thick book. She unwrapped it with eager curiosity to reveal a notebook with red velvet covers; the front cover bore the name, "Elizabeth Darcy."

She brushed her fingers over it then looked at her husband and again at the book. He opened it, his fingers lingering over hers. Inside, the pages were blank.

"I thought the new Mrs. Darcy should have a journal of her own—to make her own decisions, her plans, her projects, and to write them down. There are many clean pages for you to fill, my dear."

"William..." she was lost for words, holding the notebook, their fingers still touching.

"My love, I know that, even for someone as strong, brave, and bright as you, it might be overwhelming, even burdensome, to be constantly compared to her predecessor. I love and cherish my parents' memory, and I would be glad to know you want to continue what my mother started, but I wish you to feel free to decide whatever you like—to allow your heart and your mind to fly free and to remain loyal to yourself before others. That is the meaning of my gift."

"I never felt burdened, nor unfree—perhaps overwhelmed at times—but it helps me to know how well you understand me and how easily you read my thoughts, even those that I hide from myself. Your trust allows me to fly and to remain loyal to myself while being loyal to you. Thank you, my love."

They remained embraced—her back resting against his torso, the notebook on her lap—watching every moment of the sunset. Then a full, bright moon took its place in the sky, mirrored in the lake while countless, bright stars shone in the serene sky.

"Are you not hungry? It is quite late." He caressed her arms to warm her; then his hands lingered on her shoulders.

"No...perhaps later...I do not want to move a single inch from your arms."

"Then you shall not."

His lips tantalised her neck, her earlobe, her jaw, and she turned her head to allow more room for his caresses.

"I want you to love me," she whispered. "Now...here..."

"Elizabeth..."

He gently lowered her dress so her entire shoulder was exposed to his kisses. His hands slowly touched her full breasts then closed around them. She moaned, and her body arched, pleading for more and whispering his name.

Carefully, Darcy lowered her onto the blanket then leant atop her. He was aware of her scent and the smell of fresh grass as he allowed his passion to be released upon her in countless kisses and eager caresses.

Elizabeth's soft moans disturbed the silence of the night, soon joined by Darcy's groans. The fresh air chilled her bare skin before his touches heated it again. Threads of grass tickled her hands, her legs, and her nape, and above her, the sky was gleaming. The song of the crickets and the soft whisper of the summer breeze was the music on which their bodies joined in an ardent rhythm.

They reached their pleasure, shattering together in delight, then remained tightly embraced, allowing their hearts and their breathing to steady. She looked at the stars, the moon, and the lights of Pemberley through heavy eyelashes while he only gazed at her beautiful face and sparkling eyes.

Around midnight, they were still reluctant to leave, but the stars were shadowed by clouds and a cool wind began to blow, forcing them to hurry home.

When they arrived at Pemberley, the rain had started again, and the moon and the stars could hardly be seen.

But Elizabeth's eyes were still glittering, smiling at her husband. And the notebook was still held closely to her chest.

MAY PASSED WITH MORE RAIN AS WELL AS PLEASANT, WARM WEATHER. AT the end of the month, Maud and her family arrived at Lambton in a carriage generously sent by Darcy. They leased, at an affordable rent, a lovely house, rather small but comfortable.

Maud owned nothing but the money earned during her short time of working in Darcy's house and another small sum from selling most of their belongings in Oxfordshire; yet, she succeeded in settling the entire family with it.

The general knowledge about Maud was that she was employed in Mr. Darcy's house in London and that her mother, Mrs. Jenny Lovell, had worked as a seamstress in Paris, a fact that raised moderate interest in the neighbourhood.

As soon as Maud started her new assignment, both Mrs. and Miss Darcy selected the finest of Mr. Martin's fabrics and ordered one dress and two bonnets each. Also, Mrs. Reynolds brought several gowns to be altered. Induced by the silent recommendation of the mistress of Pemberley, other requests came in, although slowly; people were still reluctant to patronise a newcomer in their village. However, a fortnight after her arrival, Maud and her mother earned enough to ensure a modest living for the next two months.

The first morning of June, Darcy was in the library, reading his correspondence, when Elizabeth entered. It had become their small ritual to spend half an hour together before breakfast, enjoying coffee and tea while discussing their plans for the day.

He greeted his wife and hurried to take her hand. She sat on the settee, wearing a smile that he found even more beautiful than usual. Her bright eyes narrowed as she looked at him intently.

"Good morning. Am I disturbing you?"

"You never do, my love. I was only reading some letters. I received some surprising news from Robert."

"Really? Good news, I hope?" The smile did not leave her lips or her eyes.

"As I said—surprising. Robert departed for his regiment, but my aunt and uncle arrived safely at Matlock, and our cousin Anne is with them! I cannot recollect her ever spending the summer anywhere but at Rosings. It appears she came to Town with Lady Catherine, and she was too weak to return to Kent."

"Miss de Bourgh is ill? I am very sorry to hear that."

"I am not quite certain of that. The tone of Robert's letter is far from grave. He inquired whether we would like to visit his parents one of these days, but I know both you and Georgiana are quite busy."

"I look forward to seeing Lord and Lady Matlock and becoming acquainted with Miss de Bourgh, but perhaps we should wait another week or so. I hope they will join us when my relatives are here. It will be a pleasure to be all together."

Darcy looked at his wife with increasing interest, caressing her face. "My love, is there anything else you wish you tell me? Your eyes say that there is."

"You always read my mind." She smiled; then her tone became hesitant. "I am not entirely sure whether there is anything to tell, but earlier this morning, I realised we have been married for three and half months and…"

"Yes…"

She blushed, slightly embarrassed to raise the delicate subject.

"Do you remember the first week after our wedding, when I…had to keep to my bed for a few days? It was quite an awkward and distressing moment…"

He laughed, placing a lingering kiss on her palm. "I do remember. It was a peculiar moment indeed."

"Yes…but do you remember the second time it occurred? The following month?"

"Yes, it—" He frowned, concentrating on answering her. His fingers were caressing her hands; then suddenly his movements stopped. His eyes searched hers, meeting their sparkles.

"I do not remember either," she said. "Because it did not happen—not in the second month or in the third or the fourth—it never happened again."

"Elizabeth, what—? I do not understand."

"I have been such a simpleton. For almost a month, I have been sick and dizzy and lacked my normal appetite."

"You are still ill? Why did you not tell me? We must call Dr. Baring immediately—"

She put her hand over his mouth. "It would be worth calling the doctor just to prove me right. I am still unwell, but I believe I know why. My aunt warned me about this possibility, but with everything that happened to Maud, with the Almack's Ball and our travelling, I somehow did not give it enough thought until this morning."

"Elizabeth…" His face showed complete disbelief, then disturbance, then pallor and flushing, all in a few moments.

She barely restrained her tears. "My love, I believe I am carrying our child!"

Shock held him still and silent, staring at her in disbelief. Finally, the words came in waves, barely coherent, while he stroked her face and wiped her tears with tender kisses.

"My beloved Elizabeth, what are you saying? Should we hope? Is it possible that it happened so soon? I am being silly—of course, it may happen so soon—but I never thought…this is so unexpected…"

He slowly knelt to the floor in front of her, holding her hands tightly. She touched his hair; then her lips pressed his. Tears threatened them both, but they never broke their gaze, the master of Pemberley still kneeling before his wife.

"But…how are you? You said you are unwell. What should we do? You must rest now. I will not allow anything to trouble you further. May I help you in any way?"

Elizabeth laughed through her tears. "I do not believe we should do anything special. I remember my aunt's carrying my cousins. I was old enough to remember the times with Margaret and Becky. She was quite her usual self. The only thing you must do is to stop worrying. I am fine. And I am happy. I am beyond happiness. I carry our love inside of me. What else can be more wonderful than this?"

"I still cannot believe it. I will be happy too—I promise—as soon as Dr. Baring comes to see you. He is an excellent doctor, just like Dr. Harris. Should we bring Dr. Harris too? Yes, I will send for Dr. Baring right away! Should I take you to your room now?"

He tried to rise, but Elizabeth would not release his hands. He sat beside her, and she cupped his face, her forehead leaning against his.

"My dear Mr. Darcy, you are truly the silliest man in the world. Do as you want—fetch Dr. Baring if you insist—but please leave the rest of the doctors in England alone. No other woman has been finer than I am—nor happier."

The entire day became a tumult of laughter and tears, hopes and fears, joy and concerns.

Immediately after breakfast, Dr. Baring was summoned. His impromptu visit brought comments, speculations, and peeking around corners from the Pemberley staff until Mrs. Reynolds severely censured everyone and demanded they return to their tasks.

The doctor needed less than half an hour of private discussion with Mrs. Darcy to confirm her suspicions. He estimated the heir of Pemberley would come into the world around Christmas time, and he arranged to visit the young mistress twice a week.

A more difficult conversation followed with Mr. Darcy. He held poor Dr. Baring captive in the library for more than an hour—asking countless questions and demanding details and recommendations. At the end of the meeting, when the doctor was sure nothing remained unclarified, Darcy still had some uncertainties, which he agreed to postpone for a later occasion. Dr. Baring showed full confidence that Mrs. Darcy was in perfect health and there were no reasons for concern about her condition, but words were not enough to put Darcy completely at ease.

When the doctor left, Darcy and Elizabeth went for a stroll in the garden, arm in arm, still trying to become accustomed to the astonishing news.

The flowers had blossomed into an enchanting harmony of colours, and Elizabeth enjoyed the scent and the view while walking along, musing that, next summer, her child might play among the flowers.

"I know that I am happy, but I do not dare to feel it yet," Darcy said. "Are we truly expecting our first child? I believe I frightened Dr. Baring. He promised me he will visit you twice a week, but I think he would say anything to escape from me."

Elizabeth chuckled. "You are quite frightening sometimes, sir. But the doctor promised me the same, so I trust his words. He repeatedly said I have no reason to worry and there is nothing special I have to do."

"He told me the same. He insisted on allowing you to do anything that gives you pleasure as long as it does not put you in any danger."

"Then I shall only stay with you—that is what gives me pure pleasure. As long as you are with me, I feel safe and protected."

"I have long ago told you that you belong in my arms," he answered. "I promise I will not worry foolishly anymore if you promise you will let me know of any discomfort you may have."

"It sounds like a reasonable arrangement," she replied, and they continued to walk until they found a small bench on the edge of the lake and rested on it, enjoying the prospect.

Then Elizabeth turned to him and added in a lower voice, "Dr. Baring said we need no extra precautions of any kind. I am quite confident about what he meant, but I shall ask my aunt Gardiner more on that subject."

"Yes, he indicated the same to me, but it would not hurt to ask Mrs. Gardiner too—just to be certain. She is a very wise lady."

"Yes, she is. Now, shall we return inside? I look forward to sharing the news with Georgiana. And we should also inform Mrs. Reynolds, but I will ask her to keep the secret until we tell our families."

It was dinnertime when Miss Darcy received the excellent news about their growing family. The restrained and always proper Miss Darcy could hardly temper her joy and enthusiasm. Although there was a long road ahead, Georgiana eagerly anticipated the moment of holding her first niece or nephew in her arms and started thinking of a proper name for the youngest member of the family.

Later on, alone in their room, neither Darcy nor Elizabeth could find rest. They chatted until close to midnight, wondering about the miracle that was about to happen. When she eventually felt tired, Elizabeth cuddled to her husband and sighed when his arms encircled her.

"William, your heart beats rapidly and loudly," she said, placing a gentle kiss upon it.

"That is because it is too small for the happiness that fills it, my beautiful Elizabeth."

Two weeks later, the peaceful silence of Pemberley was broken by the sound of horses, carriages, voices, and cries of surprise, coming together with the arrival of the Bennets, Gardiners, and Bingleys.

Darcy, Elizabeth, and Georgiana, along with Mrs. Reynolds, waited in front of the house.

Six carriages stopped at the main entrance, and small steps running along the alley announced the presence of the Gardiner children. Thomas and Henry bowed solemnly to Mr. and Miss Darcy then hurried to embrace Elizabeth. After them, Becky appeared, looking around with curiosity then stretching her hands toward Darcy as a sign for him to lift her in his arms.

"Have you travelled well, my dears?" Elizabeth asked, kissing the girl.

"We did; Pemberley is very far away. Lizzy, I missed you. I could not wait to be finally here. I kept asking Mama how long we still had to travel. Mr. Darcy, is this your house alone? It is as big as ten Longbourns. Now I see why Mama says you are a very important man. Do you have some biscuits, please? Did you know that eating in the carriage makes you even more hungry? And sleeping in the carriage makes you even more sleepy. Mr. Darcy, did your hair grow since I last saw you?"

Before any of them had time to answer Becky's flow of questions, Mr. and Mrs. Gardiner, together with Margaret, greeted them, thanking their host for the invitation. The Gardiners' awe for their surroundings was as obvious as their uneasiness.

"Lizzy, my dear, I can hardly believe we are here. It takes my breath away only thinking I am at Pemberley. Oh, but you look just beautiful!"

"Dear Aunt, welcome. We are happy to have you here."

There was no time for other words as Mrs. Bennet's cries of admiration burst from inside her carriage.

"Mr. Darcy, what an honour to be here! At Pemberley? Who could guess you would marry Lizzy after you refused even to dance with her? And to bring her here? Kitty—come here, child, and help me get out of this carriage."

Bingley offered to support his mother-in-law, but he was not rewarded with much attention. Mrs. Bennet hurried to meet her second daughter. "Oh, Lizzy—pardon me, Mrs. Darcy—let me see you! What a lady you are! And of all this you are the mistress? This is more than an earl, I am sure. Oh, look, what a lake! I must write to my sister Philips tonight. Nobody in Meryton can imagine what you have here."

"Mama, I am happy to see you. I trust your journey was not too difficult."

"It was horrible, but I would gladly bear ten times worse for what I see around me. Mary, pay attention and write down everything. I want to be sure I do not forget anything by the time we return to Longbourn."

Elizabeth finally managed to embrace her three sisters and her father then invited the guests inside.

"Come, Mama, let us all enter. You must be hungry and tired."

Servants hurried to help everyone find their rooms while Mrs. Reynolds discreetly supervised every move.

In two hours, all were settled in the comfort of their own chambers. At their mother's demand, the four children were almost forced to eat and to rest. Any opposition was defeated by Mrs. Gardiner's determination, and not even tears were enough to convince her otherwise. The prospect of playing and visiting the horses was enough inducement to finally accept their "cruel fate" as Becky repeatedly pointed out, and all her siblings agreed with her.

Mrs. Bennet's nerves calmed miraculously under the assistance of a personal maid, and she refused any other entertainment for the time being. Three days on the road were enough to defeat even her interest in Pemberley's magnificent interior.

Kitty and Mary benefited from Georgiana's company to see the house while Elizabeth and Darcy took the Gardiners, the Bingleys, and Mr. Bennet on a tour of their home. Elizabeth held her father's arm, enjoying his surprise and wonder.

"My dear Lizzy, for once I can find no fault in your mother's loudly expressed appreciation. Until now, my understanding of your new position and responsibilities was far from the reality. One might easily envy your husband, but I certainly do not. It must be the work of a lifetime to be the master of such a vast estate."

"It is, Papa, but for William all of this means home. And it is the same for me now. He is the best master and the best landlord, and no effort is too much for him to accomplish his duties. I feel proud to be at his side."

"And so you should be, my dear child."

They walked together, following the others. From time to time, Darcy cast a glance at his wife to be certain she was well.

Mr. Bennet turned to his favourite daughter and whispered, "If I am to be honest, I rather envy Bingley. He has less than half of Darcy's income and surely less than half his responsibilities. His only reasons for distress seem to be his sisters and your mother. Quite a relaxing life this young man has. I confess I am quite fond of him; he is an excellent hunter."

"Please do not make sport of poor Mr. Bingley. He is your only son-in-law who lives near you."

"Yes, I know that—poor fellow. Quite unfortunate."

"Papa, you are incorrigible! Mr. Bingley and Jane look very happy together. I have no doubt he is the perfect match for her."

"Well, they seem happy, but I cannot be certain; they both smile all the time. Now, how long do we have until we reach the library? You may abandon me there; I will not complain. No dinner for me—some cold meat and a glass of wine would do perfectly well."

"I will let William have the pleasure of taking you gentlemen to the library while I talk to Jane and Aunt Gardiner. I hope we will still have your company for dinner, Papa. The library will still be there."

Chapter 20

June stood for "joy" at Pemberley.

The presence of such a large party changed the entire schedule, starting with breakfast and ending with dinner, but the general happiness was a most worthy reward for the master and mistress of the house.

Two days in a row, Darcy took their guests to visit the estate—the ladies and the children riding in two phaetons and a carriage, and the gentlemen following them on horseback. Mr. Bennet reluctantly left the library, which he declared to be the room of his dreams, but could not oppose all his daughters' insistence and his wife's nerves.

"My dear Mr. Bennet, you cannot possibly refuse to visit Pemberley," his wife said. "What will you tell Mr. Philips and Sir William and Mr. Collins when they ask you how large the estate is and how many tenants work on it? Surely, you cannot talk about the library only—nobody cares much about the library. And Kitty—please stop coughing, my dear. We are at Pemberley now; nobody coughs here!"

The grandeur of the estate and its natural beauties aroused the visitors' curiosity and interest, as well as their profound admiration. Mrs. Gardiner had vivid memories from the occasions when she had seen those grounds several years ago, but the view from the mistress's phaeton—having the master as a guide—was more astounding than her recollections.

They passed near a stream where, Mr. Darcy informed the gentlemen, there was an excellent spot for fishing. Therefore, plans were immediately made for a fishing party in the following days.

For the children, long tours in a carriage under the strict supervision of adults were not their cup of tea. But they were beside themselves with joy when Darcy presented them with Shetland ponies for the girls and gentle colts for the boys. From that moment, Thomas, Henry, Margaret, and Becky spent several hours daily in the company of their new friends and declared that riding was absolutely their favourite activity.

After the first week of excitement, life at Pemberley slowly settled down. Mr. Bennet's days were dedicated to reading; Mrs. Bennet divided her time between resting in her room, sitting on a small bench at the edge of the lake with her sister Gardiner and her daughters, and dictating to Mary long, detailed letters for her sister Philips and Lady Lucas.

Lydia and Mr. Wickham were rarely mentioned by either Mrs. Bennet or Kitty. Mrs. Gardiner mentioned to them some long past disagreements between Wickham and Mr. Darcy, and from that moment Mrs. Bennet took a clear side. No matter how much she liked her first son-in-law's charms and uniform, she favoured by far Mr. Darcy's handsome features and his amazing estate, and she would not risk upsetting him for anything.

Georgiana discovered that she enjoyed a noisy and crowded Pemberley exceedingly. Along with her warm relationships with Mrs. Gardiner and Mrs. Bingley, a new friendship blossomed and grew between Miss Darcy and the two Miss Bennets. Miss Darcy's practising at the pianoforte was admired every day by Mary and Kitty. Slowly, Mary started to evaluate her own performance more objectively and to ask Georgiana's advice in becoming more proficient. Kitty had no interest in learning to play, but she was enchanted to listen to the outstanding music. And both of them were astonished by Georgiana's knowledge of art, literature, and theatre and were fascinated simply to listen to her. Moreover, Miss Darcy was very proficient in riding—a sport that Kitty and Mary began to learn at the same time with their younger cousins.

The Bingleys, Gardiners, and Darcys became closer with each day, spending most of the time together, both indoors and out. Elizabeth had not shared her great news with them yet. She planned to host a small private ball for the entire family, including the Matlocks, and they chose that occasion to make the official announcement.

Despite the large company and busy schedule, Elizabeth and Darcy still managed to steal at least few minutes of privacy for themselves every day.

In the evening, when they finally retired to their suite, the delight of being alone was even greater and always ended in passionate lovemaking and deep, restful sleep.

A week before the party organised by Elizabeth, Lord and Lady Matlock, together with the colonel and their niece Anne de Bourgh, arrived at Pemberley.

Despite her mother's demand to behave, Becky ran and greeted her ladyship with so much genuine eagerness that she caused Lady Matlock to shed a few tears.

Elizabeth and Darcy welcomed them, and Darcy formally introduced his wife and his cousin.

"Mrs. Darcy, forgive me for my impromptu visit. I hope I am not intruding," Anne said hesitantly. "And please allow me to apologise for the incident caused by my mother a few months ago—"

Elizabeth touched her arm and stopped her with a warm smile.

"Miss de Bourgh, I am very pleased to finally meet you. We are all family now, and I trust you will consider Pemberley your home too. Please, let us enter; the others are waiting," she directed them, taking her husband's arm.

Becky held Lady Matlock's hand tightly. "I missed you very much, Lady Matlock. I hope you do not mind if I say that. Mama told me you are a very important person and I should not upset you. But I really missed you."

"You never upset me, my dear Becky. I have missed you too."

"Mr. Darcy gave me a pony, and I learnt to ride. May I show you how good I am? But I must ride like a girl; for the boys it is much easier to ride. Miss Georgiana said I could ride like a boy if I want because I am very young. I love my pony."

Lady Matlock laughed and patted her small hand. "I am glad you enjoy yourself, my dear."

"I also used to ride astride when I was very young. My father taught me," Miss de Bourgh suddenly said, to everyone's surprise. Becky immediately discovered a new point of interest and turned to the young lady who was walking arm in arm with the colonel.

"You did? Truly? Is it not much easier?"

"Yes, it is. But if you have a proper saddle and a good riding gown, it might be easy either way."

"I do have a special saddle. Mr. Darcy gave one to me and one to Margaret.

Mr. Darcy is very kind—I am his third favourite after Lizzy and Miss Georgiana. And he is my favourite too after Papa," Becky informed Anne, who was slightly overwhelmed by the gush of information.

"Indeed, Mr. Darcy is a very generous and kind gentleman."

"Yes he is. And he is very pretty too because he has dimples," the girl whispered to a perplexed Anne.

Lady Matlock laughed. "You better become accustomed to this, Anne, because Becky is very proficient at making compliments. She might surprise you several times a day."

Once inside, the introductions were made. The Matlocks addressed the Bennets and Bingleys with kindness and greeted the Gardiners with warmth and familiarly. Mrs. Bennet was more restrained than ever in the imposing presence of Lord and Lady Matlock, and her manners were mostly an example of decorum.

Anne de Bourgh behaved reservedly and spoke little, mostly to Georgiana or the colonel. However, Elizabeth easily observed that she was by no means proud—only quite shy.

Lady Matlock found a few moments to speak privately with Elizabeth.

"You look lovely, my dear. Every time I see you, you look more beautiful than before."

"I thank you—your ladyship is very kind. It must appear so because every time we meet I am happier than before." Her genuine smile met Lady Matlock's approving gaze.

"That might be the reason indeed. I hope you do not mind that we brought Anne."

"Of course not—quite the contrary. I confess we were worried for her: Had she been ill? She looks quite charming now."

"I think she pretended she was worse than she actually was. Catherine brought her to London, and she was seen by three doctors. Nobody found anything particular, only a general weakness. Then she insisted she was too ill to travel back to Kent and preferred to stay with us for a couple of months. Catherine made a huge scene, but Anne would not alter her decision. She was strangely determined in comforting Catherine. It is also true that she had Lord Matlock and Robert standing by her side, but still…"

"It is quite a relief to know she is well."

"She is; the doctors confirmed that. And she looks very well too. I have not seen Anne this animated in years—before Louis de Bourgh passed away."

"She must enjoy living with you. Are Lord Buxton and Lady Beatrice in good health? Did they leave London too?"

"Yes, they are at their estate in Berkshire. It seems they have several friends invited there for the summer. I see Bingley did not bring his sisters this time?"

Elizabeth did not miss the change of subject. "Miss Bingley and the Hursts preferred to remain at Netherfield, I was told."

"Wise choice—I doubt it belonged to them. Elizabeth, did Maud move to Lambton after all?"

"She did. William sent a carriage for them. They live in Lambton, and she has already started her new employment in Mr. Martin's shop."

"This is lovely news. I hope Mr. Martin offered her a fair arrangement."

"William settled things with him. He provides the fabrics, the rooms, the needles, and everything else needed, and he takes two-thirds of their earnings. Maud and her mother are giving their hard work and taking one-third. They have had a very encouraging start."

"I am content to hear that. I may visit Lambton tomorrow. Now, may we have some tea, please?"

By dinnertime, the new guests had adjusted perfectly to the happy company. The five courses were accompanied by spirited conversation, and afterwards, both Georgiana and Elizabeth delighted the party with playing and singing.

Sitting in a corner, a glass of brandy in his hand, Darcy admired his wife's beautiful smile while he marvelled at the twist of fate that brought together Lord and Lady Matlock and Anne de Bourgh with the Bennet family of Hertfordshire and their relatives from Cheapside, all happily reunited at Pemberley. That was the description of happiness for him.

MR. MARTIN, THE OWNER OF LAMBTON'S CLOTHING SHOP, WAS SHOCKED to see Lady Matlock—together with another lady and two young girls—enter his store one morning. He bowed deeply, struggling to regain his composure.

"Lady Matlock, what an extraordinary surprise! I have not seen your ladyship in Lambton in more than six years. You are very welcome."

"Mr. Martin, I am glad to see you in such good health and with such an excellent memory."

"May I help your ladyship in any way?"

"Actually, you may, sir. I understood from Mrs. Darcy that you have extended your business lately."

"If you are referring to the new seamstresses, indeed I have, ma'am."

"I believe it was an excellent idea—this neighbourhood needed such service. I have come to order a few outfits. Is it possible? I warn you my requests are not simple."

"Yes, of course it is, ma'am. Anything for you. Let me fetch Maud. It will only take a moment."

Maud soon appeared, and she paled instantly on seeing Lady Matlock. Behind her was an older lady—her mother.

"Your ladyship, allow me to introduce to you Maud Lovell and her mother, Mrs. Jenny Lovell."

Lady Matlock nodded in a small gesture of acknowledgement.

"Miss Lovell, Mrs. Lovell, I am pleased to meet you both. I was curious to see Mr. Martin's new partners, especially since my niece Mrs. Darcy was very content with your services."

"It is an honour to meet you, Lady Matlock," Maud eventually answered, barely holding the lady's intense look.

"I hope you have adapted well to Derbyshire. You were from Oxfordshire, I understand?"

"Indeed, ma'am," Mrs. Lovell answered.

"You have worked in Paris, I heard? For how long?"

"Yes, your ladyship. For almost four years."

"Do you know how to make any type of gown?"

"I am trying, ma'am. Mrs. Darcy was pleased with the dresses we made for her."

"I was informed about that too. I wish to place several orders, starting with proper riding costumes for these young ladies. Let me tell you exactly what I have in mind."

After a long discussion filled with many requests and specific deadlines, Lady Matlock and her companions left the store.

Several hours later, three additional orders were registered for Maud and her mother—and two other customers were waiting to be served.

THE PEOPLE GATHERED AT PEMBERLEY WERE AS VARIED IN CHARACTER and preferences as they were similar in amiability and mutual respect. Shared tastes brought people together in small groups and allowed everyone the pleasure of choosing their company.

The gentlemen amused themselves either in the library or on riding or fishing parties—except Mr. Bennet, who rarely left the house and only after the united insistence of all four daughters.

The ladies found great enjoyment in conversation, walking, riding, and music. Anne de Bourgh slowly accommodated to her new and old acquaintances; her complexion improved, and her manners became shyly engaging.

Darcy, Bingley, and the colonel often split their time between the gentlemen's group and the ladies'. Darcy and Bingley claimed every occasion to be close to their wives, providing many opportunities for mockery by the other gentlemen. Mr. Gardiner mostly kept a wise moderation, avoiding any risk of displeasing his wife.

Darcy was careful to inquire about Elizabeth's state several times a day in brief, private interludes that—they were certain—nobody would notice. They were rather eager to inform their relatives about the happiest of news but also enjoyed keeping the small secret just for themselves.

Two evenings before the ball, as everyone enjoyed drinks after dinner, the colonel suggested they go fishing in the stream at a spot situated rather far from the house.

"We may either ride or take the carriages. It is less than an hour at a steady pace. It will be worth the effort; the place is lovely and rich with trout. There is also a small waterfall. I am sure the children will enjoy that too. It will make a nice memory for everyone."

"The place is lovely indeed," Darcy answered. "However, we should consider that it is quite far away and the weather is very warm. It might be tiresome—especially for the ladies and the children."

"Yes, but there are trees and shade to protect us from the heat. And we will surely take food and drink with us," the colonel insisted.

"I would like to go," Georgiana said, and immediately Kitty, Mary, Jane, and Bingley supported her.

"I would not oppose it, either," Mrs. Gardiner agreed. "I am certain the children will be delighted."

"I would also like to join you," Miss de Bourgh added.

"Then it is settled—we will all go." Elizabeth smiled. "William already took me to see the waterfall, and I can testify that the colonel was correct in his praise.

"I am certain it will be a lovely day for you young people. Of course, one cannot expect that I will spend a full day outside wandering through the woods and streams, regardless of the weather," Lady Matlock pointed out.

The earl also declined. "I am confident that I saw that place some years ago, so I would rather stay home with a book and a glass of wine. Mr. Bennet, you will keep me company, I suppose?"

"I will, sir, without a doubt."

"I will stay and rest too. And I still need to finish my second letter to my sister Philips. My nerves would not bear an hour-long ride in the middle of the summer," Mrs. Bennet said.

Darcy took his wife's hand. "My dear, I am thinking that you should stay home too. You have already seen the place, and perhaps your presence will be needed here. There must be things to be done for tomorrow night's ball."

Elizabeth looked at him in disbelief. "Surely, you are joking. Why would I stay home? All the arrangements for the ball are complete."

They held each other's gaze for a moment; then Darcy lightened his tone. "Perhaps we should discuss this later," he whispered. "Now, may we have some music, please?"

The awkward moment had almost passed when suddenly Mrs. Bennet turned to her daughter and said animatedly, "Lizzy, Mr. Darcy is right: you should stay home. I know you always had a wild inclination and liked to roam the fields. But in your present condition, you must be careful. A lady in such a state should mostly keep to her bed to assure her safety."

Darcy's jaw dropped, and Elizabeth's face coloured instantly. They exchanged astonished glances then looked around at their relatives, who all wore serene expressions. The young, unmarried ladies kept their eyes on the floor.

"Mama, what do you mean? What condition?"

"Your condition of being with child, of course. You must be very careful, my dear. I stayed in bed must of the time with you five girls. My nerves and weakness did not allow me to do hardly anything; however, my situation cannot be compared in any way to yours. You are carrying the heir to Pemberley—just look around. You girls were hardly that important, so you must take extra care."

All eyes turned to Mrs. Bennet at such a statement, but she remained untouched. Elizabeth was completely shocked, struggling to speak further.

"But, Mama, how did you know?"

"How? It is quite obvious. Everybody could see that. Now, Kitty dear, will you bring me another cup of tea?"

Mrs. Bennet's calmness and the others' apparent knowledge of what they thought they kept secret disconcerted both Elizabeth and Darcy. They glanced at each other again and then at their relatives in a state of growing distraction.

"Lizzy my dear, is anything wrong?" Mrs. Gardiner inquired with worry.

"No…I was only surprised. We planned to give you all the news at the ball. Was it so easy to notice?"

"It was easy enough," Mrs. Gardiner answered, embracing her. "Please do not distress yourself. We are all happy for you."

"We did not say anything since you did not bring up the subject," Jane added. "I hope you do not mind, but Mama is right. You should be careful."

"Oh, you wished to keep it a secret?" Mrs. Bennet asked, surprised and puzzled. "Why would you do that? I planned to write to my sister Philips right away. I told Lady Lucas that you would be with child before Charlotte although she married sooner. Surely, one cannot imagine that Mr. Collins could compare with Mr. Darcy."

"Mama!" cried Elizabeth, flushing with shame while the others averted their eyes, uncertain how to react to such a statement.

"Oh, do not be so missish, Lizzy. Everybody knows I am right. You should be happy. If you only give Mr. Darcy a boy, he will be happy too."

"Mrs. Bennet, I assure you that we will be happy whether it is a boy or a girl," Darcy said, still astounded by the turn of the conversation.

"Well, if there are no further secrets to be revealed, perhaps some music would be in order," Mr. Bennet intervened wisely.

Georgiana quickly headed to the piano, followed by Mary who turned the pages for her.

While everybody enjoyed the beautiful music, Mrs. Gardiner and Jane sat next to Elizabeth, trying to calm her distress.

Darcy filled a glass with brandy and retired to a corner, joined by his cousin and uncle.

"Well, one thing is beyond a doubt with your mother-in-law: you never know when and what to expect," Lord Matlock said. "She is quite the mistress of improper conversation."

"Surely, she does not surpass Lady Catherine," the colonel intervened.

"True," the earl admitted after a brief hesitation. "I pray they are never together in the same room."

The colonel patted Darcy's shoulder. "I am sorry that your surprise was ruined, but we noticed the changes quite soon after we arrived. Elizabeth looks a little different—in a most enchanting way. You were always whispering to her, helping her do the smallest things. There were quite a lot of clues."

"You must be right. We did not intend to keep it secret. We only wished to be all together when we made the announcement."

The colonel filled his glass then whispered to Darcy, "You have at least the consolation of knowing you are much better than Mr. Collins."

Darcy cast him a sharp glare then gulped some brandy to cover a laugh. He looked at his wife and met her unsettled countenance, but she forced a smile to show him she was well. He smiled too and returned his attention to his cousin.

"Only gentlemen who are married and have a child are entitled to make sport of me, Cousin."

"I completely agree with you," the earl intervened. "In this, you are in no way better than Mr. Collins, Son. I am only surprised that Mrs. Bennet has not mentioned that yet. The opportunity is not lost, though."

An hour later, when Georgiana completed her performance, the entire party retired for the night.

Elizabeth and Darcy were the last to leave. She took his arm and climbed the stairs in silence, and when the door closed behind them, Darcy dismissed both Molly and Miles.

Elizabeth lay on the bed and covered her face with her hands.

"I do not even know what to say...Mama is so...I know she means well, but I wish she were more careful about what she says. I wonder what Lord and Lady Matlock thought—and Miss de Bourgh. Not to mention the exposure of Georgiana, Kitty, and Mary to such a conversation."

He moved her hands away and spoiled her face with tender kisses.

"Your mother did us a favour. Can you imagine our embarrassment if we had kept the secret two more days and then made a solemn announcement, only to discover everyone had been aware of it for days?"

Her tears mixed with peals of laughter.

"You have quite a point here," she struggled to reply while he kissed her neck. "And now I am slowly becoming relieved. At least I can talk to my aunt and my sister about this delicate subject if I want to."

"Precisely. As I said, your mother did us a favour, you must admit. Not to mention her generosity in preferring me over Mr. Collins."

He continued to kiss her, despite her loud laughter, and gently removed her clothes then his.

Darcy lay beside his wife and wrapped the sheets around them, and she cuddled to his chest.

"But my love, this brings us back to the point where the discussion started. I truly believe you should not ride an hour to visit a place you have already seen and spend even more hours in the heat of a summer day. "

"William, I am not ill—truly. Do you know how many women who carry a child are working hard in the fields, rain or shine? And with the Lord's mercy, they are fine."

"My dear, I feel pity for all the women who suffer, and I am willing to help anytime I can. But this would certainly not inspire me to expose my own wife to danger."

"I understand your concern, but you cannot keep me inside, alone, for the next months."

"You are perfectly right. Therefore, I will stay with you. I am sure Bingley and Mr. Gardiner will manage to organise the day without me."

"That is even more ridiculous. Of course you will go. So, you insist I should stay home—even if Dr. Baring did not forbid me to be outdoors."

"He cannot forbid you anything, my love, but your husband can if necessary. A short walk on the lawn and beside the lake would be acceptable. If you need to go anywhere, I would gladly join you in the phaeton. But these activities will suffice for now. Would you not indulge me, please?"

She sighed; the corners of her lips turned into a smile, and her tone became lighter. "Very well, I cannot but obey the master of Pemberley. I will keep company with your uncle and aunt and with my parents. We cannot allow the Matlocks and my mother to be alone at home anyway."

"Thank you, my love." He kissed her hands then her face.

"You are in my debt, sir," she murmured. "You must find a way to compensate for separating me from the enjoyment of fishing."

"Please allow me to try to earn your forgiveness, my dear wife," he whispered. Then he dedicated all his attention to reaching that goal.

THE FOLLOWING MORNING, THE DIN IN THE HOUSE WAS JUST BEARABLE. The preparations—baskets with food and drink, fishing rods—the children's cries of joy, the voices, the hurry, and finally, the silence following the group's departure marked the start of a special day at Pemberley.

After breakfast, Mrs. Bennet returned to her room and Lady Matlock to hers. Mr. Bennet happily resumed his usual place in the library, followed by Lord Matlock.

Once alone, Elizabeth spent a little time talking to Mrs. Reynolds then went to her room and slept an hour. Later on, as the house was still silent, Elizabeth headed to the library. Inside, she found only her father.

"Lizzy dearest, come in."

"Are you alone, Papa?"

"Yes. Lord Matlock has gone to Lambton; I am not certain why."

"I see. Are you well? Do you need anything?"

"I am exceptionally well. I believe these are among the happiest days of my life."

"I am glad. I will only search for a book and then allow you to read in peace."

"You are still displeased that you remained home?"

"No. But I do feel that William exaggerates the danger. I see no point in raising an argument, though. He does everything for my safety."

"You are as wise as I expected from you, Lizzy. I am glad to see you do not resemble your mother, God bless her soul. Her nerves started to torment her when she was carrying Jane, and it grew harder to bear during the next years. By the time Lydia was born, your mother's best friends were her smelling salts, and mine were my books. I confess I was not at all the caring and thoughtful husband that Darcy is."

"Papa, I know you have great affection for Mama and for us; do not be so harsh on yourself. However, you are right about William. I am as grateful to him as I love him deeply. I will only confess to you that lately he has been a real challenge to my nerves with his demands."

Mr. Bennet's eyebrow rose in challenge while the left corner of his lips lowered. Elizabeth watched her father's expression. Her own words sounded faulty to her, and she started to laugh.

"Oh...now I understand what you mean. I believe my nerves will calm with a little walk in the garden."

"I believe the same, my dear. Now let me read; I have so many books to finish during my stay at Pemberley that I fear I have not enough time. That means I will have to return very soon or not leave at all."

"Whatever you choose, Papa," she said, kissing her father's cheek.

She decided to take the stroll she planned, but when she reached the main hall, a chorus of voices startled her. A servant entered and bowed to her in trepidation.

"Mrs. Darcy! Ma'am, Lady Catherine is here and she demands to talk to someone. I did not understand her very well. With her daughter, I believe. Or with the master."

Elizabeth needed a moment to recover from the shock of such news. Recollections of her previously horrible confrontation with Lady Catherine made her quiver.

She briefly considered that she should fetch Lady Matlock—after all, Lady Catherine's daughter was in her care.

Then she breathed deeply, straightened her back and said, "Let Lady Catherine wait a few more minutes then show her to the drawing room."

Chapter 21

A ngry steps sounded along the halls until the door opened to admit Lady Catherine.

Elizabeth's heart raced slightly, but she had no time to greet her ladyship before the woman started to shout.

"I am here to talk to my daughter. Send for her this instant! She has no business being here! I was led to believe that she was staying with my brother's family, only to discover that she is living in the most dreadful company that someone of her rank could bear."

Lady Catherine held an umbrella in one hand while she waved the other in the air to emphasise her words. Her eyes narrowed in anger, and her lips spat with fury.

Elizabeth gazed at the unexpected guest, and her distress and apprehension slowly diminished. She straightened her shoulders and smiled while trying to keep her voice calm.

"Lady Catherine, welcome to Pemberley. Your visit is entirely unexpected. Did you by any chance write to Mr. Darcy of your intentions? Perhaps he forgot to inform me."

"I do not need to announce a visit to my sister's house! And I certainly do not need any approval to come and see my daughter. Where is Anne?"

"Would you like to sit down?"

"No, I would not! I am in no disposition for polite conversation with you!"

"It is such a pity that your ladyship seems never to be in the disposition for polite conversation," Elizabeth said sharply, and the smile vanished from her face. "However, this is the only sort of discussion we carry out here, and as you are a guest, I would expect your ladyship to follow the rules of the house."

"How dare you! I have been welcomed in this house since long before you even knew it existed. You have no right to even speak to me! Where is my daughter? I demand to talk to her at once! I do not wish to be anywhere around you or that fool who polluted the shades of Pemberley by bringing you and your unworthy family here!"

"Lady Catherine, nobody can demand anything from Mrs. Darcy, except for Mr. Darcy himself." Elizabeth's voice was icy, but her eyes cast flames at the intruder. "You once managed to burst into your nephew's house to offend me in every possible way and to harm my sister—your own niece—in a way that the cruellest stranger never would have done. But no longer. You are not speaking to Miss Bennet now but with Mrs. Elizabeth Darcy. I am the mistress of this house, and either you will respect my position or I will ask the servant to show you the door without delay!"

"You dare not speak to me as if we are equal! You are still nothing but a country nobody."

Lady Catherine raised her voice enough to be heard from outside, and Elizabeth took a step closer, keeping her composure.

"I hoped we could talk civilly so as not to make us the laughingstocks of the household. If your ladyship insists on exposing herself to ridicule, I will certainly not keep you company. You should leave now and return later when Mr. Darcy, Miss De Bourgh, and the rest of our guests have returned home. They are presently on an excursion."

"I will not leave, and you cannot force me to! Everybody knows who I am! I am Lady Anne Darcy's sister!"

"I do not deny that. However, this surprises me exceedingly as I have heard only praise about Lady Anne's kindness, elegance, and impeccable manners—quite different from what I have seen of you on the two occasions we have met."

"I have never witnessed such impertinence! You offend me after you refuse to allow me to see my daughter! What kind of dreadful scheme are you carrying out here?"

"As I feared, our conversation is rapidly passing into complete absurdity. Miss de Bourgh is certainly here by her own free will, and we are happy to host her as a member of the family. She is under the care of Lord and Lady Matlock, and you may speak to all of them soon. Until then, it is my duty to attend to the comfort, peace, and tranquillity of my family and friends. No disturbance will be accepted—not even from one related to the family."

"You dare to call me a disturbance!"

"Not your ladyship but your behaviour, which nobody could name otherwise. Let me make myself clear one last time. We are hosting a large party, including Miss de Bourgh, Lord and Lady Matlock, and Colonel Fitzwilliam. Most of the guests are on a long ride and will be away for several more hours. In the meantime, I will gladly offer your ladyship some refreshments and a room in which to rest in exchange for improved manners on your part."

"Improved manners? I—Lady Catherine de Bourgh? I will reveal your impertinence to my nephew and my brother as soon as I see them."

"You may do as you please. However, Lord Matlock is—"

"I need to hear nothing more, and I wish nothing from you! I will not stay here with you alone. I would rather wait in my carriage, which is at the front door. You cannot convince me otherwise." Lady Catherine's face was red from anger, her voice trembling.

The smile returned to Elizabeth's face, and she shrugged her shoulders, answering lightly, "I do not intend to convince your ladyship of anything. I am sure three or four hours in your carriage in full sun will pass in no time. Let me ring for someone to show you out."

Lady Catherine's eyes widened in disbelief; then her face coloured even more, and she hastened out, babbling obscure words that only she could understand.

Elizabeth breathed several times to calm herself then glanced outside and spotted the impressive carriage—waiting precisely in the full sun.

She rang and asked for some tea and sweets. It was a truly hot day, and the argument had sharpened her appetite.

Lord Matlock returned to Pemberley after a short call in Lambton, eager to return to the coolness of the library and Darcy's excellent brandy. He was astounded to see his sister's carriage in front of the house and immediately imagined the worst. He hurried inside, and on his inquiry, he was informed that Lady Catherine was in the drawing room with Mrs. Darcy.

He headed in that direction but was even more shocked to see his wife in the hall, indicating that he should be silent. Lady Matlock pulled him into a dining room. From the other chamber, the voices of both Elizabeth and Lady Catherine could be heard clearly.

"I saw Catherine's carriage from the window, and I heard her voice," Lady Matlock whispered. "I came to support Elizabeth, but she seems to be handling the situation very well. I believe we should not intervene. It is Mrs. Darcy's duty to solve such annoying problems."

The earl intended to act, but his wife held his arm tightly. "Elizabeth must prove her strength in front of your sister alone."

"I understand your point, and I hope we are doing the proper thing. Catherine's rudeness is appalling. Upon my word, I do not know from where she took this trait."

When the voices ceased and Lady Catherine's steps indicated her departure, Lord and Lady Matlock waited another minute then exited to the hall and entered the drawing room by the main door.

Elizabeth was near the window and startled at their entrance. She smiled politely with slight uneasiness.

"Lady Catherine is here," she said. "She wished to speak to Miss de Bourgh. I am afraid we had quite an unpleasant argument. She is now outside in the carriage awaiting the return of Miss de Bourgh and William."

Lady Matlock touched her arm to comfort her. "We know, my dear. We heard her. We did not interfere as we thought the mistress of the house should settle the situation to her liking. And from what I heard, you did it remarkably well."

"Mrs. Darcy, I must apologise for my sister's lack of civility," the earl added. "She is mostly upset because Anne refused to return to Kent and chose to spend the summer with us. But there is little she can do: Anne is of age and is the heir to her father's fortune. Even Rosings belongs to her. I sympathise with my sister for remaining alone, but Anne's health is undoubtedly improving in our company. It is such a pity that we placed you in the middle of this conflict. Darcy will be rightfully angry when he finds that you have been exposed again to Catherine's unreasonable behaviour."

A maid entered just then carrying a tray with tea, fruits, and sweets. Once she left, Elizabeth answered brightly.

"Lord Matlock, your concern is much appreciated but not needed, I assure you. Apparently, Lady Catherine has many other reasons to hate me besides Miss de Bourgh's presence at Pemberley. It is her right to do so as it is mine not to allow any misbehaviour in my home. Now, would you like to join me for some tea?"

Lady Matlock's eyes narrowed in amusement. "I completely agree with you. And yes, some tea would be lovely."

While they enjoyed their drinks, Elizabeth added in the same light conversational tone, "Lady Catherine might be unaware that you are both here. I tried to inform her, but she chose not to listen. If your lordship talks to her, perhaps you should also take her some tea or fresh water. It is quite warm outside."

Lord Matlock poured himself a glass of wine, glanced at his wife, then at Elizabeth, and said with perfect calmness, "Well, if she wished to know where we were, she would have asked or at least listened to you. I will speak to her—eventually. For now, I have something to discuss with Mr. Bennet in the library. It is such a cool room, perfect for a summer day. Then I might rest for a while before talking to my sister. In the meantime, you might consider drinks for the coachman and fresh water for the horses. None of them should suffer from my sister's obstinacy."

Elizabeth's amusement matched her surprise at Lord Matlock's manner of punishing his sister. She hurried to give the orders the earl suggested, wondering why she had not thought of it herself.

Lady Matlock swallowed some tea in her elegant manner then smiled at her husband.

"I find this to be a perfect plan, husband. I will rest a little too, and so should you, Elizabeth. Warm summer days can be very fatiguing."

Two and a half hours later, Lord Matlock finally went to talk to his sister, and as a result, Lady Catherine moved to the Lambton Inn, even if against her will. She was too weak to oppose her brother and too thirsty to argue.

When the large party returned, noisy, tired, full of joy, and with their cheeks red from the sun, Anne, Darcy, and the colonel were discreetly informed by Lady Matlock about the impromptu visit.

Darcy's anger was increased by his concern for Elizabeth, and he hurried to her, abandoning the others. He was astonished and relieved to find her preparing for dinner in excellent spirits and happy to see him.

He embraced her then covered her face with small kisses and held her close.

"My dearest, I cannot believe that again I abandoned you to my aunt's rudeness. It is a nightmare that it happened the same way and precisely when I was not here to protect you. I will talk to my aunt without delay. This will never happen again. How are you feeling? You must tell me everything."

She looked at him with bright eyes and a large smile.

"I am perfectly well. Please rest assured that today's discussion with Lady Catherine was nothing like the first one. I will tell you everything. However, I would say it was rather a comedy than a nightmare. You should talk to her; she cannot keep making a fool of herself every few months. But you should be patient and pity her. She must be frightened at the prospect of losing her daughter too."

"I cannot be so generous and forgiving. I understand my aunt's fears, but her present loneliness—including Anne's decision to remove herself for a while—is only the result of Lady Catherine's unreasonable behaviour and her insistence on always having her way. We have all learned some lessons in the last six months. It is time for her to do the same or bear the consequences. Her staying three hours in the oppressive heat of the carriage is only the beginning."

That same afternoon, Darcy, Lord Matlock, and the colonel accompanied Anne de Bourgh to meet her mother and to inform her that Anne did not want to return to Kent for the time being. Lady Catherine refused to listen to such a decision and demanded that her daughter return with her. The argument lasted for almost an hour and reached no positive result. Anne maintained her decision, and Lady Catherine answered that she no longer considered she had a daughter.

"In that case," Lord Matlock replied, "you should consider the possibility of moving to your house in London directly. Let us not forget that Rosings belongs to Anne, and she is free to use it as she likes."

That statement fell like a thunderclap on Lady Catherine, and she was unable to move or to speak—but only for a moment. The terrible exchange of reproaches and accusations that followed brought Anne to tears, and she left the room, unsteady on her feet, taking the arm kindly offered by the colonel.

Darcy unsuccessfully attempted to moderate the discussion and help his aunt to see reason Soon Lady Catherine's anger turned on him, and new insults against Elizabeth followed. That was enough for Darcy to lose his temper and to declare his intention to cut off all connections with his aunt.

The party returned to Pemberley, leaving Lady Catherine at the Inn. On her way back, Anne de Bourgh's eyes were tearful and her face pale with distress. She repeated several times that she regretted leaving her mother alone, but her determination to remain with her relatives did not change.

Lady Catherine de Bourgh left Derbyshire that same evening with the promise of never returning.

THE FIRST PRIVATE BALL HOSTED BY ELIZABETH DARCY WAS ENTIRELY A family affair. Only those who were already guests were invited. However, this did not deter anyone from treating the event with care and interest.

The doors between the drawing and dining rooms were fully opened, turning the space into a large ballroom, which was beautifully decorated with fresh flowers. The musicians were placed in a corner and the dinner table in another. Ten courses and a great variety of drinks were prepared to satisfy every guest's taste.

"I say, Darcy, this is much better than at Almack's," the colonel said while having a glass of wine with the other gentlemen in the house. "Better food, better drinks, elegant arrangements, and only lovely faces."

"Not to mention that we can dance with our wives as much as we like," Bingley added enthusiastically then suddenly paled. "I hope Lady Matlock will not force us to follow any rules."

The colonel laughed. "It is good that we are in Darcy's house and he makes his own rules. And those we will surely follow respectfully."

"Do not worry, my friend," Darcy reassured him. "I intend to dance with my wife the first and the last sets—and more in between. So you are free to do the same."

Mr. Bennet tasted some brandy then spoke without hiding his amusement.

"It is astonishing how marriage affects people in various ways. Most gentlemen lose their interest in dancing once they marry while others become more attached to it than before."

Darcy laughed. "I see your point, sir. In truth, I remember myself once telling Sir William Lucas that every savage could dance and that dancing was a compliment I never paid to any place if I could avoid it. Such a pompous fool I was."

"Well, I cannot argue with that," Bingley said. "This is your well-deserved punishment, I would say. Once you refused to dance with Elizabeth, and now you struggle to find a way to do so."

"Having the entire Bennet family here for three months is an excellent way of redeeming yourself," Mr. Bennet said conciliatorily.

The ladies' appearance interrupted their teasing conversation as both Darcy and Bingley hurried to meet their wives. All of them glowed in beautiful ball gowns, matched with sparkling jewels and exquisite hair arrangements.

Kitty and Mary, although having attended numerous other balls in Meryton, were more nervous than ever before. They stood close to Miss Darcy, whose beauty was enhanced by her confident smile.

Miss Anne de Bourgh looked lovely in appearance but rather awkward in manners, and she confessed to Lady Matlock that she did not remember having attended any ball since her father passed away.

Lady Matlock encouraged her and complimented her beauty while the colonel asked for the privilege of the first set. Anne de Bourgh accepted, but she warned her cousin that she was not certain she remembered any steps.

Darcy kissed Elizabeth's hand, and his eyes gazed deeply into hers. She was wearing a creamy satin dress and the ruby set of jewels that he offered to her on their engagement. They both understood the meaning of it: a gift prepared by Lady Anne Darcy for the new mistress of Pemberley—a bridge from the past to the future.

"You are wonderful," he whispered and kissed her palm once again. Chills travelled from the place where his lips touched her skin, along her arm, and down her spine, and a slight blush coloured her cheeks.

"I am happy," she murmured, oblivious to the pairs of eyes that were following their little interlude with either amusement or curiosity.

The entire group gathered around the table with food and drink, and the din of voices and laughter began again.

For the early part of the evening, the four Gardiner children were allowed to participate in the first ball of their lives. They sat in line next to their mother, well behaved and intrigued by what was happening around them.

Henry and Thomas were gentlemanly attired while Becky and Margaret looked charming in their beautiful dresses, white gloves, lovely curls and elegant slippers. Margaret's delight was evident; she stood by her mother's side, glancing around as if she could not believe where she was.

Becky, however, appeared sullen and sad.

Darcy and Elizabeth approached them and could not keep from asking Becky why she was so upset.

The girl lifted her tearful eyes to them. "Because my life is destroyed, and I am desperate."

They both stared at Mrs. Gardiner, worried at such a serious statement, but met the lady's amused countenance.

"Becky is not herself this evening. She is not unwell, only displeased. My dear, why do you not tell Lizzy how your life has been destroyed?"

The girl jumped down from the chair and made a large reverence, pointing to her clothes.

"Do you not see how I look, Lizzy? Look what mama made me wear!"

"You look charming, my dear—one of the most beautiful young ladies I have ever seen."

"Precisely! How can I be a lady, when I am only a small child? Am I already at the age to go to balls? Is my entire childhood gone forever? How can I ever play again in such a dress?"

Elizabeth barely held her laughter as she kissed the girl.

Mrs. Gardiner replied in earnest, "I already assured her she has no reason to worry. She is far from being at an age for these kinds of parties; in truth, I do not intend to allow her to attend any ball until she is eighteen. She is rather upset because I asked her to behave like a 'young lady' tonight. I trust she will return to her usual self tomorrow morning."

Becky sighed and returned to the chair, resigned. "Now I have worn these shoes, I will never be myself again. I feel too grown up."

She was comforted with more kisses and encouragement, but Becky's disposition did not change for quite some time. However, when the music started and her parents lined up on the dance floor together with the other pairs, Becky discovered that her slippers were not uncomfortable enough to prevent her running through the great halls. By the end of the second set, her gloves were smeared with chocolate and her curls in great disorder—and she felt confident about her life once again.

Sitting on a sofa in a corner of the room, Lady Matlock watched the dancing pairs with interest. Her husband, the earl, took a seat near her, holding a glass in his hand.

"Are you well, my dear?" he inquired. "It is rather a particular ball, quite different from what we are accustomed to, but I would say it is pleasant nevertheless."

"It is pleasant indeed—perfectly fitting after the fight with your sister yesterday."

"True. I am content to see Anne bearing the entire situation so well."

"I was looking at Anne too. Her improvement is remarkable. She is so at ease—and smiles so much. She and Robert seem very comfortable with each other."

The earl glanced at his wife. "Is there anything you mean to imply? I easily recognise this tone."

"Not quite—I am just a little worried. It would pain me to see an unequal attachment between them. I hope Robert is careful not to hurt Anne."

Lord Matlock watched the dance floor in silence for some time. The set ended, and the colonel danced the next with Miss Kitty Bennet then again with Anne.

An hour later, the earl returned to his wife. "Would it be possible for all this to end in an alliance between Robert and Anne? I never thought of such an outcome, but his attentions to her seem more than mere concern for a cousin in distress."

"I have noticed that for a couple of weeks now. I intend to talk to Robert about the entire situation. I would not want him to enter into a marriage that would offer him the security of Anne's fortune and position without any true affection for her. One son trapped in an unhappy marriage is already too much. "

"Oh, come now, Ellen. Thomas is neither more nor less unhappy than most gentlemen in his situation. As for Robert—if he is willing to treat Anne kindly and she is partial to him and agreeable to spend her life with him, I see no inconvenience. It would be a most favourable arrangement for everyone—including Catherine—I am sure. What else could we hope for?"

Lady Matlock glanced at the couples then back at her husband. "What could we hope for? To have Robert looking at his wife as Darcy looks at his, and to have his wife melting under his gaze just as Elizabeth does with her husband. To see them happily expecting their child and spreading joy and blessedness around them. To watch them building their felicity and their future together. Am I silly? Is that too much to ask?"

The powerful Lady Matlock spoke in a trembling voice, and her eyes moistened. She swallowed a little wine, and her husband kissed her hand.

"You are not silly and surely do not ask too much, my dear Ellen. Although perhaps we did not share the same flame that seems to burn between

Elizabeth and Darcy, we did have all that and much more. I still look at you with my eyes and my heart."

Her ladyship smiled at the harsh, aloof man who had stood by her side for more than thirty-five years. "I know you do, and I still melt under your gaze."

She then added, her voice turning sharper, "But you must agree, husband, that whenever we argued, you were always wrong and I was right every time. You still have to admit your error in judging Elizabeth. Your behaviour was not far from your sister's, and it was quite fortunate that I was wise enough to confront you. Not that I have lost any confrontation with you in more than thirty-five years."

Lord Mattock laughed and finished his glass of wine. "I cannot possibly contradict you, Lady Matlock. And I do admit my error, and I will say as much to Darcy and his wife. Now, would you do me the honour of the next set? I have wanted to dance with you for quite some time. I agree with Darcy and Bingley about the ridiculous fashion of not dancing with one's own wife at a ball."

"It would be my pleasure, sir. As for the rules, I recently learned that some of them are made to be broken—occasionally."

IT WAS WELL AFTER MIDNIGHT, BUT EXCEPT FOR THE CHILDREN WHO RE-luctantly retired to their rooms, the party had not lost its spirit in the slightest. Dancing balanced the conversation and the enjoyment of rich food.

Mr. Darcy was a perfect host. He invited his sister—as well as his cousin Anne and both Miss Bennets—to dance, which made Mary and Kitty freeze in panic and forget many of the steps.

The other gentlemen also performed their duties admirably and made sure that every lady in the room that wished to dance had the chance to do so.

Darcy was at Elizabeth's side each time he found a spare moment. His eyes followed her around the room every other minute, and they were rewarded with her constant loving gaze.

When the last set began, Darcy took Elizabeth's hand, kissed it tenderly, then directed her to the dance floor. The rest of the world vanished as they stepped around each other, their gazes locked, their hands touching and lingering together.

Elizabeth bit her lower lip, and a mischievous sparkle lit her eyes.

"Mr. Darcy, do you know that it has been only eight months since we met at our first ball and you found me 'tolerable, but not handsome enough' to dance with me?"

"I do know, my dearest Mrs. Darcy. I also know it has been almost seven months since I fell in love with your fine eyes and since you first refused to dance with me at Sir William's party."

They took a few more steps, then their gazes locked again and he continued. "And seven months since my life changed after spending a few rainy hours with you in a cottage."

"True...only seven months, and they bore as much felicity as a lifetime."

The music made them separate and turn in a large circle. Following the rhythm, they passed by Mr. and Mrs. Gardiner, Jane and Bingley, the colonel and Anne. The rest of their family watched them from the side.

When their hands and eyes met again, the music came to an end, but neither of them noticed. While the others returned to their seats, Elizabeth and Darcy remained on the dance floor, their fingers still entwined and their eyes still locked, paying attention to nothing else except each other.

"Is it not strange that it was rain that brought sunshine into our lives, my dearest Mr. Darcy?"

"Not at all, my beloved Elizabeth; it is just as it was meant to be. Happiness that started in a cottage in Hertfordshire is growing to fulfilment at Pemberley. And this is only the beginning of it."

Epilogue

Five years later

On a sunny June afternoon, two large carriages travelled at a steady pace through the green, blossoming woods towards Pemberley, followed by two smaller ones.

Inside the first carriage, Lord Matlock, Colonel Fitzwilliam, and Mr. Gardiner, together with his two sons Thomas and Henry, discussed plans for the next several weeks, pleased and relieved to have finally reached their destination after three days on the road.

In the second and largest carriage were Lady Matlock, Mrs. Gardiner, Becky and Margaret Gardiner, and Anne Fitzwilliam (nee de Bourgh), holding her two-year-old son, David.

The party would join the Bennets, the Bingleys with their two children, the Hursts, and Mrs. Caroline Hodge with her husband.

Miss Georgiana Darcy was also there with her friend, Miss Kitty Bennet. Also expected to arrive were the former Miss Mary Bennet with her husband, a successful lawyer, and their young son as well as Mrs. Lydia Wickham with her two daughters. Mr. Wickham could not be spared from his military duties.

The happy event that brought everyone together was the christening of young Elizabeth Anne Darcy, four months old, born more than four years after her elder brother, Alexander Bennet Darcy.

"I look forward to seeing my nieces again," Mrs. Gardiner said. "Since Jane and Mr. Bingley purchased their estate in Derbyshire, she and Lizzy are often together, but we do not see either of them as much as we would like to."

"We have seen them quite often when we stayed at the Matlock estate," Lady Matlock said. "It is only a twenty-mile journey and quite a pleasant one. But since Anne and Robert moved to Rosings for the winter, we also returned to Town."

Anne smiled. "Mama insisted on doing so, and Robert agreed. He is the kindest of men and so very patient with us. I know she behaved terribly with everyone, but she is still my mother, and I cannot abandon her. She has grown very fond of David."

"Well, who would not be?" Lady Matlock replied, caressing the child's handsome face. "He is one of the sweetest boys I have ever seen."

"Your ladyship also has a beautiful granddaughter if I am not mistaken," Mrs. Gardiner said.

"I do—Thomas's daughter. They named her Mary Ellen. A blessing for her parents—and for us. God has been good to them just when they had lost any hope." After a short pause, Lady Matlock continued with an apparently completely different subject.

"I will order several gowns at Maud Lovell's shop this week. I am pleasantly surprised by how this young woman has extended her business. She has become quite famous in the county and beyond."

"True—Elizabeth and Jane order most of their dresses from her," Mrs. Gardiner replied. "She is very dedicated to her business and her family, or so I hear from my relatives in Lambton."

"It is remarkable how the Darcys have changed this young woman's life," Anne said.

"Indeed. But again, they have done quite a number of remarkable things since they married. I am very proud of the position Elizabeth has gained among the ton. And she has also built a true community around her in Derbyshire—quite an achievement. She has honoured Lady Anne's legacy beautifully."

"Everything she achieved is well deserved," Anne added. "I remember when we were both introduced at St. James's, I almost fainted from distress, but Elizabeth kept her composure and her smile the whole time. I admire her strength and self-confidence so much."

"I remember that evening very well." Lady Matlock smiled. "You were both admired, each in your own way. And I am proud of your fairness in praising Elizabeth, my dear Anne. That also speaks highly of your character."

"I am very happy that Lizzy has a daughter, but I am not sure what we will call them since they are now both Lizzy," Becky intervened into a conversation that she found rather dull. "I like Alexander too, but boys are not quite as good as girls."

She then turned to the young David and kissed his cheeks. "Oh, do not worry, I like you too. You are a very sweet boy."

As the carriages approached the house, Becky glanced through the window and suddenly cried, "Mama, how is Pemberley so coloured? Is seems like somebody painted it!"

They all looked outside and were amazed to see the impressive stone building warmed by a beautiful gathering of flowers of all colours, as lovely as a painting.

"It is Pemberley's front garden," Lady Matlock said. "Elizabeth is very fond of it, and Darcy does everything to keep it alive."

"It is so beautiful," young Margaret whispered, looking outside with her sister.

Becky's eyes widened in surprise as the revelation struck her. "Mama, it is a rainbow!"

"Where, Becky?"

"The garden—the flowers! They are rainbow colours—all of them!"

The ladies returned their attention outside, and a smile spread over their faces.

"So it seems, my dear," Lady Matlock said.

The carriages soon stopped in front of the main door, and all were welcomed by a burst of joy and happy voices.

Elizabeth walked carefully, holding her daughter in her arms and greeting the new guests with a warm smile.

"You arrived a little early; please come in. William took a short ride to check one of the tenants' houses. He will be home in no time. Alexander is with him, and I keep looking after them."

"My nephew is always very scrupulous with his duties," Lord Matlock said while he politely kissed Elizabeth's hand.

"Elizabeth, I am so happy to see you, my dear. You look truly lovely," Lady Matlock said.

Affectionate embraces, compliments, and greetings followed.

"We were admiring your flowers from afar, and they look even more beautiful from here," Lady Matlock continued. "They are more admirable every passing year. I have rarely seen such richness of colours. Becky says it is like a rainbow."

Elizabeth blushed with pleasure. "It was meant to be a rainbow, indeed. William made this beautiful flower arrangement for me. He hired a special gardener and purchased all kinds of flowers from different greenhouses in the country and even from abroad. He started when we married and ordered new flowers every year. Some of them grew in previous years; others did not. This is the first time they are all blooming. It is exquisite and astonishing. It gives me such joy to admire it every day.

"What a lovely story—and a very thoughtful gift," Anne said. "Robert is also very caring and attentive, but I never thought of asking him for something like this."

"I did not ask for it either. It was a promise William made me at the beginning of our marriage. ."

Becky took her hand. "Lizzy, from afar it looks like a rainbow! Do you have a rainbow in the yard?"

"Yes, I have, my darling. A rainbow in my yard—and in my life," she answered, and the other ladies smiled, exchanging affectionate glances at the tenderness that filled Elizabeth's words.

Becky, however, listened to only half of her words. She ran, crying joyfully toward the main gate and waving to the rider who galloped toward them.

Darcy's impressive posture was easy to recognise, and in front of him on the saddle was a small bundle that soon took the form of young Master Darcy, holding the reins tightly and pulling on them to stop the impressive stallion.

After more greetings and embraces, the entire party walked toward the house, proudly led by Alexander Darcy.

Darcy took his daughter into his arms and kissed her forehead; then he did the same with his wife.

"Are you well, my love?"

"Yes, I am glad to see you both home. Let us enter; we have a full house expecting us," Elizabeth said with a laugh.

As she walked, holding her husband's arm, her free hand gently touched the flowers.

"Everyone is admiring my garden. I still cannot believe that you truly gave me a rainbow that I can see every day—a rainbow in my garden. I do not think any other man ever offered so much to his wife."

"You know I always keep my promises to you. But my dearest, loveliest Elizabeth—you have given me so much more."

She laughed, tearful. "We will not quarrel for the greater share of 'blame' for our present felicity. If strictly examined, we will see that both of us made every effort to accomplish what we agreed to on our wedding night: to be the happiest couple in the world."

Mr. Darcy of Pemberley answered nothing more, but he stopped and turned to face his wife. He tenderly embraced her with his free hand and let himself be lost in her sparkling eyes for a moment, then his lips claimed hers in a kiss of shared care, trust, love, and passion, which lasted until it left them both breathless—right there in front of their families, in front of their home, and in the middle of their rainbow garden.

CPSIA information can be obtained at www.ICGtesting.com
Printed in the USA
BVOW03s1026180816

459424BV00004B/60/P